The Bridges I've Burned

A BY THE BAY NOVEL

USA TODAY BESTSELLING AUTHOR

J.L. BERG

ALSO BY J.L. BERG

THE WALLS SERIES

Within These Walls

Beyond These Walls

Behind Closed Doors

The Cavenaugh Brothers - A Box Set

THE LOST & FOUND SERIES

Forgetting August

Remembering Everly

BY THE BAY SERIES

The Choices I've Made

The Scars I Bare

The Lies I've Told

The Mistakes I've Made

The Secrets We Keep

The Bridges I've Burned

By The Bay Series: A Box Set (Books 1-4)

STANDALONES

Fraud

The Tattered Gloves

The Affair

PROLOGUE

Zander

Five minutes.

Five minutes, and I'd be free.

I hadn't been able to sleep a single wink. Since the sun had sunk into the horizon, I'd been pacing the worn carpet in my tiny room.

Just waiting.

I checked my watch again. Never in my life had I been this obsessed with my watch. Well, there was that one time…

Last year. New Year's Eve.

I'd met this girl, visiting the island with her family. She was pretty, blonde, and way out of my league. She wanted to be a doctor. I just wanted to play guitar. We'd snuck off to a remote part of the beach before the fireworks began. I could feel the excitement in the air as the second hand ticked closer to midnight.

A kiss on New Year's was a pretty sure thing after all.

Ten, nine, eight…

I didn't even remember her name. I barely even remembered the kiss.

Tonight, however, was a night I'd never forget.

The second that clock struck midnight, I was getting out of this place.

Out of this tragic little house, out of this suffocating town, and away from my fucked-up family.

For good.

I'd been planning this for months. I squirreled away money, clothes, and even my birth certificate, slowly packing my brother's old pickup truck so the old man wouldn't notice. Not that he ever noticed much beyond the drink in his hand. But I couldn't risk it. Any whiff of suspicion, and he'd have my keys and cash in his back pocket faster than I could start the ignition.

It wasn't that he cared about me. He just hated the idea of being publicly humiliated.

He'd already had one son bail on him…

So, I'd been careful. Cautious.

Now, all I had to do was wait.

Two minutes to go…

I sat on my twin bed and took a long look around the four walls of my bedroom. The pale moonlight streamed through the dingy curtains, casting a ghostly shadow that only seemed to magnify the emptiness surrounding me.

But that was how everything in here felt since Macon had left.

Empty.

When Mom had died, it was supposed to be the two of us together, against the world. Against…*him.*

But now, it was just me. And I couldn't face him alone anymore.

I rose from the bed, the springs letting out a deep groan. I froze, listening for any movement beyond my thin walls. Usually, the asshole was passed out by now, but I wasn't taking any chances.

After a few seconds, I was able to move again. Looking down at my watch, I let out a silent, deep breath I hadn't realized I'd been holding.

It was midnight.

Happy fucking birthday to me.

I was eighteen, at last.

Grabbing my brother's scattered letters off my bed, I shoved them into my guitar bag and took one last look around my room.

And then I made myself a promise.

I would never step foot in Ocracoke again.

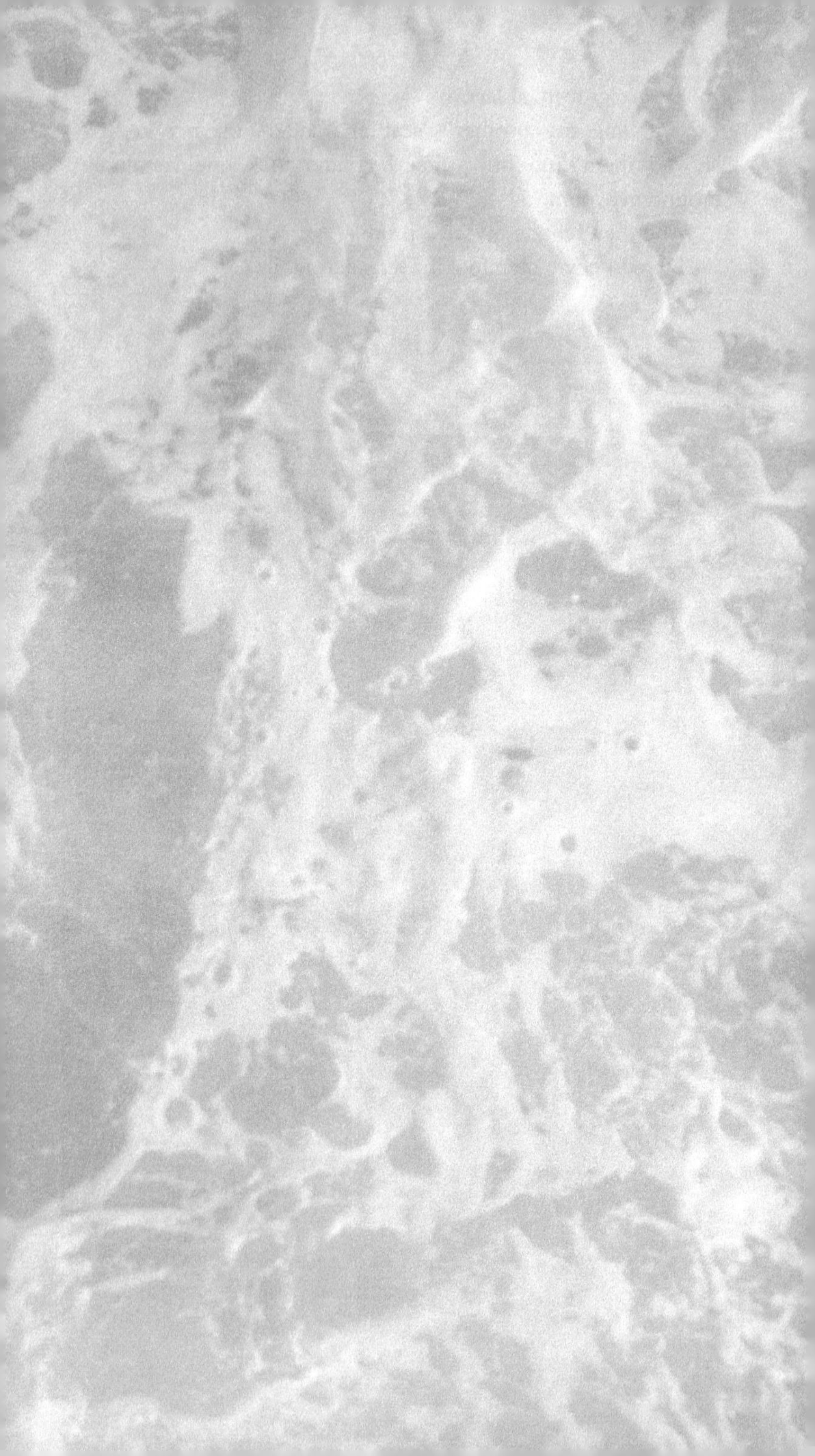

CHAPTER ONE

Elena

It was Wednesday night. I was on my second blind date of the week, and I was having a serious case of déjà vu.

The guy sitting across from me looked eerily familiar.

But the recognition seemed to be fairly one-sided because as I sat there, scrutinizing his short brown hair and hazelnut eyes, he simply stared back at me with nothing more than a polite smile.

Weird.

Maybe he just has one of those faces.

This had been a setup between coworkers, so when I'd said "blind," I'd meant it. No dating app pics to go by. No profile to scrutinize. I usually despised this sort of thing, but after the streak of bad luck I'd had, I figured, how bad could it be?

I should have known not to throw that question out to the universe.

"Have you lived in Richmond long, Elena?" the mystery man asked.

"Since high school," I answered, trying not to stare too overtly at him.

But seriously, was he famous? A local weatherman maybe?

When I'd first walked into the upscale restaurant, the recognition had been so strong that I thought maybe he was an old coworker or friend.

Come to find out he was actually my date.

Awkward.

Last month, I'd run into an old classmate in the grocery store. Strapped with a baby on her hip, that woman pulled me into a rib-splitting hug and talked my ear off for a solid fifteen minutes about how excited she was to finally reconnect after all these years.

I should have received an Oscar for my performance that day. I still had no idea what her name was.

But this? This was so much worse.

"Really?" he answered. "And you never thought about leaving? Spreading your wings?"

"I went to school in North Carolina. Undergrad and law school. I didn't actually plan on coming back here, but when you get a good job offer…" I shrugged my shoulders, causing him to laugh.

A woman at the table next to us turned her head, checking him out.

I did the same, and I had to admit, with his sharp jaw and easy smile, he wasn't hard on the eyes. Maybe I should just focus on that.

"That's what brought me here, too," he admitted. "Although I do enjoy living in the city."

I nodded in agreement, although I couldn't remember the last time I had done anything fun in the city that didn't have to do with work or meeting underwhelming men on dates.

"So, what do you do, John?" I asked, quickly changing the subject as I leaned forward.

His gaze lingered on the subtle cleavage I had going on. I'd gone with a V-neck blouse, designer jeans, and heels. It was a solid first-date option, and it was clearly working for him.

"I'm a professor," he answered, swishing his wine around in his glass.

My eyes tracked the movement as I listened to the deep cadence of his voice. The tone.

The déjà vu hit hard once more.

I'd heard him say that before.

"I teach art history downtown," he went on.

It was like unraveling a word caught on the tip of my tongue. One minute, it was hidden behind a steel plate door, and the next—

He'd been younger the last time we met, but then again, so had I.

My date to a friend's wedding had bailed on me at the last second, so I ended up going solo. Seated next to me was John, the professor. He was a colleague of the groom and fairly new to the area. The city intimidated him, so I offered a few recommendations.

We talked and danced. He told me about his classes and his love of ancient art. I complained about my intense new job and how I never had time to do anything. I couldn't even remember the last movie I had seen.

We had been drinking, and then he'd invited me over to his place…

I looked up at him. A comfortable smile spread across his face as he talked about the university and art department politics without a hint of recollection.

Oh my God. I'd slept with this guy.

I'd slept with him, and…

He doesn't fucking remember?

I realized then that he'd stopped talking. Shit, had he said something?

"What?"

"I asked if you'd seen any good movies lately."

My eyes flashed up to his. Was he serious?

But nope. There was nothing there.

"Um, no," I managed to get out before my phone began to buzz in my purse.

About damn time.

"I'm sorry," I explained, pulling out my phone. "I have to take this. It's my best friend and—"

He waved his palms, giving me a pass.

I quickly answered. "Hey, what's up?"

"Elena!" Marin's panicked voice replied. "I need help."

My eyes widened as I looked up at my date.

Is everything okay? he mouthed, concern marring his handsome features.

Don't be nice to me right now.

"What's wrong?" I asked, shrugging my shoulders in response to John's question.

"Macon and I had a fight." Her sobs were so loud that even John leaned back, trying to get away from the shrill sound coming from my speaker.

"Oh, Marin," I answered, consoling her. I looked up, and our eyes met.

An understanding smile tugged at the corner of his lips, and he gave a curt nod. "Go," he said softly.

"Are you sure?" I whispered.

"She obviously needs you. We can do this again," he insisted.

No thanks.

I bit the corner of my lip, feeling the slightest bit of guilt. But I took him up on the offer and grabbed my purse.

Thank you, I mouthed, bolting before he could get another word in.

Marin was going on about Macon's pigheadedness as I stepped onto the street and took a left toward my car.

"Okay, I'm out."

"Oh, thank God. I was running out of things to say." She laughed, all traces of sadness gone from her voice.

"You really should have pursued acting," I told her. "That was your best performance yet."

"My fiancé agrees. Although his pride is a little wounded at the moment."

"You called me an insensitive bully who wouldn't know a peony from a primrose," Macon hollered in the background. "Like you fucking know!"

"Wow, cutting below the belt with the wedding flower insults. Harsh."

She laughed. "He's not wrong about that. I have no clue."

"That's because you're an easy bride," I told her.

The weather was humid and hot. Summer had officially hit Virginia, which meant I was instantly sweating.

How long until fall?

"Tell that to your dates. They all think I'm bridezilla."

This wasn't the first date she'd SOS'd me out of this week. I hated being one of those women who needed a friend to bail her out of a date, but it was a jungle out there, and a girl could only take so much.

"Yeah, well, they were all douchebags. Like, I'm truly convinced you snagged up the last good man on earth, Marin. They're all gone. Every single one."

"That bad, huh?" she asked as I walked up to my BMW parked along the curb.

"You know when you go on a blind date, and you realize the guy sitting across from you has actually been inside you?"

"No…" she said, drawing out the word in complete horror as I hopped into my car and started the engine.

"Yep," I answered. "I have fucked my way through the entire city. It's official." Her laughter filled the small space as I pulled away from the curb. "This isn't funny, Marin. This is tragic. And to make matters worse, he didn't even fucking remember me! I am a forgettable lay."

How had my life become this tragic?

"Maybe he has a bad memory?" Marin offered as I drove down Main Street and made my way home. "Maybe he's the one who's actually fucked his way through the whole city, and he's such a player that he can't remember all of them."

"Gross," I answered, suddenly grateful for my dry spell. And my clean bill of health. "That doesn't make me feel any better. Now, I just want a shower."

"Take a bath," she suggested. "Go home and sit in that ridiculously large bathtub of yours and try and relax."

Relax. Right…how did that go again?

"And seriously, let this go. It's his loss. I mean, was he even good?"

I tried to think back. *There was champagne, and did he have a cat?* "I'm not even sure I remember, to be honest."

More silence filled the air.

"I rest my case."

<hr>

I threw my keys on the table the second the front door shut behind me. Wine was calling my name, and I didn't want to waste another second thinking about my shit date and his shit memory.

I'd bought this apartment a few years ago after my first big bonus. It was an old warehouse-style building with high ceilings and brick walls. Buying it had made me feel like a grown-ass woman, but now, walking around the cavernous space, I just felt…

Empty.

I could never fault Marin for finding happiness in North Carolina, but she'd been my person.

My best friend, my sister-in-law, and my grieving partner.

When my brother had died in a ferry accident six years ago, we'd clung to one another. She'd lost a spouse, I'd lost a sibling, and we'd leaned on each other in a major way.

And now, she was gone, too.

Not gone, I tried to remind myself.

Marin was getting married, and tomorrow, I would be traveling to the small island she and her fiancé called home and be by her side through all of it.

Every single minute.

All three weeks of them.

Jesus.

This Friday was Macon and Marin's engagement party, and the wedding would follow three weeks after. Why so close together?

Why the hell not?

They'd originally planned on a fall wedding with the engagement party a couple of months earlier in the summer. But when the two crazy lovebirds couldn't wait any longer, they just decided to move everything up and have it all together.

Personally, I think the whole thing was arranged just to force me to take a vacation, especially when the bride so expertly guilt-tripped me into it.

"I took a vacation last…" I tried to remember. Shit, when was the last one? *"I'm planning one, I swear. I'm going to go to Paris."*

I could practically hear the eye roll.

"You've been saying that forever."

"I'm trying to learn French. It takes time," I argued.

She let out a sigh. "Like. the whole language? For a vacation?"

"No, just for fun," I told her. "It's a hobby."

"All right, then enlighten me. Say something right now. In French."

I let out an aggravated groan, and she laughed, knowing she'd caught me. I was pretty sure that the language app on my phone had uninstalled itself from lack of use.

"Years, Elena. It's been years since you took a proper vacation. Don't think I haven't noticed."

Not since Daniel…

"I've been busy," I deflected.

"Take the time," she pressed. "You deserve it, and I want you here. You can stay in one of Macon's rentals."

. . .

Macon Green was Marin's fiancé—better known as Sheriff Green if you were in Hyde County, North Carolina. He'd won the position in a special election after the previous sheriff was sent to prison for a whole bunch of illegal shit.

He also happened to be married to Macon's ex-wife.

Scandalous, right?

And people say nothing ever happened in a small town.

After dropping my purse on the counter, I quickly kicked off my heels and headed to the fridge. Opening the door, I grabbed the half bottle of pinot grigio and poured myself a healthy glass before heading to my office.

Sliding into my ridiculously expensive leather chair, I opened my laptop and pulled up my email. I had about a dozen or so new messages and answered the slew of questions that had come in since I'd left the office. It wasn't lost on me that I was replying to email after I already set up my *out of office* reply for vacation.

I took a sip of my wine and continued, working through a few more things as the wineglass emptied and the hour slipped by. Eventually, I looked up at the clock and closed my laptop, knowing I was putting off the inevitable.

I needed to pack.

I also needed to make a call.

Okay, I didn't need to make the call. But I should.

She might care to know where I was going to be for the next three weeks.

Who am I kidding?

Letting out a sigh, I pulled out my phone and stared at it for far too long. "Just do it," I told myself.

I tried to remember how long it'd been since I'd talked to her. Six weeks? Seven? Longer? I'd made the suggestion to come visit over Easter, but she'd said there was no need and to just save the money.

As if I was pinching pennies in my luxury condo and Louboutins…

I swallowed the lump in my throat, looking over at the small picture frame that sat at the corner of my desk. My heart ached as I looked at his lazy smile as he hung his arm around my shoulders, messing with the tassel of my graduation cap.

I'd always wanted to be just like him.

He was effortlessly good at everything. He had the sort of charm that couldn't be faked. You couldn't help but be a little blinded by his presence. In a house that always felt cold, he was still the favorite.

I'd never understood why.

Until he'd died.

I gathered up the courage and dialed the number. It rang and rang. I let out a heavy sigh, feeling defeated until, finally, I heard a hesitant voice on the other end.

"Hello?"

"Hi, Mother," I answered. The title felt all wrong, but what else was I supposed to call her after all these years?

A pregnant pause filled the silence. "Elena, how are you?"

So formal. So polite.

"I'm well," I replied, looking up at the ceiling as I sat and leaned back in the chair. I pulled my legs to my chest and turned my body away from the picture of Daniel. "I am actually leaving for Ocracoke tomorrow."

"Oh."

"Marin is getting married—"

"I know," she cut me off. "We were invited."

"Oh. Okay."

The tone of her voice told me everything. They were *not* coming. It didn't surprise me. She'd used her grief as a weapon against Marin for years, just like she'd used me against my father.

"How is my father?" I asked, hoping to change the subject.

"He is well," she simply said. Nothing more.

This was how it always went when we spoke. Since Daniel

had died, she dropped any pretenses that she loved me, and both of them had moved back to Texas. She'd lost her only child.

I was just the unpleasant reminder of my father's sin against their marriage.

"Okay, well, I just wanted you to know where I'd be for the next three weeks. You know, in case."

"In case of what?"

"Nothing. Just never mind," I said, realizing this was a waste of time. "I guess I'll talk—"

"Three weeks?" She seemed appalled by the idea of it. "Are you sure that's wise to take that much time off?"

Those were the most words I'd heard her utter in months. And of course, it'd be over concern for my job.

It was the only time she ever showed interest in my life— when it affected hers.

She might hate me, but to the outside world, I was still her daughter, and I would not sully the family name.

"I have over three months of vacation saved up," I said through gritted teeth.

"Okay, well, it just sounds sort of frivolous to me."

My eyes rolled. Frivolous. That was what she'd said about dance lessons and football games. Senior prom. Fucking frivolous.

"Tell Dad hi for me," I said, just to piss her off.

"Good-bye, Elena."

The line went silent, and I was left alone once more, curled into my office chair, wondering why I even bothered—with any of it.

The phone calls, the visits, the constant worry over what she thought of me.

I knew I was never going to be good enough.

So, why the fuck did I try?

I'd worked my ass off for years. I'd fallen asleep at my desk more nights than I could count, seen the inside of a courtroom more than my own bedroom, and yet *I* was frivolous.

Well, fuck that.

It was time to go have some fun with my best friend.

No shitty dates, no parents, and absolutely no drama.

Paradise, here I come.

CHAPTER TWO

Zander

"Y ou know, I've heard if you stare at something long enough, it will spontaneously combust."

I tore my eyes away from the wedding invitation and scowled at my best friend. "Fuck off, Hendrix."

He grinned, taking a seat on the leather sectional next to me. He had an ice-cold beer in his hands as he propped his scuffed black boots on the coffee table. "Made a decision yet?" He motioned to the heavy card stock in my hand.

Macon and Marin are getting married! was written in bold script above a black-and-white photo. It was all very modern and casual with the date and details listed on the back.

The handwritten note that had come with it was unexpected.

> *Zander,*
> *I know it's been a while, and I know it's a big ask. But please come.*
> *Dad is gone for good, and I miss my brother.*
> *Macon*

"I didn't go to the last one. Why should I go to this one?" Hendrix gave me a sideways glance as he arched his brow at my harsh tone. It was times like this that I really wished I lived alone. A man should be allowed to be petty in his own damn house.

"Don't act like that."

"Like what?" I looked out the window and tried my best to ignore him.

A mother pushed a stroller down the street with one hand while typing on her cell phone with the other.

How very LA of her.

"Your brother's first wife cheated on him. It's not like he's going through wives like disposable cups." Hendrix had done some serious Ocracoke snooping when this arrived in the mail.

Or arrived at the bar, rather.

"Disposable cups?" I turned and quirked a brow. What a random fucking thing to say.

"My dad was ranting about them at the bar the other day. We use them sometimes for big events like St. Paddy's Day, and, man, he hates it. Goes on a tirade every fucking time about the waste and its impact on the environment."

"Yeah, that sounds like him." I laughed, shaking my head. "He knows he can say no, right? It's his damn bar."

Hendrix grinned, shaking his head. "You know he's been trying to take a step back. Hand off the reins and all that."

A grunt rumbled out of me. "Well, tell him he's doing an exceptional job."

"You tell him," he grunted. "You talk to him more than I do."

Hendrix's family owned a bar. Well, they owned a lot of things. But the bar was their baby. It was also where I'd met the Creed family and found a place to call home here in Southern California.

"You should go," Hendrix said, motioning to the invitation.

"Yes, you've made your opinion quite clear. I think I heard you the first dozen times." I rolled my eyes.

Hendrix knew my family history. We'd been friends for years. There weren't many secrets between the two of us, and so he knew just how long it'd been since I'd seen my brother.

It'd been years. Fourteen to be exact.

I could still remember the utter shock I'd felt when I turned around and saw him standing in his military uniform, looking completely out of place in Creed's.

"What are you doing here?" I said, not even bothering to drop the equipment still clutched in my hands.

"I came to see you," he said simply.

He looked so different. Older, sure, but he carried himself differently. His eyes were sharp, piercing. The buzz cut the army had given him made his features look severe. Cold even. His eyes lingered on the ink that now covered my skin.

"I sent you letters...before..." His voice trailed off.

Before you ran away.

I swallowed the lump in my throat. "How did you even find me?" I asked.

It wasn't like I'd left a forwarding address when I stole his truck and boarded that ferry out of town. I'd bounced around for months, going from state to state, draining my cash, living on fast food while sleeping in my car until I finally landed in LA. That had been a while ago though.

"It wasn't easy."

I caught a flash of pain in his eyes just before he shifted his gaze away from me.

Hendrix always tried to convince me that Macon still cared for me.

In my anger, I'd lash out at him and say he had no idea what he was talking about. After all, he'd grown up in a normal, loving family.

Me, however? Not so much.

Thankfully, my best friend wasn't easily offended, and he'd remind me of those letters—the ones Macon constantly wrote, even when I refused to reply. The letters I carried with me everywhere.

I looked at my big brother, so official-looking in his Army fatigues. It'd nearly broken me the day he told me he was leaving. But I'd survived.

I'd more than survived. I'd fucking thrived.

Maybe it was time to show him.

I finally set the amp and cable down, settling my nerves. The movement caused his gaze to shift downward.

"So, are you a roadie or something?"

I suppressed a bitter laugh. Not because roadies were beneath me. If he'd visited sooner, I very likely would have answered yes. I'd done everything in this bar—from cleaning the toilets to serving drinks and hauling in instruments. Nothing was beneath me. What angered me was the fact that he'd assumed.

I'd been glued to a guitar since the day he'd shoved that old acoustic in my hand. He knew it was all I'd ever wanted to do since. But he was the big brother with the military career, and I would always be the little brother who had run away.

"Something like that," I managed to spit out.

He looked around the bar, checking out all the framed portraits and photos on the walls.

"I've got to get back to work," I said, not wanting him to look too closely. There were likely a few notable people he'd recognize on that wall, and I didn't need a reason for him to stay any longer than necessary. "Besides, I have nothing more to say to you."

He visibly winced, and I tried not to let it affect me.

I couldn't afford to let him in again. Not now, not ever.

I'd burned that bridge a long time ago. There was no use in rebuilding it now.

I stared down at the photo invitation. My brother's smiling face was fixed on his gorgeous fiancée. He looked happy and content.

Complete.

He didn't need me.

"I don't want to do the whole wedding thing," I said. "There will be tons of people, and you know what a big deal it will be for me to show up after all this time. No one needs all that drama. Besides, I just got home. I'm fucking tired, and it's not like I have a lot of downtime if I decide to take them up on the offer."

Hendrix gave me a knowing look. Yes, I was making excuses.

No, I didn't care.

"Then, at least go to the engagement party," he suggested. "Less pressure than going to the wedding. Fewer people, and it's three weeks earlier. So"—he gave me a stern face—"you'll have plenty of time to rest up for that tour you haven't decided on."

I'd been making a name for myself as a session guitarist for years. I liked the variety, bouncing around from one gig to the next. I'd filled in for some amazing bands and equally amazing venues. My last gig was crazy. Like life-goals kind of shit. The band—Manic at Midnight—was a household name. The US tour was insane, and I thought nothing could top it.

Until they asked me to come on full-time. Yep, that was right. A permanent member of one of the biggest bands on the planet. Most people would just say *fuck yes* and then roll around in the pile of cash that was thrown at them. But there was a reason I'd chosen this career path.

I liked being a ghost. I enjoyed the anonymity of showing up and playing the part and then disappearing. I got to enjoy the perks of the job with none of the pitfalls. Of course, the money wasn't as good, but considering where I'd come from, I was doing pretty fucking well.

But this? This could set me up for life.

It could also be my downfall.

"Doesn't mean I want to be out of town right before I possibly leave again for months," I said, knowing I was full of shit. I was anything but a homebody. Last year, I'd seen the inside of a hotel room more than my own bedroom.

"What the fuck does it matter if you're in North Carolina or LA? I'm pretty sure they have airports out there. Also, I feel no sympathy for a man who will be spending months traipsing across Europe with a rock god like Asher fucking Knight."

I rolled my eyes. "Asshole."

"No," he countered. "I've just become an expert at recognizing Zander Green bullshit. I should be certified by now." He thought he was fucking hilarious. "I could go with you," he offered. "Maybe hook up with some cute bridesmaid. Or one of those hot tourists you used to talk about."

I rolled my eyes, remembering the time I'd drunkenly told him about losing my virginity to a girl who had been driving a wayward golf cart. She'd nearly run me off the road. She made up for it by giving me a blow job on her parents' boat. Pretty sure she was just using me to rebel a little, but I didn't care. I was sixteen, and she was hot. I'd learned a whole lot from her that week.

"I tell you way too much when I'm inebriated."

"Yeah, you're kind of a lush."

"You're just not gonna let this go, are you?"

"He's your brother, Z."

"I don't need a brother." *I have you.*

I didn't say it, but I didn't need to. As much as I'd resisted them at first, the Creeds had dragged me into their crazy little family and adopted me as one of their own.

There was nothing for me back in Ocracoke.

"If you don't want anything to do with Macon, at least go back and say your piece. You owe it to yourself, if nothing else. Give yourself that closure, and then you can finally say yes, make us all proud, and then promptly forget us all, like all famous people do."

I purposely ignored that last part. "When I left, I promised myself that I'd never go back."

He gave me a wry grin. "When I was eighteen, I promised my sisters I wouldn't sleep with their friends." He gave a half-hearted shrug. "Some promises are meant to be broken."

I roared with laughter. Eventually, the room became silent again, and I looked over at him, my arms folded across my lap. "You think I'll have regrets if I don't go?"

"I think you'll never be able to put your past truly behind you until you face it. You either need to forgive and make amends, or say what you came to say and walk away."

I looked down at his messy handwriting. "So, shit or get off the pot?"

He chuckled at my choice of words. "And my parents wonder why *I'm* still single."

<hr>

"Jesus fucking Christ." The words came rushing out of my mouth the instant I stepped out of the Norfolk Airport.

It was sweltering.

I'd forgotten how suffocating the humidity here could get around the summer months. I could not fathom why anyone would willingly choose to have their wedding in this kind of weather. I couldn't really fathom why anyone would choose to get married in the first place, but that was an entirely different conversation.

With my duffel bag in tow, I managed to locate my rental, and I was on the road in no time.

I already wanted to turn back and go home. But I knew I would never hear the end of it if I did. Hendrix was a glass-half-full kind of guy. He had two parents, a fuck ton of siblings, and thought the world began and ended with the word *family*.

He hadn't lived the kind of life I had—with a poor, deadbeat dad throughout a childhood that could only be made worse with the death of a mother. I'd spent the first few months of my adult life trying to put as much distance as I could between me and my father.

Just knowing I could be anywhere near him darkened my mood and made my heartbeat kick up a notch. Macon had said in his note that he was gone, but hadn't elaborated.

Was he dead? Did he move away? Incarcerated?

Maybe I didn't want to know.

After a couple of hours, I'd made it most of the way down the coast. By the time I hit Hatteras, it was evident that summer was in full swing. Minivans and SUVs lined Highway 12 as people made their way to Ocracoke. The closer I got, the more my anxiety started to take hold. By the time I finally got into the queue for the ferry, I was sweating.

And it had nothing to do with the heat.

"Fuck," I swore under my breath.

I glanced around as the line trudged closer to the shore. It was now or never. I could either keep going or I could turn around and forget this had ever happened.

Macon wouldn't even know I was here.

My heart pounded in my chest.

It had been fourteen years since I'd stepped foot on that island.

Fourteen fucking years since I'd walked out the door of that shitty little house.

I'd sworn I'd never go back. If I never heard the sound of that ferry or smelled the salty brine of the ocean through my car window, I'd be just fine.

More cars shuffled up the road as the sun began to set. Macon's engagement party was tomorrow. If I didn't go now, I never would. I'd turn this car around and not stop until I saw palm trees.

Eventually, my indecision made the decision for me. I got to the front of the line, and I was directed onto the ferry.

The last one of the day.

I swallowed the lump in my throat as the boat carried me home for the first time in years.

It was dark by the time the boat docked on the other side.

Driving off the ferry, I felt numb.

I wasn't sure what the correct emotion should be. Should I feel angry? Nostalgic? Happy? Whatever I was supposed to feel, I didn't.

I just felt…*nothing*.

My phone started to vibrate next to me, and I hit the Answer button on the steering wheel, thankful I'd synced it before I left.

"I just saw you got off the ferry. You doing okay?" Hendrix's voice came through over the speaker.

"What do you mean, you just saw I got off the ferry? You're tracking me now?"

Our friendship was very strange.

"Do you remember when my dad had us all download that app last year?"

I tried to think back to the Creed family Christmas. I'd had a lot of mulled wine and spiked eggnog, and then my memories got a little fuzzy after that.

"Anyway, he had all the kids join his 'circle' or whatever so we could keep tabs on each other."

All the kids. The Creeds had a way of adopting a lot of strays. Me included.

"So, wait." I paused for dramatic effect. "He can track us? Anywhere?" I let that sink in for a second. I wasn't sure if that was a good thing or a bad thing in my situation.

"You know, I'm not gonna think about that right now. We're focusing on you."

I let out a snort as I tried not to glean too much joy in his discomfort. Hendrix wasn't exactly known for being a saint.

"I'm okay," I tried to assure him. "I boarded the ferry like a good little rock star, and I'm headed into town as we speak."

"Aww, listen to you calling yourself a rock star. So cute."

I rolled my eyes. "I did that for your benefit. I just wanted to prepare you for the imminent brush-off."

He laughed. "Gotcha. Good plan." Silence settled before he spoke up once more. "So, you've made up your mind then? About Manic?"

I let out a long, dramatic sigh. "Yeah, I have. I signed the papers and everything."

My agent was ecstatic, to say the least.

"Jesus. It's about fucking time. Do you know how big of a deal this is?"

Yes. Yes, I did.

It wasn't every day a band like this had an opening. Their lead guitarist had fucked up. Badly. And they wanted to distance themselves from the scandal as quickly as possible and move on. When I came aboard to fill his spot at the beginning of the US leg of their tour, I thought I was just another hired gun, as usual.

But something had just clicked.

Working with those guys was like filling a missing part of my soul. If it was just about the music, I would have said yes before the question even left my agent's lips.

But it wasn't. It was so much more.

It was press tours and photo shoots. Groupies and paparazzi. All the shit I'd avoided since I'd started this job.

All the shit I hated.

"This is great news, Z. It's gonna be epic, I promise."

"You sound like Saul." My agent.

"Yeah, well he's a smart dude. It's why my dad set you up with him."

The sign for Ocracoke loomed ahead of me.

"Speaking of your dad, can you tell him?"

There was a pregnant pause.

"You don't want to do that yourself? Isn't this, like, a special moment or some shit?"

Lance Creed was more than just an adopted sort of father figure to me.

He was also my manager, my mentor, and the man who'd molded me into the musician I was today.

"Yes, but you're his assistant." I grinned.

"Oh, fuck off." He tried to sound irritated, but I could hear the amusement in his tone. "You know I'm only helping him out until I figure things out. Besides, it has one perk."

Like insider information on potential deals. It was nice, not having to keep this from my best friend.

"You headed straight to your brother's house, or are you checking in somewhere?"

The thought of seeing Macon tonight made my stomach lurch. "I think I'm gonna find some food, and then I'll figure it out from there."

I didn't mention I didn't actually have anywhere to go. Accommodations in Ocracoke came mostly in the form of private rentals. Hotels were few and far between and booked months in advance.

I'd known this when Hendrix talked me into going, but I hadn't mentioned it. It wasn't the first time I would be showing up somewhere without a place to stay.

Although it was sort of ironic.

Back in my hometown with nowhere to sleep but my car. Just like the good old days.

"Okay, good luck."

"Thanks."

I was going to need it.

I drove around town for what felt like forever.

In reality, it was probably five minutes.

Ocracoke was a lot of things. Big was not one of them.

It felt like nothing had changed, and yet everything was different.

Maybe I was the one who had changed. Maybe a bit of both.

I was apprehensive about stopping somewhere for food. What if I was recognized? *Not in that way.* I highly doubted anyone here would recognize me from a concert. I just didn't want any locals to see me and word to get around to Macon that I was here before I had the chance to see him. I hadn't exactly RSVP'd.

But a guy needed to eat.

Driving down the main road, I found a restaurant I didn't recognize. Some sort of taphouse. The parking lot was full, and when I pulled in, I could hear live music coming from inside.

Well, live-ish.

Karaoke.

I inwardly shuddered. But where there was karaoke in Ocracoke, there was a large crowd of tourists. Most locals would avoid this shit like the plague. But just in case, I threw a baseball cap on and grabbed a hoodie.

Just as I was about to go inside, I got a text from Lance.

LANCE

Congrats, kid. I'm proud of you.

I sent a quick text back.

ME

Thanks. It's all thanks to you.

LANCE

No, I just helped you shine. You've always been a diamond.

I didn't really know how to respond to that. As a kid who had never received praise growing up, I had become an adult who didn't really know how to accept it. Luckily, he knew this about me and simply followed up with another text.

LANCE

Enjoy your time away. Just don't forget, you signed an NDA. You can't tell anyone until the official announcement is made.

ME

Got it, boss.

I was only going to be here for a day anyway.

The less I told my brother, the better. It would make it easier to leave all this behind.

Slipping my phone in my pocket, I headed inside.

I was used to loud bars. I liked loud bars. They were my lifeblood and my church.

But this? This was like walking into the middle of a rabid catfight on speakerphone.

God, my ears are bleeding.

Whoever thought it would be a good idea to give drunk people free rein to a microphone was truly evil.

The person currently up on the tiny stage was massacring a Johnny Cash song. I had the sudden urge to pull out my phone and record it for Hendrix's older brother, who was named after the singer.

But even I wasn't that mean, even though the grouchy fucker kind of deserved it.

I headed straight for the bar, opting for a drink first.

This might not have been my smartest idea. But then again…it wasn't like there was a drive-through Taco Bell in Ocracoke.

Like the rest of the place, the bar was packed. I squeezed myself between a guy in a Hawaiian shirt—clearly on vacation—and a gorgeous woman. At first, I thought they might be together, and I quickly pulled back, not wanting to interrupt a date. But then I noticed the body language and something else that caught my eye.

A flash of white hidden behind the woman's dark hair—an earbud.

Had I not noticed that she was alone, in a karaoke bar, I probably wouldn't have been so hung up on that one tiny detail.

People wore earbuds for all sorts of reasons. Music, audiobooks, podcasts—all valid reasons. But some also found they helped with sensory issues. We had a bartender back at Creed's who never worked a single shift without a pair.

But then why wouldn't she just leave? Why willingly sit in this musical nightmare?

I examined her a bit closer. In a sea of flip-flops and shorts, she stuck out like a sore thumb. Her black jeans fit her like a glove, accented her generous, feminine curves. Everything she wore screamed money—from the manicured nails to the Louboutin bag that hung beside her.

Hendrix had sisters. They told me things.

Her dark hair was styled perfectly with soft waves that brushed the olive skin on her bare shoulders.

She was flawless.

Flawless and perfect.

And she probably knew it.

Living in LA, I'd met dozens of women like her, and I swore, once you met one, you'd met them all.

I stepped forward, intent on one thing and one thing only—getting my hands on an ice-cold beer. If I was going to make it through the next twenty-four hours, I was going to need it.

The guy in the Hawaiian shirt to my left was talking loudly, his *actual* date—or wife—indulging him as he complained about the cost of groceries while he flagged the bartender for another overpriced drink.

The irony.

I glanced over at the earbud woman, who was still seated quietly to my right. As I turned, my elbow accidentally nudged her phone, causing the screen to light up. My eyes instinctively glanced down.

I'm a nosy motherfucker. What can I say?

Miss Louboutin was, in fact, willingly sitting in a karaoke bar, by herself, drowning out the bar with her earbuds. But that wasn't the most interesting thing about her.

And her music taste was...*startling.*

Metallica's *S&M* album cover looked up at me while I tried to keep my mouth from gaping open. Maybe it was just a fluke. Maybe she just hadn't bothered switching the song between Taylor Swift singles.

No hate on T. Swift. That woman was a legend. But she had a type of fan, and Miss Louboutin over here fit the mold perfectly.

The polished princess took a sip of her red wine, and then the song flipped.

The Smiths.

Her gaze finally turned toward mine.

And my night just got a whole lot more interesting...

CHAPTER THREE

Elena

There was a difference between being one hundred percent happy for your best friend and her fiancé and actually wanting to witness that happiness.

Okay, that sounded kind of bitchy.

Let me rewind.

I'd arrived in Ocracoke with little to no issues. Well, unless you considered a fuck ton of traffic an issue, but I had been prepared for that. I trudged down the coast at a snail's pace, stuck in between what I was sure was every family on the eastern seaboard. But I had a plethora of audiobooks and all the snacks a girl could want, so there were little to no complaints.

When I rolled off the ferry and drove the short distance to Macon and Marin's little bungalow house, I thought surely this would be when the excitement kicked in. I hadn't seen my best friend in months. She was getting married, and I had three weeks away from work.

But the second I saw the two lovebirds, all wrapped around each other like those live oak trees Marin loves to paint, all I could see was green.

I didn't want to be jealous, but damn was I ever.

Maybe it was just residue from that awful call from my

evil stepmother, and I just needed a night to clear my head. Then, I'd be the best, most supportive maid of honor the world had ever seen.

I made an excuse, saying I was tired from traveling, which they totally bought. Macon gave me the key code to my rental, and I bolted out the door. A few minutes later, I was hauling my shit into the ridiculously cute little house Macon owned, and not ten minutes after that, I had gotten...*bored*.

So, I got in my car and drove around until I ended up at the taphouse I'd heard Marin mention a few times. Macon had a love-hate relationship with the place. He enjoyed the food, but kind of hated the owner.

Apparently, Gavin—that was the owner—was a little too open with his *appreciation* of Marin, which drove Macon crazy. I'd spoken to Gavin a few times during my visits to Ocracoke, and Macon truly had nothing to worry about. That guy was a relentless flirt. He'd bat his eyes at your eighty-year-old grandma just to coax a smile out of her.

I instantly regretted my decision the second I walked into the place.

Karaoke night.

I briefly considered turning around and finding somewhere else, but there weren't many decent bars in Ocracoke. So, I headed for the polished wood grain bar and found an empty stool, ignoring the idiot on the stage who was singing an off-key rendition of "The Sign" by Ace of Base.

I flagged down the bartender, a good-looking guy who looked like he spent more days in the water than on dry land. With tanned skin and sun-kissed hair, he was a surfer-boy fantasy come to life.

Just not mine.

"What can I get you?" He gave me a lazy smile, his eyes dropping to my empty ring finger.

"Just a glass of red. Whatever is good."

"No problem. I'll hook you up." He winked, giving me a once-over before sauntering away.

I let out a sigh and looked over the bar menu before deciding against ordering anything more. My car snacks were still holding me over, and I honestly didn't want to talk to the flirty bartender any more than I had to.

I had a strict man ban for the duration of this vacation.

Did I just rhyme?

For the next three weeks, it was all about Marin. She was my priority.

Did that mean I hadn't packed provisions? No. Of course not. My favorite battery-operated boyfriend was safely tucked away in my suitcase, ready to take care of my needs, just like it had for the last…

God, how long has it been?

Just then, the bartender returned with my drink, along with his charming smile. "The owner thankfully expanded the wine list over the last year, so we've brought in some good brands. Hopefully, I picked out a winner."

"Is this your favorite?" I asked. I didn't know why. I didn't want to give him any false hope.

"I'm more of a white-wine guy myself. I've never understood the idea of drinking something room temp. What's up with that?"

I laughed—a real, honest laugh—and his face lit up. Shit. I needed to shut this down fast.

"I get that." I had several segues I could have gone with. Most of them flirty, a few serious if I really wanted to get to know him.

But I didn't.

I wasn't looking for a fling.

When I saw the wisp of hair and a hand up in the air, I thought the universe was throwing me a lifeline.

I should have known better.

"Looks like your bartending skills are needed elsewhere," I said, motioning toward the twenty-something bombshell behind him.

His gaze followed to where I was pointing, and his mouth fell open.

"Duty calls." He sped off toward the blonde, and I swore it was like witnessing Ken meet Barbie.

Their eyes met, and he was instantly smitten. So much so that the rest of the patrons in the bar and I were instantly forgotten.

So much for getting food.

After about thirty minutes or so of people-watching and listening to my stomach growl, I wasn't sure how much more karaoke my ears could take. Surely, in a room this big, there had to be at least one good singer, right? The math alone should prove that.

But either the talented people in the room were holding back or life simply was that cruel.

When the trio of women got up and butchered "Girls Just Want to Have Fun," I'd decided this girl had had enough.

I just had to wait for the bartender to pull himself away from his new love interest long enough that I could pay for my drink. After a quick search, I found him nearly nose to nose with her. His fingers flipped a piece of her hair, and she laughed.

God, it's like love at first sight.

I rolled my eyes.

I reached into my bag, looking around to see if I had any mints or, by some miracle, a cookie. When that turned out to be a bust, I decided to just fuck it all and pull out my AirPods.

If I was going to have to sit here and wait for the bartender to come back before I paid my tab, I could at least save myself the sanity.

I pulled up my music app and scrolled through my playlists. When Marin and I had first met, she'd found my taste in music…lacking.

• • •

"What is all this?" she said, staring down at the old CD collection I kept hidden from my parents—the one I'd inherited from Daniel before he went to college.

She picked up AC/DC's Back in Black *album by the tips of her fingers like it was a poisonous snake. I laughed.*

"You don't know who AC/DC is?"

"I mean, I've heard of them. I think my dad might have mentioned them. Why do you listen to this stuff?"

When she'd found out the reason, she didn't mind so much. She learned my hot older brother—her words, not mine—had gotten me hooked on it, and suddenly, she'd had an overnight interest in it. Of course, she was still a diehard *NSYNC fan and a proud Swiftie, but at least she wore the Guns N' Roses shirt I'd bought her, and she could actually name most of their songs.

I felt someone brush my arm, and I immediately turned. The bar was pretty packed, so it wasn't the first time someone had squeezed in to try and flag down the distracted bartender.

It was, however, the first time I'd been rendered nearly speechless by the interloper.

He was everything I avoided.

Hair so dark that it was almost black. The ball cap he wore covered most of it, leaving only the tiniest raven-colored tendrils peeking out. He was tall. Damn tall. He wore a slim-fitting black hoodie, the sleeves pushed up. Every inch of his thick forearms was covered in ink.

And his face. Chiseled cheekbones, intense emerald-green eyes, and a freaking eyebrow piercing.

If Adam Levine had a doppelgänger, it would be this guy.

That studded brow rose as those green eyes darted to the earbud he'd clearly noticed, and then he smirked, almost challenging me.

Look away, Elena.

Look the fuck away.

But I didn't. Like an idiot, I pulled the AirPod out and cocked an equally challenging eyebrow. *See, Mr. Bad Boy, I can do it, too.*

He seemed to like that, his grin widening. "You know, some might consider that rude." He pointed to the AirPod in my hand. "Downright offensive even."

His eyes sparkled with mischief. He was goading me.

Flirting even.

"And are you one of those people?"

"Might have been if I hadn't seen your playlist." He motioned down to my phone. I hadn't pressed stop yet, so the music rambled on. It was in the middle of "Wonderwall" by Oasis. "Didn't peg you for a Metallica fan."

Metallica? How long has he been watching me?

"And you're basing this assumption on what?"

His eyes drifted down my body so leisurely that it gave me chills. He chose not to answer and instead asked, "Can I ask why you're willingly in a bar, during karaoke night, when you clearly don't want to be?" He again pointed to the AirPods.

"You can," I answered with a shrug. "Not sure I'm going to answer though."

That grin returned.

Does he have freaking dimples?

My insides flip-flopped, which was a definite sign I should walk away. No good could come from a bad boy with dimples and a panty-melting grin. But instead, I just asked, "What about you? Are you a fan of karaoke? Gonna get up there and sing a little 'Sweet Caroline'?"

"Karaoke really isn't my thing. I'm just here for the food, which appears to be lacking. Wanna head over to a table and try out our luck there?" He pointed behind him to where an empty table sat.

Huh, why hadn't I thought of that?

"Then, maybe I can find out just how good your taste in music is."

"I have excellent taste in music. Maybe it's your taste that's lacking."

Man ban. I have a man ban.

Why was I still talking to him? It had been easy enough to shut down the flirty bartender. This should be no different.

"We'll see." He motioned with his hand, cocking that pierced eyebrow. "You coming?"

This was my chance to say no.

I could politely decline and still find somewhere else to eat. Maybe.

But instead, I got up and followed him to the empty booth.

As we were walking to the secluded booth in the corner, I did not notice the way his jeans clung to his tight ass. And I definitely *did not* look at all those tattoos on his arms and wonder what others he had hiding under all those layers of clothing.

Nope. Because he was not my type.

Not. At. All.

And it didn't matter anyway. This wasn't a hookup.

It was just two strangers enjoying a meal together.

Sure, keep telling yourself that.

There were times when I really wished I didn't have an inner monologue. That bitch was annoying as hell.

I watched as he slid onto the bench across from me. There was something almost familiar about him, but I couldn't put my finger on it. Maybe he was local, and I'd seen him around during my many visits to Ocracoke.

No. I would have definitely remembered a guy like him.

He seemed to notice me staring at him, and his lip curved upward into a wolfish grin. My cheeks flamed, and I awkwardly looked down at the menu in front of me.

Did I just blush?

I was not the girl who got flustered in front of a guy.

I was the woman who brought men to their knees—both in the courtroom and the bedroom.

This…this was not acceptable.

"So," he began, bringing my attention back up to his emerald-green gaze, "do you always hang out in annoying karaoke bars? Or was this a desperate attempt to get away from something? Family reunion? A minivan full of kids? A husband you regret marrying?" His eyes glittered with amusement.

"Do you really think I'd agree to dinner with you if I had a *husband* somewhere, waiting for me?"

He shrugged. "I don't know anything about you. You haven't even given me your name."

He was right. I hadn't. Jesus. How reckless of me. Not even twenty-four hours into my man ban, a couple of dimples and a sexy grin, and there I was, having dinner with some nameless guy.

"You haven't given me yours."

His mouth opened. "It's—"

I put my palm out, stopping him. "Nope. I don't want to know."

His brow cocked. "You don't want to know my name?"

I shook my head, my hair tickling the bare skin on my shoulders. "Nope. No personal questions. This is just dinner. No hooking up."

His grin widened as he leaned forward on his elbows. "I don't believe I offered. Are you always this forward?"

"I—" I rolled my eyes. "Just order some damn food."

He laughed, and I tried not to notice how the sound sent shivers down my spine. Or how those dimples made his whole face light up.

God, he was pretty.

I was done denying it. Our time together was fleeting. An

hour, maybe two. And then we'd part ways, and I'd never see him again.

Might as well enjoy the view.

He flagged down a waiter, who was thankfully very attentive and took care of adding my bar tab to my ticket. He ordered a double cheeseburger with extra fries and beer. He probably didn't even think twice about it. I, on the other hand, stuck with the Caesar salad. I might be on vacation, but I had to squeeze into a formal gown in three weeks, and I'd already had my final fitting.

After the waiter left, a deafening silence settled between us until he finally spoke up. "Are you here on vacation? Solo, or—"

I angled my head, giving him a sharp stare. "No personal questions, remember? And how do you know I'm on vacation? Or alone?"

His grin widened. "Well, other than the fact that you're not denying it?"

He crossed his arms in front of him. I tried not to stare at the ink spread across them, but it was difficult. The word *Creed* stared back at me in bold, blocky script, written along the entirety of his left forearm.

His name? Last name?

Doesn't matter.

Don't care.

"You don't look like a local," he stated matter-of-factly. "You stick out like a sore thumb."

My brow rose. "And you'd be an expert? You don't exactly look like an O'Cocker yourself."

He seemed impressed I knew the term locals used. He clearly did.

"You'd be surprised." His expression darkened.

What was that supposed to mean?

Doesn't matter. Don't care, remember?

"So, you never answered my question before." He met my gaze. "Why come to karaoke night if you're not gonna listen?"

This was why I'd been discreet about the earbuds. "You'll think it sounds stupid."

That seemed to pique his interest. "Try me."

"I wanted to be alone, but not—"

"Alone?" he guessed.

"Yeah."

Our eyes met, and something passed between us. A mutual understanding. I shivered.

"A bar gives you that, you know? You can be by yourself, but melt into a crowd and not feel isolated."

His eyes softened. "Yeah, I know."

I believed that he did—know, that was. Some people would just agree to placate you, but I had a feeling he got what I was saying on a deeper level. I'd ask him about it— except for that pesky *no personal questions* rule I'd instated.

"What about you? You don't seem like the karaoke type. What brings you here?"

"Besides hot dinner dates?"

He meant it as a joke, but the way his eyes heated, even for just a moment, sent a zing of electricity down my spine.

And it had me seriously reconsidering my man ban.

I laughed, trying to cover the flutter of nerves he'd caused in my belly. "Right. Besides that."

"Nothing nearly as deep. I needed food. And like you, I have a fondness for bars."

"Why am I not surprised by that?"

He sucked in his bottom lip, slowly dragging it between his teeth, and I swore I felt it between my thighs.

"Why did that feel like an insult? Are you saying I'm the type to frequent bars, Louie?"

"Louie?"

"Well, my first inclination was to call you Miss Louboutin, but it's a little long, and I just can't get that accent right, you know?" His gaze drifted to my handbag before that wicked gleam settled on me. "Gotta have something to call you when I think about you in the shower later."

Damn.

I bit down on the inside of my cheek, trying to keep my stupid grin from showing. "Oh, you're trouble."

"I've been called worse, but if that's what you're sticking with, I'm down." He gave me a little wink.

"I'm not—" I gave an exaggerated sigh as he laughed.

I would not be thinking about him while I—

Probably wouldn't.

Okay, jury was still out.

It was like he could see the internal argument going on in my psyche, and he loved every second of it. His grin widened. "It's okay. I won't tell anyone."

"Jesus."

"Nope," he said. "Not even close."

I rolled my eyes.

Our waiter chose this moment to deliver our food, and I thanked the heavens for the interruption.

His intense stare was…

It was intense. There was no other way to describe it.

It made my stomach flip-flop and heat pool in the apex of my thighs. I tried to tell myself it was simply the change of scenery. It would be like eating the same boring cereal for breakfast every day and then suddenly going to IHOP. Everything would look good after that.

I'd been dating straitlaced suits for too long.

The bad boy sitting across from me was just a stack of decadent chocolate chip pancakes, and I was dying to sink my teeth in for a bite.

Okay, bad metaphor.

"So, you like Metallica, and I saw Oasis on that playlist. Tell me, Mystery Girl, what else floats your boat?"

"You first," I challenged.

"All right," he agreed, his hand sliding off the table. It came back a second later with his phone. "Pull up your music app. Show me your top songs from last year. We'll compare."

"But—" Those apps were a lot like social media.

"Just scroll past your username, Louie. I'm not trying to out you." He gave me an amused, lopsided grin.

"Fine." I grabbed my phone from my bag and did as he'd instructed, navigating to my playlist and scrolling down until the first song was at the very top and my name was hidden. I didn't know why I didn't want him to know my name.

I liked the feeling of being anonymous. I could be anyone at this moment.

Like a choreographed dance, we both placed our phones down on the table and shoved them forward at the same time, never breaking eye contact. A wry smile tugged at the corner of his lips as the tips of our fingers brushed against each other.

Sparks. There was no other way to describe it.

His eyes widened ever so slightly.

Did he feel it, too?

His throat bobbed before he tore his gaze away and looked down. I did the same, and a moment later, he was laughing.

"I really thought you were bluffing." He shook his head.

"What?" I looked at his playlist, and it was eerily similar to mine. A healthy mix of classic and alternative rock from the last four decades—including some new bands I'd latched on to. "Did you think I was trying to impress someone, sitting there by myself?"

"No—I mean, I hoped not because shit, what a fucking surprise."

"Good surprise?"

His eyes crinkled. "Great surprise."

We ate in companionable silence for a few minutes. He scarfed down his burger while I enjoyed my salad.

"How does a bougie little thing like you get into music like that? Are you secretly a groupie, posing as a trophy wife? Is there a tramp stamp under there I should know about?"

"You're funny." I eyed his French fries with envy.

"I know." He shoved his plate of fries to the middle of the

table, and I my brow furrowed before I looked up at him. "No one should come to a bar and order just a salad. Not when bars have the best fries."

I let out a sigh. "Fine."

He looked at me expectantly, waiting for me to answer his previous question. It fell into the personal side of things, but I decided to answer it anyway.

"My parents were very strict. Still are, I guess," I said, always feeling awkward when I spoke about them.

"You are not my daughter."

The words assaulted my memory every time I thought of them.

"My brother and I were never allowed to listen to music unless it was in church. My brother was as straitlaced as they came. He never did wrong, he got the grades, and as far as my parents were concerned, he really did exist just to lick their ass."

He laughed.

"It must have been around the time I was nine or so because he was ten. I was walking toward my room, and I heard something."

I'd never forget that moment because the sound made me falter. I had never heard anything like it within the walls of our house.

"I crept up to his room and put my ear to his door, and sure enough, there was music playing. I didn't even knock. I was a nosey little shit, so..." I shrugged, and he grinned. I was still a nosey little shit. "I'm pretty sure he jumped a foot off the ground when I appeared in front of him. I thought for sure he was going to yell at me. Instead, he shut the door, pulled me into his lap, and showed me all of his old CDs. I thought they were the coolest things I'd ever seen, and of course, by default, my brother was the coolest for owning them. Music was our thing."

A sad smile ghosted across my face.

"You must have loved him very much."

I looked up at him, my face blanched.

"You said *was* when you were referring to him."

I swallowed, biting my lip. I didn't need to say anything. He already knew, so there was no need to confirm it.

"Guess I broke my own rule, huh?"

He shrugged. "You know what they say about rules…"

He looked like the kind of guy who broke all sorts of rules. *And hearts.*

"How about I tell you something personal and even the score?" he suggested.

I swallowed, biting the side of my lip before giving a slight nod. I watched as his gaze shifted downward. I could see his eyes lose focus, as if he was deep in thought, sifting through facts and memories, trying to pick the right one to offer up to the stranger sitting in front of him.

"I'm here for a family reunion of sorts," he confessed, but the words were strained.

"You don't sound happy about it."

He shrugged, blowing out a breath. "Not sure it's gonna be a happy sort of reunion."

"You don't think they'll like seeing you?"

"No," he countered. "I think they'll be thrilled to see me after all this time, but I'm not here to mend fences."

"Too late for that?" I stared across the table, a deep hollow settling in my chest.

"Yeah, something like that."

"Families are complicated." I knew that more than most.

He merely nodded.

A moment passed and then another as the sound of someone singing an off-key version to "Baby Got Back" went on behind us.

"You want to get out of here?" His eyes blazed, stirring a fire in my belly.

I didn't hesitate. I just simply nodded and said, "Yeah, I do."

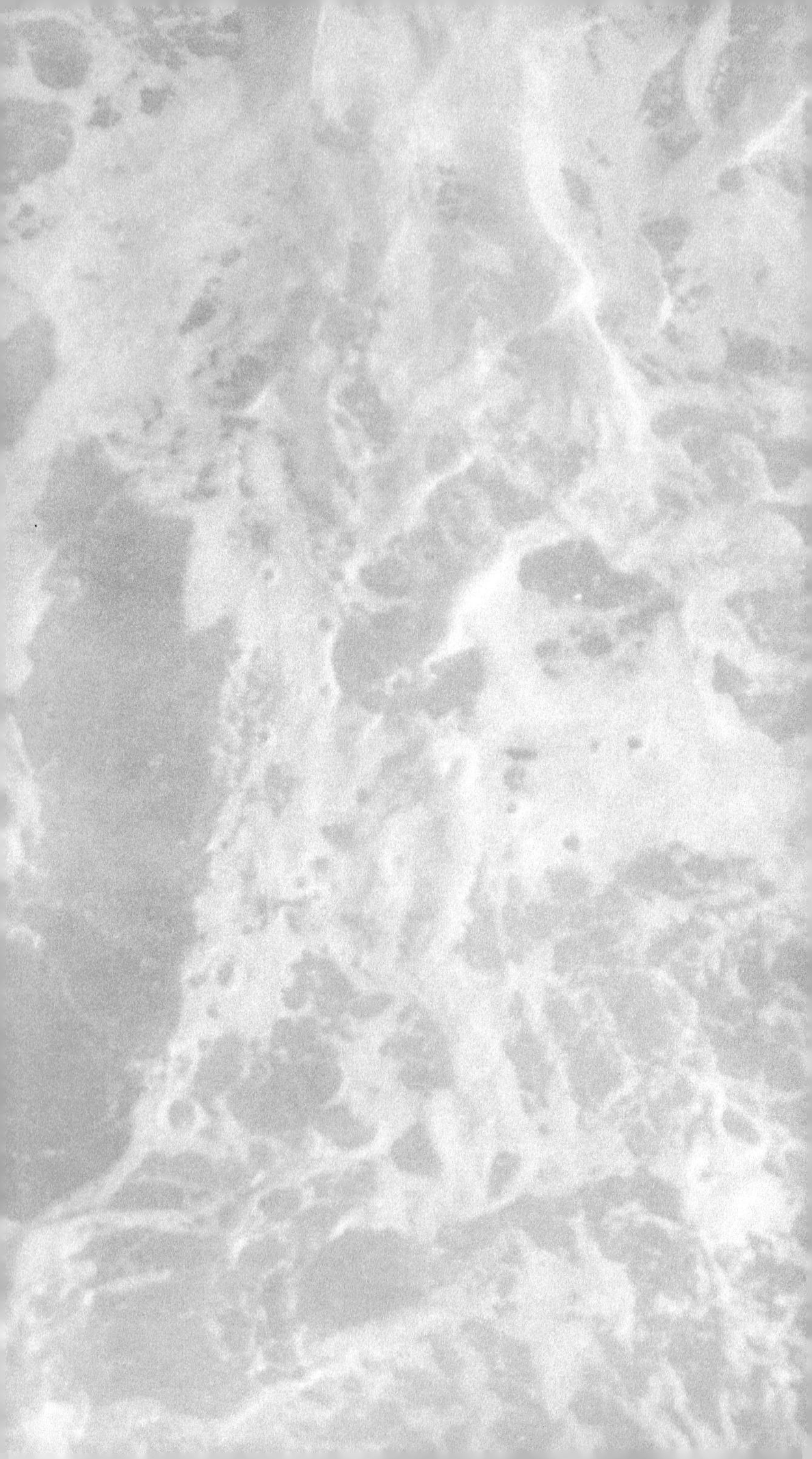

CHAPTER FOUR

Zander

I awoke with a startle.

Why am I so fucking hot?

And what the…

My fingers touched the ground next to me because it was definitely ground and not a bed.

Is that sand?

I opened my eyes, the bright morning light nearly blinding my retinas as I adjusted to my surroundings. The blue ocean winked in the distance. Lazy waves made their way to shore. I was on the beach.

I slowly sat up as the night before started to come back to me.

Waking up in a strange place always took a moment for me to acclimate to. You'd think after several years of traveling, I'd be used to it by now, but whenever I woke up in a strange hotel or tour bus, I always needed a moment or two to adjust.

Although I had to admit, waking up on the beach was a bit unusual.

Kind of nostalgic though.

"You want to get out of here?"

It'd been a spontaneous request, asking her to leave with me.

She'd made her intentions clear.

Hell, she'd even laid down a fucking rule book.

No personal questions. No names.

It was ridiculous. And kind of hot.

I'd thought I'd be okay with the idea of *not* getting to know her. After all, most of my encounters with the female variety as of late didn't go beyond a night or two, and there generally wasn't much talking involved. With the type of work I did, relationships were never really on my radar.

My life was music. There wasn't a lot of time for anything else.

When I'd walked into that bar, I hadn't expected much more than a mediocre burger and a bit of hearing damage. She was a damn good surprise, and I was happy for the distraction.

I enjoyed teasing her. I really enjoyed flirting with her. She was easy to talk to and was a hell of a lot better than eating alone in my car. But when she told me that story about her brother, I suddenly didn't want the evening to end. I found myself wanting to ask her a dozen other questions.

Where did you grow up?

Why are you in Ocracoke?

What's your name?

So, I asked her to leave with me.

And like she'd been doing all night, she surprised the hell out of me by saying yes.

I got up to pay our bill, a cheesy-ass grin plastered across my face as I imagined the look of pure shock on Hendrix's face when I told him I'd picked up a woman at a karaoke bar of all places.

Without even exchanging names.

But then I remembered her somber face when she'd spoken about her brother, and I felt oddly protective of her.

Maybe I would keep this one to myself…

It didn't take long to pay the tab, and as I turned back toward the table, I came to an abrupt stop.

It was empty.

I looked around, my eyes going from one side of the restaurant to the other.

I swallowed hard as I took in the face of every single person.

She was gone.

Maybe she'd gone to the restroom.

I headed back to the table to wait, and that was when I saw it. Written on the back of an old receipt was a single word that had twisted my heart in an unfamiliar way.

Sorry.

I looked out at the ocean, the morning sun steadily rising over the horizon. I wasn't sure why I was taking her rejection so hard.

Maybe it was just that—the rejection. It wasn't something I was used to. Doing what I did for a living, it wasn't hard to find a warm and willing bed. Even when I was a hired gun in a band, I was still part of a band, and where there were musicians, there were women.

Maybe it was simply because I still didn't know her name. That tiny detail bothered me more than it should.

Whatever it was, I'd left that karaoke bar feeling number than the moment I'd walked in, and I strongly considered just saying *fuck it* to this whole thing.

You still could.

The urge to flee was strong. I could just catch a ferry, and no one would even know I was ever here.

It was only eight in the morning, but it already felt like someone had turned the fucking furnace on and forgotten about it.

I wiped my brow and rose to my feet.

After I'd been ditched at the taphouse, I'd driven around a bit before heading here.

It was a place Macon and I had liked to go to when we were younger. A little off the beaten path and not known to many, except locals. I knew it'd be a good spot to camp out for the night.

I tried to sleep in the car, pushing the seat all the way back with the windows down, but it was too damn hot.

So, I'd slept on the beach. It hadn't been the first time.

"Come on, Zander," Macon said, pulling me from the truck. "We're gonna sleep on the beach tonight."

"Why?" I looked past him.

I could hear the waves, but the moon was barely a crescent tonight, and it was hard to see past my own hand.

I shuddered. Twelve-year-olds shouldn't be afraid of the dark.

"Because I said so," he snapped.

He scrubbed his hand down his face and sighed. He looked tired. He always looked tired. He'd gotten a job at the marina a few weeks ago, and I heard Dad yelling at him a lot more.

"Because I thought it would be fun," he offered.

"Fun?"

"Yeah." His expression softened a bit. I tilted my head. "We can be pirates, like Blackbeard." He had my full attention, and he asked, "Did you know this is the beach where Blackbeard died?"

I gave him a blank stare. "It is not. That's over by Springer's Point."

He grinned, clearly impressed. "Okay, so you do pay attention in school. I was worried since all you seem to do is play that guitar."

His words sounded like a reprimand, but his eyes were filled with pride. He loved seeing me play that guitar, not just because he had gotten it for me, but because I was actually getting pretty good. Or at least that was what he told me.

I rolled my eyes. "When it's about pirates, yeah. It's the only cool thing about living here."

"That and the tourists."

"What?" I scrunched my eyebrows. What was so great about tourists?

"Never mind. You'll find out when you're older." I made a gagging noise, and he laughed. "Anyway, tonight, we're gonna sleep under the stars like the pirates did. Sound fun?"

I met his gaze and smiled. "Yeah, sounds fun."

I had six figures in my savings account, just signed with one of the biggest bands in the world, and yet here I was, sleeping on the beach like I was a scared kid again.

Life really could come full circle.

I had no idea what my brother's schedule was on the day of his big engagement party, but I figured I should show my face sooner rather than later. Nothing ruined a party more than your estranged brother dropping right in the middle of the champagne toast.

So, I decided to vacate my beach accommodations and head into town. My first order of business was getting some food in my belly and caffeine in my veins. Fourteen years ago, Ocracoke hadn't had a coffee shop, so when I saw a sign for one, I hoped I might luck out and fly under the radar like I had last night.

The moment I stepped through the door, I knew I was screwed.

"Is that—" the older woman's gaze sharpened as she stared me down from behind the counter. "No, it couldn't be. Zander Green?"

Shit. Could I pretend I was someone else?

I merely smiled as sweat trickled down my back.

"Oh my goodness! It is you! My, how you've grown!" She threw her hands up in the air like I was her long-lost grandchild and beckoned me forward. I had no fucking clue who she was. "Come here!" she crooned. "Come here and give me a big old hug!"

Somehow, I managed not to roll my eyes.

God, I miss LA.

It took me a good ten minutes of mind-numbing chitchat before I was able to place an order.

"Where do you live?"

"What do you do?"

"Are you married? Kids?"

I answered as vaguely as I could because even though I hadn't lived here in over a decade, I still remembered how this place worked. News spread like wildfire, and if I didn't get my ass to Macon's ASAP, the whole fucking town would be at his doorstep, announcing my arrival before I even had the chance to drive the five minutes to his house.

By the time I had my latte and breakfast sandwich in hand, I felt like I'd run a marathon, under water, while carrying lead weights. I slumped back in my rental car and breathed out a long breath.

"One more day," I reminded myself.

By this time tomorrow, I'd be on my way back to the airport, and soon, I'd be rid of this place.

Once and for all.

I smiled, though it didn't reach my eyes.

I ate my sandwich in record time and pulled out of the parking lot, driving down the main street toward Macon's. I hadn't planned on going to his house this early, but the crazy lady in the coffee shop kind of forced my hand, and it wasn't like I had anything else to do.

Might as well go drop a big old bomb on my brother's happy day.

It took less than five minutes to get to the address given on the invitation. I parked along the curb, my eyes sweeping over the manicured lawn and the bright yellow door. It was a far cry from the house we'd grown up in, and I guessed that made me feel...*something.*

I could leave here, knowing he was happy and doing well.

It was more than both of us could have ever hoped for.

I stepped out of the car and shoved my keys in my pocket, my coffee in my other hand. I'd changed in the car before I left the beach, so although I didn't have the luxury of showering, I at least had fresh, sand-free clothes on.

Sleeping on the beach is not fun anymore.

Walking up to the driveway, I felt my belly flutter in anticipation.

What did I say when he pulled that door open?

Oh, hey, Macon. Long time no see?

Just came to say good-bye. For good.

God, this was gonna suck.

I stepped up to the door, swallowing down the heavy lump in my throat. I should have left my coffee in the car. Now, I looked like a total jackass, standing here in front of my brother's front door, holding a damn latte like it was just another Tuesday.

Fuck.

I heard a chorus of female laughter, and I felt a slight sense of relief. At least no one was sleeping. Raising my hand to the door, I forced myself to knock.

No turning back now.

"Can you get that, Elena?" I heard someone shout. "I need more coffee for this shit."

I grinned, realizing that voice probably belonged to my soon-to-be sister-in-law. A moment passed and then another until finally the door creaked open.

My world tilted.

"Louie?"

"Hey, Trouble."

Her name was Elena Mendez.

The mystery woman from the bar, who I'd playfully nicknamed Louie, was actually named Elena, and she was currently staring at me from the opposite side of the threshold.

I knew Ocracoke was small, but this?

This was fucking insane.

Marin, my brother's fiancée, recognized me immediately, her eyes widening as she took in my massive frame from across the room.

Does my brother have pictures of me?

I must have stunned her slightly because she wordlessly motioned me in, meeting me in the middle of the living room like we were old friends. She wrapped her arms around my stiff body while I silently tracked Elena as she stepped into the kitchen.

"I can't believe you're here," Marin said, her eyes misting with unshed tears. "I have to go call Macon. I'll—I'll be right back."

She rushed down the hall, leaving my not-so-mystery dinner date and me alone.

"So," I said, running my tongue along the back of my teeth. "Elena, huh?"

She bit the inside of her cheek as her arms folded in front of her. "Yep. And you must be Zander, the long-lost brother?"

I merely nodded.

An uncomfortable silence settled between us, one that hadn't been present the night before. I took the opportunity to look around, noticing the oil paintings that hung on the walls and the photos that lined the mantel.

"I take it, you're one of Marin's friends?"

"Best friend," she corrected. "And sister-in-law."

My brow rose in confusion, and then I remembered the one personal detail she'd managed to reveal to me. "Your brother?"

She gave me a solemn nod. "Marin's first husband. He died in the ferry accident six years ago."

Jesus. My brother was marrying a widow? I took another turn around the room, realizing how little I knew about him.

It doesn't matter.

You're leaving tomorrow anyway.

Marin chose that moment to reappear, coming from the hallway and into the kitchen. She was just as stunning in person as their engagement photo. Tall with slim curves and dark brown waves. In her casual leggings and blouse, she was Elena's opposite in almost every way.

Looking like she'd just stepped out of a Parisian cafe, Elena's version of casual was a pair of black linen pants that cinched at the ankle, highlighting her chunky sandals and perfectly painted toes. Her tight white tank top accentuated her abundant curves and bronze skin. And if I didn't stop staring, I was sure both women would start to notice.

"Macon is already on his way home," Marin informed me. "He was at the station, but it's technically his day off." She paused, her cheeks flushing red before she added, "Macon's the sheriff. I guess I should have led with that."

"I know," I answered, attempting to ease her nervousness. "I haven't kept up on everything, but I heard about that."

I left out the part about my nosy-as-fuck roommate.

Silence engulfed the room as we all tried to find some common ground.

Before things started to go from awkward to downright uncomfortable, the door burst open. I turned, and for the first time in years, I found myself staring into the familiar gaze of my big brother.

"Zander," he said, a bit breathless. He must have broken a law or two to get here that fast.

"Hey, Macon," I greeted him. My chest felt tight as I tried to maintain my smile.

He looked frozen in place, like he couldn't quite believe his eyes. I tried not to let that affect me.

He left you.

He chose to walk away.

Now, you will do the same.

I swallowed back the hard lump in my throat as I watched Marin walk toward him, offering a hand and pulling him toward her. It was then that he seemed to snap out of whatever trance he had been in. He turned toward her, his expression morphing into something so personal that I had to look away. I noticed I wasn't the only one. Elena's brown eyes found mine just then, and she gave me a hesitant smile.

I knew I was here to talk to my brother, but that one smile made me want to take her hand and drag her into one of those empty rooms at the end of the hallway and demand answers.

Why did she leave?

Did she regret it?

Did she think about me?

But she wasn't my priority.

And now that I'd learned who she was, I knew she'd done us both a favor by walking out of that bar.

This was far more complicated than either of us had ever anticipated.

"Are you—" my brother began. His words were hoarse, and I noticed Marin's hand slip into his.

"I'm here for your engagement party," I said. "If you can fit one more, that is. I know I didn't RSVP."

He looked visibly wrecked, his eyes glassy, as if he was trying to hold in a dozen emotions. I dug my fingernails into my palm.

Don't react. Don't react.

"We absolutely have room," Marin finally answered, not even trying to cover the tears streaking her cheeks. "We'd love to have you."

"Great."

"Elena." Marin turned to her friend as she wiped the moisture from her eyes. "Why don't we head to the coffee shop and grab some refreshments? I see Zander's already made a stop." She motioned to the forgotten coffee cup I'd placed on the kitchen island. "But there is never enough coffee and pastries, right?"

Her gaze quickly shifted to Macon and then mine. She gave a tentative smile. God, she was horribly transparent. It'd be annoying if she wasn't so wholesome about her intentions.

"Right," Elena agreed, giving me a sideways glare.

What did I do?

Both Macon and I stood there, awkwardly staring at each other, while the women moved about the house, grabbing keys and purses.

Elena finished first, and she brushed past me, toward the door, briefly stopping at my side. Her words were barely audible, but I heard them nonetheless. "Do not ruin this day for him."

She remembered what I'd said last night.

"I'm not here to mend fences."

She didn't even wait for any sort of acknowledgment. I watched as she gave Macon a dazzling smile and patted him on the shoulder.

I felt a twinge of jealousy, seeing how at ease she was with him.

"Take care of my girl," he told her.

"Always do, Hot Cop."

He rolled his eyes, chuckling under his breath.

Marin followed close behind, and I once again looked away as the two lovebirds whispered sweet nothings in each other's ear and kissed each other good-bye. The door finally shut, and then it was just the two of us.

Nearly a decade and a half worth of silence settled between us. A clock ticked somewhere in the house. A bird passed by the window and cawed.

I let out a huff.

"Your accent is gone," he commented. "There's not even a hint of twang anymore."

I shrugged. "Got me laid for a while." I grinned. "West

Coast girls love a Southern boy, but I eventually just sort of lost it."

More like dropped it. On purpose.

After a few years of living on the West Coast, I had gotten tired of being asked where I grew up every time I opened my mouth. It had been like being dragged back to that sad little house over and over again.

"Got a few more tattoos since I last saw you." He motioned to my arms, making my gaze drift downward. I had no idea why. It wasn't like I didn't know they were there.

I'd ditched the hoodie today, and I was sporting a vintage Rolling Stones tee, ripped black shorts, and a pair of Converse. With that much skin showing, all the tats were out on display.

"Once you get one," I said, "it's kind of hard to stop. I'm surprised you never got one, being in the military."

He shrugged. "Never really had anything I wanted to put on my body permanently," he confessed. "Although I've been thinking of getting something before the wedding as a surprise for Marin."

I winced. "You want to get your fiancée's name? Isn't that a little risky?" I mean, the guy already had one divorce in the rearview.

"Nah," he said, a wide grin spreading across his face. "We're a done deal. She's it for me."

Although our parents' marriage had been a train wreck, I knew others were not. Lance and his wife, Tilly, had proven that to me. I knew real love existed out there, and I hoped, for my brother's sake, that he'd found it this time around.

"I can't believe you're here," Macon said softly as we both headed over to the living room. He went and sat in an over-sized gray chair, and I took the sofa directly across from him. "I hoped you'd come, but I never—"

"I wanted to come to the wedding," I lied. I didn't want to come to the wedding. Not even a little. "But I've got a lot of things going on right now, so I wanted to at least show up for this."

He looked up at me, his expression shredded. "You can't make it to the wedding?"

I shook my head. "Sorry, man."

He visibly pulled himself together as he sank further into his seat. "No, it's okay. You're here now. That's all that matters."

I winced. He was being way too nice.

"Where are you staying?" he asked, throwing a foot over his knee.

He was in better shape than the last time I'd seen him, which was something, considering he'd been just a few years out of boot camp then. He no longer had the intense buzz cut or the severe edginess that had surrounded him though.

When the wedding invite had first come, I'd looked at that picture of the two of them and thought, *No way*—there was no way two people could be that happy.

But sitting across from him now, I realized it wasn't an act.

He looked like he'd scored the fucking jackpot.

"Oh, um, just one of the hotels in town," I answered, looking at one of the oil paintings on the wall. "Is that local?"

"It's Marin's," he answered matter-of-factly. "What hotel?"

"Uh, The Cozy Motel." My gaze was still fixated on that painting. "Marin's an artist? She's good. Does she showcase in town?"

A moment of silence followed, then another.

"Did you know you still avoid eye contact when you lie?"

My eyes snapped to his. "What do you mean?"

His hands rested on his lap, his shoulder back as his intense gaze pinned me in place. At that moment, he looked every bit the authoritative sheriff he was. It was intimidating as fuck.

"The Cozy Motel hasn't been in business for years."

Shit. I should have noticed that last night. I'd been too focused on finding food.

"So, I'll ask again," he said. "Where are you staying?"

"You know where we used to sleep like pirates?"

"You're sleeping on the fucking beach, Zander?" His voice was filled with shock, but there was also a hint of regret, too. Maybe those were conflicting memories for him, too.

"This was kind of a spur-of-the-moment trip for me," I explained, hoping he wouldn't ask why.

"A letter arrived for you today at the bar," Hendrix said.

I lay sprawled out on the hotel bed, freshly showered but utterly wiped. Five months, twenty cities. No fucking sleep.

"At the bar?"

"Yeah." He hesitated. "It's from your brother. Looks kind of fancy."

My stomach tightened as I stared up at the ceiling. "Just leave it in the stack with the rest."

"You don't want me to open it?"

"No," I answered. "It's not important."

It had taken me another three days after I got home to break the seal.

I avoided his gaze. "There isn't exactly a lot of options in Ocracoke for accommodations in the summer."

He let out a sigh. "No, there isn't."

"It's no big deal," I told him. "I'm leaving tomorrow anyway. And it's not like I've never slept on the beach before."

"It is a big deal," he countered. "We're not helpless kids, trying to avoid one of Dad's benders. I can find somewhere for you to stay."

"Macon," I sighed. "This is why I didn't want to tell you. You've got enough on your plate, and unless you went and bought a hotel I don't know about, there's really nowhere for me to stay. And I'm not staying here—that would be just fucking weird."

"It wouldn't be weird," he argued.

I gave him an incredulous stare. "On the night of your engagement party? Come on, brother. I know it's not your wedding night or anything, but no one wants that kind of cockblock. I've met your fiancée. She would make it her life's mission to be hostess of the year."

He laughed. "You're not wrong about that. But I've got other options. Just give me a little bit of time. I'll figure something out, okay? We're family," he said, his warm gaze meeting mine. "We take care of each other."

Family...

That single word made my heart squeeze, and as much as I wanted to argue with him, I simply nodded, remembering Elena's plea. "All right. Whatever you want."

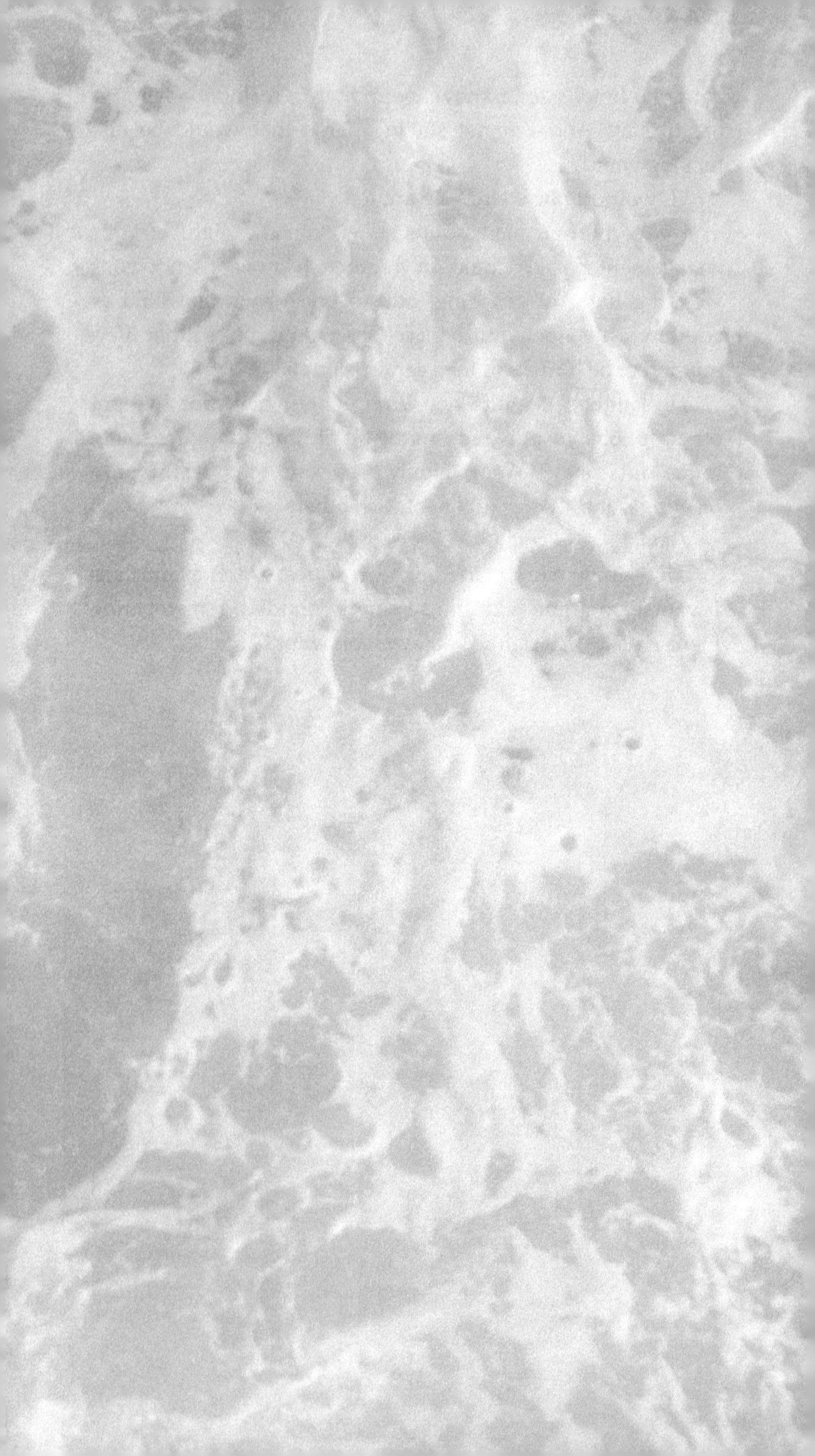

CHAPTER FIVE

Elena

'd been in Ocracoke for only a handful of hours, but I was already racking up an alarmingly long list of regrets.

Number one on my list was saying yes to dinner with a smoking hot mystery man who turned out to be Marin's future brother-in-law.

A close second was choosing to tell her about it.

"I can't believe the guy at the bar turned out to be Zander!" she nearly squealed as we sat, huddled together, on one of the plush velvet sofas in the coffee shop, waiting for our order.

"You already said that," I muttered.

She'd said it more than once actually. In the car. On the way here. In the line before we ordered.

It'd taken her a few minutes to get over the roller coaster of emotions she was riding in regard to her fiancé's long-lost brother returning, but once she processed all of those, the focus had quickly shifted to me and the long-winded story I'd told her just an hour earlier about the hot guy I'd ditched at karaoke night.

. . .

"So, wait," Marin said, her back turned as she scooped coffee grounds into her fancy coffee maker. It was a gift from Macon. Coffee was kind of their thing because it reminded them of their meet-cute. It was adorable as hell—in a barf-inducing sort of way. "I thought you went to the rental after you left here."

"I did," I assured her, already knowing where this train of thought was leading. "But a girl needs food, Marin."

"We could have fed you." She looked a little forlorn as she turned back around, having set the machine to brew.

"I know that, babe. But I am going to be here for three weeks. I don't want you to get sick of me right off the bat."

She rolled her eyes. "I'm not going to get sick of you," she promised, leaning against the cool granite.

I smirked as I took in her long black leggings and oversized blouse. Only she could pull that off and still look put together.

"We've been friends for half our lives. Pretty sure if I was ever going to get sick of you, it would have happened during those years we shared a bathroom."

I grimaced. "Don't remind me."

To save money, the three of us—Marin, Daniel, and I—had thought it'd be a brilliant idea to share an apartment.

Spoiler alert: it was not.

Sharing a space with a couple, especially a couple that included my brother, was like willingly subjecting myself to torture every night.

Or day. Or mid-afternoon. 'Cause those two fucked like damn bunnies in heat.

I'd heard things. So many things.

"So, you went to get food and ended up at Gavin's place? On karaoke night of all nights?" Marin asked, rerouting the subject back to my crazy night.

I'd come over here to help her with the seating chart for the wedding, and we were both doing an A+ job of avoiding it.

"Yeah, well, Macon said the food was good," I lied, not wanting to explain my weird need to be surrounded by people when I wanted to be alone.

She shrugged. "Billy's is better than Taps, but go on."

Billy's was better, but it was also familiar. There was no way I could disappear at a restaurant owned by her next-door neighbor.

"Anyway," I went on, "I took a stool at the bar and ordered a glass of wine, and this guy came up to me and started talking to me about music, and eventually, we got a booth."

That was the Reader's Digest version of what had happened, but it would do.

"This sort of shit always happens to you." She gaped at me.

Now, it was my time to roll my eyes. She thought stories like this were thrilling, like I was Carrie Bradshaw and this was my real-life version of Sex and the City, but she wasn't the one who went home after endless bad dates, feeling miserable and alone.

There was nothing glamorous about it.

"He seemed nice, and it wasn't like I was going to sleep with him," I reiterated, mostly for myself.

"He was hot, wasn't he?" A knowing grin spread across her face.

I looked anywhere but at her, but finally caved. "Yes, okay? He was fucking gorgeous. Like, Adam Levine fine."

"Tattoos and everything?"

I nodded.

"Wait, are we talking blond Adam, sophisticated Adam, or, like, shirtless-rock-star Adam?"

I stared at her blankly. "I didn't realize you had such an Adam Levine fetish."

She laughed. "I'm just asking." She paused. "For reference. I need to make sure I get the right picture in my head. Details are important."

I smirked. "Mmhmm. Well, he definitely wasn't blond. Or shirtless."

"Well, that's unfortunate. For you," she clarified with a laugh.

"He actually looked kind of like he was hiding. Maybe he was a celebrity." I giggled. "You know, with how they wear baseball caps and hoodies."

"You mean to tell me you could have hooked up with a celebrity and you didn't?"

"I told you," I huffed, sitting up straighter on the stool while she moved around the kitchen, grabbing us mugs. "This was not a hookup, and he was not a celebrity." At least I didn't think he was.

She glanced back at me, giving me a mischievous grin.

"Besides, I have a man ban for this vacation."

She fully turned, two mugs frozen in her hands. "A man ban?"

I nodded. "Yep. No dates, no hookups. Just me and my trusty battery-operated boyfriend."

She grimaced. "Gross."

"Self-care is not gross, Marin. How many times do I have to tell you this? Just because you have a permanent man in your life now doesn't mean you don't have to stop—"

She held out her hand, silencing me. Marin had always been a little shy when talking about sex, which always amused me—because like I'd said, I'd heard things, and Marin was not innocent.

Not. At. All.

"So"—she overemphasized the word, making me laugh—"you and this mystery man just ordered food and talked? What was his name?"

I shrugged. "I told him I didn't want to know. No names, no personal stuff."

"That's…weird."

"It was nice." Although I was a little sad about it now.

"And then the two of you just parted ways?"

I bit into my bottom lip. "Well, not exactly. He asked me to leave with him, and in a moment of weakness, I said yes."

Her eyes perked up. "I knew it! Man ban be damned!"

"I ditched him." I grimaced. "When he was paying for our food, I wrote a note, apologizing, and ran out before he could come back."

Marin stared at me, speechless.

"I know. I'm horrible. But I freaked, okay? All I could think about was all the horrible dates I'd been on recently, and then the last conversation with my mom about how frivolous I was came roaring back and—"

Her face softened as she placed a mug in front of me. I'd finally gotten the courage to tell her about my true parentage six months ago. I'd been carrying the secret for years, unwilling to burden her with anything more. She'd taken it better than I'd expected, although I worried that I'd caused an even bigger rift between her and my parents with the revelation.

"It's okay. Honestly, it was probably for the best," she said.

"Oh, yeah?"

"Well, if you'd met some awesome guy and started a passionate affair, who the hell would help me with this seating chart?" She grinned, and at that moment, I couldn't love her more.

"All right. Let's do this thing," I said just as the doorbell rang.

"Why did he call you Louie?" Marin asked as our order was called, and we walked to the counter to grab our food and coffee.

I held up my bag, and she laughed.

"Miss Louboutin," I explained. "Stupid nickname he picked up when I wouldn't give him my name."

"That's adorable," she said with a familiar gleam in her eye.

"Don't you even think about it," I warned.

"I knew Ocracoke was small, but, damn, running into Macon's brother the night he arrives in town? That's—"

"Awkward?" I offered as I swiped the drinks off the counter.

Marin grabbed the giant bag of pastries, and I tried not to roll my eyes. I knew we had vacated the house to give the men time to talk, but did she have to buy out the entire store? A few bear claws would have sufficed.

"No," she argued. "Awkward would have been if you'd slept with him and then found him standing at our front door this morning."

At least I would have gotten a good orgasm out of it.

'Cause that guy looked like he knew his way around a—

Nope, not going there.

He was Macon's brother and Marin's future brother-in-law.

As if that wasn't complicated enough, his words from last night kept coming back over and over.

"I'm not here to mend fences."

I chewed on my bottom lip as we headed back toward Marin's car, my mind a minefield of emotions.

"So, what are you going to do?" Marin asked.

"Me?" I asked as we both hopped in.

She placed the big bag of pastries in the back seat as I held the drink carrier in my lap, hoping and praying nothing sloshed on my expensive linen pants.

"Nothing," I answered. "I'm going to do absolutely nothing. He's only here for the next day, right? That's less than twenty-four hours. I can act like an adult for that long."

What was it they said about famous last words?

"No, absolutely not!"

"Doesn't he have somewhere else to stay?"

We both spoke at the same time, and I jerked my head across the living room and found Zander staring at his brother with a look of total outrage.

Wait, what?

Why would he say no?

This wasn't his idea?

Marin and I had no sooner walked back through the front door than Macon hit me up with a ridiculous request—asking if I would mind sharing the rental house with his brother.

Is he crazy?

"My other two rentals are booked. Besides, it's just for a day," Macon added. "And…" His eyes turned to Zander.

"Don't, Macon," he warned, begging his brother to stay quiet.

"What?" I demanded. "What am I not getting here?"

Zander must have noticed the moment his big brother had decided to rat him out because he groaned loudly, his palms digging into his eye sockets.

God, even that was attractive.

Shut up, Elena.

"He doesn't have anywhere else to stay."

"What?" My eyes went wide, staring at him as he tried to avoid my gaze. "Where did you go last night after—"

Macon's eyes went wild, darting between his little brother and me. "Last night?"

Marin's face turned the color of a tomato as she turned to her fiancé. "That was something I didn't exactly get a chance to explain over the phone."

Macon's expression hardened, and he instantly morphed from loving fiancé to intimidating officer of the law. His intense stare pinned me down, even though he directed his words at Marin. "Explain what?"

If this was what it was like to be interrogated by him, just throw the cuffs on me now.

"Marin and Zander kind of met last night." She swallowed as she fidgeted with her hands. "At the taphouse."

"You…met?" Confusion turned to horror as his gaze ping-ponged between the two of us. "Did you—"

"No!" both of us exclaimed as we ignored each other.

Macon stared at us, and I could tell he wasn't at all convinced.

"We met at the bar, grabbed a booth, and had dinner," I told him. "That's it. I didn't even know his name until this morning."

"Do you usually not ask your dinner dates their names?" Macon asked before he held up a hand. "You know what? Not important. Getting Zander off the beach for the night? That's my focus right now."

I fought the urge to turn toward him, imagining him all alone on the beach while I slept in a big house, all by myself.

"He can stay with me." I relented.

"No—" Zander tried to argue before Macon cut him off.

"Good. It's settled." He grinned, looking pretty damn pleased with himself. "Let's eat. I'm fucking starving."

After the four of us sat around Marin and Macon's kitchen island, awkwardly drinking coffee and munching on pastries, I offered to take my new roommate to the rental so he could get situated.

He reluctantly agreed, and after a quick good-bye, we drove separately to the little yellow house Macon had aptly named Ochre Bay.

"I can't believe Macon owns rental property," Zander said the moment he stepped out onto the curb.

He reached into the back of his car and pulled out a black duffel bag and a large guitar case. I tried not to stare as his biceps bulged, the ink wrapping around his arm in a stunning piece of artwork that demanded attention.

"Why?" I asked as he slung the duffel over his shoulder.

No baseball cap today. With his messy hairstyle and mirrored sunglasses, he somehow looked even hotter than he had the night before.

If that were possible.

"We didn't exactly have the easiest childhood," he said as we headed down the walkway. "I don't think either of us would have imagined..." He paused, staring at the house in front of him, his eyes distant.

I turned to him. "What you said last night..." My words were hesitant as I blew out a breath, trying to gather the courage I needed. Usually, I didn't need it. I never had a problem being brazen with my opinion. Until him, it seemed. "You can't do that to him, Zander. He—"

A brief flash of pain painted his features before he gave a hollow shrug. "It is what it is," he said, and then he walked away, leaving me there in the middle of the driveway.

With the code Macon had given him, he made it clear he didn't need a tour guide and let himself in, not bothering to even glance back over his shoulder.

I let out a sigh and headed inside. As soon as I was through the front door, I searched for my new housemate but found myself alone.

I guess he is settling in just fine.

Looking around, I suddenly felt antsy. I wasn't used to the feeling of having nothing to do. I'd brought him here to show him around, and now that I no longer had that task, I felt…useless.

I went to my bedroom and grabbed my laptop. Maybe I'd just check up on a few things while I had time.

Yeah, I know. I was on vacation. But…

Heading back into the living room, I tucked myself into a cozy chair and opened my computer, trying not to feel guilty for the four emails I'd already responded to.

It will only save me time in the long run, I told myself.

I heard him before I saw him.

"You doing anything important?" he asked as I turned my head.

I did a double-take. He was still in those black shorts and rock tee, but he had a sleek black guitar strapped across his chest.

I swallowed audibly.

What is it about a guy with a guitar?

"Uh, um… no. Just catching up on some work emails," I answered, ashamed of myself for the girlish stuttering.

He is just a guy, Elena. You've literally met hundreds of them. He is not *special.*

Get a fucking grip.

"Aren't you on vacation?" he asked as he took a seat. He positioned himself on the edge of the cushion, propping the instrument on one thigh, as if it was second nature. "Sorry, am I allowed to ask personal questions?" His flirty comment was a complete contradiction to the broody man who'd left me in the driveway less than an hour ago.

"Seeing as we're living under the same roof now"—I rolled my eyes—"I'll allow it."

"All right, so you like to work on vacation?"

"No," I answered too quickly before adding, "But I can't just ignore my responsibilities while I'm gone either."

"And what is it that you do that's so important you can't take a little time off?"

"I can take time off," I argued.

"Clearly not," he countered.

I huffed. "I'm a lawyer. Criminal attorney."

That pierced brow lifted, and suddenly, I was left wondering if he had any other piercings. My eyes dragged down his body, and I felt heat sear my cheeks before I finally looked away.

"What do you do?" I asked, trying to focus my attention on my screen for half a second before giving up and looking up at him again.

His fingers began to pluck out a familiar tune, and before I got lost in the melody, I realized what he was saying.

"You're a musician?"

"A guitarist." He grinned. "I thought a lawyer would be smart enough to decipher what kind of instrument this is."

I let out a sigh "I didn't want to assume. You could play other instruments."

"I can, actually. I play a little bass, and I can bang on the drums decently, but they only pay me to do this," he said, strumming the guitar almost effortlessly.

This time, it wasn't anything I recognized, but it sent shivers down my spine, and I found myself setting my computer down and turning to face him.

"So, are you in a band or—"

"Session guitarist."

"I don't know what that means," I confessed. "I dated a

guitar player in college, but it was only a week, and honestly, he wasn't much of a talker."

"So, you *are* a groupie. I knew it."

I laughed, shrugging. "I will admit, I did meet him at a concert, and he was in a band. But it was a one-time thing. After he stole shit from my dorm room while I was sleeping, I found myself miraculously cured of my"—I made air quotes with my hands—" 'groupie phase.' "

"Until last night, that is." His grin was shameless.

God, those fucking dimples. How many women had he charmed into his bed with those?

"Whatever, Trouble." I folded my arms across my chest, like I didn't trust myself to stay put."You asked me to dinner. Not the other way around."

"I'm not denying that, *Louie*," he said, bending down over his guitar as he strummed out a melody. He looked up at me once more. "I knew what I wanted."

That zing of energy pulsed between us. It was just as potent as the night before, but more intimate because, now, I knew him.

And that made it more dangerous.

"But"—he cleared his throat, placing his palm down on the strings, silencing the notes with the touch of his hand—"I guess it's good that you decided to leave." He didn't look at me, his gaze fixated on the instrument at his chest. "It would have complicated things and—"

"When are you going to tell him?" I asked, knowing this would most likely be the end of our conversation, considering the way it had gone last time I brought up Macon.

"Tomorrow," he answered. "Like you said, I don't want to ruin today for them."

I nodded, my head turned toward the window.

"You won't..." He paused, clearly sorting out his words. "You won't tell Marin?"

I let out a pained laugh.

He was asking for a lot. Every time I had seen that hopeful

smile on Marin's face this morning, after hearing those words Zander had said last night, it'd felt like a betrayal.

"No. It's hard to keep something like this from her, but I don't want her to carry that burden today."

"Thank you."

"Look, I don't know what happened between the two of you," I started. "But could you at least—"

But just like before, he rose from his spot on the couch and headed toward the hallway. "I'm gonna go rest up before the party. I'll see you later."

But unlike before, he never returned. He stayed in his room, and I didn't see him for the rest of the day.

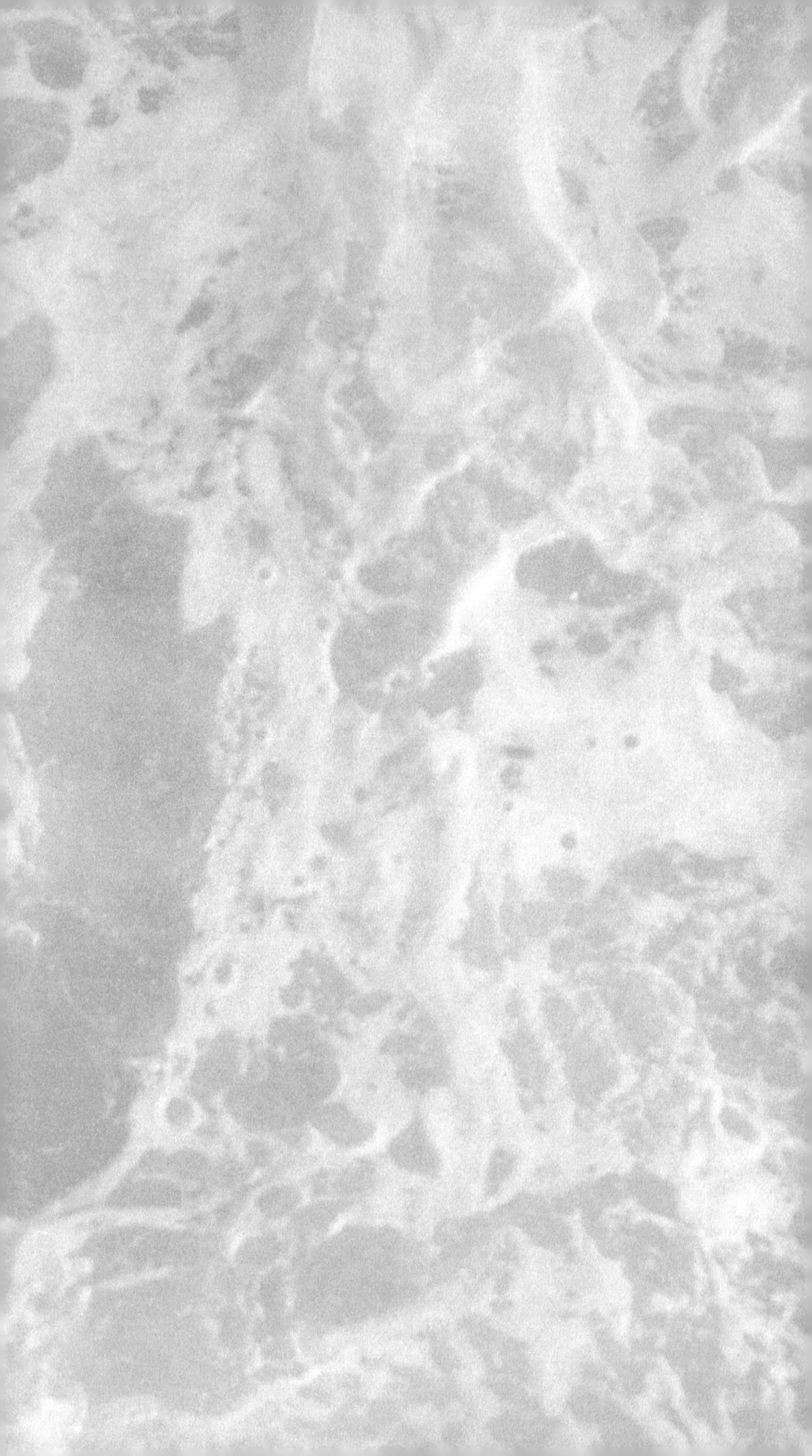

CHAPTER SIX

Zander

"Why the fuck are you FaceTiming me?" I asked the second after I answered.

Hendrix was a diehard texter, who only called when it was necessary—so, basically, when he was in the car, or vice versa.

"Damn, you look fine," he said, ignoring my question altogether, as a wide grin spread across his face.

I'd been in the middle of getting ready for the party when my phone started to vibrate from across the room. He'd caught me in the middle of trying to tie my tie, which was difficult in its own right but more so when I didn't have a proper mirror to use.

The round teak mirror above the dresser was nice but way too small when you were a towering six foot three. Clearly, Macon hadn't designed this rental for himself.

"While you're here," I grumbled.

I held the strip of fabric out in front of me. He sighed.

"Put the phone on the dresser," he instructed. "I don't know why you still can't fucking do this."

"I don't know," I answered. "Maybe it's one of those things that if you're not taught at a young age, you simply can't do it."

"Bullshit. Presley can do it, and she learned from a YouTube video in five minutes."

Presley was one of the Creed sisters, and, yes, if you couldn't tell, they had all been named after famous musicians.

Their family was…*unique*.

"I confess," I deadpanned, "I just like asking you for help."

"I knew it. We've been living together so long that you've become dependent on me. What will we do when you finally con some poor woman into marrying you? How is she going to compete with all this?" He motioned to himself in a dramatic fashion.

"Well, since that's never gonna happen, I guess it doesn't really matter, does it?" I said, but the moment I did, Elena's face popped into my mind, and I felt my insides twist.

I hadn't seen her since I'd walked out of the living room earlier today.

Her questions regarding Macon didn't anger me.

They made me feel exposed.

Like she'd peeled back the thick layers I'd so carefully constructed around myself that no one else managed to reach.

And…I didn't know what to make of that.

So, I'd hightailed it out of there and hidden in my room for the rest of the day.

Really mature, Zander.

Now, it was nearly time to go, and I had about a hundred different emotions going through my head. I was on edge at the very idea of showing up at a party in my hometown after all this time.

Who would be there? What would they say?

I still hadn't thought about what I was going to say to my brother tomorrow. How did I tell him good-bye? I'd been so confident when I got here yesterday, but after seeing his face today, so heavy with emotions, it had made me waver.

And the one that had me in the most knots…I couldn't

stop thinking about the fact that after I hopped on that ferry, I'd never see Elena again.

"Oh, damn." A familiar feminine voice came on camera. "Is that my long-lost brother from another mother?"

"What the fuck?" Hendrix said, turning to his sister with a mixture of surprise and horror. We had just been talking about her. "Did I somehow summon you here? Where the hell did you come from?"

She just grinned, her freckled face beaming up at me. "Your door was open, and I came to say hi. Siblings do that, asshat." She turned her attention back to me.

"Hey, Presley." I grinned as she shoved her legitimate brother over to make room for herself.

She was nearly a foot shorter than him and half his size. But he made a grunting noise as she slammed into him and retaliated by pushing her back. I shook my head at their antics.

"You look hot," she commented. "And I mean that in a completely platonic, sisterly way." She held her hand palm up, as if it pained her to even utter the words.

"Noted."

Hendrix had *never* had to give me the *don't fuck my sisters* talk because I'd never once looked at any of the Creeds as anything but family. I found Presley about as attractive as a baby kitten. Or a potato.

Not that she looked like a potato. Never mind.

"Are you trying to tie that?" she asked, pointing to the train wreck wrapped around my neck.

"He doesn't remember how," Hendrix explained. "I was going to refresh his memory."

She rolled her eyes. "Oh, please, Hen. You barely know how to do it yourself."

Her brother seemed to scoff at that.

"If you want a woman's opinion, get rid of it. Unbutton that top button, maybe the next one, too? And it will look much better."

I didn't argue. I liked ties about as much as I liked taxes, so anything to get me out of them sounded like a fantastic fucking idea. I pulled the tie over my head and tossed it on the bed behind me, already feeling more like myself. Just as I was done undoing the buttons, a knock came to my door.

"Uh, come in." I looked at my phone, a tiny bit of panic settling in, and two sets of blue eyes were glued to the screen like I was in some sort of live-action soap opera.

I hadn't exactly had time to explain to Hendrix where I was or who I was with…

Elena walked in, and I swore I stumbled. Standing seemed like an impossible task, but the room sort of shifted nonetheless.

Holy hell.

This woman could kill a man in that dress.

And what a way to go…

It was red, tight, and made my mouth fucking water. With tiny straps and simple lines, it accentuated her abundant curves. The hem hit just below the knee. Her legs looked endless, and the sky-high heels she wore would no doubt be starring in my dreams tonight.

"Uh, hey," I managed to say.

Did my voice just crack?

Her gaze lingered on me, moving up and down my body before she noticed the phone perched on the dresser. She did a double take. "Am I interrupting something?"

I turned just in time to see my best friend and his sister wave, both sporting wide grins.

Jesus.

"Um, no. Just checking in back home."

Her eyes seemed to widen slightly as her gaze darted between me and the two people on my screen, and soon, I realized how she could have misinterpreted what I said.

"That's my best friend and his *sister*."

Not my girlfriend.

"Oh, hi," she said awkwardly, although she did seem to

visibly relax at my clarification. She bit into the bottom of her red lip for just a second before stopping herself. "I just came in to see if you wanted to go to the party together." She paused, her cheeks turning a gorgeous shade of pink. "I mean, not together, but you know what I mean. Do you want to share a ride—a car?!"

God, she looked flustered and kind of miserable.

It was fucking adorable.

I grinned. "Yeah. I'd like that. Give me a second, and I'll be right out."

"Yeah, of course. No problem."

She made a beeline to the door.

"Bye!" my idiot friends called out, both waving again like idiots.

Gonna kill them both.

So very slowly.

She glanced back and waved back, clearly amused. I waited until she left before I turned around.

"Who the hell was that?"

"Where the hell are you?"

Both questions were thrown at me in unison. Compared to the other Creed siblings, Presley was closest to us in age and at that moment, they'd never looked more alike. Sandy-blond hair, striking blue eyes. Mischievous grin.

I let out a long-suffering sigh.

Would they forgive me if I just hung up and turned off my phone?

"When you sent me that text this morning that said all was well, did you forget to mention something? Or some-one?" Hendrix prodded.

"Look, it's kind of a long story. One that I obviously don't have time for, but to answer one of your questions, I'm at one of Macon's rentals."

"One of?" Hendrix's brow rose. "I thought your brother was a small-town sheriff. How the hell does he own multiple properties?"

I shrugged, grabbing random shit, like my wallet and keys, and shoving them in my pockets. "Hell if I know. How does a runaway with mediocre talent get to travel with world-famous bands?"

"Dude, nothing about you is mediocre," Hendrix said, staring at me intently.

Presley and the rest of the Creed family didn't know about my offer, and it unfortunately had to stay that way for the foreseeable future.

"I second that," Presley chimed in, looking up from her phone as she typed something out.

If she's texting the rest of the family about this...

"If that's true, it's because of your dad. He made me into what I am today."

Hendrix shook his head. "Nah, he merely coaxed it out of you. You can't squeeze blood from a turnip."

"What?"

"You've never heard that saying?" He seemed appalled.

"No." I laughed as I finished getting ready. I didn't do dress shoes unless I absolutely had to, so I went with a nice pair of boots.

Presley must have noticed me reaching for the blazer I'd thrown on the bed because she suddenly interrupted the conversation again. "Did you bring your bomber jacket?"

I turned toward the camera. "It's like the seventh circle of hell out there, Pres."

She merely lifted her brow.

I sighed. "Yeah, of course, I brought it."

There were two things I never left home without—my guitar and my leather jacket.

I was a walking cliché, and I knew it.

"No one is gonna wear those stuffy suit jackets when they all get inside anyway, so you might as well look hot for..." She pressed her lips together. "What's her name again?"

"I don't think I told you, and it's not like that."

"Okay." She grinned, not believing me for a second. "Wear the jacket, Z."

"Wait, are you two, like, sharing that rental?" It was like I could see the light bulb flipping on above his head.

"Yep."

"Dude," they both said in the exact same way.

Regular siblings were weird. Creed siblings were on a whole other level.

"Wait, what happened to your other accommodations?"

"Fell through," I lied. "Macon helped me out."

"That's like a sign from God," he said as I slipped the bomber over my shoulders and finally grabbed my phone off the dresser, eager to get this call over with so I could go see Elena in that dress again. "You sharing a roof with that hot piece of—"

"Hendrix," I warned him, "don't."

His brow shot up. Yeah, that was new.

I'd never shut him up over a girl before.

"Well, at least think about it. Maybe think on it for a while. A day or two. Maybe a week."

"You know I am leaving tomorrow," I reminded him.

"Yeah, but what if you didn't? It's not like you have anywhere you need to be."

"Yes, I do," I argued. "I need to be home, which isn't here. Not anymore."

<hr>

Stop. Staring. At. Her. You. Creep.

I'd managed to get us safely to the restaurant without crashing into a tree or swerving into oncoming traffic, but it wasn't without difficulty.

That damn dress.

Being on the road for so long had done something to me. I'd grown leaps and bounds in my professional career, but my personal life had taken a hit. I couldn't remember the last time I'd gone on an actual date or felt any sort of real connection beyond a few fleeting moments with a random stranger.

But the moment Elena had walked into my room in that dress, everything in my body had risen to attention, reminding me what it felt like to truly want another person.

No, not want.

Need.

"This used to be a pizza place when I was a kid," I commented as we walked up to the restaurant named Portofino.

I grabbed the door, and as she stepped in, my hand slid to her back as I followed her in. I didn't even realize I'd done it at first, but the moment I felt the heat of her skin burning through the thin fabric of her dress, I pulled away.

My hand fisted at my side like it was angry with me for forcing it away from her.

First my friends, and now, my own body was betraying me?

I let out a slow, measured breath.

If I could just get through tonight, then all this would be over. No more Ocracoke, no more family drama.

No more Elena…

My heart galloped a little at the thought, and I immediately shoved it aside, choosing to take a look around instead. The venue was small and intimate. With brick interior and low lighting, it came off as upscale and romantic. We were mostly on time, so a healthy number of people had already arrived. The restaurant was closed for the event. Macon's best friend and his husband were the owners, and he'd said tonight was their wedding gift to the couple.

Pretty damn nice gift…

"Do you want to check your coat?" Elena asked, bringing my attention back to her and all those lush curves. There was a tentative note in her voice.

"There's a coat check? In the summer?"

A tiny grin tugged at the corner of her bright red lips. "I

suggested it. I've been to tons of events, and no one ever thinks to offer a coat check when it's warm, and if the venue is small like this, well, let's just say, everyone benefits when there's a place for the men to stash those suit jackets." She held her palm up. "And before you say, 'Why don't you just drape it over the back of your seat?' let me just tell you that no one wants pictures with a room full of jackets."

She had a point.

I chuckled at the way her face grimaced. "Not even sure why people wear them in the summer in the first place."

Her gaze slipped down my chest. "Says the man in the leather jacket."

My hands smoothed over the supple leather. "This is my safety blanket. It knows no seasons."

She shook her head, clearly enjoying the easy way in which we'd slipped back into this lively banter we had going. "A man with a safety blanket. Now, if that's not a red flag, I don't know what is."

"Yeah, but it's a manly safety blanket 'cause it makes me look hot. So…" I shrugged, causing her to laugh, but I didn't miss the way her eyes lingered.

Take your fill, Elena.

"So, will you be able to part with it? Do I need to hold your hand or…" she teased as she showed me the way to the coat check.

A young girl, probably in her mid-teens, was already busy taking tweed blazers and suit jackets in various shades. Elena shot me a triumphant grin.

It was a brilliant idea. No one wanted a room full of sweaty dudes.

It only took a minute to get up to the front, and the poor girl nearly dropped the whole roll of tickets on the floor when she looked up at me. Her eyes widened, and that was when I spotted it—the black bracelet around her wrist.

A *Manic Fanatic*—their term. Not mine. Basically a diehard fan, usually of the teen variety. Although Asher had told me some wild stories involving some meet and greets and stay-at-home moms.

"Are you…" she stumbled on her words before she could out my stage name to Elena.

I shrugged my coat off and shoved it into her arms, giving her one of my most panty-melting smiles. "Could you make sure to give this one extra attention, darling?" I normally avoided my North Carolina twang like the plague, but right now, I'd do anything to keep this girl quiet.

And that included making a teenage girl blush.

"Yes!" she nearly squeaked. She pulled the coat to her chest, and I tried to ignore the way she breathed in the smell of the leather. She glanced up at us when she realized what she'd just done. Her face went cherry-apple red. "Here's your ticket!" she said, ripping one off the large roll and handing it to me.

"Thank you." I gave her a wink, and with a hand on Elena's back, I got us the hell out of there.

"A fan of yours?" she asked, a mischievous grin on her face.

"Nah," I said casually, shaking my head. "She probably just confused me for someone else."

Elena eyed me suspiciously. "She seemed to recognize you pretty quickly."

Yeah, that was because she had. It wasn't the first time it had happened. I'd toured with some big bands in the past, but not long enough to be recognized.

Not until Manic.

The first time had been standing in line for coffee in Melrose. The girl was in her mid-twenties and gorgeous. She walked up to me with a hesitant smile. I returned it tenfold, wondering if it was my damn birthday or something.

But then she'd asked, "Are you Zander Tate?"

It was a name I mostly saw on paper—a decision Lance and I had made a long time ago to separate me from my career.

And my career from my past.

Hearing it out loud…

I didn't know if I'd even answered the girl.

I just remembered leaving the coffee shop, knowing my life would never be the same. It was about to get a hell of a lot worse.

"I've toured with a few bands that are pretty notable." That was the understatement of the century. Manic at Midnight had just won a Grammy for the fourth year in a row despite losing their lead guitarist. "It's possible she saw me with one of them."

"How notable?" she probed.

Think, think, think.

"I did a few concerts with Vertigo," I said casually.

Her eyes widened. "No shit?"

I nodded. Vertigo was an up-and-coming band. Their first single hit the charts and not too long ago, and since then, they'd been gaining notoriety. Clearly, Elena was a fan.

I was, too. They were a good group.

"I love the lead singer's voice. She reminds me of a young Amy Lee."

I was once again blown away by her musical prowess. "They actually did a cover of an Evanescence song at the end of one of their shows I did."

"Seriously?" Her voice was nearly an octave higher. I loved it.

"Yeah, it was pretty epic," I replied, now kind of regretting it. Had I given her too much information? That concert could be found with a Google search.

"Elena!" someone said behind us.

She turned, and I caught the side of her face light up with recognition.

"Molly!" she exclaimed, pulling the blonde into a tight hug.

I watched the encounter with a mixture of trepidation and curiosity.

How often did Elena come to Ocracoke that she knew its residents so well?

The two women pulled back, and Elena turned. "Not sure if you remember—"

"Zander." She said my name like she was seeing a ghost.

I kind of wanted to respond by leaning forward and whispering, *Boo*, but I didn't.

"Hey, Molly."

Before I could barely get the words out of my mouth, the woman reached out and pulled me into a tight hug. I nearly groaned.

No one has any fucking boundaries in this town.

"All right, Mols. I think that's enough. You're gonna suffocate the poor guy."

I'd been so focused on Elena and Molly that I hadn't even noticed the man hovering nearby. I looked and found another familiar face.

Molly took a step back. My eyes went wide. Apparently, she wasn't the only one seeing ghosts tonight.

"Jake?"

"Hey, Zander," he said, swinging a possessive arm around Molly.

"You two…" I didn't even know what I was going to say, but they both held up their ring fingers.

"Married," Jake said with a wide grin. "Four years. Two kids."

Hadn't these two broken up, like, eons ago? Jake had packed up and left after graduation, which broke Molly's heart. It was literally all anyone could talk about for months. I remembered it vividly because it happened to be the same time Macon left for boot camp, and no one seemed to give a flying fuck about that. Well, no one but me…

Had I stumbled into some alternate universe?

"I think I need a drink," I said, making both of them laugh.

"It boggled my mind, too, when I came back, but shit actually does happen when you're not here," Jake joked as all four of us made our way to the bar.

I suddenly turned. "Wait, *you're* at my brother's engagement party?" I questioned.

He sighed. "Yeah. Weird, right?"

"Does he know?" I smirked.

Jake and Macon had never gotten along. He never really explained it to me, but it went way back. If something had changed between the two of them, it had to have been major.

"He knows," he said as we waited for the bartender.

Elena and Molly stood on the other side of Jake, quietly chatting. I tried not to get distracted by the way her ass looked as she leaned over the bar.

"Marin and Molly are really close. Molly's even in their wedding."

Well, I guessed that would classify as major.

"So, because they're friends, you were able to put years of bad blood behind you? Just like that?" I didn't know who I was asking for—him or me.

"No," he confessed as I steepled my fingers along the polished wood. "Not just like that. But little by little. It helps to see Marin and Molly so happy when we're all together. But we've talked some, and honestly, we're just kind of letting things play out."

"How so?"

"By realizing the past is just that—in the past—and there isn't shit we can do about it. So, instead, we just have to focus on what we can control, and that's right now."

"But how do you forget about the past?"

He looked over at me, keenly aware that I wasn't talking about him and Macon anymore. I knew I was his brother, but I was not that invested in the future of Jake and Macon's friendship.

"No one's asking you to forget. Hell, no one is even asking you to forgive. But at the end of the day, you have to weigh your trauma against whatever motivates you now—

love, loyalty, the desire to make amends and see what wins."

I let his words settle for a moment before I replied, but never got the opportunity. Elena and Molly joined us.

"We took matters into our own hands," she said, handing me a beer. It was the same brand I'd ordered the night before.

"Beauty, brains, and you know what kind of beer I like? You might just be the perfect woman."

"You wouldn't say that if you heard about my last few dates."

The thought of her on a date with another man conjured up irrational thoughts of jealousy, and I instantly shoved them down. "I think that reflects more on them than you, Louie."

"You're really sticking with that ridiculous nickname?" She shook her head. "I'm wearing Chanel today."

I grinned. "Chanel just doesn't have the same ring to it, you know?" I leaned forward, my lips brushing her ear. "And, yes, I'm keeping the nickname."

"God, you really are trouble."

"Oh, you have no idea."

We stared at each other, and suddenly, the room felt so damn small. And so fucking hot. Just then, someone rang a bell, pulling us out of our trance. I cleared my throat, and she blinked.

Fucking focus.

I kept reminding myself I was leaving in mere hours, and yet somehow, every time I opened my mouth, I indeed got myself into trouble.

This was a disaster.

Everyone began to take their seats like fucking cattle, and I let out a slow breath. As I looked around, I realized how intimate this party was. Considering Macon was now the sheriff, I had expected the whole damn county to be here. But in actuality, there were less than fifty people in attendance.

That didn't mean all fifty pairs of eyes weren't staring at me. They definitely were.

"On a scale of one to ten, how awkward do you feel right now?" Elena asked as she leaned over.

She smelled like jasmine and citrus. I inhaled, and I had to stifle a moan. I wouldn't be surprised if the mere whiff of an orange gave me a damn hard-on for the rest of my godforsaken life.

"Oh, definitely an eleven. Maybe a twelve," I answered, nervously running my hands through my hair.

"Want me to go get your jacket?" she teased.

Now that you mention it…

I rolled up my sleeves, feeling stifled by the rigid material. But if I was being honest, it wasn't the shirt.

It was the people.

I'd felt comfortable with Molly and Jake, but this? All the tentative glances and whispered conversations. I felt like I was on display, and all I wanted to do was bolt. I let out a staggering breath as I felt Elena's hand come to rest on my thigh. My eyes jerked to hers, but before she could say anything, Macon stood, and everyone quieted.

"Oh, good." He let out a chuckle. "I was really hoping I wouldn't have to tap a glass to get your attention."

"Believe me, so were we," a bearded man next to him muttered, and everyone laughed. "No one wants to clean that up."

"I—oh, sorry." Macon hesitated before reaching down to grab Marin's hand. She looked up at him with such devotion and affection that it made my chest ache. "*We* were going to do this at the end of the meal, but knowing how all you fuckers drink, I suggested we do it now while you're all still sober—"

"Speak for yourself, Green!" someone hollered toward the back.

A chorus of laughter followed.

"I knew I should have uninvited you, Millie." Macon shook his head, a smile tugging at his lips.

Molly's little sister was here, too?

Before I'd left, Macon had hated all these people. Now, they were at his engagement party.

Part of me wanted to be jealous or angry. While I had been gone, he'd built an entire life here—one we would have killed for while growing up in our lonely little house. But mostly, I was just relieved. I could leave here tomorrow, knowing he was taken care of.

He would be fine without me.

"First of all, we want to thank all of you for coming," Macon continued. "Even the loud ones." He gave a pointed stare in Millie's direction, and this time, I turned and found her.

She'd been hot when we were young, but now? Damn. She was sitting next to a man I was surprised to recognize. I'd read about him after the memorial the town had commissioned after a ferry explosion several years earlier. That ferry explosion had made national news, and I'd never forget how my hands shook while I looked up the victims' names on my phone.

I'd never been so relieved *not* to see Macon's name in my life.

I hadn't realized the artist had become a permanent resident of the island. Or Millie's husband.

"I know some of you had to travel to be here tonight, like Marin's parents and siblings."

Marin smiled down at an older couple sitting next to her, and then she turned her attention back to Macon and squeezed his hand.

"And my brother, who flew in from Los Angeles to be here tonight."

Macon's voice had grown hoarse at the mention of me, his eyes finding me in the crowd. The room grew quiet.

Oh God, why did I come?

How could I do this to him?

I suddenly wanted to flee. But Elena's hand squeezed my thigh, bringing me back to the present, and I placed my palm down on top, taking a deep breath.

"I know a lot of you had planned on a fall wedding," he went on.

That was news to me, and my brow lifted. They'd moved up the wedding?

"No one more than my pumpkin-latte-loving bride, but sometimes, life throws little curveballs, and you have to adjust."

They both looked at each other, grinning.

Marin took over as I noticed my brother's eyes grow wet with tears. "Our little curveball is due in December—"

The restaurant went wild. Gasps, shouts of joy. Marin's mother burst into tears, and among all that, Elena's hand flipped over, and her fingers wrapped around mine.

Did she know?

I snuck a glance at her, but she seemed just as shell-shocked as me.

"If you'll do us all a favor," Macon's voice boomed, quieting everyone instantly as he smiled ear to ear, "and lift your plates, Marin is dying to know what color to paint the nursery."

Everyone raced to lift their plates, but I turned to Elena instead, her hand still wrapped around mine like a lifeline. She reached for her plate at the same time as me.

Discreetly taped under the plate, there was a heart.

And that heart was pink.

The news hit me like a bullet train.

I'm going to be an uncle.

CHAPTER SEVEN

Elena

'm sorry," I quickly apologized, blinking a few times in an effort to force myself back into the conversation. "What did you say?"

The older woman across the table seemed unfazed and repeated the question. "Is there anything you recommend us doing in Richmond when we visit?"

She was a relative of Marin… An aunt maybe?

Shit, I can't remember.

"Oh…" I covered my mouth with my napkin, even though I'd barely touched my food. All I could think of when I stared down at my food was the pink heart that was taped underneath. My stomach swirled. "There are, um, tons—museums, parks, amazing restaurants. Are you Poe fans?"

Her sparse white eyebrows furrowed.

I guess not.

I pulled out my phone and slid it across the table. "Give me your number," I suggested, trying to smile even though all I really wanted to do was tell her to fucking google it, throw down my napkin, and run. "I'll send you a list."

She seemed pleased with the suggestion, and I let out a staggered breath. I looked around the table, noticing how everyone was engaged in animated conversations, their moods happy and jovial.

Like yours should be.

The woman finished punching in her phone number and handed it back to me, and she opened her mouth once again. "So what—"

"How is Texas this time of year?" Zander interrupted her, making my head turn.

He leaned over the table and smiled. The woman's eyes raked over his edgy, dark haircut with the shaved sides, the pierced brow, and all those tattoos covering his forearms.

And she freaking *blushed.*

"Oh, it's miserable," she answered, fiddling with the pearl buttons on her sweater cardigan.

Was there a single woman on this planet he couldn't charm? I'd be mad about it if it wasn't for the fact he'd purposely distracted her from interrogating me any further.

I didn't know how I felt about that. He shouldn't know me so well.

Someone laughed, and I turned. Macon was kissing Marin's temple, laughing at something her sister had said. Her parents were huddled over something—was that a sonogram picture?

"I'll be right back," I said suddenly as I rose from my seat.

Zander looked up, a note of concern flashing across his face.

"You okay?" he questioned.

I nodded. "Just need to use the restroom," I assured him.

He didn't seem convinced, but let me go anyway.

It wasn't like he could follow me to the restroom.

I was thankful that mostly everyone was still mid-meal, and I had a clear path across the restaurant. After my last conversation, I was at my limit for idle chatter at the moment. I followed the signs to a small hallway, and there, I found the ladies' restroom. I pushed the door open and let out a sigh of relief when I checked the three stalls and found them all empty.

I went to the sink and stared at myself in the reflection. My red lipstick was mostly gone, but outwardly, I mostly looked the same as I had when I left the house less than two hours prior.

Beautiful, polished, and put together.

Inside, I felt disgusting and ugly.

"What the hell is wrong with you?" I whispered, my lips quivering as I said it. My arms wrapped around my middle as I tried to will myself back together.

A quiet knock sounded at the door.

Cocking my head toward it, I froze. Why would someone knock? Did they not know it was a multi-stall situation up in here?

I took a few tentative steps, and before I made it to the door, Zander stepped in, his eyes sweeping over me like he was checking for bodily harm.

"Are you okay?"

Say yes, Elena.

Say yes.

"Can you take me home?" The words were out before I could stop them.

"Yeah," he answered right away, not even bothering to ask why.

He closed the distance between us, wrapped an arm around my shoulders, and ushered us out. The hallway was quiet and empty, but I heard the sound of laughter as the party went on without us.

"Why did you come after me?" I asked as he pushed the door open and we headed for the exit.

"I don't know," he answered honestly. He sounded just as surprised by his actions as I was.

We made it to his car without being noticed. Everyone was still too wrapped in the food, the booze, and the happy news...

I bit down on my bottom lip as Zander opened the passenger door and guided me in.

"I'm good," I assured him.

He seemed reluctant to let me go but did once I had my seat belt in hand. The car door shut soon after, and a few seconds later, he was in the driver's seat, and we were on the road.

A deafening silence settled between us as I watched trees and street signs pass by us. A chill went down my spine as a blast of cold air from one of the vents hit me, and then I remembered.

"Your jacket!" I said, sucking in a breath.

"It's fine," he assured me. He didn't seem fazed, which surprised me. The jacket seemed pretty important to him. "I'll text Macon."

"Do you even have Macon's number?" I asked.

"No," he confessed, the tiniest smirk spreading across his face. "But I'm sure you can remedy that for me."

I decided not to point out that once his brother had his phone number, the ability to cut and run would become a little more difficult. But maybe he'd thought about that already.

Maybe he hadn't.

Either way, it didn't matter. He was leaving regardless.

"I take it, you didn't know?" Zander's voice was quiet. Tentative.

"No," I answered as I fiddled with the clasp of my clutch, running my fingers over the cool metal as I tried to come up with something else to say. But what else was there?

Why hadn't she told me?

Why had she held on to such a big announcement and decided not to share it with me privately? From the reactions in the room, it appeared that they hadn't told anyone, not even Marin's parents.

So, why would I assume I would be an exception?

Because she was always mine…

Zander pulled into the driveway of Ochre Bay and shut off the engine. I didn't say anything as I tugged off my seat belt and exited the car. Soon, he joined me, and we walked side by side up the walkway until we reached the doorway, and he punched in the code.

I flipped on a light and immediately kicked off my heels.

"Do you want anything?" he asked as he headed straight for the kitchen. "I noticed you didn't eat much."

"I—" He had been watching me? "I'm good," I answered. "I'm going to go change. I'll be right back."

He nodded, already pulling out what looked like fixings for a peanut butter and jelly sandwich.

"Do you want me to text Marin, or…" *Please say no.* I couldn't pretend right now.

He shook his head, already diving into the peanut butter with a butter knife. My stomach growled.

"No, I can do it."

I reached into my clutch and placed my phone on the counter. "You can grab Macon's number. I don't want them to worry."

A wry grin ghosted his lips as he drew his thumb into his mouth and licked a bit of peanut butter off of it. I watched far too intently.

"I doubt they are worried in the way you think." He stared at me for a moment longer.

Oh, right.

"I'll let you get changed." He turned away.

I didn't bother saying anything more. Heading down the hallway, I opened the door to my room and stepped in. It was dark, and for a few breaths, I just stood there as all my awful thoughts came rushing back at once.

She should have told me.

Why do I feel jealous?

Why isn't he here?

A sob tore from my lips as I tried to muffle the sound with

both hands. Tears burned my eyes, and in that moment, I hated myself.

Hated my insecurities.

My selfishness.

"Elena." A soft voice sounded behind me.

I turned to see Zander framing the door. The light from the hallway surrounded him like a halo, and he stepped into the dark room and wrapped his arms around me.

He didn't say a word. He didn't ask any questions as I let the tears fall, all that guilt and shame staining my cheeks as the sound of my sobs filled the room. His hand gently stroked my hair. My head rested against his chest, and I felt the steady, comforting rhythm of his heartbeat.

"You must think I'm an awful person," I finally said, my voice barely a whisper. "My best friend announces she's pregnant, and I burst into tears."

"That is the last thing I'm thinking right now," he assured me, his voice deep and even. "And for the record, you're allowed to feel and react however the fuck you want."

"I want to be happy for them," I said before amending my words. "I *am* happy for them."

"You can be happy for someone and also feel sad—"

"I feel—" I swallowed, hating myself for even thinking it. "No, I can't."

"Sometimes, saying it out loud helps. You're only feeding the monster by keeping it in."

"The monster?"

"Trauma, rage, depression. Whatever your demon is, it feeds off of all those self-doubts and intrusive thoughts. The less we acknowledge them, the bigger those monsters grow inside our head, and pretty soon, there's not a whole lot of room left for us."

"You sound very well-adjusted for someone who can't talk to his brother."

For once, he didn't pull away. "It's one thing to offer advice. It's another thing to follow it."

I tried not to think about how much that resonated with me. How many times had I given Marin advice over the years, only to do the opposite in my own life?

I took a deep breath, letting the air leave my lungs slowly as I gathered the courage to speak. "It's not like I've never thought about Marin having kids. Logically, I knew when she and Macon got engaged, this would happen. I guess I just hadn't prepared myself for the type of emotions it might conjure up. When I saw her up there, elated and beaming with joy, I wanted to be happy, like everyone else. Instead, the first thought I had was, *It should be Daniel standing there beside her*. And then I got so angry with myself for even thinking it." The words made my eyes sting, and I fought the wave of emotions threatening to take over. "God, I really am an awful friend."

"No," he argued. "You're a good sister. One who still misses her brother."

I squeezed my eyes shut, a myriad of images flooding my mind—sitting on the floor of Daniel's room, listening to music; dropping him off on his first day of college; seeing his face when Marin walked down the aisle.

"He would have been an amazing dad," I said. "He always thought Ocracoke would be a great place to raise kids."

Zander grunted, and the deep sound vibrated against my chest. "I feel like I'm the wrong person to make that assessment." He paused before adding, "But I don't doubt Macon will do his damnedest to give his family everything we didn't have."

I looked up at him. "I love Macon," I assured him. "I do."

"You don't have to convince me." His eyes turned away.

"Your brother's a good man, Zander."

"I know," he said quietly, pulling back. His arms dropped to his sides. "You okay to get dressed now? I made you a sandwich. Don't say you're not hungry."

Still avoiding the Macon topic. Got it.

"Yeah, and thanks." *For everything.*

"Anytime."

We both knew that wasn't true.

"So, is the PB and J, like, a specialty, or are you trained in other childhood delicacies?" I teased him as I sat cross-legged on the sofa.

Despite the dig, it was really good. The perfect balance of peanut butter and raspberry jam. I couldn't remember the last time I'd had something so simple and satisfying. Zander was on his second—or was it third?—sandwich while I was eating at a more leisurely pace and still nibbling on the first half of mine.

"That's a lot of mocking for someone who didn't say thank you." He smirked.

And then I swore he shoved an entire half of a sandwich in his mouth.

That should not be adorable.

He'd changed after he left my room, switching out his all-black look for a fitted gray T-shirt and sweats. I'd never really been a big fan of sweats, always associating them with my father's frumpy pajamas, but these were not your papa's PJs. They hung low on his hips, and the tapered fit made his ass look fucking edible.

I'd tried not to stare when I came out of my bedroom and he walked out of the kitchen, carrying my sandwich.

But there might have been some blatant ogling—I wasn't gonna lie.

His large body seemed to dwarf the oversize chair as he leaned over the coffee table and continued to inhale his dinner…snack? *Whatever.*

I attempted to cover my grin but failed miserably. "Thank you. I was actually hungry."

"Clearly," he mocked, motioning to my half-eaten sandwich.

"Not all of us have the metabolism of Superman," I said. *Or the body.* "And the maid-of-honor dress I picked out is not forgiving, so I'm trying to behave."

His gaze raked down my body. I was dressed down in yoga pants and a cropped fleece hoodie.

"I'm sorry I'm going to miss that." His words sounded genuine. "But if the dress is anything like the one you wore tonight, I don't think you'll have any problem, Louie." His eyes darkened, causing me to flush.

Part of me was relieved he wouldn't be here. I wasn't sure how much longer I could withstand this sexual tension between us.

A soft knock caused me to jump, and Zander's eyes jerked to the door.

"Expecting anyone?" he asked.

I shook my head. As he was just starting to get off the couch, a familiar voice came from the other side of the door.

"If you're naked, could you just let me know? Like, give me a signal or something?"

Zander and I looked at each other.

It was Marin.

"Maybe just a knock on the wall? Or you can just…" She paused, and I could just picture her at the threshold, staring up at the sky, begging any deity she could think of to give her strength. "You know what? I'll just come back in the morning."

"Should we save her from her misery? Or let her go?" An evil grin spread across Zander's face.

I was already getting up and headed for the door. "She doesn't need that kind of stress," I told him. "Or nightmares."

He laughed.

Pulling the door open, I found my best friend on the other side, one face shielded by a familiar article of clothing—Zander's leather jacket.

"Is it safe?" she asked, her voice slightly muffled by the leather.

"Oh my God." I swatted at the jacket, getting her attention. "You are ridiculous."

She finally dropped it to her side, and her eyes opened. "You're dressed." She seemed…shocked.

"Of course, I'm dressed!" I exclaimed. "Didn't Zander text Macon?"

"Well, yes, but he told Macon he took you home 'cause you didn't feel well."

I looked at her, my expression blank as I waited for her to respond. I looked over at Zander, who was casually leaning against the arm of the couch with his arms folded across his chest. I looked back at Marin, and her mouth formed a big, round O.

"Oh, so that was true? I just assumed it was code."

I rolled my eyes and stepped aside to let her in. She caught sight of Zander, taking in his casual appearance, but apparently chose not to say anything.

"So, are you feeling okay?" she asked as I returned to my seat on the couch. She took the seat next to me and turned so we were facing one another.

I swallowed, unsure how to respond. I didn't want to lie. I had technically left the party because I felt unwell. There just wasn't anything physically wrong with me.

"Uh, I'm gonna go check in with…" Zander grabbed the back of his neck as he pushed off the couch, clearly uncomfortable with giving Marin too much information about his life. "I'm gonna go make a phone call."

His eyes met mine, and I knew immediately what he was doing. He was giving us time to talk, and once again, I found it strange that he could understand me so well after such a short time.

She was still in her dress from the party. It was romantic with a delicate floral pattern, and now that I looked at it, I realized it was also deceptively good at covering her midsection.

It also made me think back over the last twenty-four hours in a new light.

"So, I have to ask you a serious question," I said, getting straight to the point.

She nodded, her eyes avoiding mine, obviously nervous.

"Did you or did you not serve me decaf coffee this morning?"

She burst out laughing, and I held out my hands in an exaggerated shrug and said, "What? I need to know 'cause I'm not sure our friendship can handle this deception."

I knew we had other stuff we needed to talk about, and we would, but right now, I needed to laugh with my best friend.

So, that was what we did.

"I'm going to plead the Fifth," she finally answered.

"You bitch!"

Her eyes were leaking with unshed tears from our giggling. "It's why I ordered a matcha latte this morning at the coffee shop, too."

I grimaced. "Gross. You know that shit tastes like grass, right?"

"Well, right now, that 'grass' is the most caffeine I'm allowed to consume, and even that makes Macon nervous. He's overprotective on a normal day. Now? He's freaking insane."

I swallowed nervously. "So, how did this all happen? The baby, I mean. Was it planned?"

"No!" she answered with a laugh. "But it's not unwelcome, if that's what you mean."

"That's not at all what I meant," I assured her. "I know you've always wanted kids."

Her gaze met mine, and although she didn't say anything, I knew we were both thinking of Daniel.

"I'm not sure how it happened, honestly," she told me. I

tilted my brow. "Okay, I mean, I know *how* it happens, obviously, but I don't know how exactly it happened for us."

"Explain," I said, grabbing another bite of my long-forgotten PB&J. I needed something to do with my hands.

"I'm not sure if I ever told you that Macon and Kristy tried to have a baby for a long time."

I could tell by the pitch in her voice that she did not enjoy talking about her fiancé's cheating ex. It wasn't as sore of a subject as it used to be now that Kristy had helped put her second husband, the former sheriff, behind bars.

But it didn't erase the pain she'd caused Macon.

"Anyway, I guess after she got pregnant so quickly with Hayes, Macon kind of figured it was his fault they'd never conceived."

That sounded like him. He tried to carry the blame for everything.

"So, you decided to, what? Forgo birth control because of it?" I was trying to figure out where she was going with this story.

"Not exactly," she answered sheepishly. "But I might not have been as diligent as I should have been, believing that it might never happen for us."

"Marin." I tried to sound genuine in my scolding, but how could I? They were having a baby, and if there were two people more deserving, it was Marin and Macon.

My throat constricted.

"I'm sorry I left the party," I said, my voice suddenly heavy with emotion. "I—"

"No." She held up a hand. "I should have told you. I worked up this whole gender reveal in my head and got so wrapped up in the surprise of it all that I forgot to stop and think how it might affect everyone. When the first sentence out of my dad's mouth was a fearful, 'Is she healthy?' " I knew I'd made a mistake.

My face softened. "He knows MS isn't inherited."

She nodded. "Yes, of course he knows. The rational side of

him, that is. But sometimes, when you're hit with something like that, the irrational thoughts are the ones you hear the loudest."

I nodded, understanding more than she realized. "So, that's why you showed up here, in the middle of your engagement party, willing to walk in on Zander and me?"

She grinned.

"Seriously, Marin. Did you really think I'd just run back here, emotional and distraught, and what? Use his dick as a coping mechanism?"

She snorted, her hand flying to her mouth as a laugh bubbled up her throat. "I mean, I wouldn't blame you. God, those Green genes are really something else, aren't they?"

Now, it was my turn to laugh. "That is your future brother-in-law!"

"Doesn't mean I can't acknowledge that he's hot." She shrugged. "And you're totally right. Adam Levine clone, all the way."

"Good God," I muttered. "Who are you? Is this a pregnancy symptom? I think I liked it better when you went fifty shades of red when talking about anything remotely sexual."

"Oh, I'm not completely cured. Mention a vibrator, and I turn into a tomato." It was true. She was already fidgeting on the couch and blushing.

I raised my pointer finger in the air. "You just gave me the perfect idea for a baby shower gift! Every new mom needs one."

Her eyes went wide. "Don't you dare! My mother will be there."

Giggles filled the living room, healing my soul bit by bit.

"Thanks for coming over," I said finally.

"Thanks for spending these three weeks with me. I know it wasn't easy to take the time off."

I thought those words over. "No, but maybe it should be."

"What do you mean?"

"It's just…" I let out a sigh. "Ever since Chad and I broke

up, I keep going out on these dates, hoping I'll, what? Meet someone? But what's the point? It's not like I have anything to offer them. My life is that job."

She gave me a warm smile. "Then, maybe this vacation is just what you need. Just consider you and your job officially on a break." I grimaced, and she just shook her head. "How many times have you checked your email?"

"A few times," I confessed.

"I'll go in your room right now and confiscate that laptop, I swear to God."

I pressed my lips together to stop from grinning. "You're gonna be an amazing mom," I told her. I'd never meant anything more. This was a role she'd take on effortlessly, and I couldn't wait to see her embrace it.

"And you're going to be an amazing aunt," she assured me.

I swallowed, feeling emotional all over again.

I wasn't technically going to be an aunt. But she knew that.

I also knew that she didn't care about technicalities.

"No," I corrected her. "I'm going to be the *best* aunt."

Her face broke out into a wide grin. "Well, my sister already said the same thing so—"

"Margo thinks she can beat me? Oh, it's on." I rubbed my hands together like some maniacal villain. "How do you feel about monograms? Designer diaper bag? Oh! Chandelier in the nursery!"

"Oh God, this kid is gonna be spoiled."

Hell yeah, she is.

One of the weirdest things so far about this vacation—aside from my temporary roommate—was the lack of an alarm clock. I'd woken up to that jarring sound blasting in my eardrums ever since I was a kid. Even on the weekends, I was an early riser, always heading to the gym or catching up on a bit of work before I started my day.

But when I had gotten to Ocracoke, I'd forced myself to go without. It was vacation after all, right? And vacation was all about relaxation and a disconnect from reality.

But after two days, I'd decided I really fucking hated it.

I rolled over in bed and opened my eyes to the morning sun. *The morning sun?* I never got up when it was light outside.

What time is it?

Where the hell am I?

Shit, did I sleep through my alarm?

God, I felt disoriented. I turned my head slowly, shifting in the too-firm bed, and found my suitcase on the floor across from me. The world started to make sense again.

Marin. Ocracoke. Wedding.

Pregnant.

The initial shock from last night had worn off, and although the painful reality of once again realizing that my brother was gone was still there, I was truly happy for my best friend.

And so unbelievably grateful to have her in my life.

Seeing her standing there at the door, knowing she'd left her own engagement party to come find me, had reminded me just how amazing she was.

If my brother's life had to be cut short, I was glad he at least had gotten to spend it with her.

Zander had never come back after he left Marin and me alone to talk. I wasn't sure if he didn't feel comfortable with Marin here or if he simply needed to rest. But the two of us talked for hours until Macon came by and stole her back, grumbling about the stragglers at the party and how long it took them to leave.

You give people an open bar, and suddenly, they forget where they live…

It had been late when they both headed home, but part of

me had hoped I might see Zander again. He was leaving today, and I'd wanted to have a little more time with him before he left.

To thank him.

To…

It doesn't matter.

He's leaving regardless.

I sat up and stretched, looking out the window. It was sunny, which meant it was going to be hot. For a girl who had grown up in Texas and Virginia, you'd think I would be used to this kind of weather, but I hated it. It wasn't to say I liked the cold either. Give me seventy-five and sunny any day of the week. I was not made for extremes.

I threw the covers off and quickly changed out of my pajamas. I might have packed cozy loungewear, but my PJs were the exact opposite. One hundred percent silk, this little short and camisole set was worth every damn penny, and it made sleeping feel indulgent.

Thankfully, each bedroom in this house came with its own bathroom, so I headed into mine and brushed my teeth. Catching a quick look in the mirror, I tried to tame my hair with a brush, but ended up just tossing it into a messy ponytail before heading into the kitchen.

The house was eerily quiet.

What time was it?

I realized I hadn't even checked. I made a mental note to mention that to Marin.

See, I was totally acing this vacation thing.

I went to the pantry and pulled out a bag of coffee and then pulled out the pot to fill it with water.

My eyes widened as I saw its digital clock staring back at me.

Nine freaking thirty?

I'd slept in until nine thirty?

After that startling revelation, I realized I wasn't the only one.

Zander's bedroom door was still firmly shut.

I had no idea what Zander's schedule was, but I knew he'd planned on talking to Macon today, so he had to be up at some point.

Maybe I'd make him something as a thank-you for the meal he'd bought me the other night.

I did kind of owe him for bailing right after…

I opened the fridge and stared at the stocked fridge Macon had left us. What should I make? Eggs and bacon? Pancakes? Oh, waffles!

I pulled my head out of the fridge and frantically looked around. I needed a recipe.

Shit, where is my phone?

I remembered I hadn't had it when I came into the kitchen, so I ran back to my room and found it still plugged in on the side table. Just as I was about to grab it, it started to vibrate.

I looked down at the screen. Marin was calling me.

"Hey, what's up?" I answered cheerfully.

"Hey." By the sound of her voice, I knew instantly that something was wrong.

"Are you okay? Is the baby—"

"Baby is fine," she assured me. I hope she realized she was going to be saying that a lot over the next five months of her pregnancy. "I'm calling because…" She paused. "Is Zander there?"

I scrunched my brows in confusion, and for some reason, I scanned my room like I expected him to be there. "What do you mean? Where else would he be?"

She let out a sigh. "He was supposed to meet Macon at the coffee shop half an hour ago, and he never showed."

Dread pooled in my belly as I ran to the window and pulled the curtain to the side.

The spot where Zander's rental had been parked along the curb was now empty.

"Fuck." I squeezed my eyes shut.

He wouldn't.

He would.

"What?" she asked.

"Hold on," I replied, turning around and marching out of the room.

I headed down the hallway to his room. I didn't even knock.

I knew there was no point.

He wasn't there.

The bed was neatly made, and the curtains were pulled closed. It was as if he had never been there.

"He's gone," I finally told her.

There was a long pause.

"This is going to destroy Macon."

I bit my bottom lip, hating that I'd kept this from her. "He came back," I told her. "It's a start."

But even I knew I was grasping at straws.

She said good-bye after that, needing to find Macon to deliver the news. I wandered back into the kitchen as the coffeepot beeped that it was ready.

A whole pot of coffee, just for me.

I sighed, placed my phone on the counter, and grabbed a mug. As I turned around, I noticed the notifications on my screen.

One unread text from an unknown number.

I pulled it up.

Take care of our niece.

—Z

I couldn't stop the tears that followed, and I had no idea why.

CHAPTER EIGHT

ME

Hey, Elena didn't feel well, so I drove her home. It's Zander BTW.

Also, I left my leather jacket. Do you mind grabbing it?

MACON

Okay. No problem. I'll tell Marin. Why the fuck did you bring a jacket in July?

ME

'Cause it makes me look cool. Obviously.

MACON

Says the 32yo with the eyebrow piercing.

ME

Which also makes me look cool.

MACON

<eye roll emoji> Meet for coffee tomorrow. We haven't had a chance to catch up. 9:30?

'd had every good intention of going to that coffee shop.

I'd even driven up to the damn place.

But the second I got there, I panicked.

Maybe it had been the banter between us that reminded me just how easy I could fall back into this life.

His life.

But that was the thing. I had my own life, friends. Family.

Sweat poured down my back as the car slowed and the parking lot came into view. All I had to do was turn the wheel. My heart started to race.

I can't do this.

I can't say good-bye to my brother.

So, I didn't.

I just kept driving, got on the ferry, and never looked back.

"You are a fucking coward," I muttered under my breath as I took the exit that led to the Norfolk airport.

I'd been driving for hours without a single break, like I was punishing myself for sneaking away this morning.

I hadn't even said good-bye to Elena.

Just a single text, after stealing her number when she let me borrow her phone.

Way to be both a jerk and a creeper at the same time, Z.

I pulled into a fast-food restaurant and parked, leaving the car idle as I let out a deep breath for probably the first time in hours.

I needed a minute before I drove into that airport.

Okay, maybe more than a minute.

A family walked past, the mother shouting ahead to watch for cars as the young girl and boy sipped from little apple juice boxes and pointed at something in the distance. Their parents smiled at each other fondly and reached out and clasped hands.

My parents had never looked at each other like that. I wasn't even sure I had a memory of the two of them together that wasn't coated in misery. What would Macon and I have been like if we'd had a childhood like those two kids? If our mom hadn't died? If our dad had cared more about us than booze?

Would it have made a difference?

I looked down at my phone for the first time since I'd disembarked the ferry.

I had a few messages from Macon and one from Lance. I wasn't ready to read the ones from Macon yet, so I skipped ahead to the one from Lance.

LANCE

Call me ASAP.

That didn't sound good.

He picked up on the first ring.

"Are you still in North Carolina?" he asked. No *hello*. No *hey, how are you?* Just straight to the point. That was how Lance rolled when he was working. He rarely let our personal relationship bleed into his role as my manager, and I respected the hell out of him for it.

"On my way to the airport," I answered, which was technically true. He didn't need to know that I was currently sitting in a McDonald's parking lot, having a bit of an existential crisis as I pondered my life choices and berated myself for bailing on my brother.

"Any chance you'd want to stay for a bit longer?"

Now, that got my attention. I sat up in my seat. "Why?"

"Check your phone. I just sent you another text."

He couldn't just tell me?

I pulled the phone away from my ear and tapped on a celebrity news post he'd sent.

My world tilted.

ZANDER TATE REPORTED TO REPLACE MITCH ZEGLER AS LEAD GUITARIST FOR MANIC AT MIDNIGHT.

"You still there?" he asked.

"Yeah," I answered, my voice half the volume it had been before. "I'm still here."

"We're trying to figure out who leaked it because there is no way it's a credible source. We'll get it taken down. In the meantime, I've talked to Ridge, the manager for Manic, and he'd like you to continue to keep a low profile."

In Los Angeles? That was like asking a pink flamingo to hide in a herd of cattle. People there stalked celebrities for sport.

"So, I'm on house arrest." I let out a sigh. "Do you know when the band is planning on making the announcement?"

"It sounded like they had some ideas," he explained. "But they want to do it in person, and since a few of the guys are back home in the UK, I'm guessing a couple of weeks at least."

God, I was going to go fucking mad if I had to hole myself up in my house for that long.

I looked down at my leather jacket spread across the passenger seat and tried not to imagine my brother sitting in that coffee shop this morning, waiting for me.

I said the words before I even had a chance to regret them. "You asked if I was still in North Carolina?"

I was technically in Virginia at the moment, but he didn't need to know that.

"Yeah," he breathed out. "Hendrix mentioned your hometown was remote."

"Yeah," I answered. "Ocracoke is about as remote as you

can get. Doesn't mean I won't get recognized." I already had after all.

"Do you want to stay?"

I thought about how I'd left things with Macon. Or how I hadn't…

And then my mind wandered back to that darkened bedroom, the feel of Elena in my arms.

"Yeah," I answered. "If I'm gonna be stuck somewhere for a few weeks, I'd rather it be there than cooped up inside." Especially if these were going to be my last weeks of normalcy.

"We can have Hendrix take over your social media accounts while you're away," he suggested. "I'll keep him regularly posting pics of you in LA. That way, if some Manic Fanatic spots you there—"

"They'll think I'm just some really good-looking doppelgänger," I finished for him. "You're kind of diabolical."

"That's why they pay me the big bucks." He paused, and I could hear the shift in his voice. "So, you're gonna do it then? Go to your brother's wedding?"

I swallowed the lump in my throat, realizing this was Lance, the dad figure, asking and not Lance, the manager.

"Yeah," I answered. "I think I at least owe him the chance to try and explain. He basically raised me."

"You don't owe anyone shit," he clarified. "But if you think going back there will be good for you and your soul, then you absolutely should. Plus, Hendrix said there's a hot roommate?"

"Oh, fuck him." I laughed.

"Hey, I'm just looking out for you. As your manager."

"Whatever."

His deep, familiar chuckle filled my ear. "Let me know if you need anything. And, kid?"

"Yeah, Lance?"

"Don't forget the NDA," he said. "You can't tell anyone."

Shit. I *had* forgotten about that.

"Right." I swallowed hard. "I remember."

"You going to be okay with that? Being around your family and old friends and keeping that a secret?"

"Yeah," I lied. "It's only a couple of weeks. What could possibly go wrong?"

There were several things I had not considered when I made the rash decision to turn my car around and head back to Ocracoke. The first and most glaring issue was my accommodations. Elena had been okay with me sharing her space for a night.

But three weeks?

I wasn't even sure I could handle three weeks alone with that woman. One night had been torturous. Knowing she was right down the hall, wondering what she wore to bed, picturing her in the shower—

Fuck, maybe I should reconsider that house arrest.

Secondly, I'd packed enough clothes to last me about two days, and while I could make do and buy whatever I didn't have, the one thing I couldn't replace was my equipment. If I was going to be here for an extended period of time, I was going to need more than the single acoustic I'd brought along.

I had a tour to prepare for.

Thankfully, Hendrix was more than willing to take care of this problem for me.

"Dude, does this mean I get to meet your family?"

"No," I answered when I called him to tell him about the article and the abrupt change of plans. "Just ship it to me."

"And risk my balls when you go apeshit 'cause your Strat was scratched in transit? No fucking way. I'm hand-delivering that thing."

"I feel like you're just using this as an excuse."

"Maybe." He laughed. "But you can't deny the thought

that one of your guitar babies getting injured gives you heart palpitations."

It did. I wasn't gonna lie.

Some people had fur babies. I had guitars.

So, that was how Hendrix roped me into booking him a round-trip flight from Los Angeles to Norfolk, leaving in a few days. Until then, I'd just have to make do. I tried to get him in and out in a day, but he convinced me he needed more time to recharge than that. He was staying for two.

He made sure to add how excited he was to meet my "other roommate" before we hung up.

This was gonna be a nightmare.

My stomach rolled as I drove off the ferry and onto Highway 12.

The town's welcome sign mocked me as I drove by once more.

I'd texted Macon after I boarded the ferry for the second time that day, asking him to meet me at the coffee shop. Again. I expected him to ask questions. Yell a little maybe.

Instead, he responded with:

MACON

You actually gonna show this time?

Yeah, I guessed I deserved that.

When I drove into the parking lot, he was already waiting for me. He leaned against his patrol car, both arms folded across his broad chest. I'd never seen him in uniform before.

Well, not this one at least.

He wore tan utility pants and heavy boots. A black shirt and vest with the word *sheriff* in bold script covered his upper body. He looked formidable, and I suddenly felt like I was twelve years old all over again.

Shutting off the engine, I stepped out of the car and walked the short distance to where he stood. The gravel crunched under my feet, and I could feel his heavy gaze every step of the way.

"You came back," he simply stated.

"I did."

He looked out toward the bay before turning back toward me, blowing out a breath. "I really want to fucking punch you right now."

I rubbed the barbell in my brow before answering, "You can if it'll make you feel better."

He stared at me for a moment longer before pushing off his cruiser. "Come on. Let's go get some coffee."

Guess my face is safe for now.

I followed him, and we both made our way inside. The door chimed, and since it was late afternoon, the place was mostly empty. We both headed toward the counter and were instantly greeted by the same woman I'd run into yesterday.

Does she ever leave?

She pressed her lips together, her eyes glassy, as if the sight of us brought her to tears.

"The Green boys. Together at last," she let out a huge sigh as she looked at Macon and then me.

I still had no fucking clue who this woman was.

Had he stumbled upon a long-lost grandmother while I was away?

I turned to Macon, who seemed to be making a concerted effort to be polite.

"Hi, Janet," he said with a forced smile. "Can I get a black coffee with cream and two sugars? Zander?"

"What? Oh, just black for me," I replied, enjoying the sight of Macon's discomfort. It appeared he wasn't chummy with everyone in town.

After last night's party, I'd started to wonder where my burly brother had gone.

Here he is.

"I can get it," I said, pulling out my wallet, but Macon swatted me away and threw down some cash, not bothering to ask for change. "I can afford coffee," I said defensively as Janet handed us our cups, and we took a seat toward the back. "Despite my lack of accommodations, I do actually have my shit together."

He gave me a withering stare, leaning back with one leg over the other. "How am I supposed to know that, Zander? I don't know shit about you. You've been MIA for over ten years, and then you suddenly roll into town, and before we even have the chance to sit down for more than five minutes, you up and bail? What the fuck, man?"

I tried to gather my thoughts, the warmth of the coffee heating my hands. "Look, I'm sorry, okay? This isn't easy for me."

"Do you think it's easy for me?" His voice carried through the coffee shop, and he let out a sigh. "Great, just fucking great." His eyes flew to the counter, where Janet was giving her best performance as she pretended to wipe down the pristine counters. He glared at her, and she scurried off like a little mouse.

"No," I answered, realizing we should have done this somewhere else. No one needed to know that the Green brothers were causing drama in the coffee shop. "None of this is, but I never…" I let out a frustrated sigh. "I never wanted to come back here."

"You think I don't know that?" he said with a humorless laugh. "The moment I found out you'd run off with my truck on your birthday, I knew you were never coming back."

"This was never supposed to be a reunion for me, Macon. I've been so mad at you for so long that I thought coming here would help me move on, but I couldn't even do that right." I let out an audible sigh. "You don't know what it was like. After you left. You don't—"

—know because you fucking abandoned me, I wanted to say.

The words caught in my throat, and I could barely swallow. I set my coffee down on the table and leaned forward, digging my palms into my forehead.

"Then, tell me," he said.

I shook my head.

But he persisted. "Please, Zander."

I looked toward the door. The water from the bay winked in the distance. I didn't know why I was resistant to divulging this information. It was why I'd hated him for so long. It should be easy to dump it back on him, right? To finally make him feel as shitty as I had.

"After you left, I thought it'd be the same, you know? And it was at first. And then, after a few months, I guess when he realized you really weren't coming back, he got angrier. And a lot more vocal," I finally said.

"Did he hurt you?"

"No." I shook my head. "Not physically at least. But he made sure I knew it was my fault that you'd left. Said I was too needy and you just couldn't wait to get away."

"That's not…" He let out a sigh. "He just said that because he was pissed that I was no longer there to provide him with a steady flow of cash. He hated the fact that I could hold down a job, unlike him, but it never kept him from stealing my earnings."

"It…" I swallowed. "It doesn't matter. It's in the past."

"That might be so, but it doesn't change the fact that I did abandon you. I left you with a monster masquerading as our father, and for that, I'm sorry. I've waited a long time to tell you that." His gaze didn't meet mine. "I could have waited a few years before enlisting, but at the time, a few years seemed like—"

"An eternity."

Every day in that house had felt like a lifetime in hell.

"He eventually stopped coming home," I told him. It was funny. Sometimes, those days felt like they were only yesterday, like the pain of his words was still so raw and real that I could barely breathe. And then there were moments when he felt so far in the past that I wondered if any of it was actually real.

But that was what the memories were for, I guessed. A reminder.

A warning.

"That was a nice change of pace," I went on. "I had no idea where he went, and at the time, I was so relieved to be free of him that I didn't care. I thought I'd be fine without him, but when the lights went out two weeks later and there was no food in the house, I really started to panic."

My brother's face looked haunted. "What about the money I sent?"

My eyes shot up to his. "What money?"

We stared at each other for a heartbeat. Then another.

Finally, he cursed, "Motherfucker." He shook his head. "I sent money in every letter I sent you, Zander. I should have known."

No, I should have known.

I should have known that my brother wouldn't have left me completely stranded.

"It's okay. I got a job. The Sutherlands hired me to work on the docks. That was a good day," I told him, my voice thick with emotion.

Mrs. Sutherland was a lifesaver. Literally. Another week, and I wasn't sure what I would have done. I wasn't sure if she had seen the desperation in my eyes or heard the hunger in my belly, but she had given me a job and always happened to have "extra" food when I was around.

"It was enough until he came back. And when he did, I started stashing every penny I'd earned so I could leave."

"Was LA always your end goal?" he asked.

I shrugged. "I'm not sure that I had one, honestly. I just wanted to get as far away from him as I could, and LA was about as far as I could go without hopping on a plane."

Every city I'd ended up in never felt right until LA. I'd settle in for a bit, find a job, and after a few months, I'd get that itch to pick up and leave again. When I finally got to the West Coast, I just knew. Maybe it really was the distance, or perhaps it was just where I was supposed to be. Either way, it had become home.

"So, are you staying for a while? Or did you forget a phone charger or something?" he asked as he nonchalantly took a sip of his coffee.

"Oh, definitely the phone charger. Drove all the way back from the airport for it. Those fuckers are irreplaceable."

He rolled his eyes. "Asshole."

"I've got some time between gigs. I want to stay for a few weeks and go to your wedding, if that's all right? I'm not saying it will fix everything, but I'd like to try. I'm sick of being so damn angry."

He was silent for a moment before he bobbed his head up and down. "Okay, but I have one condition."

"Sure," I answered. "Anything."

A grin tugged at the corner of his mouth. "Be my best man?"

"But your best friend—" I began to argue.

"Will understand," he countered, leaning back in his seat, suddenly much more relaxed. "It was always the hope that you'd make it here and take his place anyway."

"I don't know, Macon."

"Look," he persisted. "I know there is still a lot we need to work through."

That's the understatement of the year.

We might be brothers, but we might as well be strangers at this point.

"But there is still no one else I'd rather have as my best man than my baby brother," he said.

God, just stab me in the fucking heart, why don't you?

"And besides"—a sly grin spread across the fucker's face —"you said anything."

Well, shit.

"Fine," I relented. "But I hope you don't expect me to plan a bachelor party in three weeks."

He laughed. "Don't worry. Billy and Eli already have that covered. All you need to do is get fitted for a suit and walk Elena down the aisle. Oh, and make sure I don't pass out."

Elena was the maid of honor…

How had I forgotten that?

"So, what did you mean when you said you were between gigs?" Macon asked.

My attention turned sharply away from Elena.

Right…

Macon had no idea what I did for a living.

How did I tell him that his little brother was a…rock star?

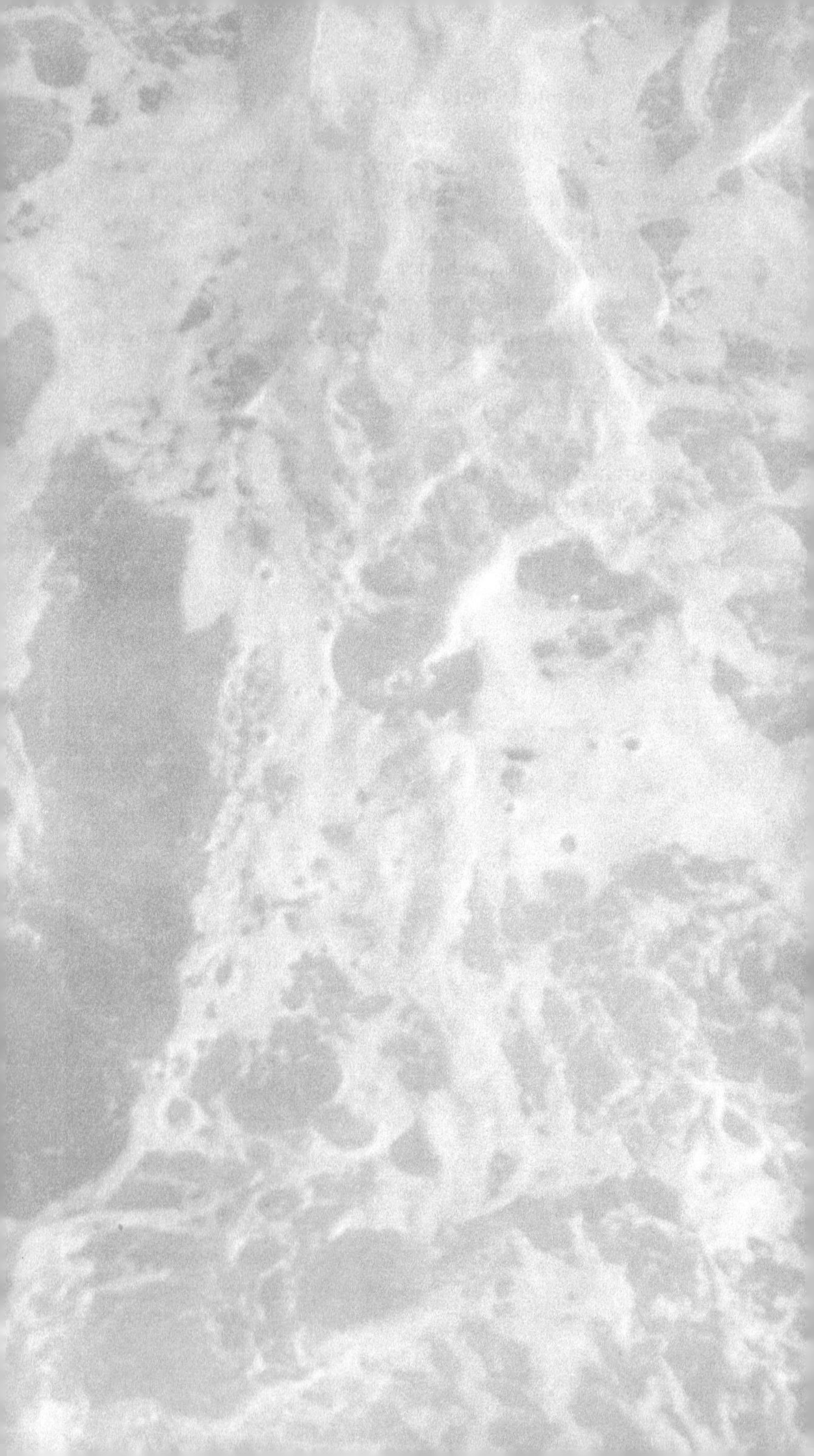

CHAPTER NINE

Elena

"Don't take this the wrong way," I said as I struggled to regain my breath. "But aren't pregnant women supposed to—I don't know—rest and shit?"

Marin grinned at me from across the room, not even the least bit winded. She was on mile five or six? I'd lost count.

"It's annoying, right?" She laughed as she took a gulp from her water bottle, not even bothering to slow down. "I never used to use the treadmill, much less visit the gym, but since I met Macon—"

I rolled my eyes. "Yeah, I know. Now, you're the workout queen."

She'd been reluctant, to say the least, when Macon challenged her to start running with him. But now, it was one of their favorite things to do together.

"Don't act like you don't go to the gym, too."

My legs burned and felt sort of like Jell-O when I stepped off the elliptical. The Ocracoke Gym—I had to give it to them on originality when it came to names—was small, but thankfully clean. With only a few machines and a set of weights, I couldn't imagine how stifling it might get in here with more than a few people.

Today, it was just the two of us.

Lucky me.

"I work out, sure," I answered, reaching for a towel from a large stack in the corner. "But I am starting to realize my definition of the word and yours are vastly different." I wiped the fluffy terry cloth over my brow and down my face. "When I go to the gym, I get my cardio in while I read or catch up on a show. You? You seem to be training for a marathon or the Olympics."

She grinned. "I just really want to beat Macon."

"You're trying to beat the guy in a race? Have you seen him run? He's ex-military. He's a freaking beast."

She shrugged. "I almost had him," she bragged before adding, "Once. But I might have cheated a little and flashed him."

Laughter filled the small space, and I reached for my water bottle and checked the time. It was late afternoon, and we'd already been here for over an hour.

Surely, she was done, right?

Marin had spent the morning at the sheriff's station, trying to console Macon. After she confirmed what he'd already suspected—that Zander had fled the island without so much as a good-bye—he was understandably upset. Marin said he was both angry and heartbroken. He'd waited years to get the chance to talk to his brother, and now, he wasn't sure he'd ever get another. He sent a string of texts to Zander that ranged from telling him off to begging him to come back, but all of them went unread and unanswered.

After Marin left Macon at the station, she texted and asked me to join her for lunch and a trip to the gym. I'd been so ready to get out of the house at that point that I practically flew out the door.

I was not handling the downtime of vacation well. I needed a hobby, and stat.

Billy's was one of the most well-known restaurants in Ocracoke. The owner, Billy Radcliffe, also happened to be Macon's best friend and their next-door neighbor. The restaurant's patio overlooked Silver Lake Harbor and was known for its laid-back atmosphere and amazing food.

Unfortunately, the shade of the umbrellas and the slight breeze from the bay had done nothing to hinder the stifling humidity of the July heat, and no amount of convincing could get Marin to eat inside, where the air-conditioning was.

"It's beautiful outside," she'd said.

"Island life has changed you, my friend." I'd glared at her as I proceeded to down my weight in water.

Now, after an afternoon in the heat and an hour in the gym, all I could think about was how gross I must smell and how much I wanted a shower.

"I can see the way you're hovering near the door, Elena."

"Come on, Marin," I begged her. "Stop torturing yourself. Think of the baby!"

The treadmill started to slow, and I felt a glimmer of hope.

"This is the time when you should be eating ice cream and pickles. Not running so much that you dry-heave."

"When did you see me dry-heave?" She scoffed.

The treadmill finally came to a stop, and I silently cheered. I watched as she stepped off and grabbed a towel, wiping it down her face and neck. It was the first time since I'd arrived in Ocracoke that I'd seen her in something formfitting, and I could already see the small changes in her body. Her normally slim, flat stomach slightly swelled out under the tight fabric of her yoga pants.

I stared at her for a moment, momentarily stunned.

There was a fucking human in there.

"You okay?" she asked, looking slightly concerned.

"Yeah, I just..." I shook my head, feeling completely bewildered. "You're fucking pregnant, Marin."

She laughed, tossing the towel in the dirty bin. "Uh, yeah. Tell me about it. Lunch today was the first time I could keep a meal down in days."

"And this is how you choose to celebrate? By torturing me?"

She shrugged. "It's the first time I've felt this good in weeks. Besides, isn't any time we spend together a gift?"

"Uh, no. I want to see the return policy."

When she moved to grab her stuff, I didn't hesitate.

Oh, thank God.

The baby bump had me thinking…

"Hey, I meant to ask you. Your wedding dress. The one we picked out a few months ago—"

"Yeah, that one's out."

She'd originally picked a gorgeous cream-colored lace gown that had a mermaid-style silhouette. It did a beautiful job of accentuating her slim curves and tall frame.

"I found something similar that is a bit more forgiving. I'm not sure how much I'll grow in the next three weeks, and I wanted something that I wouldn't have to panic over if my belly suddenly popped out."

"I get that." I wasn't even pregnant, and there were times when a little bloat could mean the difference between a dress fitting or ending up back on the rack.

"I actually need to go pick it up this week. It's at that same bridal shop we went to up the coast."

"We should make a day of it," I suggested. "Grab an early ferry and do some shopping. Have lunch?"

"That would be great," she agreed. Then, her eyes wandered to the other side of the gym. "Oh shit. I forgot to do weights."

She set her stuff back down and started making her way to the weight station. She looked over at me.

My arms folded over my chest, and I shook my head. "No way. That's a hard pass for me."

"Oh, come on! It will just be a few minutes."

"I love you. I truly do, but I've had all the endorphins I can handle for the day." I bolted for the door. "And despite what Elle Woods would say, they do not make me happy."

She snorted. "You would leave a pregnant woman all alone?"

"Don't try and guilt-trip me," I hollered over my shoulder. "That's just low. You have a phone and the sheriff on speed dial."

"Enjoy your shower!" she hollered.

"Enjoy your weights!"

And then I ran.

I stepped out of the bathroom, feeling like a brand-new woman.

It was amazing what a good shower could do. Although Macon might not agree with me when he got his water bill this month. I walked into my room, my head bopping with the music coming from the small Bluetooth speaker on the dresser. A billow of steam trailed behind me as I tugged the soft towel tight around my body. It was time to make a plan.

A plan for vacation.

I was going to be here for three weeks—okay, it was technically two and a half weeks now, but whatever. The remainder of that time, I could not be solely reliant on Marin for entertainment. Yes, I'd come here to help her with the wedding, but she wasn't going to need me twenty-four hours a day. It had become clear to me that I was going to have to find things to do by myself.

So, I decided to make a list.

A mental one, but a list nonetheless.

I plopped down on my neatly made bed, folding one bare leg over the other as I leaned back against the headboard.

What to do with myself for two and a half weeks.

Nearly five minutes went by, and I was coming up blank.

I was not used to failing…

I was staying on an island people purposely paid money to visit. Surely, I could find an activity or two. Maybe take up a hobby?

I thought back to the last few years of my life, and while I had told Marin I used my gym time to catch up on books and shows, the truth was, I usually used that time for—yep, you guessed it—work.

I couldn't remember the last time I'd actually finished an entire book.

So, maybe I could take up reading? I made a mental note to go check out the stack of books Macon had in the living room.

What else?

Fishing? One of Macon's old classmates owned a company that took tourists out on boat tours.

I scrunched my nose at the mere thought of touching a fish.

Nope.

Suddenly, my mind pivoted back to Zander.

Guitar lessons?

My mind conjured up an image of his large frame curled around me as he helped place my fingers on the right strings. His lips nearly brushed my ear as he praised my efforts...

I shivered, and goosebumps dotted my flesh.

My eyes closed as my thoughts drifted back to our brief time together. I wondered where he was right now. Had he made it to the airport? Was he already on his way back to LA?

Has he thought of me?

I'd been furious to find out he left this morning. He knew what it would do to Macon, and yet he'd done it anyway. But more than that, I was upset because he'd left me, too.

I'd felt something for him. I wasn't sure what it was, but when he'd come into my room and held me while I cried, I thought he'd maybe felt it, too.

A connection. A spark.

But then he'd left without so much as a, *Good-bye. Hope you have a nice life.*

So, now, all I had were a few fleeting memories of him and maybe a little regret. What if I hadn't run out that night in the bar? Sure, things would have gotten complicated the morning after, but would it have been worth it? To spend one night with him regardless of how things turned out in the end?

I knew without a doubt the answer was yes.

He would have taken my hand and led me out of the bar and to his car. My head would have been pounding with anticipation and nervousness. We would have driven down to a secluded spot on the beach, where no one would bother us.

I squeezed my thighs together as my body began to ache from the sheer thought of being alone with him. My nipples hardened, the slightest movement becoming unbearable as they grazed against the terry cloth of my towel. Opening my eyes, I reached for my nightstand and grabbed the one thing that could bring me relief.

Unlike Marin, I did not feel embarrassed when it came to self-pleasure. Although, if I was being honest, I did feel a little guilty when said pleasure involved fantasizing about her brother-in-law.

A new song drifted through the speakers. The sultry guitar mix filled the small space as my mind wandered back to that night.

Or at least the version I was imagining in my head.

Warm sand, hot summer night, scorching need.

I tugged at the towel and let it fall to either side of me on the bed. As my hands began to explore my body, I imagined it was his callous fingers touching my naked skin and palming my breasts. When I turned the vibrator on and used it to tease my clit, I wondered what it would feel like to have his tongue between those slick folds. Just thinking of him had me so wet that when I sank two fingers into my core, I let out a loud moan as I imagined him buried deep inside me.

"Oh God."

I writhed against my hand, dropping the vibrator on the bed as I began to wantonly grind my hips against my own hand. My heart was hammering in my chest as I chased my release. My back arched off the bed, and as I closed my eyes, I saw us on that beach. A tangled mess of naked limbs as we lost ourselves in each other until the sun came up.

I cried out as I shattered. My body shook as I rode out every last wave of pleasure. It was so intense that I felt like my body had left the earth for a moment.

That *never* happened.

Usually, my self-induced orgasms were pretty damn good, but nothing compared to the release that came with sex.

If fantasy sex with Zander was that good, I could only imagine…

I guess I will never know.

Well, if that was a mood killer…

My breathing began to normalize, and I sat up and let out a sad sigh.

Grabbing the towel, I made quick work of cleaning up my little toy in the bathroom. After it was put away, I picked out some clothes and blew my hair dry. I skipped makeup, not knowing what I was doing for dinner.

I grabbed my phone off the dresser, deciding it was time to check in with Marin, and realized she'd already texted me.

Guessed she'd finally left the gym…

MARIN

Zander came back! Macon just called me after they met at the coffee shop. Crazy, right? Anyway, he's on his way back to the rental. Just wanted to give you a heads-up!

I stared at the text for far too long.

He'd come back?

And then my eyes went wide as I noticed the time.

"Shit!" I exclaimed under my breath.

It had been well over twenty minutes since Marin had sent that text. In any normal city or town, that wouldn't be anything to sweat over. But in Ocracoke, where it took less than five minutes to get anywhere…

I took a panicked look around the room, my eyes landing on the nightstand, where I'd just tucked away my freshly cleaned vibrator.

I swallowed a nervous lump in my throat.

Surely, he hadn't heard anything. I mean, I'd had the music up really loud, and…maybe he wasn't even here yet.

I looked out the window and found his empty rental parked on the curb.

For fuck's sake. Of course, he's here.

How in the world had I not heard him come in? Had I been that into my fantasy that a fucking intruder could have marched right through the front door?

My mind drifted briefly back to that earth-shattering orgasm.

Yes. The answer was yes.

I looked down at Marin's text again and then back to my nightstand.

Oh, you know what? Fuck it.

I was a grown-ass woman, and if I wanted to masturbate in the middle of the day on my damn vacation, well then, try and stop me.

I straightened my back and flipped my hair behind my shoulder. I marched toward the door and opened it.

Remember, I thought, *you command courtrooms. You eat men for breakfast. You are fierce.*

I stepped into the hallway and turned. I slowly walked to the living room and found him sitting on the sofa, a book in his hand. He looked very comfortable, like he'd been sitting there awhile.

I inwardly groaned.

"Marin texted me that you were back," I said, squaring my shoulders.

I tried to come off as bored and unaffected by his presence. But in reality, the mere sight of him affected me.

Deeply.

"Guess I wasn't as done as I thought I was." Those emerald eyes met mine.

God, his was beautiful.

"So, are you staying long?" I asked, instantly looking away.

I maintained my detached and aloof demeanor. He pretended to be deeply invested in his book. We were both failing miserably.

"Until the wedding," he stated. "Macon asked me to be his best man."

What? He did what?

"Oh." I managed to keep my mouth from falling open.

That meant that he and I—

Fuck.

My phone buzzed, and I thanked the heavens above for the auspicious interruption. I looked down and found another text from Marin.

MARIN

Dinner at our house tonight. Come over
whenever.

I nearly wept with joy. *Time to get the hell out of here.*

"Well, it's good to see you, I guess," I said, adding the last part simply because I was still mad at him for leaving this morning. "I am headed out for dinner."

I started to turn but noticed him rising from his spot on the couch. I couldn't help but watch. He wore ripped black jeans today and another vintage tee. That bomber jacket he loved clung to his body like it had been made for him, but all I wanted to do was push it to the floor and find all those hidden tattoos.

I had not done myself any favors today.

If the sexual tension had been bad before, it was off the chain now that I'd pictured him naked while I got myself off.

The man ban was gonna suck extra hard now that he was back.

He started to breeze past me but stopped short. "They invited me over for dinner, too." He grinned.

I pressed my lips together. "Oh."

"I'll go grab my keys, and we can ride together?"

I merely nodded, my brain going crazy with the sheer proximity of him.

"Oh, and one more thing." He stepped even closer. I could feel his hot breath on my cheek as his lips curved upward into a mischievous grin. "Do you always scream that loud when you come?" he asked, and then he leaned in closer, nearly brushing his mouth against my skin. "Or is it just when you think of me?"

I forgot to breathe for a second. He was so close, his mouth a fraction of an inch away from mine, and his voice— God, his voice. And then the haze started to lift, and I registered the words he'd uttered.

My eyes widened, and I shoved him, heat flushing my cheeks, but also pooling in my thighs. My body was so confused.

"I cannot believe you!"

"Hey, I can't help what I heard. You weren't exactly quiet."

"I didn't know I had an audience!" I threw my hands up, flustered. *Why is it so damn hot in here?* "And I was not thinking about you!"

"You called out my name, Louie."

"I—"

Oh my God, please tell me I didn't

No, I definitely didn't.

Pretty sure.

Mostly sure.

Fuck.

His grin widened. "I'm just fucking with you, but good to know where your mind was."

"Oh my God." I covered my face with the palm of my hand. "You're impossible. Can we please just forget about this?"

He shook his head, pinning me with those green eyes. "Yeah, I don't think so. Those sounds are permanently etched into my brain now. Never gonna forget anything about that..."

I opened my mouth to respond, but he was already gone, walking down the hallway with a definite pep in his step.

And all I could do was watch him.

God, I was so fucking screwed.

CHAPTER TEN

Zander

"You seem to be latching on to the rock-star lifestyle pretty quickly," Hendrix teased as we stood in front of baggage claim.

He'd met me here just moments earlier with a big smile on his face, not a trace of fatigue. My Strat was strapped securely around his chest, all snug and safe in her hard case along with his base.

"Having someone hand-deliver clothes to you? That's pretty damn bougie."

A young woman standing next to us did a double take, eyeing me up and down.

"It was your idea, fuckface, and will you shut the hell up with that shit?" I said under my breath, giving him a hard stare.

He laughed, clearly unfazed and very much amused.

If there was anyone who could adjust well to the rock-star life, it would be Hendrix. It wasn't that he was a fame seeker per se; it was more his ability to adapt and the unfathomable charm he possessed. Hendrix was just a likable guy. You couldn't be around him without being drawn to his infectious personality.

Of the two of us, I'd always thought it would be him who would break out and make it big.

He'd been trained for it after all.

Music was a way of life in the Creed family. Hell, they'd all been named after musical legends. But no one had really taken to it more than Hendrix.

Like me, he could play a myriad of instruments, but his calling was the bass.

He'd been in a band since college. They slowly made a name for themselves and even got a record deal. But not all of them were willing to put in the work, and they had fallen apart before they could even release their first single. Hendrix had been sort of drifting ever since. He'd done a little session work, but Lance and I both agreed he had far too much talent to be doing grunt work for his father.

"Afraid you'll be recognized?" He playfully smacked the back of my head. "It's not like your Beyoncé."

"I already was," I told him as he bent forward and hauled a huge suitcase from the conveyor belt.

My eyes widened. How much shit had he packed me?

"Seriously?" His excitement was palpable. This was why our roles should have been reversed. He would love this. The attention. The fans. He'd take it all in stride. "In Ocracoke, really?"

I nodded. "Nearly gave a teenage girl a heart attack," I said quietly as he grabbed another bag. "Jesus, is that all?" I asked, mortified by how much stuff we'd accumulated. "You know I'm only gonna be here for a few weeks, not a few months, right?"

"Yeah, but I had no idea what to pack."

"So, you brought my entire closet?" I packed less than this for international tours.

"No, Presley did that."

"Oh, okay. That makes sense." I grabbed the handle of the largest bag.

He shook his head in disbelief. "So, it's okay if she does it, but not when I do?"

"I trust her. At least I know everything matches."

"How can it not match? All you ever wear is black."

I looked down at my hoodie and jeans and just grinned.

He wasn't wrong.

"So, tell me about your roommate."

It had been several hours since the airport, and we'd just disembarked the ferry. It was Hendrix's first experience using this specific mode of transportation, and he'd been enthralled, to say the least.

"Dude, this is, like, a real fucking ferry!"

I just stared at him, my eyes blinking. "I don't even know how to respond to that."

"I'm in a car, on a boat...in the ocean." He said it like he was Bill from Bill & Ted's Excellent Adventure *and he'd just been introduced to time travel.*

"You're my roommate." A very stoic answer.

"Okay." He grinned as we headed down Highway 12. Sand from the dunes skated across the asphalt as the afternoon sun beat down on us. "Tell me about your *temporary* roommate. The extremely *hot* temporary roommate."

I shrugged. "There's nothing to tell." *Also, don't call her hot.*

I could feel his eyes on me as I stared straight ahead, focusing far too intently on the road. "Really? Is that why you insisted on driving all the way back to Virginia today to pick me up rather than just letting me rent a car?"

"Is it a crime that I wanted to spend time with my best friend?"

"There wasn't any other reason you wanted to get out of the house?"

I kept my expression blank. Or as blank as I could manage because when it came to Elena, I had a hard time controlling my reactions.

Or my emotions.

Or the raging hard-on I got whenever I thought of her.

When I'd walked into that house several days ago, I nearly lost my damn mind when I heard her through that bedroom door. I stared at the doorknob, so riveted, that I almost dropped the duffel bag I'd been hauling down the hallway.

God, the way she'd moaned…

Music to my fucking ears.

"Nope," I finally answered. "Just wanted to welcome you at the airport and make sure you got in okay."

I knew he saw right through me. He always did. But he chose to let it pass, which worried me a little. Usually, that came to bite me in the ass later on.

"How very kind of you."

I made a sort of shrugging gesture as my hand gripped the wheel. "I'm a very kind guy."

We didn't talk much the rest of the way. Hendrix took in the sights as we traveled down the main drag of Ocracoke, and within minutes, we were pulling up to the small yellow house.

"So, did she mind sharing the rental again?" Hendrix asked as I put the car in park.

"I didn't really ask."

"You didn't ask?"

I hopped out of the car, and he followed. He met me at the trunk.

"Nope. Just sort of showed up and moved right back in."

I left out the part about how she had been locked in her room, masturbating, when I got back. Or how I stood outside her door, like a fucking creeper, and listened.

Or how I'd snuck back to the living room and pretended

to be completely unaffected by the whole ordeal, even though all I wanted to do was toss her over my shoulder, take her back to that room, and see just how good that moan sounded when she was wrapped around my cock.

"I don't think she minds," I added, which was the truth. She'd never mentioned otherwise at least. "She seemed just fine when I mentioned you would be visiting."

"Well, that's because I'm awesome." He palmed his neatly trimmed beard and waggled an eyebrow at me.

"It's a wonder you fit in the door with that big ego of yours."

"That and my big—"

I planted a hand on his chest and gave him a shove. He laughed, and we both got to work on hauling out luggage and my guitar case. With everything in hand, we headed to the front door, and I punched in the code and let Hendrix in first.

"This place is—oh, *hello*."

I'd heard him say hello to hundreds of women over the years. It was the kind of hello that reminded me of Joey from *Friends*. Hendrix had a swoonworthy baritone voice and a killer body, thanks to hours in the gym. Women loved him, and they loved his *hello*. But the moment I heard him greet Elena in his *special* way, I instantly wanted to push him out the door and slam it in his face.

I stepped in behind him and found her walking toward us from the kitchen. She wore—was she in a robe?

"Going to the beach?" It took me a moment to realize the robe was actually a bathing suit cover-up.

She'd pulled the gauzy floral fabric tight across her body, but I could still make out the thin straps of a bikini tied around her shoulders.

"Oh, um, yes. I was actually about to text you, in case you wanted to meet us there when you got back."

"Well, now, I'm back."

Her curious gaze wandered over to the man next to me.

"This is my best friend, Hendrix."

Elena took a tiny step forward, probably to offer her hand.

Hendrix being Hendrix dropped everything he was carrying and swung an arm around her shoulders. "What's this I hear about the beach, darling?"

Darling? What the fuck?

She grinned, making my mood instantly sour. When was the last time she'd smiled at me like that?

Before you left like a fucking coward with your tail between your legs....

She'd been doing her best to ignore me over the last few days. It was a stark contrast to the flirting banter and easy conversations we'd had going before I left.

It was also annoying as hell.

"I would think you'd be familiar with the idea. You know, sand, waves, lots of half-naked girls," she teased.

"Oh, you're feisty. I like it."

My teeth ground together. "Come on, *Hen*," I said, purposely using the annoying nickname his sisters liked to call him. "Let's go drop this stuff over in our rooms and leave Elena to finish getting ready."

He turned his head so his mouth was incredibly too close to her ear. "I think he might be a little jealous. You've gotta stop flirting with me, darling."

She laughed but stepped out of Hendrix's embrace and started to grab a large beach bag and keys that were stashed on the kitchen island.

I gave him the death stare.

"Oh, do you want me to wait for you?" She stalled. "I don't mind."

"No." I waved her on. "You go ahead."

I've got a best friend to kill.

After a quick tour of the house, Hendrix dropped his shit off in the empty room across from mine, and we both went our separate ways to change for the beach. Presley had thankfully come through on the packing side of things, and I found a pair of trunks tucked neatly in my suitcase, along with just about everything else I could possibly need for…well, ever.

Probably need to send her a thank-you text.

Less than five minutes later, I opened the door and nearly ran into Hendrix in the hallway. The two of us did not fit side by side, so there was a momentary shuffle of who went first, and I finally relented, letting him take the lead.

Two seconds later, he stopped. "Is this Elena's room? Why wasn't this on my tour?" He looked back with a wolfish grin.

"Keep walking, Hen."

"I bet it smells good in there. Did you notice how good she smells? Kind of citrusy, no?"

"We're gonna be late," was the only response he got out of me.

"Wasn't aware the beach was something you could be late to." But he just shrugged and kept moving.

I took one last glance at her door and marched forward.

The urge to throw my body in front of that stupid hardwood frame and bar my best friend from entering had been ridiculous.

I wanted to tell him to fucking cool it.

But I hadn't.

I just got in the car and started driving and reminded myself of all the reasons I needed to chill when it came to Elena Mendez.

One, she wasn't mine, and it wasn't like I was jonesing for a relationship, especially a long-distance one. *No thank you.* Two, Hendrix was a flirt. It was a known fact, and me harping on him for it wasn't going to change that. Three, I knew the second I called him out on it, I'd never hear the end of it. *Ever.*

Elena had texted me their location—a popular local spot I'd frequented as a kid. Like everywhere on this little blip of land, it didn't take long to get there. We pulled off the road and grabbed towels and the snacks Hendrix had found when he raided the kitchen. As we started to track through the dunes, I suddenly stopped.

"About Manic," I said, looking out toward the sparkling blue water. I just spotted Macon out in the distance, standing near a cluster of umbrellas, grabbing a drink from a cooler.

"What about it?"

"You know we can't say anything," I told him, trying to spot Elena in the group but failing.

He dropped the bag of snacks on the sand and looked over at me. "Of course I know." He cut me with his stare. "I signed my goddamn life away on that NDA."

I let out a frustrated breath. "I know. I'm sorry. I just—this is harder than I thought it would be. I didn't plan on being here this long and all the lying I would have to do."

His brows knit together, and he nodded. Hendrix was rarely serious. I wasn't sure if it was an avoidance tactic or if he really was just that well-adjusted. But when he did flip that switch, it was intense.

"So, what did you tell them then? So we have our stories straight."

"I told Macon I'm a session guitarist. And I even told him about some of the bands I'd worked with, but I just left out the part about Manic."

"So, basically, the truth."

"Minus a very important detail, Hendrix." I pinched the bridge of my nose, the heat already making my shirt stick to my back. "Is it bad that part of me is kind of relieved? That I don't have to tell them because at least I get to enjoy a few more weeks of—"

"Normal?" His arms folded across his chest, showing off the same Creed tattoo that every member of his family bore— even the adopted ones like me.

"Yeah."

"No, it's not bad," he answered. "The choice is out of your

hands regardless. So, you're doing the best you can. You could have just left, but you chose to come back and try to work things out with your brother. I think, if given the option, he'd take that over a little white lie."

It was a bit more than a white lie, but I could see what he was saying.

In a few weeks, I would forever be known as Zander Tate, lead guitarist for Manic at Midnight. Even to my family.

Right now, I was going to enjoy being Zander Green just for a little while longer.

We started heading down toward the beach again. The roar of the waves grew closer as I kicked off my flip-flops and went barefoot. Thankfully, the sand wasn't so hot that the bottom of my feet was burning.

That was never a good time.

"You know it's gonna be okay, right?" Hendrix said. His face was pointed dead ahead, his eyes focused on the water. "The fame and shit?"

"Yeah, I know." I tried to sound convincing.

"You're just the guitarist anyway." His words were laced with humor. "It's not like you're the *real* star. When you stand next to Asher, no one even knows you exist, so—" He lifted his shoulders and shrugged, making me laugh.

"I'll tell him you said that."

"Don't bother. He already knows. Founding member of the Knight Rider Fan Club right here. I've even got a T-shirt."

"I bet you do." I knew he was trying to make me feel better, but all my mind could focus on was my face on T-shirts and rabid fan clubs. My stomach fluttered with nerves.

We finally got to the part of the beach my brother had claimed. Elena hadn't been really specific on details, so I wasn't sure who had been invited, but it was safe to assume it wasn't just the four of us.

Well, five now that we had Hendrix.

There were several umbrellas all lined up in a row,

creating a large barrier from the sun, and they had set up at least six beach chairs that were all facing away from us.

Marin waved us over, and Hendrix noticed her immediately.

"Jesus, she is—"

"My pregnant sister-in-law," I cut him off.

"Yikes, okay. Got it." His eyes widened. Nothing made him squirm more than talking about marriage or babies. "Guess I should have recognized her from that invitation you stared at for a week straight."

"I did not stare at it for a week straight."

Three days, tops.

"Whatever." A wide grin spread across his face as he swung an arm out to greet my brother.

"Glad you could make it," Macon said, shaking Hendrix's hand.

"Thanks for having me."

"From what Zander told us the other night, you two are more like family, so you're welcome anytime."

That dinner had been a special sort of hell.

Marin and Macon had been elated to have the four of us all under one roof.

Elena? Not so much.

She pretended like I didn't exist.

I pretended like it didn't bother me.

We'd kept up this ruse ever since.

"Let me introduce you to some people," Macon suggested.

We dropped our towels on top of a large stack, and Hendrix reluctantly let go of his snacks.

"This is Billy." Macon gestured to the man in the chair on the other side of Marin.

I recognized him from the engagement party. He reminded me of a lumberjack with wide shoulders and plaid-print swim trunks. His dark brown hair was a bit overgrown, like his beard. He had a kind smile and immediately held out his hand to greet us.

"Thanks for showing up and relieving me of best-man duties." He used his other hand to block out the glare from the water, resting it just above his brow as he glanced up at us.

"I feel like kind of an asshole, coming in at the last minute when you've already done everything."

"No, it's all good. Besides, Eli is the one who's done most of it anyway," he said, turning an adoring gaze to the man sitting next to him. "I was just planning on taking the credit for it all."

"Isn't that what you always do?" The man sitting next to him, presumably Eli, was about as far from a lumberjack as I could be. With olive skin and the trim body of a swimmer, he had a regal quality to him that screamed sophistication.

"Hey, you knew what you were getting involved with when you married me."

"Mmm, yes, I did."

They smiled and stared at each other so intensely that I had to turn away.

God, married people are gross.

Macon motioned toward Eli. "That's Billy's husband. They're newlyweds. And a nightmare to live next to right now."

"Oh, *puh-lease*," Billy objected. "At least we keep it inside. On the patio furniture, Macon? Really? You don't even have a fence."

I heard a choking sound and turned to find Marin sputtering soda and doing a piss-poor job of trying to cover it with her hand.

"I could have gone my whole damn life without hearing your dirty talk," Eli added.

I'm gonna go drown myself in the Atlantic now…

"A lot of good keeping it inside does when you don't close your cur—" He paused. "You know what? Never mind."

"So, where's Elena?" *Dear God, can we change the subject?*

"Oh, she went to cool off. She doesn't handle heat well," Marin answered, having recovered from her Coke incident.

She wore a bright pink bikini and was sitting cross-legged, munching on a bag of caramel corn that was wedged between her legs. Macon, who sat back down next to her, reached out and snatched a handful. She smacked his hand, and he laughed.

"She'll bounce back and forth between here and the water until we leave."

My eyes tracked the coastline, trying to spot her, but all I saw were half a dozen kids on boogie boards and one very disturbing group of teens trying to record some sort of synchronized dance on their phone.

"You can take the two chairs at the end." Macon gestured with his hand.

I recognized Elena's beach bag resting against one of the chairs, and just as I was about to claim the one next to it, my best friend plopped his sorry ass down in it. He looked up and grinned.

Fucking traitor.

I reluctantly took the one at the end and got settled in. I put on some sunscreen and grabbed a beer from the cooler. Just as I was starting to get into a conversation with Eli about the restaurants they owned in town, I turned my head and saw her.

She rose from the tide like a fucking sea goddess. Her tan skin glowed under the summer sun.

And she was wearing my favorite color.

If that red dress had ruined me, this black string bikini fucking slayed me.

Full, round breasts, curvy hips, and, shit, was that a...*tattoo*?

"Dude, you got a little drool." Hendrix leaned over, rubbing at the corner of my face.

"Shut the fuck up." I smacked him away.

"I don't know what's wrong with you." He just shook his

head. "If I was stuck in a house for three whole weeks with that"—he motioned to where Elena was making her way toward us—"I sure as hell wouldn't be fighting it."

"Believe me." I rolled my eyes and kept my voice low. "I know exactly what you'd do, but this is complicated. She's Marin's best friend. My *sister-in-law*'s best friend."

"So?"

"What do you mean, *so*? You're the one who keeps pushing for me to make amends with my brother. How well do you think that's gonna go if the first thing I do is hook up with his wife's best friend?"

"Hooking up doesn't have to equal a broken heart and hurt feelings. Grown-ups *can* fuck and then move on and be friends later on in life."

I pictured running into Elena years from now at Thanksgiving after she'd moved on with some sophisticated asshole. He'd boast about the giant ring he bought her while simultaneously bitching about the cost of his yacht maintenance and lazy employees.

The guy wasn't even real, and I already hated him.

"I don't think she's a hookup kind of girl," I argued as I tracked her every step up the beach.

I could see it now. The floral black ink that hugged her right hip, and flirted with the edge of her barely there bikini bottom.

"Did you ask her?"

"No, but she told me she had a ban on dating or whatever. Women only do that when they're burned out on finding *the one*."

"All the more reason for her to let loose, don't you think? She's not looking for Mr. Right, so why not swoop in and be her Mr. Right Now?"

"That was cheesy as fuck," I told him, rolling my eyes. "Also, shut the hell up. She's coming."

I sounded like a teenage girl, gossiping between classes,

but the last thing I wanted was for her to hear us whispering about her behind our beer bottles.

"How was the water?" Marin asked as Elena bent forward and grabbed her towel off the chair.

My mouth watered as I caught a glimpse of her ass.

I didn't even try to look away.

"Good," she answered. Her eyes met mine ever so briefly, as if she was making a concerted effort to avoid my gaze. "Although, now, I'm covered in sand."

"You know"—Hendrix's flirty voice was back, as was my urge to kill him—"I could help you with that later. I've been told I'm quite skilled with a bar of soap."

"You're awful." She laughed, wrapping the large towel around her hips. She grabbed a bottle of water and took a seat, digging her feet in the sand.

Does she like him?

Or is it just harmless flirting?

Not knowing annoyed me more than I could stand.

"So, how did you and Elena meet, Marin?" Hendrix asked.

I instantly went on alert, my breath sucking in through my teeth. I probably should have told him about the whole *Marin being a widow* thing.

But Marin didn't seem fazed. It probably wasn't the first time she'd been presented with this kind of question, and she took it in stride. "Elena moved to Richmond during our senior year of high school, and we became instant friends, even through college, when I started dating her brother."

"You dated her brother?"

She nodded, a hint of sadness in her smile. "Married him, too."

The conversation suddenly halted, and before Hendrix could put his foot in his mouth, I leaned over and quietly said, "Marin's a widow."

"*Oh.* Oh shit," he said under his breath before quickly recovering. "So, you were okay with your best friend marrying your brother?" He directed the question to Elena, keeping the topic light while still acknowledging her loss. " 'Cause I gotta say, if Z and one of my sisters hooked up, I'd need to go to therapy. Or jail."

Everyone laughed. Including me.

"There were some uncomfortable moments when we shared an apartment, which I will not elaborate on for the sake of Macon's mental health—"

"Thanks for that." He saluted her with his Coke Zero.

"Oh, fuck off," Marin cut in, laughing under her breath. "I have my own *uncomfortable moments* from that time, too, you know. You love to tell everyone how traumatizing it was to live with your brother and his fiancée. But I had to live with my best friend and two hundred thirty-two hookups."

I tried to school my features and not react.

Hendrix did not, and he immediately asked, "Hold up, is that a real number? Also, can you repeat it?"

"She is exaggerating. Obviously." She looked offended, but, like, not *that* offended. She waved off Marin's accusation with her hand. "It wasn't that bad."

"But how much is she exaggerating?" Hendrix teased her, his body angled toward hers in his chair. "Give me a ballpark number."

"Why?" she fired back, arching a brow. "Wanna compare?"

"A gentleman never tells."

"I don't think there is anything gentlemanly about you."

His voice dropped an octave. "Oh, baby, you have no idea."

I didn't even remember standing up, but suddenly, my beer bottle was wedged into the sand, and my ass was off the chair. "I'm gonna go swim for a while," I announced, and then I took off without another word.

Fucking Hendrix.

I knew what he was doing.

He'd never make a move on Elena, not when he thought

that there was even the slightest chance I had an interest in her.

Which I didn't. Obviously.

She was hot. Ridiculously hot. But I couldn't go there.

Want. To. Lick. That. Tattoo.

Fucking hell.

It wasn't because of some bro code or family loyalty that kept Hendrix in check.

He was just a good guy.

So, the fact that he kept flirting with her was all for my benefit. Ever since I'd stumbled into Creed's begging for a job fourteen years ago, Hendrix had been occupying the roles of best friend and brother, and he took the roles seriously. He was constantly trying to meddle in my life.

And right now, his meddling mission was to make me as miserable as possible.

It was working.

My feet hit the cool, wet sand as I waded into the water, dodging a loud group of girls sailing in on boogie boards. I'd spent so many years on the other side of the country that I'd forgotten how warm the Atlantic could be in the summer.

Growing up, I'd always assumed the beaches in California were nicer than ours.

According to The Beach Boys, everyone wanted to be there, right?

But the first time I'd gone to Malibu, I'd found out very quickly that the Pacific was cold.

Like ball-shriveling cold.

Turned out, those wetsuits I'd always seen Dylan wearing in my Mom's *90210* reruns weren't just some weird '90s fashion trend.

When the water got to my waist, I dived under, wetting my hair and the rest of my body. I resurfaced and looked back at the beach.

"I love your tattoos."

I turned to see the group of girls I'd noticed on the shore.

The waves on this beach were shit, and all three of them were now using their boogie boards as floaties.

Jesus, are they stalking me?

They kicked a little closer, which caused me to drift further back.

"Thanks," I answered, trying to mentally calculate their age. College maybe?

Too young—that was for sure.

"Are you an artist?" one of them asked.

She was the same one who had spoken before and seemed to be the ringleader. Her sun-bleached hair, tanned skin, and flawless body meant that she probably never had to try too hard for male attention and therefore expected I wouldn't be any different.

"My sister's boyfriend is a tattoo artist, and he's covered like that, too."

"Nope," I answered, finding this conversation tedious. Mostly because I'd had it already.

I'd lost count of the number of people who had commented on my tattoos over the years with no actual interest in them. In reality, it was just a vapid attempt for attention or an excuse to force their opinion on me.

Neither of which I wanted or asked for.

"So, are you from here?" the blonde asked.

"Yeah, we could really use a tour guide," another added.

Now, they were all getting bold. Great.

I grabbed the back of my neck in frustration and caught something in my peripheral vision.

Not just something. *Someone.*

"Sorry, *girls.*" I made sure to emphasize that last word. "My wife looks lonely. Gotta run."

Arrow straight to the heart. Their faces fell as if I'd physically wounded them. I swam off, feeling triumphant.

I found "my wife" not too far off. Elena must have just waded into the water. Her hair was still partially dry from the sun, and she was scooping handfuls of water onto her arms and shoulders like her skin was on fire.

Elena wasn't a big fan of the heat.

She must have heard the water slosh as I swam over because just as she looked up, I wrapped my arms around her. I didn't give her even a second to react.

"I'll buy groceries for the rest of the week if you pretend to be obsessed with me for the next five minutes," I whispered in her ear.

"And why would I do that?" she asked, but didn't attempt to pull back.

"Because I just encountered the deadliest creature in the water, Elena, and I need protection."

She didn't turn her head, but she must have seen them. That or she'd noticed me with them before. "You're running away from college girls?"

"Hell yeah, I am," I answered. "There are so many of them."

Her head tilted slightly. "Seems to me like there are only three." She grinned. "Cute, too."

"Just shut up and hold me. Can't you see I'm distraught?"

She rolled her eyes, but didn't let go. I moved my hands down to her waist, so she could wrap her arms around my neck. The position was a bit more comfortable since my large arms weighed her down, but it also forced us closer together.

So much closer.

When I felt her nipples brush against my chest, I started to realize what a horrible idea this was.

My cock, however, was as happy as a motherfucker and ready to say hi.

"It was nice of Hendrix to fly out here and bring your things," she said.

My grip on her waist tightened at the sound of my best friend's name on her lips.

"He's a nice guy," I answered. "Plus, he's been dying to visit this place ever since he found out I grew up on an island.

He thought that was the coolest fucking thing." *Spoiler alert: it was not.*

"Has it lived up to his expectations?" A wry smile tugged at the corner of her mouth.

And now, I'm staring at her mouth.

"The ferry blew his mind."

"Why does that not surprise me?" She laughed as I started to draw slow circles on her stomach with my thumb. I couldn't help it. She was too fucking soft. "How did you two meet?"

"You seem to be very interested in my best friend." I lifted a brow.

"No, I'm just curious—" Amusement swiftly spread across her face. "You're jealous!"

"I am *not* jealous," I said as convincingly as possible. *I am so fucking jealous.* "You and Hendrix are both free to do whatever you want."

"Really?" she pressed, her arms pulling me closer as her voice grew husky. "So, you wouldn't mind if I invited him to my room later? Don't worry; I'll try to be quiet this time."

My face blanched, and her head tipped back in laughter.

"You're right. Definitely not jealous."

A mischievous grin spread across my face, moments before I lifted my hand out of the water and dunked her. I heard her gasp in surprise a split second before she went under. Her revenge was swift. I felt her legs wrap around my torso, and a moment later, she was dragging me under with her.

In other circumstances, I would have been seriously impressed by leg strength, but at the time, all I could think about was the feel of her body pressed against mine. Her arms circled my neck as we rose to the surface. Our eyes met as we took our first breath, and the playful humor turned into something else entirely.

I should let her go, I thought.

But I didn't.

My gaze dropped to her mouth as my hand moved down her back, grazing the edges of her bikini bottom. Her eyes flashed with desire, and she drew in a quick breath of air. Her fingers dug into my hair.

I knew I was toeing a line. Damn near crossing it.

But I couldn't bring myself to care.

I bent my head, my heart ramming in my chest.

"You guys are the cutest couple."

We both froze. Looking to our side, I found the three college girls, all clustered together as they swam back to shore.

I felt Elena try to pull away from me. I held her close.

"Thank you." I smiled through my teeth as I tried to keep up the ruse and savor every last second she was still in my arms.

The girls swam by, and I wasn't sure whether to thank them or curse them for the interruption.

Because when it came to Elena Mendez, nothing ever made sense.

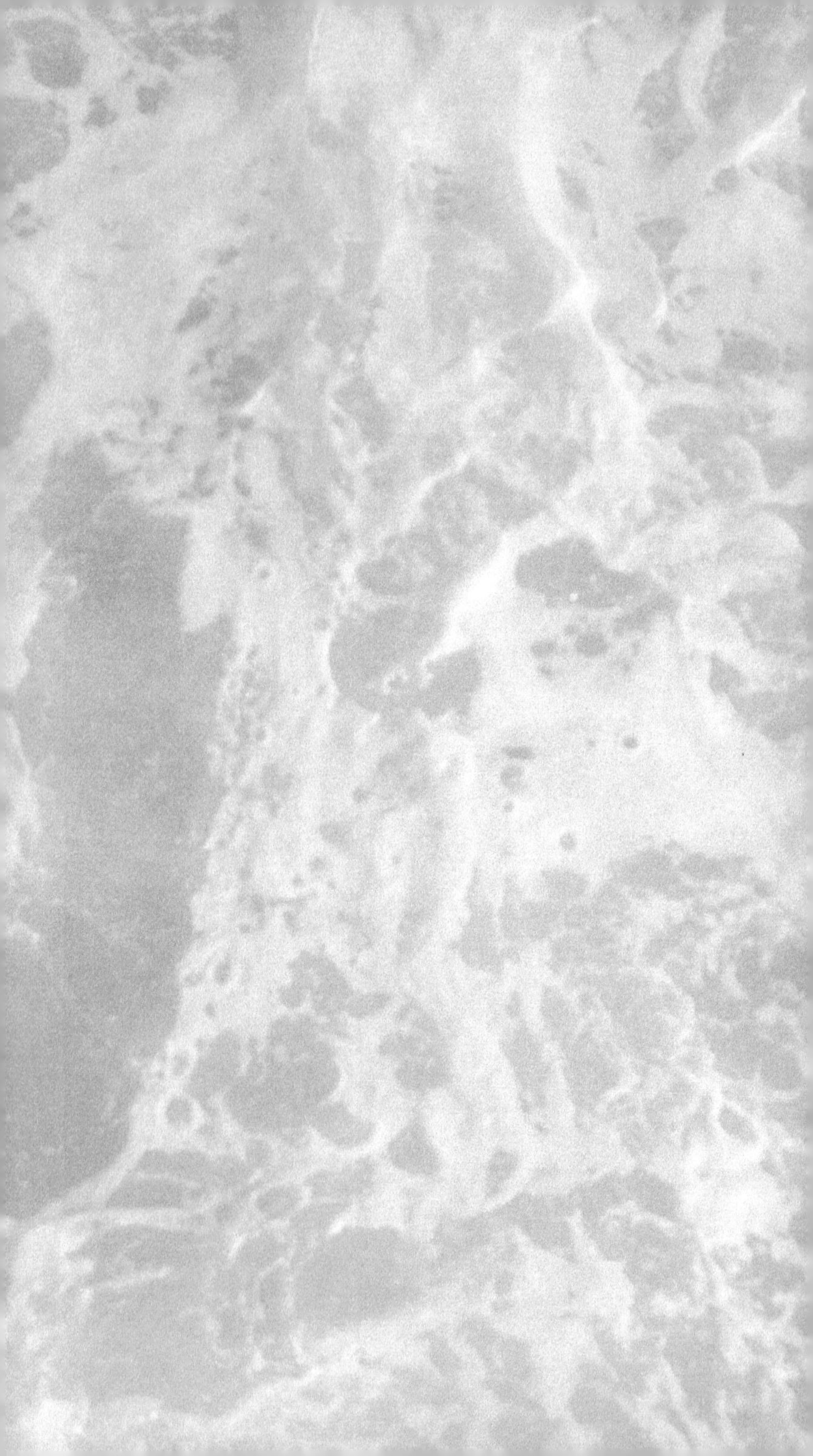

CHAPTER ELEVEN

Elena

MARIN

I saw you.

ME

I don't know what you're talking about.

MARIN

Don't play dumb with me. I saw you and Zander in the water.

ME

You saw nothing.

MARIN

You would lie to a pregnant woman?

ME

You're pregnant…not a freaking priest! <eye roll emoji>

MARIN

Honestly, I think I deserve sainthood for surviving my first trimester. I've never thrown up so much in my life. So. Much. Vomit.

ME

> You should consider being a spokesman for abstinence. Teen pregnancy rates would plummet.

MARIN

You're avoiding the subject. What the hell happened with Zander? And don't lie!

ME

> Nothing....much. Okay, fine. We almost kissed. But it was a total mistake. Definitely won't happen again.

MARIN

OMG. No. Do it!!! Marry Zander, and then we can be sisters-in-law again!

ME

> Wait, I thought you didn't want me to hook up with Macon's brother?

MARIN

Eh. I'm over it. I mean, who could blame you? Did you see all those tattoos? <drooling emoji>

ME

> I'm so gonna tell on you.

> Also, who else saw us...doing absolutely nothing in the water?

MARIN

No one. They were all busy talking about Macon's super-secret bachelor party. Which reminds me...

ME

> Yeah, yeah. I'm on it.

tried not to think about that moment in the water with Zander.

I definitely tried.

But I couldn't say I succeeded.

We'd almost kissed. I hadn't imagined it.

If we hadn't been interrupted by those very nosy college girls, I was nearly positive I would now know what it was like to be kissed by Zander Green.

Kinda hate those bitches, if I am being honest....

Because now, all I could think about was that almost kiss and the man who was responsible for it. The memory of his piercing green eyes seemed to follow me all the way back to the rental, through the door, and to the bedroom. I couldn't help but remember the way his hands had felt on my hips as I stepped into the shower, and it took every ounce of willpower I possessed not to reach down and soothe the ache between my legs, thanks to those stolen moments in the water.

After I rinsed away all the sand and washed my hair, I wrapped myself up in a towel. I took my time getting dressed, choosing leggings and a cropped hoodie again. When I resurfaced an hour later, I found Zander and Hendrix in the living room, both freshly showered, surrounded by guitars.

"Hey," Zander said as he moved about the room with ease. "We ordered pizza. Hope that's all right?"

"Perfect," I answered.

We'd all decided to give Macon and Marin some alone time tonight, and I was thankful for the night in. The sun had been draining, and I needed some time to recharge.

I watched as Zander plugged cords into an amp and sat down on one of the couches, positioning a foot pedal. He'd dressed down in a pair of black sweatpants and a gray T-shirt that said *I'm with the band*.

"We were gonna play for a bit. Do you mind?" he asked as his eyes met mine, waiting for an answer.

"Um, no," I answered, suddenly unsure of what I was supposed to do. Turn around? Sit down? God, I hoped he didn't expect me to join in.

If he thought those singers at karaoke night were bad...

"You can stay," he clarified with a knowing grin.

"You should stay," Hendrix added. "I love an audience."

"That's an understatement." Zander laughed as I headed over to the oversized chair that sat diagonally from the couch.

I noticed the way his eyes followed me, like a predator tracking its prey. It sent a shiver down my spine.

"Hey"—Hendrix shrugged—"not all of us can be rock stars."

Zander glared at his best friend before he turned to me. "He's kidding. He's just jealous 'cause the only session work he's done is in the studio."

"Someone's gotta stay home and keep the plants watered."

"You guys live together?" I guessed.

Zander nodded. He'd switched out his acoustic for an electric guitar today. I'd noticed Hendrix haul in a large guitar case, and I'd wondered what was inside. "Yeah, we've been roommates forever, but we were sick of renting, so we went in on a place together a couple of years ago."

"That's impressive. The housing market in California is insane."

They both nodded as they got situated. Hendrix also had an electric guitar strapped around his chest. Or was it a bass? I was a little rusty. It'd been ages since I had been in front of a live band and not just listening to one through my earbuds.

"How about you, Elena?" Hendrix asked. "You own a big old house in Richmond?"

He knows where I'm from? Zander must have filled him in.

I shook my head, laughing. "Hell no. I barely see the inside of my apartment. Why the hell would I want an entire house? But I do own it—my apartment, that is. Paid for it in cash."

"No shit?" Hendrix was impressed. "You must be a damn good lawyer."

As usual, my mom's cutting words came to mind.

Not good enough, apparently.

My face must have betrayed my emotions because Zander turned to his friend. "Let's get this going, yeah?"

"Yeah." He grinned. "Any requests?"

"Oh, um…what do you know?" I asked. "Give me a few to choose from."

They both just looked at each other and then back at me.

Zander feigned shock. "You wound me, Elena."

"What? What do you mean? It's a valid question."

"No," he argued, "it's not. Now, try again. Any requests?"

I let out a huff of frustration. There was no way the two of them could possibly know every freaking song on the planet. " 'Stairway to Heaven'?"

"Too predictable." Hendrix looked insulted. "Try again."

"Fine," I sighed, wondering just how vast their song catalog could be. So, I went for something a bit different. " 'Wicked Game.' " Chris Isaak's voice was fucking hot.

A *wicked* smile spread across Zander's face. "Done."

They both fiddled around with dials on their amps and their instruments, and then a minute later, Zander gave Hendrix a nod. With one foot on the pedal and the other bouncing out a beat, they started.

For most of us, a career was just something we did during the day to put food on the table at night. For Zander, his career was an extension of his soul. From the very first note, he had me.

Hendrix came in a moment later with the bass line, and it was perfection.

Until Zander did something so totally unexpected that I had to keep my jaw from dropping to the floor.

He started singing.

Because *of course*, he could sing.

The man sounded like liquid sex, and even though his

attention was focused on the song, I couldn't help but feel like every word was meant for me.

A voice like that should come with a warning label.

By the time he uttered the last lyric, I was completely spellbound.

"Okay, what else?" Hendrix's exuberance cut through the haze, and it was then I realized they'd finished.

I double-blinked and tried to focus. " 'No Rain,' " I said almost immediately, needing something a little lighter.

"Blind Melon?" Hendrix chuckled.

"That album cover is legendary. Tell me you didn't want to dress up like a bee for Halloween."

"My sisters definitely did," Hendrix confirmed.

"See!" I rest my case.

"I am not singing that one." Zander groaned, but his face was full of amusement.

Hendrix made a dramatic hand gesture and slicked back his long hair. "Prepared to be amazed, darling."

Zander set the beat and then executed the iconic intro flawlessly. I was instantly transported back to my brother's childhood bedroom. I swallowed back a lump in my throat.

When it was time for the lyrics, I learned one thing very quickly.

While Hendrix had a sexy speaking voice, the guy definitely could not sing. He could play the shit out of the bass, but his vocals were absolute crap, and he knew it. In fact, he might have been a little proud of it.

He got to the chorus, and his voice cracked at the high note. I could see Zander trying to keep it together, but I couldn't. My head fell back as laughter exploded from my lips, and Zander joined me.

"Okay, assholes. You sing along if you think you can do any better," Hendrix said over us.

He got around to the chorus again, and as Zander's eyes met mine, I let out a huff of resignation, and we both belted out the lyrics to the '90s classic.

Despite Zander's complaints about the song, he sounded surprisingly good.

Me, on the other hand?

"Dear God." Hendrix feigned disgust. "Is there a cat being tortured nearby?"

I threw a pillow at his face. "Fuck off. You're not any better."

"What?" The song came to an end. "My mom told me I have the voice of an angel."

It was the most fun I'd had in forever. By the time the pizza had arrived, they'd played a few more songs, I'd fallen more in love with Zander's voice, and I'd laughed so hard that I was in danger of cracking a rib.

"You seem to know a lot of music," Hendrix said as we gathered plates and napkins for our meal.

"I know a little." I shrugged.

"She knows more than a little." Zander started lining up the pizza boxes on the counter and opened them.

"What's your poison?" Hendrix asked. He handed me a plate and a napkin. "Hard rock? Metal? Alternative?"

"I grew up listening to a little bit of everything—whatever my brother could get his hands on. He'd sneak off to this record shop in town, and they had a small CD section, and he'd buy whatever they had—within reason," I added with a grin. "I think after a while, the owner took notice and saved stuff for him."

"Did he ever play? Your brother?"

I shook my head. "He never really got the option, growing up, but I think he would have liked to."

We all started fixing our plates. I was happy to see they'd ordered a salad in addition to the pizza and plopped down a large amount next to my single slice.

We all took a seat in the living room and sat in companionable silence as we ate.

Finally, Hendrix looked up and asked, continuing our

conversation from earlier, "Do you like anything modern? Or do you mostly just stick to the classics?"

I wiped my mouth with my napkin, catching Zander's gaze. "I listen to modern stuff."

Hendrix, having finished his pizza ages ago, absently plucked out a tune on his bass.

"Is that Manic at Midnight?" I asked him, and I swore Zander grimaced.

"Yeah. You a fan?"

I shrugged. "They're all right. Their earlier stuff is pretty good," I said.

Daniel had actually tried to get tickets to one of their concerts when they came to a small venue in Richmond a long time ago, but it sold out too quickly. Even back then, they had been crazy popular.

"Are they even still together? You know, since—"

"Since their lead guitarist knocked up a seventeen-year-old minor and then tried to pay her off to say it wasn't his?" Hendrix interjected.

"Yeah, that." I winced. I'd already known that, but even hearing it again out loud made me sick. "Seriously, who does that?"

"You'd be surprised," Hendrix said. "My dad works in the music industry and has heard it all. But Mitch is one of those guys who let it all go to his head. He wasn't always like that, and unfortunately, he didn't give a shit who he took down with him when he spiraled."

"I guess fame doesn't always bring out the best in everyone."

"No, it doesn't."

Zander had been suspiciously silent during this whole tangent of conversation, leaning back against the sofa with his head slightly bent, as if he were an observer rather than a participant.

"I, um, really like Vertigo," I said, hoping to redirect the conversation. "I was actually telling Zander how jealous I was that he got to tour with them. I love their album."

"They're great," Hendrix said. "And their lead singer? So fucking hot. Zander was an idiot to pass on that, but he's a stickler for his 'rules.' " I didn't miss the way Hendrix made little air quotes around the last word and rolled his eyes.

"Rules?" I didn't know why I was probing for more information regarding this particular subject. It wasn't like I wanted to know more about Zander's sexual exploits on or off the road. In fact, the mere thought of it made the pizza in my stomach start to churn.

"I don't mix business with pleasure. It never ends well," he simply stated, setting his plate on the coffee table before settling back into the plush sofa.

"So, you're saying two consenting adults can't have a casual relationship?" Hendrix pressed.

"You know that's not what I meant," Zander argued, shifting in his seat as he eyed his friend. "But when you add the element of working together, it can blur the line of professionalism, and that's when it gets messy."

"I agree with that." I nodded.

"Yeah?" Hendrix set his bass down and headed to the kitchen for more pizza.

"I had this thing going with a coworker years ago before I started dating—" I realized neither of these men knew anything about my dating history, so mentioning my previous long-term boyfriend who was no longer in the picture was pointless. "Anyway, it was great for a while." Fucking hot, actually, but I didn't need to go into detail. "And then we got put on the same case. When he started slacking and I had to call him on it…"

"I bet that went over well." Hendrix grimaced, returning with four pieces of pepperoni piled high on his plate.

I looked at the flat, washboard abs pressed against his tight T-shirt. *Where the hell does he put it all?*

"No, it didn't. His ego did not recover well from that one." I looked up and found Zander staring at me.

"But would you say it's possible outside of the workplace?" Hendrix asked.

"What?" I pulled my gaze away from Zander.

"A casual relationship."

"Oh, sure." I shrugged.

Hendrix's face broke out into a wide grin, and Zander…

Zander just kept staring at me as if I was a puzzle he couldn't solve.

<hr>

The next day, I had promised Marin my undivided attention. There were still a lot of details to work out regarding the wedding, and with the unexpected arrival of Zander and the baby announcement, things had understandably gotten a bit…derailed.

We spent the morning at By the Bay Inn, discussing ceremony and reception details with Molly, who was seriously the most organized person I'd ever met. Her lists had lists. She showed us pictures of past weddings held at the inn, including her own, and made sure Marin was comfortable with every choice, down to the very last cream puff.

"If you had told me a few years ago that I'd be sitting here, planning Macon Green's wedding at our family inn of all places, I would have never believed you," she told us as we headed out.

"Not just planning it—a bridesmaid, too. Don't forget that part." Marin grinned.

Molly laughed. "Oh, I haven't." She gave me a wink.

"Life has a way of surprising you, doesn't it?"

Marin had originally met Molly on the way to the hospital after the ferry accident. Molly had been engaged to Jake's best friend—which was a whole other story—and they both caught a flight from a local pilot to get there as quickly as possible. Marin had never thought she'd see Molly again.

"Sometimes in the most amazing ways."

Molly pulled her into a tight hug, and after I wiped away the dust that had somehow lodged itself in my eyes, we headed out to Billy's for a much overdue lunch, where my best friend tried to badger me again about my almost kiss with Zander.

"I don't know what to tell you other than it won't happen again."

God, how I wanted it to happen again.

"Why?" she challenged.

"What do you mean, why?" I scoffed. "He's Macon's brother. I can't just hook up with your brother-in-law!"

"Why?"

"Are you a broken record today?"

She grinned. "Just don't rule it out. I know you have your man ban or whatever, but Zander could be good for you. You could be good for him."

"Or…it could be a cataclysmic disaster," I countered, rolling my eyes. "Zander is already a bit of a flight risk. I don't need to give him one more reason not to come back here."

"I'm hearing a lot of excuses, but I haven't actually heard you say you don't like him." A wide grin spread across her face.

I didn't have a comeback for that one because she wasn't wrong.

Liking Zander had never been the problem.

Liking Zander too much? Now, that was a problem.

The rest of the day was spent working on the dreaded seating chart and making sure the out-of-town guests were all accounted for. Marin had insisted on making these ridiculous welcome baskets for each of them, and we drove all over town, gathering items to put in them. In addition to all the rooms at the inn, one of Marin's other new friends, Lani, had offered up discounted rooms at her upscale hotel as well.

Marin assured me that this was going to be a small affair, but it felt like the whole island had been booked up solely for this event. By the time we finished everything on Marin's to-do list and ordered dinner, I fell asleep almost the second I got home and didn't check in with the boys until the next morning.

"Rough night?" Hendrix grinned as I stumbled into the kitchen after the smell of coffee lured me from my bed. He was in a pair of loose pajama pants that sat low on his waist, and the black tank he wore clung to his muscles like a second skin.

"I didn't see it coming, but Marin is a borderline bridezil-la." I set my phone on the counter as he handed me a mug. I grabbed it out of his hand like it was the holy fucking grail.

"Marin? Really? She comes off so chill."

I turned to see Zander strolling into the kitchen. Shirtless.

I nearly dropped my whole damn mug right there on the tiled floor.

I want to trace those tattoos with my tongue like he's a treasure map...only it's not gold I'm seeking...

"Um, what?" Those were the only words I managed to get out before my brain caught up with my vocal cords, and I finally said, "Oh, yeah. You would think. But she's about the details—centerpieces, floral arrangements, fucking seating charts."

"Seating charts? Like we had in school?" Hendrix chimed in.

I leaned against the center island as Hendrix finished up his coffee, clutching my mug as I watched Zander open the fridge and check the contents before closing it again. "Sort of, but more strategic because you've got to figure out where to put Aunt Rose so that she's close to the bathroom, but not anywhere near Uncle Leon because they're not on speaking terms."

He squeezed by me, and I felt his hand brush my bare thigh as he went to grab a mug of his own. Without even asking, Hendrix plucked it from his hand, filled it, and then handed it back to him.

I guessed he wasn't a milk and sugar type of guy.

"That's insane," he said, stepping aside to allow me access to the coffeepot.

I didn't miss the way Zander's eyes tracked me.

I tried to ignore his heated gaze and focused on filling my cup. "If I ever get married, I'm never doing a seating chart. Ever. People can just sit wherever the fuck they want. It will be chaos, but who cares? Actually, you know what? I'm just gonna elope."

"Sounds perfect." A lopsided grin tugged at his lips before he brought his coffee cup to his mouth, and I watched his throat bob as he swallowed.

Why did my stomach do flip-flops when he did that?

My phone started vibrating on the counter, and Hendrix wordlessly handed it to me. I thanked him as I saw Marin's name flash across the screen.

"I still have an hour," I said the moment I answered, staring at the time on the microwave. Was it already eight thirty in the damn morning? I wasn't sure if I should be proud of this new ability to sleep in or be slightly horrified. "I'm not late yet."

"I know you're not. That's not why I'm calling."

"Please don't make me go buy you another matcha latte. They make my car smell like microwaved grass."

The guys laughed.

Marin joined in. "It does not. And no. Although—"

"No more caffeine!" I heard Macon yell in the background.

"This is what I get for being lazy and putting you on speakerphone." She sighed. "Speaking of which, can you put *me* on speakerphone? I need to talk to you and Zander together."

"*Okay*." The word was dripping with suspicion as I placed

my phone on the counter and tapped the right button before turning to Zander. "Apparently, Marin would like to talk to us both."

His brow lifted as he casually leaned against the counter, one leg over the other, looking effortlessly cool. "All right," he said, taking a sip of coffee before he folded his arms across his chest.

"Okay, we're both here," I told her.

"Oh, okay. Great! Morning, Zander!" she said in a sisterly sort of way. A little annoying, kind of sweet.

"Morning, Marin," he mimicked, a wide grin on his face.

Good God, that's adorable.

"So, I wanted to run something by both of you."

Our eyes met as we waited for her to elaborate. He smirked, and suddenly, my stomach felt like it was doing a cliff dive off the Empire State Building.

"Zander, I know you are taking Hendrix back today, right?"

"Yep," he answered. "Leaving in about an hour."

"Right," she answered, and I swore I could feel her grin from here. "Well, Elena and I had planned on driving up the coast to pick up my wedding dress. And since you still need to get measured for a suit, I thought maybe—"

"You want Zander to pick up your wedding dress?"

An amused expression painted his handsome face.

"No." She laughed. "I want you to go together."

"What?" I stared down at the phone like I expected her to pop right out of it and explain herself.

"This just makes sense, honestly. Zander's already gonna be up that way, and Macon hates the idea of me being that far away from him—"

"It's a few hours up the coast," I protested. "And doesn't he travel all over the county for work?"

"He does, and don't remind him. He's already threatened to drag me with him the next time he boards that ferry."

"It's not a threat, Marin. It's a promise," he growled in the background, making me roll my eyes. "The swan quarter ferry takes two and a half hours to get back here."

That man was going to drive her nuts through her entire pregnancy.

"*Anyway*," she went on, "you're the only one I trust to pick up my dress, and while you're there, you can help Zander out as well."

"I thought we were going to have a shopping day," I complained.

Everyone needed one of those while on vacation, right?

Plus, what the hell? Who did she think she was? Marin the Meddler?

"I know." She sighed heavily into the phone like breaking this news broke her heart. She wasn't fooling me in the least. "But yesterday really wore me out, and it's probably best if I rest. *For the baby*," she emphasized.

Man, she was laying it on thick.

It took everything in me not to roll my eyes. I looked up at Zander, and that same sly smirk was plastered across his face.

"No problem, Marin. We'll take care of it," he answered. "Go take care of yourself."

"Thank you, guys." She acted relieved. "I'll see you when you get back."

Marin hung up, and I grabbed my phone and finished the last sip of my coffee.

"Looks like we're going on a road trip." Hendrix grinned.

"And I'd better go get ready," I added. "Don't want to make you guys late."

"You okay with this?" Zander asked as I set my coffee cup in the sink.

I placed my hands on the counter and turned to him. "Depends," I deadpanned.

His eyes searched mine. "On?"

"Who gets to control the music?"

They both started laughing.

Do they think I'm joking?

"You know, I think I'm actually going to miss him," I said as we headed back down the coast.

"But not more than you'd miss me though, right?" he teased.

"Eh." I tried to keep a straight face but only lasted a second.

We'd said our good-byes to Hendrix at the airport, and even though Zander had made him swear to behave, he'd done the exact opposite.

"I can't believe he picked you up."

"And twirled me around. Don't forget about that part." He laughed.

"You two act like brothers," I commented as I watched the trees go by the window.

"We are," he said confidently. "As much as Macon and I are. Maybe more so." I could tell admitting that came with a little guilt. Maybe some leftover anger. "Isn't that the way it is with Marin and you?"

I nodded. "Yes. I mean, not enough to get Mueller tattooed on my body, but they've always been good to me." *Better than my own family.*

He grew silent for a moment before he finally said, "I didn't even know that was Marin's maiden name."

"She hasn't used it in years," I told him.

A heartbeat later, he tapped out a beat on the steering wheel. "Just makes me realize how much I've missed."

"There's a lot to look forward to though," I reminded him.

He looked briefly in my direction, and I saw doubt lingering in his eyes. Suddenly, I was on high alert. My nerves twisted as I feared the worst.

"Please tell me you're not leaving again, Zander."

"No," he said firmly. "No. I just…" He breathed out in frustration. "My job is chaotic. So fucking chaotic, and I worry I'll still miss everything and let them down. I can't decide which is better—to be the forgotten brother or the disap-pointing one."

"You were never forgotten," I assured him. "There's a reason Marin recognized you the second you showed up at that door. And honestly, you're starting at ground zero as far as your brother is concerned. So, you can really only go up."

My attempt at humor lightened his mood instantly.

"So, what you're saying is, the standards are low?"

I grinned. "Very."

"All right. I can work with that."

Our conversation just flowed from there, and I realized how easy it was to talk to him. Since that moment we'd shared in the water, things had been easier between us. I stopped trying to ignore him, and although the sexual tension was still through the roof, I was glad I could finally talk to him again.

I'd missed that more than anything.

We made good time and arrived at the bridal salon around mid-afternoon. Thankfully, since most rentals emptied out on Saturdays, the traffic gods had been on our side.

The door dinged as we stepped inside. The air smelled sweet and floral, and although the decor was tasteful, I remembered why I'd hated this place the last time I was here. Everything was understated yet somehow over the top at the same time with accents of gold and muted shades of pink. It screamed feminine, which was usually my jam, but this just felt nauseating.

I knew a lot of women dreamed about their wedding from a young age, but I hadn't been one of them. Don't get me wrong; I loved fashion, shoes, and makeup as much as the next girl. But the idea of a traditional wedding with the white dress in a stuffy church with a bunch of people staring at me sounded more like a nightmare than a fairy tale.

Maybe it was First Communion flashbacks. Maybe it was a fear of commitment. Maybe I just really hated tulle. I had no idea.

"Whoa. That's a lot of white," Zander said, holding a hand to his eyes like he'd been blinded.

I laughed. "They should really give you sunglasses before you come here."

He glanced around, his tight black Metallica shirt and fitted jeans a stark contrast to all the frilliness that surrounded us. "I feel like I'm walking into someplace I shouldn't, like that time I accidentally walked into the girls' restroom on a field trip."

I snorted, grabbing his hand and pulling him forward. I tried to focus on the warmth of his skin or how his fingers intertwined with mine. "I'm not a fan of this place either," I whispered like I was keeping a secret from the walls themselves.

"Yeah?" That seemed to perk him up.

"Yeah. I mean, why white?" I said, looking around. His brow lifted. "Okay, I know *why*. But if I were to get married—which I'm not saying I am."

"Course not." He humored me.

"But if I were, I wouldn't want to dress up like some virginal sacrifice. It's an outdated tradition, and besides, I look horrible in white."

"All right. So, what color would you want?"

A ghost of a smile played across my lips, but before I could answer, a woman came from the back. She was around my mother's age, but far more stylish. Her gray hair was swept back in a low bun, and she wore a pink tailored pantsuit.

Of course.

"Hello!" she greeted us with a wide smile. "I'm so sorry to have kept you waiting." Her gaze drifted down to our still-linked hands, and I noticed she softened a little. "Oh my, what a beautiful couple. What can I help you two with today?"

"Oh." I blushed, instantly turning to Zander as I began to

pull away. But before I could, his grip on my hand tightened, locking me in place.

"Thank you." A wicked grin spread across his lips as he pulled me closer. I had to hide the sharp inhale as my back collided with his chest and a firm hand snaked around my waist.

What the hell is he doing?

"We're actually here for two reasons," he told her. "My brother is getting married in a few weeks. I'm the best man, and my girl here is the maid of honor."

His girl? The fuck?

"Oh, that's lovely." The woman's eyes were as round as saucers as she gobbled up his bullshit.

"So, the first order of business is picking up the bride's wedding dress, and then since I got into town late, I need to be fitted for a suit."

"That's simple enough," she said. "My husband usually handles the suit and tuxedo side of things but I'm sure we have everything for the wedding party on file. What else?"

"Well..." His hold around my waist tightened, and my belly started to flutter as he leaned forward. I felt the tip of his nose brush past my ear and down the nape of my neck. He barely touched me, but the act of it felt incredibly intimate and sent shivers down my spine. "We haven't told anyone because we don't want to steal my brother's thunder—hence the lack of a ring—but I just asked this beautiful woman to marry me, and she said yes!"

What?

I faked the biggest smile I could manage while I quietly plotted Zander's murder.

"Oh, how wonderful!" The woman was so far under his spell that she was nearly jumping up and down in joy in her pretty pink pumps.

"Now, we're not one for tradition," he told her, and although I couldn't see him from this angle, I could just feel the panty-melting smile he must be broadcasting across the room 'cause the poor woman looked like she was about to overheat. "So, we're not planning on doing a big wedding like my brother."

"Oh, that's all right," she said, making a gesture with her hand like her entire life didn't depend on people doing that very thing.

"But that doesn't mean I want to miss the opportunity to see her in a wedding dress, you know?"

"Oh, absolutely!" she agreed, eyeing me from head to toe like I was a giant Barbie doll.

"You think you could help us out with that? I'd love to see her try a few on."

I looked up at him, intent on glaring, but when I saw the heat in his eyes, all I could do was stare.

"Don't worry about a thing, honey. I'm sure we can find something perfect!"

I double-blinked, turning back toward her.

So, this was happening then?

"Excellent," Zander replied.

The woman introduced herself as Gretchen. She was also the owner, and her enthusiasm told me she'd clearly picked the right career path. She ushered us deeper into the lion's den to begin our search. She was so excited about the dresses that she suggested we do everything else after I played dress-up.

Fan-freakin'-tastic.

I would have felt bad for pulling this woman's chain, but she looked so damn thrilled about the whole thing that I was pretty sure Zander had actually made her day.

"Do you have anything in mind?" she asked, making me blanch.

We were surrounded by tulle and lace and *so much white*. I caught Zander absently leafing through dresses like he was flipping pages of a book.

"Didn't you tell me once you had a specific color you

wanted, babe?" he said, squeezing my hand before looking up at me and smirking.

"Color?" Gretchen questioned.

"Um, yes," I answered in a steady voice. "Black."

"Black?" Gretchen tried to hide her surprise, and Zander had the biggest shit-eating grin on his face, like I'd just made him the happiest boy in all the land.

"It's a family thing," I explained quickly, feeling slightly exposed. "My dad's family is from Spain."

My *abuela* and many generations before her had always been married in black, which symbolized the bride's commitment.

Till death do us part.

She'd obviously known of my father's transgression and never treated me differently because of it. When she'd shown me family photos and the many brides dressed in black, I knew it was the one family tradition I'd want to uphold if I ever got married.

Especially when I found out my mother had been the one to break it when she married my dad.

I also happened to look fucking hot in black.

"Is that going to be an issue?" I asked, hoping I'd just found a snag in Zander's ridiculous game.

"Oh, no," she assured me with a bright smile. "I actually have a few in stock, and many of the dresses on the floor come in black or ivory. I don't have many brides requesting that color." She clapped her hands together. "How exciting!"

Yay me.

Zander followed us around as Gretchen helped me pick out several dresses. He seemed to take a step back, and I wasn't sure if it was because he felt out of his element or if he just enjoyed watching me squirm.

Either way, once I had a good selection, we headed to a massive dressing room, and Gretchen gave me a robe—pink, of course—to change into and told me she'd be back. I stared at myself in the mirror for a moment while I removed my sandals and shorts, thinking about my conversation with Marin regarding Zander.

I did have a million and one excuses when it came to Zander, but not a single one of them had anything to do with liking him.

In fact, liking him was the sole reason this whole thing was so fucking complicated. If I'd just found him attractive, he'd be easy to pass up. Hendrix was hot as fuck, but I didn't want to rub myself all over him like a damn cat in heat.

So, did that mean I wanted more? And an even bigger question…did he?

And if so, what did that even mean? A few hookups until the wedding? A long-distance nightmare?

I let out a sigh just as Gretchen called out from the other side of the dressing room door, asking if she could enter.

"Yep," I answered. "All ready."

Or at least as ready as I can be for…whatever this is.

I'd obviously never tried on a wedding dress, but I'd been here a few months ago when Marin picked out her first gown—Gretchen must have been out that day—so I knew what to expect.

When it came to putting on a dress of this magnitude, you had to be prepared to leave your modesty at the dressing room door. I took off my robe and proceeded to stand there in my black lace panties and bra while Gretchen helped me step into a mermaid-style gown with a plunging neckline and gorgeous beaded overlay. She had to cinch it slightly at the waist with clips, but when I looked at myself, I nearly gasped.

"Would you like to show him?" she asked, a knowing smile on her face.

I nodded, still staring at my reflection.

She patted me on the shoulder. "It's okay, honey. Most brides are a little emotional when they see themselves in a wedding gown for the first time."

Her words shook me out of whatever I was feeling, and I waited for her to grab the train before I opened the door.

"Your bride, sir," she said as if announcing a queen.

I felt all sorts of ridiculous as she placed me up on a large pedestal like a prized hog.

But then my eyes met his, and suddenly, I didn't feel quite so ridiculous anymore.

In fact, I watched him stare at me in the reflection of the mirror as he sat, one booted foot over the other, like he'd just been handed the keys to the kingdom.

I felt powerful. Sexy. Special.

His gaze raked over every inch of me, lingering on the curve of my hips and the valley between my breasts as he leaned forward and dragged a single thumb over his bottom lip.

Gretchen finished primping the skirt as he continued to watch. "You could easily add a veil to this or go without." She stepped back, obviously happy with her work. "It'd go beautifully with a—oh!" She startled as Zander rose from his seat and hopped up on the pedestal behind me.

I caught the sight of her eyes widening just as his arm snaked around my waist.

I didn't think she was used to men in her domain. And I didn't think anything could have prepared her for Zander Green.

"You look stunning," he whispered in my ear, making my knees weak. "I want more."

Why did I feel like he wasn't just talking about dresses?

"Thoughts?" Gretchen managed to say. She sounded out of breath as she looked at him.

Join the motherfucking club, Gretch.

"What do you think, babe?" he asked as I looked at us in the mirror.

His tall frame was curled around me like he'd done it a million times. That possessive hand splayed across my stomach made a statement—*mine*—and my traitorous body liked the sight of that a bit too much.

"I don't think this is the one," I said, never taking my eyes off his. "Too formal?"

Not sure what the dress code was for our nonexistent wedding, but I'd had to say something.

"Yeah, I agree. You look like a bride, but not *my* bride," he said with a cocky grin.

He placed a soft kiss on the hollow of my neck before returning to his seat. I felt it all the way down to my toes, and I couldn't tell if he'd done it for the sake of appearances or if he'd just wanted to.

It was all I thought about as Gretchen helped me off the pedestal and back to the room. I replayed it in my mind, like a damn VCR tape, over and over as she helped me out of the dress and into a new one.

When I came back out in a gauzy A-line number and watched him do nearly the same thing, my hopes began to dwindle.

Maybe it *was* all just a game for him.

As we headed back to the room for the last and final gown, I tried not to think about it and just focused on the dress. I saved the best for last after all. It was black satin and had a slit all the way up the way up my damn thigh. The A-line waist and the corset-style back made my boobs look fucking amazing.

It wasn't even in the realm of traditional, and I felt like a pure badass in it.

Gretchen gave me a motherly sort of smile and a moment to admire myself before scooping up the back of the skirt and helping me out the door.

I heard Zander before I saw him.

"Fucking hell."

I looked up to see his eyes drinking in every detail—from the high slit to the tight waist and silky fabric. We got to the pedestal, and just as Gretchen was about to help me up, Zander was there.

"May I?" he asked.

A blush tinted her cheeks, and she nodded.

Somehow, I thought this woman would allow him to get away with just about anything at this point.

He held out his hand and offered me a lopsided grin. Biting my bottom lip in an attempt to keep from laughing, I took it as he helped me up. His hungry gaze lingered on my bare leg as I stepped onto the pedestal.

He took over for Gretchen completely, walking around and adjusting the skirt with precision. He was very dedicated to his task, and I watched as his eyes roamed all over me, making me instantly flush. I felt like I was being prepped for a meal, and God help me, I couldn't wait to be eaten.

When he got to the front, he even bent down and positioned the fabric at just the right angle. As he rose, his hand slid up my bare thigh, his thumb barely grazing my tattoo.

I was so turned on by the tiniest touch of his hand; it was embarrassing.

"What do you think?" My voice sounded a little breathless.

"I think I want to marry you in this dress," he said, his eyes unfocusing for a moment, as if he was a little shocked by that statement.

Maybe he just realized we'd have to pay for it…

"But we don't know when that will be yet," I said, directing my words toward Gretchen.

"Oh, that's no problem," she scoffed. "No problem at all. We can work all those details out later."

I turned back to Zander, who was still looking at me with that Zander brand of intensity. He hopped off the pedestal and whispered something in Gretchen's ear. That blush came roaring back to her face, and then she nodded before walking away. Zander proceeded to walk toward me and offer me his hand.

I cocked an eyebrow at him, but he just smirked, so I took it. It was then that I realized he was the one who was escorting me to the dressing room.

Gretchen had walked away.

My heart started to beat wildly in my chest. Was he going in there with me?

I stepped into the lavish space, the other dresses now gone. All that remained were my own clothes that I had neatly folded on a chair in the corner. I looked up at the mirror and watched as he stepped in and closed the door behind him.

Okay, that answered that question.

I started to turn around, but his hand curled around my waist, and I was pinned against his chest.

"What the hell are you up to?" I asked, still entranced by the sight of him. Of us.

His large body made the once-spacious dressing room feel incredibly small.

And hot. *So very hot.*

"I told Gretchen that I needed to educate myself on the logistics of my bride's gown." He grinned.

My mouth dropped open. "And she just agreed?"

"I can be very charming," he whispered next to my ear. "And she's a romantic."

"And what if I'm mad at you?" I asked, eyeing him curiously. "For putting me in this in the first place?"

"I don't think you are." His voice was so fucking sexy.

His fingers found the strings that tied the corset, and he slowly began to pull. I let out a gasp.

This was definitely not a game anymore.

The bow came loose, and he tugged the satin laces free. My breath grew ragged as I watched him, his eyes never leaving mine. With his arm locked around my middle, he kept the dress in place as the bodice began to loosen. I could feel his hard body against mine. His need for me.

He spun me around to face him. We were so close; I could feel his heart beating in his chest. He kept one hand firmly around my waist, still keeping the bodice pinned to my body, which surprised me.

I was supposed to be undressing after all.

His other hand drifted back up my leg, thoroughly enjoying all the other benefits of this dress.

"Seems like you are more than capable of untying a few laces," I quipped.

"Turns out, they aren't that different from shoelaces."

"So, what you're saying is, you really didn't need to come here at all."

"Oh, no." He grinned. His eyes seemed almost brighter under the fluorescent lights. "I definitely did."

"Why?"

" 'Cause I needed to do this."

His mouth closed over mine, and I let out a gasp. Or maybe it was a groan. All I knew was that my body felt like it was going to combust if I didn't get more of him.

Nothing should feel this good.

I wrapped my arms around his neck as he parted my lips with his tongue. My hands dived into his hair like it was my last dying wish. That hand of his that had been hanging out on my thigh suddenly started climbing, digging into my ass as he hoisted me up. My legs curled around his waist just as the dress shifted, and the thigh slit suddenly took center stage, parting the dress like the Red Sea.

At least my lace panties matched the dress.

He pushed me up against the mirror as his fingers dug into my waist. My thighs tightened, and I could feel him, hard and ready beneath his jeans.

Zander kissed like a fucking pro. Like a man who knew exactly what to do with his mouth. He scattered kisses down my neck, along my collarbone, until we were both nearly breathless.

His forehead rested against mine. "I should have never come in here."

I stiffened at the sound of his words. *What?*

He looked up at me and smirked. "I don't think Gretchen

would approve of all the things I want to do to you in that dress."

My heart stuttered as he slowly pulled back and my feet touched the floor.

"And if I don't leave, I'm pretty sure she'll find out."

I raised an eyebrow. "You think I'd let you fuck me in a dressing room?"

He chuckled, and the sound of it was like a warm caress over my skin. "Ten seconds ago, I'm pretty sure you would have said yes to anything."

He's not wrong.

But like hell I was telling him that.

"Are you always this cocky?"

He grinned. "Yes," he answered. "Especially when there's something I want."

"And what do you want?" I asked, my mouth mere inches from his.

"You, Louie," he breathed out. "I want you."

And then he stepped out of the dressing room, leaving me with one single question.

But for how long?

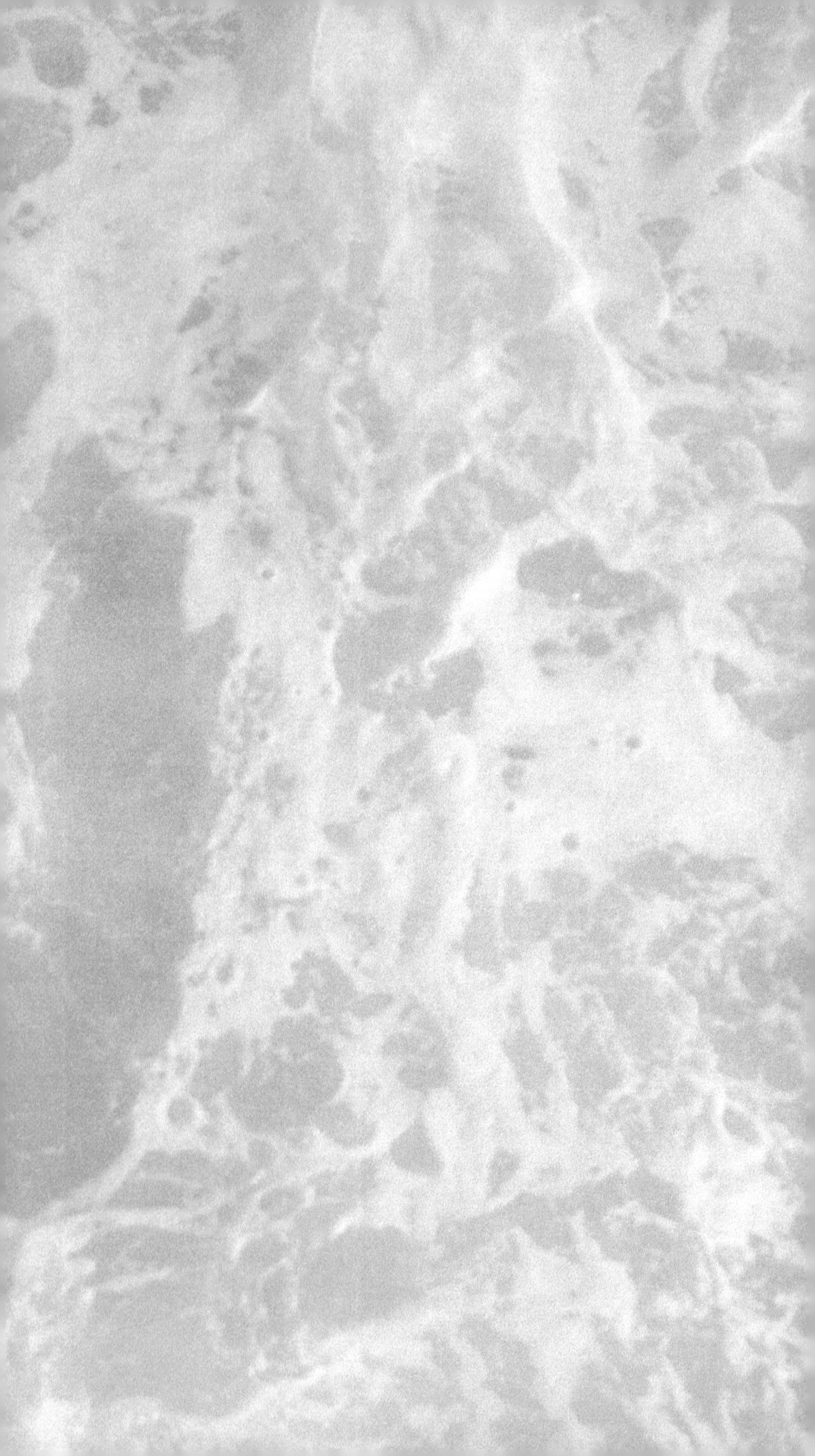

CHAPTER TWELVE

Zander

I stood in the kitchen the next morning, staring at the coffeepot, willing it to hurry up.

I was fucking exhausted.

After that make-out session in the bridal shop, I'd slept with one eye open and a semi all fucking night, just hoping I'd hear the telltale sounds of creaking floorboards as Elena snuck into my room.

But she hadn't.

And now, I was bleary-eyed, exhausted, confused, and horny as fuck.

The two of us had gotten into Ocracoke late last night, barely catching the last ferry of the day. Elena had fallen asleep in the car, and I lost track of the number of times I had to stop myself from sneaking a glance at her while she slept. By the time we got home and I woke her up, her eyes fluttering open in confusion, I knew it was time to call it a night. I helped her into the house, and she gave me a sleepy good night at her bedroom door. I went to my own door and tried not to overthink everything that had happened that day.

That obviously didn't happen.

I'd replayed every damn minute—from the drive to the shop and the fucking dressing room.

It had all started off as a game.

But when it came to Elena Mendez, I was quickly starting to realize that this game had no rules and the stakes were high.

When I told myself she was off-limits, I only wanted her more. When I tried to convince myself she was just another hookup, I'd picture her in that damn wedding dress, and my heart started to race.

I wanted to run away from her and hold her tight at the exact same time.

Nothing in my life was normal anymore. The moment I'd said yes to Manic, I had given up any semblance of normal, and I knew this time in Ocracoke was merely a countdown before the madness started. It was wrong to start something with her when I was forced to lie. And yet I still couldn't walk away.

I blew out a breath as I grabbed a mug from the cupboard, just as my phone started to buzz. I turned to grab it off the counter, hoping it was Hendrix.

It wasn't.

I swallowed nervously and looked down the hallway. Finally, I picked it up.

"Hey, Ash," I answered.

"Z," he greeted in that familiar Scottish brogue that had made him a household name. It had that rough quality that all rock stars possessed, but the deep, sophisticated timbre of someone who'd been classically trained. "Hope I didn't wake you up."

"Me?" I chuckled. "You're the one on West Coast time." I looked at the clock on the coffee machine. It was around five in the morning in Los Angeles.

"I like to get my day started early," he confessed.

"That's not very rock and roll of you," I goaded him, peaking down the hallway. Still clear.

"Yeah, well, I've always had to be the grown-up of the lot. Even more so lately." I could hear the pain in his voice still.

Manic at Midnight had always been a tight group. They'd formed the band young and grown up together. They were the kind of success stories people fell in love with. Losing Mitch hadn't just been personal; it had been devastating and nearly destroyed them.

It was a choice they'd had to make, but it hadn't come easy.

"Listen," he said, changing the subject quickly. "I wanted to run something by you."

"All right."

"The guys and I have been asked to do a charity concert in a couple of weeks. It will be recorded in front of an audience and broadcast live."

Live? My stomach churned. *Shit's getting real.*

"Ridge and I thought it might be the perfect time to make your grand introduction."

"On national television?" I was pretty sure my voice jumped an octave.

He laughed, "We don't do many television appearances, other than award shows, and with all the press still surrounding Mitch, we want to try to redirect that." His voice dipped like it physically pained him to say his name.

"I get it," I said.

Mitch had not only fucked over the band; he'd ruined a young girl's life in the process. Since she'd recently turned eighteen, her name had been leaked, and she'd been dragged through the mud by the press. Asher and the band were doing everything they could for her, including trying to redirect the headlines.

"So, what do you think?"

"Uh, what day?" I asked, grabbing the back of my neck as I paced the kitchen.

He rattled off the date, and I realized it was the day after Macon's wedding. A pit in my stomach formed. I knew I was going to have to leave here, but now, it all seemed so…final.

"How soon would you need me?" I asked, explaining to him my time crunch.

"You could fly out the day of, as long as you get there early enough for sound check."

How was I going to explain this to Macon? To Elena?

I was just going to board that ferry without being able to say a word and then show up on national television the next day?

Fuck my life.

"All right," I agreed nonetheless. "Sounds good."

"Great. I'll have Ridge set up the rest and contact you and Lance with the details. I just wanted to be the one to call and ask," he explained. "I know you probably feel like you're being thrown into a shitstorm, but we're glad you're joining us."

I thought back to my months with them, and I smiled. "Yeah, me, too."

"Enjoy your brother's wedding. And the last few moments of peace." He said it sort of jokingly, but I couldn't miss the hint of sadness in his tone.

I'd always known I was leaving. I only had three weeks in Ocracoke and that time was dwindling quicker than sand in an hourglass. But for some reason, that phone call had just made everything feel so real.

This had an end date.

Was it even fair for us to start something?

Kind of too late for that…

I blew out a breath, took a sip of my coffee and set it down. I texted Hendrix to see if he was awake.

ME

You never texted me when you got home.

His text back to me was almost immediate.

HENDRIX

Are you my mommy now?

ME

Your mom is a lot meaner than I am. What the fuck are you doing up?

HENDRIX

What the fuck are you doing, texting me, if you didn't think I was up? Also, I'm on East Coast time.

I snorted. *East Coast time.* What the actual fuck?

ME

You can't be on East Coast time. You were here for two days.

HENDRIX

Tell that to my brain. Now, what the hell do you want?

ME

Damn, Jet-lagged Hendrix is grumpy. I need advice.

HENDRIX

Is it about Elena?

ME

Maybe.

HENDRIX

<eye roll emoji> Okay, here is my advice...

I decided to text Hendrix later about the charity concert when he was more awake and less snippy. I hesitated as I pulled up the chat history I had with my brother. We hadn't texted each other since that day I'd come back on the ferry, and I wondered if we had the kind of relationship that included this type of thing anymore.

I used to ask him for advice all the time, but that was when I was a kid and I needed to know which action hero was better—Wolverine or Spider-Man.

Wolverine, obviously.

A part of me really wanted to just stay here and wait for Elena to emerge from her bedroom so we could continue whatever the hell we'd started in that dressing room.

'Cause, fucking hell, that had been hot.

But I also knew I needed to sort a few things out of my head before I went near her because if I managed to catch her alone again? All bets were off, and I owed it to her to figure out what I wanted first.

I sent a quick text to my brother before I could second-guess myself.

ME

You busy this morning?

Macon also texted back almost immediately. Everyone was glued to their phones today.

MACON

Nope. Covering for one of the deputies in the PM, so I'm off this morning. What's up?

ME

Want to meet for coffee?

MACON

Sure. Give me thirty?

ME

Sounds good.

It was just enough time to shower and change.

By the time I was walking back down the hallway, I could hear Elena stirring in her room. My stomach fluttered with the memory of her body wrapped around mine, and the urge to stop at her door was strong.

But instead, I kept walking, and when I got into my rental car, I sent her a text, letting her know I was meeting Macon and that I'd be back later. By the time I got to the coffee shop,

I had a thumbs-up emoji from her and a request for a bear claw.

I couldn't help the dumb grin that spread across my face.

Macon's truck was already in the parking lot, so I headed inside to find him. The door chimed as I opened it, and I scanned the tables, eventually finding him at the back of the line at the counter. The place was fairly busy, but not so bad that I feared we wouldn't find a place to sit.

"Morning," I said as I took a place next to him.

"Morning," he parroted. "How was yesterday? I heard you didn't get in until late."

I raised my brow, and he chuckled.

"First thing you've got to know about Marin and Elena is, they talk. All day, every day. About everything and anything."

"And what Elena tells Marin, she tells you?"

He shrugged. "Some of it. But, no, she doesn't tell me all of Elena's secrets."

"And I'm assuming she told you—"

He just grinned. "Dressing room, huh?"

I rolled my eyes.

"Nice."

"So, are you gonna tell me what she told you? Or am I gonna have to bribe it out of you?"

"You're asking me to breach my wife's confidence?"

Someone said hi to Macon as they headed to the exit, and he gave a friendly nod.

"She's not your wife yet. Also, uh, yeah," I said plainly, "spill the tea."

"Jesus, you are a West Coaster now, aren't you?"

I just laughed as we moved forward in line.

Finally, he let out a sigh. "Fine, but only because you're my brother and also 'cause I don't want you to mess this up. But I want the biggest fucking latte they make and at least three doughnuts. It would have been six, but Marin spared me the gory dressing room details. Thank fuck."

"Done. Although, if that's what we're basing it on, I think you owe me a few doughnuts after having to hear Billy's lawn furniture story. Seriously, I might never be able to go to a cookout again."

He snorted. "Probably shouldn't sit anywhere in our house then."

Dude, gross.

"Also, we applied for the marriage license, and I bought the ring, so she's my damn wife."

His logic was flawed, but I didn't think anyone could argue when he had that dopey smile on his face.

We got to the counter, and I found myself face-to-face with none other than the Manic Fanatic teen from the engagement party. Her eyes latched on to me, grazing over the leather bomber I'd specifically worn to cover my tattoos in public. Her face scrunched in confusion. Finally, Macon got her attention, and I let out a sigh of relief. Hendrix had been keeping up the ruse on my social media that I was in LA, so when we finished ordering and the girl moved on to the next customer without bothering to look up, I knew it must be working.

We found a table near the back and settled in while we waited for our order to be ready. Macon leaned back in his chair, his overgrown haircut such a contrast to the military buzz cut I remembered him with. I'd thought that would be the last time I saw him.

I was glad it wasn't.

"So, you got a fetish for women in wedding dresses?" he teased as his arms folded casually across his chest. He was dressed down this morning in tan shorts and a dark blue shirt that sported the logo for Billy's restaurant.

I wonder if they have those in black...

I shook my head and shrugged. "I blame Billy Idol, honestly."

My brother chuckled. I thought about the way her eyes had come alive when I asked her what color wedding dress she'd choose.

"I just wanted her to have a bit of fun. I get the feeling that she doesn't have a lot of it."

He looked pensive. "She works a lot," he stated.

"So do I. So do you," I answered. "Are you saying she works a lot and you don't think she enjoys it?"

He didn't answer.

"Does she date?" I moved on, hating the question before I even finished asking it.

"I feel like these are things you should be asking her." He gave me a pointed stare.

This is not three doughnuts' worth of tea.

"Okay, fair," I relented.

His loyalty to Elena surprised and delighted me. It was annoying as fuck, but I was glad to see someone stand up for her.

Even if it was against me.

"So, what's your plan with all this, Zander? 'Cause I know where you live and I know where she lives…"

I shifted in my seat. Okay, whose big brother was he? Hers or mine? I thought I liked Hendrix's *just go for it* form of advice better. These pointed questions were making me squirm.

"Hell. I don't know," I answered honestly. "Up until yesterday, I had a solid plan of steering clear of starting anything with Elena."

"So, what changed?"

"Fuck if I know," I said. "I can't think clearly when I'm with her. She's…" I stalled.

"What?"

"Different. She's different, okay? God, I sound like a fucking tool."

"You kind of do." He grinned. "But hold that thought." He got up and headed for the counter to grab our food and drinks.

I sat back in my seat and waited, letting my mind wander for a moment. Okay, not exactly wander. It was definitely going back to a specific moment in time—when I'd had Elena pinned up against that mirror. The skirt of her dress had shifted, baring her legs and her black lace panties.

Jesus.

It had taken all the willpower I possessed to keep my hand from slipping underneath them and finding out just how wet she was for me.

"Oh my God, is that Zander Green?!" someone shouted behind me.

My whole body stiffened as I remembered those parting words Asher had said to me this morning.

"Enjoy your brother's wedding. And the last few moments of peace."

Were they already over?

My eyes shifted downward as I tried to burrow into myself like some sort of damn turtle.

Then, my mind finally caught up to the actual words that had been spoken.

Zander Green. Not Zander Tate.

I swiveled around to see Millie McIntyre walking up with my brother, looking like she'd just flown in from Milan or some shit. I'd thought Elena dressed to impress. Millie looked like something out of a magazine ad with mile-high stilettos, a trendy floral dress, and a matching purse.

My gaze darted over to the cash register and I let out a breath of relief when I saw the Manic Fanatic employee was somewhere in the back, out of earshot.

It wasn't like our Mama gave Macon and me common names like John or Robert.

"Millie McIntyre," I greeted her, standing to give her a hug.

"Damn, you grew up nice," she said, blatantly checking me out. "And it's Millie Fisher now." She grinned, showing off the giant rock on her hand.

"That's right." I nodded. "The artist?"

She beamed, taking a seat next to us as Macon handed me

my coffee and did the same. "Yep. Somehow, I managed to move back here and bag the only British guy in a hundred miles. Fucking hot, too."

"A hundred miles? Did you conduct a survey?"

She punched my arm affectionately. "Oh, shut up. But enough about me and my amazing life. How are you? Marin told me you're a musician?" She eyed me intently.

"Yep, I've done all right for myself."

"More than all right," Macon boasted, and I couldn't help but notice the way Millie watched me for a reaction. "You should hear some of the bands he's worked with."

He'd only known of a few of them when I listed them off, but I got the feeling that even if he hadn't, he would have still been impressed and proud.

And didn't that make me feel like an asshole?

"That's...awesome." The remark came slowly as she seemed to be mulling something over. Whatever it was, she seemed to put it aside, beaming up at us. "I still remember you walking all over town with that old guitar strapped to your back."

Macon and I shared a sad smile, remembering how hard he'd worked to get me it.

"And so you're here for the wedding? As the best man?"

"Yep," I confirmed.

"And you and the maid of honor...you're both staying at Macon's rental? Together?"

"Uh-huh..."

She crossed her legs, smirking. "You're totally sleeping together, aren't you?"

"Jesus, Millie." Macon looked to the heavens like he was asking for strength. "Some days, I think I miss being the town grump."

"Oh, you're still the town grump, Macon. We just support and love you for who you are now," she said, batting her eyelashes. "It's called acceptance." She made a heart sign with her hands.

He rolled his eyes and then looked over at me. "Ignore her and maybe she'll go away."

"This is so fucking weird." I made a motion, pointing at the two of them.

"What is?" they both asked at the same time.

I looked side to side. "The two of you," I started. "Macon having an engagement party with half the fucking town—including Jake Jameson of all people. It's like I'm in some alternate twilight zone version of Ocracoke."

"I know," Millie agreed. "This place has definitely changed over the last few years—thank God; otherwise, I don't think I'd survive living here again. But it's still Ocracoke. People will tell you they live here to escape the drama of the mainland, but then gossip about their neighbors all day long."

"People love talking trash about each other. That's universal," I told her. "It just spreads quicker here."

"I don't know." She stared intently. "Pretty sure the internet has us beat." She paused, and my heart fluttered. But before I had a chance to dwell on it, she moved on. "And you can thank Marin for Macon and Jake becoming besties—"

"We are not—"

She cut him off, eliciting a growl from my brother, "She made his grinchy heart grow a few sizes, and now, he's much more tolerable. I think the fact that he's getting laid regularly helps, too."

"Marin needs new friends." He shook his head, a slight grin tugging at his lips.

"While we're on the topic..." Millie said, stealing one of Macon's doughnuts from right under his nose. He went to protest but instead just rolled his eyes. "Let's get back to you and Elena."

"I don't remember inviting you to join us for coffee," Macon said.

"Really? Weird." She just grinned and turned to me. "Anyway, are you sleeping together?"

I looked at my brother, and he just sighed in defeat. I turned back toward Millie.

Fine. Maybe a woman's opinion wasn't the worst thing in the world.

"No, we're not," I replied, leaning back in my chair. I took a sip of coffee and ran my hands through my hair, feeling like I was suddenly under some sort of weird interrogation.

"But you want to?"

My silence was damning.

"Okay, that's a yes." She laughed. "So, what's the holdup? Is it Macon? Is he cockblocking you 'cause she's Marin's best friend? Macon, are you cockblocking your brother?"

"Fuck my life," he muttered under his breath.

"No," I answered for him. "No one's…cockblocking." *Kill me now.*

"Oh." She seemed relieved. "So, then what is it? Can't be a problem with attraction. 'Cause you're both shit hot, and I saw you eye-fucking the hell out of each other at the engagement party."

My eyes had been all over Elena that night, and I hadn't exactly been subtle about it. Good to know it had been reciprocated.

"It's timing," I admitted because if I didn't fess up soon, we'd all be here until next week with the way she was rambling. "The two of us are only here until the wedding, and then she goes back to Richmond, and I—"

"Ah." She nodded, not waiting for me to finish. "The distance dilemma."

"Yeah," I confirmed.

"So, obviously, what you feel for her is more than a casual hookup."

"I don't know."

"That wasn't a question," she stated. "If you didn't, you wouldn't be concerned about a time or distance constraint. In fact, you'd probably be looking forward to moving on to someone new."

Someone new?

My chest tightened as I imagined her at a restaurant, laughing at a joke her date had just told her.

"Don't like that idea very much, do you?" She observed me.

"I hadn't really thought about it until now."

"But now, you are, and you want to rip this faceless fucker's face off?"

"Yeah, a little," I confessed, looking up at her like she was some sort of wise Prada-wearing Buddha.

"I've done the distance-dilemma thing." Her face seemed to be haunted by a painful memory. "Eventually one or both of you will have to make a choice."

"What choice?"

She gave me one of those looks. The kind mothers gave their toddlers when they couldn't figure out how to open a banana. "A distance dilemma can only be solved if one of you decides to close the gap. Or meet in the middle—that's what Aiden and I did."

My gut churned because I knew my fate was already set. I'd signed a binding contract making it so, which only left—

"Aren't we getting a little ahead of ourselves?" I questioned. "We're still getting to know each other, and you're talking about uprooting lives."

"It's just something to think about."

I let out a sigh. "I don't know if that's even what I—"

"Then, just go in with an open mind," she suggested.

"So, I'm just supposed to go in with absolutely no plan, assuming that if this is meant to be, it will all work out?"

Macon was the one to answer this time. "Isn't that what we do most of the time anyway? Just figure it out as we go and hope for the best?"

"Well, yeah, I guess. I was just hoping for something a bit more concrete."

They both laughed, and then Millie said, "You can't start a relationship, thinking of all the reasons it might fail—because it will fail. There is no plan when it comes to this kind of thing. You simply have to decide to try." She gave me a wry grin. "Love is chaos. Surrender to the madness."

After Billy's overshare at the beach, the last place I wanted to be was anywhere near my brother's backyard and all the mental images it brought up. But, that weekend, he and Marin decided to host a cookout.

"Just a few people," he'd assured me. "Bring whatever."

Considering my last few days had been virtually Elena-free, I was willing to basically attend any event—tainted lawn furniture be damned—if it meant I got to see her. If Marin didn't give Elena some time off soon, I'd be forced to steal her a way for a day or two. We were running out of time.

ME

Do you want to drive to the cookout together? I'm running to the market to pick up something to bring, but I can swing by.

ELENA

I'm actually already here. But could you pick up some extra dessert? Marin is hormonal.

ME

And brownies will fix that?

ELENA

Well, coffee would be her first choice, but…

ME

Bring all the brownies. Got it.

I swung by the coffee shop and managed to swipe the last of their brownies and homemade potato salad. I also threw in a dozen cookies and a few Rice Krispies treats.

I wasn't sure who I was trying to impress more—Marin or Elena. Either way, I was stocked up on sweets.

I also dropped by the local market and picked up a small gift for Marin and Macon. Weren't you supposed to always show up to a party with a gift?

Our parents hadn't exactly sent us to etiquette classes or whatever, but it seemed like the right thing to do.

I'd spent the morning trying to convince myself that I could keep pace with my brother in the North Carolina heat. I did my fair share of running and weight training back in LA, but if it was hot, my pampered ass ran on a treadmill.

This—*this*—was bullshit.

My brother ran in one hundred percent humidity like it was a frosty day in December. The sweat rolled down his back while I panted and begged for water. The fucker seemed completely unbothered.

I knew he was ex-military, but even this seemed unnatural.

I'd spent the rest of the day answering a few emails, signing some documents Saul had sent over, and squeezing in some much-needed practice time.

Pulling up to the curb of Macon's house, I collected all the food and the small gift and headed toward the door. A home-made sign was taped to it that said, *Drop the food in the kitchen!!! We're in the back!!!*

So many exclamation points…

I followed the instructions and headed inside. Macon and Marin's kitchen island was covered with food. Everything from ribs and hot dogs to guacamole and chips. I dropped the desserts near a plate of cupcakes and squeezed the pasta salad somewhere in the middle with everything else. I headed outside with the gift clutched tightly between my hands, already regretting it.

I should have known by the number of cars outside that this was no small cookout.

Half of Ocracoke seemed to be crammed in this tiny backyard.

"Zander!" several people shouted and waved.

Drunk, too, by the sound of it…

I scanned the yard, looking for my brother, and recognized several friendly faces—Jake and Molly, Billy and Eli. I finally found Macon with his arm slung over his fiancée, drinking a Coke Zero, as she munched on a plate piled high with chips, talking with Dean Sutherland—who had also gone to school with Macon—about some Netflix show. I caught his attention, and he waved me over.

"So, this is just a few people?" I looked around with a grin.

He shrugged. "It's Ocracoke. None of these fuckers have anything to do." He laughed. "And if you offer them free food and drinks…"

My eyes tracked back to that Coke in my brother's hand, and I realized I'd never seen him with a drink in his hand since I'd arrived. Our dad was an alcoholic, and although I'd never felt particularly overwhelmed by the presence of it in my life, I wondered if my brother had.

I held out the gift I'd brought to Marin. "I, uh, never got a chance to give you guys a housewarming gift," I said awkwardly. "Or any gift actually." I offered the bouquet and the bottle of sparkling apple cider, grateful I'd decided to go for something nonalcoholic for Marin.

Both of them just stared at the flowers. I started to feel uncomfortable.

"Shit, sorry. I didn't get a vase. Do you have one?"

They all burst out laughing.

Like, every single one of them…

The fuck?

I looked up at them, my brows knitting together in confusion.

"Sorry," Marin apologized. She had to breathe through one word to the next, her eyes wet with tears from her laughter. "Inside joke."

I pressed my lips together and looked around. "I think I might be the only one on the outside."

"Be glad for that," Dean said, slapping his hand on my shoulder. I'd forgotten he was a survivor of the ferry explosion, losing an arm because of it. "I can never look at a vase anymore without picturing that son of a bitch naked." He motioned with his head toward my brother, who was headed inside with the flowers and apple cider.

"This town is weird as fuck."

"And LA isn't?"

I turned to see Elena walking up to me like she'd just materialized out of thin air. She was wearing a gorgeous ankle-length dress in a muted green. It had buttons all the way down the center, and every single one past her mid-thigh had been left open.

"Oh, no. LA is definitely weird, but it's a brand of weird I've gotten used to. I barely raise an eyebrow when I hear someone at Starbucks talking about which spa has the best vampire facial or how you will not believe how awesome this new cleanse is," I answered, trying not to blatantly stare at her legs. Those buttons were taunting me.

She looked like a damn present, ready to be unwrapped.

Maybe I can convince her it's my birthday.

"Vampire facial?" Marin blanched, a chip halfway to her mouth.

"I could explain it to you," Elena offered, taking a sip of her glass of wine. "But it would just gross you out."

Dean turned to—God, was that his brother? "Taylor, your wife had better not start offering shit like that at the salon."

Yep, definitely Taylor Sutherland. I'd recognized him at the engagement party, but I'd sort of had my attention on other things.

I owed their family a ton of thanks. Without the help of

their mom, I wasn't sure I would have ever earned the cash to leave all those years ago.

Taylor chuckled, taking a sip of beer. "Don't give her any ideas. You know how she loves a good theme."

"Lord help us," Dean muttered.

"Where is Lani? I miss her." Marin pouted as Macon appeared once more, wrapping his arms around her and presenting her with a whole new plate. "Ooh, chips!"

He'd told me this morning that Marin had been suffering from some severe morning sickness. He might be going a little overboard to compensate for it.

"At home with Matthew. Cora and Lizzie are there, too." He chuckled as Marin dived into her food. "Girls' night. Mostly."

"Cora brought over an entire season of *Doctor Who*," Dean added with a grin before turning to me. "Cora is my wife. Lizzie is our daughter."

"Is everyone married?" I asked, looking around the yard at all the couples grouped together.

I hadn't thought of anyone here in fourteen years. I'd compartmentalized my childhood and put everything and everyone in it in a sort of time capsule. Coming back and seeing Macon and my classmates with spouses and families reminded me that life here had gone on whether I thought about it or not.

"Not everyone." Dean laughed. "But close. Our friend Gavin there is the eternal bachelor, but you wouldn't know him. He's a transplant from the mainland."

"He owns Taps." Elena gave me a meaningful look, making me grin.

"Speaking of, what's up with that, Zander?" Marin asked around a mouth full of chips. "Why the hell would a professional musician walk into a bar on karaoke night?"

I shrugged. "It was packed, and I was hungry. I didn't want anyone in town to see me before you did, and I figured it'd be a good place to melt into a crowd," I explained. "Even at the expense of my hearing."

"And instead, you found Elena."

"With earbuds on," I added with a touch of amusement.

"You weren't there when the couple got up there and sang 'Barbie Girl.' " She grimaced. "In character, guys. It was on a whole other level of weird."

"This is kind of making me want to go, honestly." Marin laughed.

"No!" everyone shouted.

"So, I keep meaning to ask you"—Macon swiftly changed the subject—"when do you go back on the road? Headed out with anyone we might know?"

I went rigid, hating that I couldn't tell him.

"Yeah, the beginning of September," I said as they all stared. *Jesus, is it getting hotter?* "But I, uh, can't say anything more. Contractually obligated and all."

They all groaned.

"Seriously?" Macon exclaimed. "Don't you know we're all living vicariously through you now?"

"I'll tell you soon," I told him, wondering if there would be any way I could tell my family before that concert. "Promise."

"What's it like? Touring with bands?" Taylor asked. "It's got to be a wild lifestyle. Like, do you actually sleep on a bus?"

"Sometimes," I offered. "Depends on the band and the length of time I'm with them. The lifestyle is not for the faint of heart. I'm never home, I keep insane hours, and I basically run on caffeine."

"That sounds like Elena's job," Marin joked.

"But I doubt hers comes with an endless supply of hot chicks." Taylor gave a salute with his beer, and everyone chuckled.

"I'm gonna go grab some food," Elena announced abruptly, suddenly pivoting toward the house.

Marin tracked her long strides, and I noted the look of concern on her face.

Is she upset?

"Uh, me, too."

A look of approval spread across Marin's face as she watched me follow her best friend.

I headed toward the kitchen, but when I stepped through the sliding glass door and took a look around, Elena was suspiciously absent. I hovered near the island for a moment, wondering whether to run off after her or give her a few minutes. Women needed those from time to time, right?

Fuck it.

I'd only been to Macon and Marin's a few times, but the layout wasn't complicated. It was a ranch-style with a single hallway, much like the rental Elena and I were currently occupying.

There were only so many places she could be, and when I found the guest bathroom wide open, that narrowed things down significantly.

A few more steps down the hallway, and I found her in what would normally be considered a spare bedroom, but it had been transformed into something else entirely.

"Wow," I breathed out as I stepped inside. "Is this Marin's studio?"

Elena was in front of a large easel, her eyes fixed on an unfinished painting of the harbor. At the sound of my voice, those chocolate-brown eyes drifted toward me.

"Yeah." She nodded. "Macon helped her with it. Pretty great, right?"

I took a look around, noticing the sink they'd installed in the corner and the flooring that would stand up perfectly to paint. "It's perfect," I stated, walking toward the wall of cabinets near the door that looked like they housed every damn paint color known to man. "I thought you came inside to grab some food?"

"I was. I am," she insisted, moving toward the door. "I just needed a minute."

"Why?" I prodded.

Her mouth opened, but no answer came. Instead, she tried to squeeze past me to leave. I took a step back, grabbed the handle of the door, and swung it closed.

The lock clicked in place with the push of my thumb.

Her eyes widened, and I asked one more time, "Why?"

She visibly swallowed. "Because, Zander, this…is confusing." She motioned between the two of us. "I don't know what the hell it even is, and I'm not used to feeling like this."

"Like what?"

"Out of control," she confessed. "Powerless."

I took a step forward, and she took one back.

"I like casual relationships," she stated like it was a fact from one of her cases. "I think I might even prefer them because looking back, even my ex was basically just a long-term friends-with-benefits arrangement."

Hearing her talk about a boyfriend, even an ex, had me all sorts of jealous.

"So, if that's what you want, I can do that," she tried to assure me, but I saw doubt swimming in those brown irises.

"But?" I pressed, taking another step forward.

She stood still, our bodies now mere inches from each other.

"But when I think about us leaving here in a week and you going on the road in September with groupies and hot musicians, I get—"

My fingers closed over her chin, and I tilted her head toward me. I couldn't help the smirk that spread across my face. "Are you jealous, Louie?"

"No," she scoffed, tearing her chin from my grip. Her arms were closed around her chest in a frustrated movement as she turned away from me. "Okay, fine, yes! And this is what I mean about feeling out of control. I am not a jealous person. Especially over a guy I've known for two fucking weeks."

My smirk turned into a wide-toothed grin at this point.

I was beginning to think I was the only person in the world who could upend Elena's world this spectacularly. It was only fair though because my life had been completely upside down since the moment I'd stepped into that karaoke bar.

I closed the distance between us once more, her back now to my front. "I don't know where this is going either," I said, leaning over her. "But, I'm right there with you on the jealousy thing. The very mention of your ex has me feeling murderous."

She snorted out a laugh.

"I don't know what will happen in a week, let alone two months, but after that moment in the dressing room, I sure as fuck don't want to waste any more time worrying about it when we have so little to begin with. Do you?"

She turned to face me, her eyes alight with fire. "No."

"Good." I palmed her cheek. "There is just one little thing we need to take care of though."

Her brow furrowed as I stepped back and grabbed the back of my shirt, removing it with one swift tug. Her eyes widened and then heated.

"I can't have you feeling powerless, Elena."

Her gaze wandered over every hard ridge of muscle, every line of ink. I held my arms out wide and did a slow turn in front of her.

"You're used to commanding courtrooms and being in charge." I dared her with a hint of mischief in my voice. "So, do it. Command me. Take back that power."

I half expected her to give me a pat on the head, command me to stay like a dog, and confidently walk back out to the kitchen to make herself a sandwich.

Would that technically count as far as the challenge went? Yes.

But it wouldn't be nearly as fun.

From the wicked gleam in her eye though, I knew she was leaning toward the fun side though, and hallelujah for that.

She began to circle me like a predator, her fingernails grazing my shoulder and across my back. My whole body came alive with that single touch.

"They're gonna start to wonder where we are," she whispered softly as she walked behind me.

"I couldn't give two fucks," I answered honestly.

With the way she was touching me and the sound of her voice in my ear, someone could be trying to beat down the door, and I still wouldn't open it.

She made one final turn and stood before me once again, her hands running down my chest, over the smooth lines of my abs. She traced over the large design on my rib cage. "I want you to tell me what each one of these means while I run my tongue over every single line."

Hell yeah.

"But not now." A sexy smirk fell upon her lips right before her hand dropped to my shoulder and gave me a little push. "On your knees."

There she is…

Confident, commanding, and so fucking hot.

She didn't need to ask me twice. I sank to my knees as I held her gaze, my hands running down the soft fabric of her dress.

I was itching to touch her, to bury my whole fucking face in the apex of her thighs, but I was hers to direct. Hers to use for her pleasure alone, and I wouldn't make a single move until she told me to.

No matter how much I wanted to.

"You can play the guitar pretty well—"

"Pretty well?" My hand tightened around her calf, making her laugh.

"Okay, exceptionally well. Is that better?"

"Marginally. What about my superior guitar skills?"

"Those talented hands good at anything else?"

"A few things," I answered, sliding one hand up her thigh. "I have a pretty good mouth, too. Don't forget about that."

The sex haze she was under seemed to momentarily lift. "Yeah, why don't you ever sing? Like, you could totally—" She let out a tiny squeak as I grabbed her waist, spinning us around until I had her pinned against the door.

"Elena?" There were undercurrents of amusement in my voice as I looked up at her.

"Yeah?" She sounded slightly breathless from my abrupt relocation.

I slid my hand up her smooth leg, bending it at the knee before I hooked it over my shoulder.

"Later." I grinned, looking up at her.

Damn, that's a nice view.

Her head fell back against the door with a thud as my fingers explored her. Her skin was so fucking soft, and as I began to trace every curve of her hips and scatter kisses along the inside of her thighs, I remembered the one thing I'd been dying to do.

I lifted up onto my knees slightly, finding the cluster of flowers I'd become obsessed with.

"When you came out of the water the other day and I saw this peeking out of your bikini, I got so fucking hard." I heard her take in a sharp inhale as my tongue traced the lines closest to her core. "I've been dying to do this ever since."

Leaning back down on my heels, I slid my hand under the lace of her panties, finding her wet and ready for me.

"Shit," she cursed.

"If you're worried about them finding us, you're not doing yourself any favors, Louie."

"You're not making it easy, Trouble," she fired back.

But she had it all wrong.

She was the one who was making it hard.

So fucking hard.

She felt like silk. Soft and warm, and all I wanted to do was rip that tiny piece of lace from her body and claim her over and over against this damn door.

Dude, not at your brother's house.

I already knew we were crossing a line, fucking around in Marin's studio like this. Locking ourselves in here all night to fuck was probably a giant faux pas.

Not that he didn't deserve a little payback after the things I'd had to hear about his sex life since I got here.

"Not sure if you know this," I said, sliding her panties to one side. God, she was gorgeous. I'd love to take them off entirely, but I wanted to save that for later, when I had all the time in the world to explore every inch of her. "But guitar players—*exceptional* guitar players, that is—tend to have large hands." I sank a single digit inside her. *So fucking wet.* "And very, very long fingers."

"Oh my God," she swore as I added another, thrusting deep.

Her body clenched around my fingers as I pumped them in and out, watching her writhe under my touch.

"More," her breathy voice demanded.

Yes, ma'am.

I curled my fingers at just the right spot, and she tried to stifle her moans, clamping a hand over her mouth. I doubted it did any good.

Especially when a second later, my tongue found her clit.

"Holy fucking shit, Zander."

Exactly what she said.

She tasted fucking perfect, and suddenly, I felt like a starved man, feasting on my first meal in days. I hooked my arm around that leg that I'd wrapped around my shoulder and pulled her closer, burying my face between her thighs.

Because who needs oxygen, am I right?

Her fingers dug into my hair, and her hips started to grind.

Yes.

I'd never been this turned on, going down on a woman. The moans and soft gasps alone were nearly enough to make me come in my jeans.

I felt her core tighten around my fingers.

"I'm so close."

I sucked down hard on her clit, causing her to gasp, and then her body quaked, and she fell apart, shaking and moaning my name. I squeezed out every drop of pleasure from her orgasm, licking and sucking until she sagged against the door in exhaustion.

I adjusted her drenched panties and smiled to myself, knowing she'd have to walk around with those on as a nice little reminder for the rest of the night.

Just as I rose to a standing position, a knock came from the other side of the door.

The look of horror on Elena's face was priceless.

"Yes?" I answered innocently.

She frowned, and I lifted my upturned hands like, *What?*

She swatted me in the arm. I silently laughed.

"Jesus fucking Christ," I heard my brother mutter under his breath and then sigh. A moment went by, and then he cleared his throat. "Marin would like me to ask you if you could please be mindful of the paintings on the easels. They're commission work, and she's already cashed the deposits."

Elena pressed her lips together, and I barked out a laugh.

"Also, Zander, what the fuck?"

"Sorry, Macon," I tried to say, my head buried in Elena's neck as my shoulders bounced.

So not sorry.

Elena couldn't hold back any longer. I looked up to see her smile and then join in, laughing right along with me as I heard the telltale signs of my brother's footsteps trudging down the hall.

"Wanna get out of here?" I asked, breathless.

I could still feel her heart beating wildly between us. A moment passed as we looked at each other.

Then, she said, "Race you to the door?"

CHAPTER THIRTEEN

Elena

We barely made it over the threshold before clothes began to litter the floor.

I wasn't even sure we'd said good-bye to anyone at the cookout. We'd just bolted out of Marin's studio and gotten the hell out of there.

Whatever. I'll apologize tomorrow.

Right now, I only had one goal, and it was getting the man in front of me naked. So far, I was about fifty percent there. I'd yanked off his shirt after we both kicked off our shoes in the living room. Zander though was beating me as my dress flew over my head, leaving me in just a bra and the panties, which were still soaked from before.

His eyes raked over me with a look of pure masculine appreciation. "I've wanted to strip you bare since the moment I laid eyes on you," he told me.

"No one's stopping you."

I hadn't planned on sleeping with Zander today. But I hadn't planned on *not* sleeping with him either. Sex wasn't something I ever abstained from. If I was with someone and it felt right, I went for it.

With Zander, it felt more than right.

It felt real.

"All in good time." He grinned, bending down to capture my lips.

His kiss was scorching, demanding, and all-consuming. He kissed me like he owned me, and part of me wondered if he just might in that moment.

His hand snaked around my waist, and he slowly dragged us to the couch, his mouth never leaving mine until the back of his legs hit the cushion and he fell back.

A laugh escaped from my lungs as I watched him stumble, but he quickly recovered and reached out to pull me on top of him. I fell into his lap with my legs straddling him. The smile on his face nearly took my breath away, and I couldn't help but kiss those damn dimples on his cheeks.

I felt his hand slide up my spine as his mouth met mine again.

God, I could spend days kissing Zander, and considering the way he leisurely explored my mouth while his fingers dug into my hair gave me the impression he felt the same.

That hand that still rested on my spine slowly started to drift upward, reaching for the clasp of my bra. With a slight twist, it came undone. I pulled back as he slid the straps down my shoulders and dropped it to the floor.

"Come here." His voice was rough as his eyes took me in. A hand slid under my ass as he hauled me forward on my knees. It created the perfect angle to—

"Shit!" I cried as his mouth closed over my nipple.

With his free hand palming my other breast, he ran his tongue over the sensitive bud, making me buck in his arms. His fingers dug into my ass.

"How attached are you to these?" he asked, grabbing a fistful of lace under his palm.

"I could live without—"

He didn't even let me finish, twisting the material until it shredded under his strength. He did the same thing to the other side, and they fluttered to the floor.

Those had been expensive as fuck, but, damn, that was hot.

Those emerald-green eyes were roaming my body again, mapping every new inch of exposed skin.

I looked down at the black shorts he still wore.

I'd failed miserably at my task. He was most definitely not naked.

My hands went to his zipper. *Time to remedy that.*

He silently watched as I undid the button and worked on that zipper. When my fingers reached his waistband, he lifted his hips, and together, we slid off the last piece of clothing and dropped it to the floor.

I took in every impressive inch of him.

Once, when Marin had been pretty hammered on red wine, she'd gone into some rather lengthy detail about…well, Macon's lengthy details.

I smiled. It seemed that some things indeed did run in the family.

"Shit," Zander cursed. "Grab my wallet out of my shorts."

Oh, right. *That.* I shifted in his lap, twisting around toward the floor.

"Jesus, Elena. You're killing me here," he said as I wiggled against his crotch.

I popped back up, laughing but triumphant. I handed him his wallet, and he opened it up.

"This had better not be one of those lucky condoms you've had in there since high school."

He pulled out not one, but two condoms, setting the second on the side table.

That's promising.

"No." He gave me a pointed look. "I bought these a few days ago."

Oh.

"A bit presumptuous, wouldn't you say?"

He tore the wrapper open and quirked an eyebrow as he rolled it on.

"Hopeful maybe?" he said. "Confident even."

His hand cupped the back of my neck, and he kissed me again. His lips brushed over mine like he'd done it a thousand times. I fisted his hair, rolling my hips against him.

"I need to be inside you," he whispered in my ear.

Yes.

I lifted my hips while my hands wrapped around his cock. He sucked in a breath as I angled my body. His fingers dug into my waist as I lowered myself onto him.

"So fucking tight," he cursed as I took every delectable inch.

I'd never felt so full, so overwhelmed by need.

I'd never needed to move so badly in my life.

The first roll of my hips felt like paradise. The second, nirvana. Then, his mouth closed over my nipple, and I started grinding on that cock of his like it was my last day on earth. He lifted his hips, thrusting into me as I continued to ride him.

A hand slipped between my thighs, and Zander's thumb found my clit.

"Oh my God," I groaned as those sensitive nerves hit his thumb every time I rode him.

I felt myself growing close, that fluttering feeling building deep in my belly. My hips moved wildly, and Zander rubbed his thumb in exactly the right place.

That was all it took.

I shattered, panting and moaning as my core spasmed around him, driving him into a frenzy. He grabbed me around the waist, and I suddenly found myself on my back. He pushed one of my knees forward, and I swore he sank in deeper.

He slammed into me as the sound of sex filled the room. It was fast and dirty, and when he came with a guttural groan, I couldn't look away.

It was addictive.

He was addictive.

And that was when I knew…this was far from casual.

———

My eyes fluttered open as the morning sun filtered in through the window.

That's not my window.

Wait, when did I start calling it my window?

I turned in the unfamiliar bed, and my heart fluttered.

It fucking fluttered.

Wearing nothing but a pair of black boxer briefs, Zander was propped against the headboard with a sleek acoustic guitar resting on his thigh. He had a pencil tucked behind his ear as he glanced down at a notebook balanced on his bent knee while he absently plucked out chords.

It was like waking up to my own personal erotic fantasy.

"Enjoying the view, Louie?" His eyes found mine, and that lopsided grin spread across his face, making butterflies burst in my belly.

"Mmhmm," I said, stretching languidly under the covers.

He watched every move, knowing how little clothing I had on at the moment.

Spoiler alert: it was none.

"What are you doing?" I pointed to the notebook.

"Messing around." He shrugged.

"Do you write songs?"

"I used to," he confessed. "But I haven't in a long time. I haven't had much time for it."

He seemed to want to say more, but instead, he began to lazily pluck the familiar melody of "More Than Words" by Extreme.

"Is there any song you don't know?" Amusement colored my tone, but mostly, I was just in awe of his talent.

"I'm sure there are a few." He grinned.

"How long does one have to play to be a human jukebox?"

"I don't think I've ever been called that before." He laughed as he moved on to another song—Led Zeppelin maybe? "I actually started a bit late. I'd been having some trouble dealing with our mom's death, and I guess Macon giving me something tangible to focus on helped with all those unfamiliar feelings."

My throat felt thick with emotions. I knew their mom had died. Macon had told me, but until now, Zander had never spoken about it.

"So, he bought you a guitar?"

"He said he got it from a thrift store, but since we don't have one of those around here, I'm guessing he probably worked or traded for it," he said, his expression heavy with guilt. "It was pretty beat up and worn, but I played that thing for years."

And something told me he still did.

"So, you just taught yourself?"

He nodded. "I have a pretty good ear." He shrugged. "And for a long time, I didn't even know how to read music."

"What changed?"

He chuckled. "Lance." When I looked up at him in confusion, he clarified, "The Creeds."

"Lance is Hendrix's father?"

"Yeah," he confirmed as he effortlessly plucked out those familiar first notes of "November Rain" by Guns N' Roses. "They're well known in the music industry. Lance is my manager actually, but they also own a bar."

"A bar?"

His mood was lighter when he spoke about the people who'd become his family, and I couldn't help but be drawn in.

"I'd been in LA for months before I approached Creed's— and I knew exactly who owned it. I knew what it could mean to have someone like that in my corner. I also knew I probably wasn't the first person to try and worm my way in by getting a job at the bar."

He smiled, and my eyes immediately fell on that bold tattoo on his arm that carried the family name.

"But I was willing to do anything to get in front of Lance Creed, so I busted my ass at that place—cleaning, bussing, and hauling equipment."

"And did you get it?"

"No, I totally chickened out," he confessed. "The first time I saw him standing behind that bar, I froze. And then before I could make a bigger idiot of myself, I turned and hid for the rest of my shift."

I barked out a laugh. "Seriously?"

"Yep. I'd been there for weeks, waiting for him to show his face, and when he finally came back from a long business trip, I choked."

"So, how—"

"Hendrix," he explained. "He came home from college for the summer and started working in the bar. We became good friends, and one day, he invited me over to play with him."

"And the rest is history?"

"No." He laughed. "The rest was a hell of a lot of hard work. Lance took one look at me and that beat-up guitar and knew I had no formal training. He put me through the wringer before he even considered representing me." His eyes gleamed as he talked about his manager. "I worked in that bar for-fucking-ever before I landed my first gig."

"But now, look at you," I said, my gaze raking over his body. All that bare skin.

My body came alive instantly.

"Yes, look at me." His voice was pure sex as he slowly put his guitar down next to the bed, moving toward me with purpose and a smoldering gaze.

We didn't leave the bed for the rest of the day.

———

That had been an awkward conversation.

No one liked talking about their previous…exploits.

But I'd learned a long time ago that avoiding it was worse than just suffering through the uncomfortable exchange.

My part of the conversation was fairly short. My string of bad dates meant the only action I'd seen lately was the battery-operated kind. His required a bit more explanation, but the gist was, he was a single but highly responsible guy while traveling with a band on tour.

I'd tried not to dwell on that too much.

I sat up in bed, the sound of the shower running as the late afternoon sun streamed through the window.

I'd woken up to the soft melody of his guitar again today. I had firmly decided it was the best way to start the morning until I fell back asleep and woke up an hour later with his face between my thighs.

My skin still burned from the stubble on his chin.

I grinned, feeling my cheeks heat as I thought of something to text back to Marin, but as I was holding my phone, I spotted his guitar in the corner.

Seeing him play in bed was damn near pornographic.

Seeing him in concert…

I quickly looked over my shoulder, double-checking that the shower was still running. I didn't know why, but I suddenly felt embarrassed as I typed his name in the search bar of the internet browser.

My stomach twitched with a mixture of nerves and anticipation.

Is this considered stalking?

I wasn't sure what I was expecting—but definitely not this. I scrolled down and down, and there was nothing.

Literally nothing. A few other notable Zander Greens popped up, but none of them were the hot, tattooed guitar god who was currently naked in my shower.

I let out a sigh. Maybe that was just what it was like, being a session guitarist.

Always there, but never seen.

My heart hurt at that sudden realization because if there was anything I'd learned about Zander Green, it was that he wasn't meant to lurk in the background.

He was the main attraction.

"Janet at the coffeehouse winked at me yesterday," Zander said, his husky voice in my ear as his arms pinned me to the countertop. "Fucking winked, Elena. We should have never left the house."

I snorted out a laugh as his mouth lingered on my neck.

"It's only been a few days since the cookout. I'm sure it

will die down. Besides, I'm not exactly sure who you think you're complaining to, Trouble." I grabbed a coffee mug and then went back for another. "I seem to remember it was your bright idea to lock us in Marin's studio while half the town was in the backyard." I grabbed the freshly brewed coffee and poured two cups. "Wasn't my fault."

"Yeah, but it was your loud mouth that got us caught," he countered as I turned and handed him his plain, boring black coffee.

Weirdo.

"I can't be held liable for that either." I arched a brow before returning to my own cup. I threw in a little bit of sugar and some cream. "You were already aware of the volume level associated with"—I paused, taking a sip of coffee as I pivoted around to face him—"me being pleasured, so technically, that's on you, too."

"Did you just go all lawyer on me?"

God, those freaking dimples.

"Maybe a little."

"It's kind of hot," he admitted as his eyes roamed over the Van Halen T-shirt I'd stolen from him. "Maybe we should role-play? I'll be the corrupt—but hot—criminal, and you'll be my super-sexy lawyer who just can't seem to resist me."

"Or we could just make out in the kitchen?" I suggested.

He set his coffee down and then did the same with mine. "So practical." Amusement played across his face. "I'm not sure I could pull that one off anyway, seeing that I'm so gentle-natured and innocent."

I sputtered out a laugh as he pulled me closer. "Innocent?" *If he was innocent, I was the Pope.* But sure. I'd play along.

"Wanna corrupt me?" A wicked grin spread across his face.

I wasn't really sure who moved first, but we were on each other in an instant. My fingers fisted that inky-black hair. His hands wrapped around my waist as he pulled my mouth against his. Our kiss deepened as his tongue dived into my mouth. A hand slid down to cup my ass, urging me to wrap my legs around him.

But I had other plans.

He did want to be corrupted after all.

I pulled back, scattering kisses down his neck and torso. His breath was heavy, and I could feel his heartbeat as my fingers moved down the lean lines of his abs. I looked up to find his eyes on me, watching with that intense green stare.

I ran my fingernail over his hip bone, the sexy V that peeked out of his sweatpants. His stomach muscles involuntarily flexed as I reached for the waistband and slowly lowered it, taking his boxers with it.

I dropped to my knees.

His hands tightened around the edge of the counter as I took him in. I licked my lips in anticipation.

Zander was still silently watching me, still gripping that stone like his life depended on it. But this wasn't my first time getting him off, and I knew the second my tongue grazed the underside of his—

"Jesus, fuck," he practically shouted, his head lolling back as I circled the tip of his cock, and then inch by inch, I closed my mouth around him.

"Shit, Elena."

He really had no room to talk when it came to volume control. He was quite the talker in the bedroom.

I loved every minute of it.

My hand slid up his stomach as I worked him in and out, rolling my tongue around the sensitive head while I palmed his balls. He groaned as his fingers fisted my hair. He thrust his hips forward, and I nearly gagged, his cock hitting the back of my throat.

I let my tongue flatten as he took over, fucking my mouth over and over. Our eyes held, making the carnal act that much more intimate.

"Fuck, fuck, fuck," he muttered, and I knew he was close.

I grabbed the back of his thighs, pinning him to me so he

couldn't pull away. His fingers tightened around my hair, and then he let out a groan. His head fell back as I swallowed down every drop of his orgasm.

His chest was still heaving when he hauled me up, his eyes shining bright as he pulled me in for a kiss. "Consider me thoroughly corrupted."

I grinned. "With a dirty mouth like that"—I smiled, biting his bottom lip—"pretty sure you already were."

"I don't know," he argued. "You bring out a whole new level of debauchery in me."

I didn't know if I believed that, considering he spent most of his life on tour with rock stars, but I'd let it slide.

"Speaking of"—his eyes swept over me—"you look very dirty. Want to join me in the shower?"

I couldn't help but look at his naked chest, which of course only led to me picturing the rest of him naked.

"As much fun as that sounds," I said, patting his chest, "you have plans."

He adjusted his pants, and a small smirk tugged at the corner of his lips as he noticed me checking him out.

Smug bastard.

"Right, my brother's bachelor party."

I grinned. "Yep. Do you know where you're going?"

"No, he's being weirdly vague. Should I be worried?"

I shook my hand. "With Macon?" I scoffed. "No."

"I assumed Macon was having a daytime bachelor party out of respect for Marin since you guys are doing"—he waved a hand—"whatever. Why do I get the feeling that's not all there is to it?"

I tilted my head and reached for him. "Macon's bachelor party was always low-key," I told him. "Billy and Eli planned it that way."

He stared at me intently as if he was putting the last piece of a puzzle together. "My brother's an alcoholic, isn't he?" Just saying the words seemed to pain him, and when I nodded, he flinched. "How long?"

"I think things got bad for him after Kristy cheated on him. But he's been sober for a while now. He goes to meetings. He's healthy."

He went silent. The words seemed to take time to soak in, and I allowed him the time to process them.

"I wish I'd known," he said. "I just never thought—after growing up with our dad. Macon is the strongest of the two of us, you know?"

"I think we always see our big brothers as superheroes, but they have flaws, just like the rest of us." I cupped his cheek, making sure he saw me. "And you're here now. That's what matters."

"So, what was the original plan for the bachelorette party?" he asked, leaning back against the other side of the counter, clearly needing a subject change. I handed him his forgotten coffee mug and I watched as he brought it to his lips.

God, that mouth.

"Definitely not whatever it is we're doing now," I answered, slightly distracted.

"You don't know? Didn't you just say you planned it?"

I sort of half shrugged. "If by plan, you mean did I call up Lani and say, 'Hey, can we do some sort of low-key bachelorette party at your place?' then yes."

"Lani is Taylor's wife?"

"Yeah," I confirmed. "And seriously the most gorgeous woman on the planet."

His eyes glittered as they swept over me. "Doubtful, considering she's standing right here."

"Charmer," I mused, even though I was totally swooning on the inside. "Anyway, she's Lani Hart."

His eyes widened. "As in Hart Hotels? That Hart?"

"Yep," I confirmed. "Although I think she had some sort of falling-out with her dad. I don't know all the details. Anyway, she and Taylor own the hotel right on the harbor."

He slowly nodded. "I saw it when I was showing Hendrix

around town. Used to be The Cozy Motel when I was younger. That place was a dump."

"Well, it isn't now," I assured him, remembering the time I'd stayed there after Marin moved in with Macon. "It's pretty swanky."

"So, you asked Lani to set it up for you, but you really have no idea what it is?"

"I'm pretty sure there is food involved."

"Well, that's reassuring. Gotta keep up that stamina." He gave me a wink.

I tried to ignore him, biting my bottom lip to keep from grinning. "And I'm hoping there will be at least a little bit of alcohol, but given that we switched to this low-key bachelorette party because we didn't want to bum Marin out, I'm not counting on it."

"You could have the bartender make you a mocktail," he suggested. "They've become pretty popular. I've had a few at parties if you want suggestions."

"I honestly think that would just upset her more because she'd feel like we were going out of our way for her."

"As opposed to changing the whole theme of the—"

I held out my hand. "Don't even bother. I gave up trying to reason with her the moment I found out she was pregnant. The woman is growing a human inside of her and not just any human—our niece. She's moody and a bit impractical at times, but she gets a free pass."

He set his coffee down and moved toward me, tucking a stray hair behind my ear. "You're a good friend," he told me.

"You're not a half-bad brother," I quipped, making him laugh.

I tiptoed up to kiss him. His fingers sank into my hair, tightening into a fist as his hunger for me grew.

A phone started to vibrate next to us, and he groaned.

"If that is Marin sending us on another wild goose chase, tell her we're busy."

"I don't know." I arched a brow, pulling away from him. "Our last one didn't turn out so bad."

"I know, which is why we're *very* busy."

My good mood died the instant I saw my phone screen.

"Elena, you okay?"

"Yeah. It's just my mom," I said, still staring at that screen. "She never calls me."

"Ever?"

Outside of Daniel, we really hadn't talked about my family. Not that there was much to say.

My mood darkened as I shook my head, answering the call. "Hello, Mother."

"Elena."

"Is everything okay? Is Dad—"

"He's fine," she acknowledged, but didn't provide any further information.

A second went by and then another as I waited for her to say something.

Zander watched me as I started to pace the kitchen, one bare foot in front of the other as I tried to ignore how clammy my hands felt or how erratic my heartbeat was.

"Did you need something or…" I huffed out a breath, hating that I still cared.

"I wanted to remind you that next month is the anniversary of Daniel's—"

"I know what day it is," I clipped, my body coming to a halt. "I don't need a calendar reminder for the day my brother died." My tone was harsh, but I didn't care. She hadn't chosen to call me in years, and this was the topic she'd picked.

I felt Zander's soothing presence step up behind me, and I leaned into it, seeking his warmth as he wrapped an arm around my waist.

"I just wanted to be sure since you've likely been preoccupied with Marin and her wedding." The word *wedding* rolled off her tongue like she was saying something uncouth or slanderous.

"Just because Marin is getting married doesn't any of us have forgotten him."

Her silence seemed to suggest she didn't agree.

"Anyway," she went on, "I've asked Father Thomas to come say a few words at Daniel's graveside this year, and I'd like the whole family to be in attendance." *She didn't want to look bad in front of the priest.* "Since I doubt Marin will come, it will be imperative that you do."

"You're making a lot of unfair assumptions about Marin," I said.

"It's not like she's been to his grave much to begin with."

"She lives thirteen hundred miles away. You know how much she wanted him buried close to her, but she chose not to fight you and buried him in the family plot. Do you know how hard that was for her?"

Another beat of silence.

Zander began to make slow circles with his thumb on my stomach. It felt like an anchor, and I focused on it.

I chose not to mention Marin's pregnancy. It would only anger her more, and besides, it wasn't my news to share.

"I'll check my work calendar and—"

"This is not negotiable, Elena," she said, her voice rising. "If you can take three weeks off for a ridiculous wedding, you can spare a day for your brother."

I bit down hard on my bottom lip, tears threatening to spill down my cheeks, and I took a deep breath. "Funny how I only seem to be part of the family when it suits you," I said, and before she could get another word in, I ended the call, slamming my phone down on the counter for good measure.

As I tried to breathe through my anger, Zander stood there and didn't say a word. He just held me, making those slow circles over my skin.

It was like, somehow, he could sense what I needed.

I wasn't a woman who needed a white knight. I didn't

want a man to fight my battles or take control when life got overwhelming.

I just wanted someone to be there.

I turned in his arms. "As you can see, my mother is thrilled about Marin's upcoming nuptials."

"Has she always been like that?" he asked.

"I'd love to say no—that it's just a byproduct of grief—but unfortunately, parenting has never really been her strong suit."

A sad smile tugged at his lips as he took me in. "And what about your dad?"

I let out a sigh, tracing the edge of the tattoo that covered his collarbone. "He's almost worse," I said.

"Has he—" I could see his eyes harden.

"No." My voice softened as I placed a hand on his chest. "Nothing like that. He just—" I let out a deep breath. "My dad had an affair before I was born. Or maybe it was a one-night stand—I'm not sure about the details. But he cheated. I was the result."

"Your biological mom?"

I shook my head. "No idea. She dumped me off with my father shortly after I was born and bailed. At this point, my mom—stepmom? I have a hard time now, trying to figure out what to call her."

"It's okay." He pulled me to his chest.

"Anyway, at this point, they could have done a lot of things—sane things, like divorce, or, hell, put me up for adoption—and gave me a fighting chance, but instead, they stayed together. Daniel was only a year old, so they moved to another town, started over, and no one was the wiser."

"Except them."

I nodded. "My mother has never forgotten. And she's never forgiven him. She has been using me as a way to punish him ever since."

"When did you find out?" he asked, his voice soft and soothing.

"Right after Daniel died," I said. "In one of her grief rants, she told me she'd lost her only child, and when I questioned what she meant—"

"I'm so sorry, Elena."

I pulled back so I could look up at him. "It actually made a lot of sense," I told him. "When she finally explained everything, it hurt, learning the truth, but it also answered a lot of my questions. Why I was never enough. Why I always came last."

He tilted my chin up, and my heart melted. "You're more than good enough."

"That's the first time she's called me in over a year, and it was just to make sure I'd show up and make her look good."

"I could come with you," Zander offered.

"Oh God, she'd lose her shit," I joked, but my belly fluttered at the idea of having him with me.

"What? Why?" That pierced brow rose as he grinned. "I'm a hit with parents. Look at me."

He held out his arms wide, reminding me of that day in the studio when he'd let me do whatever I wanted with him.

"She'd take one look at those tattoos, probably cover herself in the sign of the cross, and promptly disown me." I laughed. "Wait, that actually might work. Shit, we should totally get married."

"I thought we already were," he challenged. "Picked out a dress and everything."

"I don't know," I teased. "I might need some more convincing."

He grabbed me at the waist and threw me over his shoulder, intent on a shower and doing just that.

"Okay, so I might have gone a little overboard," Lani warned me.

I'd barely stepped foot into the grand lobby of Windows

Hotel and Resort when she ran up to meet me, hugging the shit out of me in a red maxi dress that made her look fucking lethal.

Seriously, could she dial it down a notch or two?

The worst part was, I knew she really wasn't even really trying. She was *that* kind of pretty with bronze skin and long, thick brown hair that fell down her back like she'd been at the salon all morning, but really, she'd probably just let it air-dry while she fed her toddler.

And to top it off, she was incredibly sweet. Ugh.

"How overboard are we talking?" I asked.

We hadn't exactly talked price when I set this up because in all fairness, I wasn't strapped for cash, and how much could one measly bachelorette party cost?

Marin had offered to foot the bill when she discovered we had to change plans because of her pregnancy, but I'd shut that down real quick. This was her special day—days?—and I was the best friend with the large savings account and zero attachments, so if anyone was going to splurge, it was going to be me.

"A little." Lani bit at her the baby pink polish on her nail before adding, "Okay, a lot, but I couldn't help it. When am I going to be able to organize another spa day bachelorette party?" She had a point. Most women hit the clubs, and Ocracoke was a little sleepy for that kind of action. "But don't worry; I'm covering all the extras. My present to Marin."

"Oh." I perked up. "That's really generous of you."

It's beyond generous.

She swept me into the dining room that had been closed for the luncheon part of the day, and the moment I stepped inside, my mouth hit the floor.

"Lani, this is above and beyond," I told her.

"I know!" She beamed, clearly thrilled with herself. "I got ahold of Marin's florist and then sort of went crazy."

Instead of the circular tables that normally adorned the dining room, she'd created a single long table for us in the middle. Small bouquets of peach roses and eucalyptus leaves lined the center with beautiful place settings and personalized menus. There was a photo wall and a custom cake.

Ten minutes later, when Marin walked in, she cried.

Not just cried, but, like, full-on sobbed. Through snotty tears, she went on and on about how much she loved each of us and how lucky she was.

I would have laughed if I didn't think she'd murder me.

"Stupid hormones." She sniffled after finally settling down and taking a seat.

"They're the worst," Molly confirmed. "The first time I was pregnant, we kept it a secret until after our wedding. I was so paranoid and was somehow convinced people could just tell by looking at me."

"If anyone had given that secret away, it would have been Jake," Cora cut in. She was the nurse at the medical clinic Jake owned and married to Dean Sutherland, Jake's best friend—Molly's ex-fiancé. Way too much drama for one tiny town. "He had a grin plastered on his damn face for weeks. I just figured he was sneaking you in during lunch for a quickie in his office."

Molly's grin suggested that wasn't totally untrue. "Well, one day, he found me sitting on the floor in my closet, sobbing because my jeans didn't fit. I told him everyone would surely find out now if I had to buy new clothes."

"Yeah, I doubt anyone would have noticed that, even in Ocracoke," Lani quipped.

"I know that now." She laughed. "But hormonal Molly was never planning on leaving that closet. So, my amazing husband dried my tears, grabbed a rubber band, and made my jeans work for another two weeks. Problem solved."

"What a great guy," Marin said, and I could already see more tears forming.

Ohmigod.

"Okay, subject change! Otherwise, Marin is gonna cry all

over her place setting," Lani announced, making everyone laugh.

"I want to know about Elena and Zander!" Millie said from the other side of the table.

"Oh, me, too!" her traitor of a sister chimed in.

"Yeah, because, apparently, you were having way more fun at that cookout than the rest of us," Millie quipped, holding her champagne glass out in a salute toward me.

"I didn't even get to go." Cora pouted while Lani added, "Me neither."

"Well, the food was lovely," Molly said. "As was the company, right?"

Everyone nodded.

"Elena especially enjoyed the company of one guest in particular," Millie teased, making me roll my eyes.

"I just want to know which one of you motherfuckers told on us." I pointed my finger at the crowd of women. "Because everyone in the town knows. Janet at the coffeehouse seriously winked at Zander yesterday!"

They all burst into laughter.

"Maybe they all just heard you." Marin shrugged, making my mouth fall open. She didn't even blush when she said it.

"In your neighborhood? I'd think they'd be used to it by now. What's one of Macon's favorites? Oh, yes. 'Scream so the whole island can hear you.' "

Now, *that* got her blushing.

"Hey, there is nothing wrong with giving your man a little vocal encouragement," Millie said as Marin's shoulders shook in silent laughter. "Of course, when there are guests around—"

Molly's face blanched. "That was one time!"

"Mmm, it was more than once, sis. You screamed his name all night long." She grinned before turning back to the rest of us. "And then she had to get up and play hostess the next day and serve them all breakfast!"

"Oh my God." Molly buried her hands in her face before

she shot back up, her eyes fixed on her sister. "You had a drunken one-night stand with Aiden when you were supposed to be looking after the inn!"

"Hell yeah, we did." Her face went all dreamy, not embarrassed in the slightest. "But we were in the family wing, which, as you know, is in the back of the house—purposely away from the guest rooms. Unlike, say, the yellow room, which is—"

"Lani and Taylor totally had sex in a restaurant!" Molly said, pointing a finger directly at her friend.

Man, she was just throwing everyone under the bus.

Several questions were thrown out at once.

"In front of other people?"

"Was it open?"

"Which restaurant?"

The last question made me laugh. Were they asking for a recommendation?

"It wasn't…" Lani's words stalled before she gave Molly a look. "We didn't have sex. Taylor…" She tilted her head and widened her eyes a bit while making a vulgar hand gesture with her fingers.

"While you were sitting at your table?" Millie sounded impressed.

Lani nodded, and a faint blush painted her cheeks. "The waiter asked me a question about my drink order, and I literally slammed my hand down on the table and practically screamed, 'Yes!' at him."

Laughter filled the room.

I could have totally pointed a finger at Marin and told everyone about the night she and Macon had snuck into the sheriff's office and had sex on his desk. But since Macon had caught his ex-wife cheating on him in that very office, I had a feeling the intent of that rendezvous had been to erase some especially bad memories for him.

That all felt far too intimate to share, even among friends.

"Okay, back to bad-boy Green," Molly said over the laughter.

"I agree!" Millie added.

"Since we didn't grow up here, we don't really know much about him," Cora said, motioning to Lani. "But I have to say, there's got to be something in the water because, seriously, what is up with the men down here?"

"Ocracoke does not get to take the credit for Zander," Millie argued. "We were a few years apart in school, and I do not remember him looking anything like that."

"I have to know," Cora asked, a look of guilt spreading across her face, "And if any of you tell my husband I asked this, I'll deny it." She turned to me. "But how far exactly do those tattoos go?"

I bit my bottom lip, remembering all the times I'd licked that inked skin. "Down his whole chest, his back. He has a few on his legs, too."

"God, that's hot," Millie said. "Why is that so hot? Like, I don't want my husband to run out and get covered in ink, but on other guys?" She made a dreamy sigh.

"I have never gone for guys with tattoos. Or piercings." I dated guys in suits. Guys who barely made nine o'clock dinner reservations because they barely left their office.

And wasn't that pathetic.

"What about musicians?"

"There was a brief phase in college," I answered, shuddering at the memory. "Not a great experience. Probably why I don't normally go for the tattooed, bad-boy look now that I'm thinking about it."

"Until Zander?"

"Yeah." I let out a little sigh.

I was starting to worry that I was seriously monopolizing the conversation. Like, shouldn't we be talking about Marin? And wedding shit?

"She likes him." Marin beamed, clearly not upset with the conversation. "We're totally gonna be sisters again."

"I think we're getting a little ahead of ourselves," I argued.

"Do you think this could be something that lasts beyond the wedding?" Millie asked.

She seemed highly interested in the topic of me and Zander. Maybe she just loved a good gossip story.

"Maybe," I answered. "I mean, I want it to. It's just—"

"What?" Marin's hand found mine, her brows all scrunched up in concern.

"It's not something we've really discussed."

"Like, at all?"

Well, he did make that comment about going with me to my parents' today, but I'm pretty sure he was joking. Wasn't he?

"I mean, a little," I answered. "In the general *let's just give this a try and see where it leads* sense."

"But you haven't discussed what happens when you go home and he goes..." Millie paused. "Where is he even going?"

"I don't know," I answered, hating how twisted my gut felt at the mere thought of him leaving. "He told us at the cookout that he's signed on to do a tour starting in the fall, but can't say who it's for."

"Hmm," was all Millie had to say about that.

"You care for him," Molly stated, her eyes softening as she looked my way.

"I think he's a really nice guy." I deflected, looking away. "But we've barely known each other for two and a half weeks. It's too soon to know what I feel."

Marin snorted, making me glance over at her.

"What?"

"It's just that a year ago, when I was falling for Macon after just a few short weeks, I said something very similar. I distinctly remember someone telling me that there were no rules when it came to falling in love. In fact, I believe she also said that if she were lucky enough to find love, she'd run toward it with open arms."

"No offense, but she sounds kind of like a cunt," I said

dryly, hating myself for my own stupid advice. "Besides, that advice was for you. Not me."

"What can't it be for you?" she argued.

"Because—"

Because I don't deserve it.

Because I'm not worth it.

Because I'm scared...

All my insecurities and negative thoughts came rushing to the surface, and I felt panicky. What if I didn't know how to love someone? What if this ended up being some epic failure and he left, like everyone else?

"I know the word *love* sounds intimidating," Cora offered. "Especially when you're talking about a person you just met. So, let's replace it with the word *connection*. You and Zander sound like you have a real connection, and something like that is rare. Don't deny yourself the chance to explore it because of fear. Believe us all when we say, we've all been there."

A chorus of yeses and uh-huhs echoed her.

"It really only comes down to one question," Millie said, and I looked at her intently. "Is he good in bed?"

Everyone roared. "What?"

She looked around, raising her hands in the air. "I'm serious! We all heard them in that studio!"

I swore a hundred sets of eyes all turned to me, and I felt heat creep up my neck.

"It's so fucking good," I admitted with a smirk.

The room erupted into cheers.

I rolled my eyes again.

"Have any of you ever tried the..." Millie started making hand gestures, but then paused. "We should totally make a group chat and exchange tips."

"Oh my God," Molly groaned.

"Just what I want—a group chat about my brother-in-law's dick," Marin joked.

"I mean, it wouldn't be *all* about your brother-in-law's

dick. There'd be others, too." Millie grinned. "Besides, Molly tells me all sorts of stories about Jake. It's really good ammo if he ever pisses me off."

"He is still so mad at you for telling Mom and Dad that the couple they heard having sex in the bathroom at your wedding was us."

"Well, it was!" She shrugged, and then she turned to me. "See, you're not the only one who has sex in other people's houses. Molly and Jake totally did it in my bathroom. We hadn't even cut the cake yet. What I don't understand is why Mom and Dad were both headed to the bathroom in the first..." She paused as a horrified expression took over her face.

"You don't think?" Molly's eyes went wide, as she probably put two and two together, remembering exactly why her and her own husband would visit the bathroom together.

I snorted out a laugh.

Lani stood as Millie and Molly tried to wipe that thought from their minds. "Well, that took a disturbing turn. Anyone hungry?"

CHAPTER FOURTEEN

Zander

So far, I was not hating Macon's low-key bachelor party.

Compared to the few more traditional bachelor parties I'd attended, this one did have its perks.

The first being that I wasn't wasted, which would seem like a shortcoming to some, but the day was young, and I still had a long list of things I wanted to do to Elena tonight. The second? Since Macon's best friend happened to be married to one seriously wealthy dude, we were currently cruising up the coast in one sweet-ass boat.

Seriously, this thing was insane. Growing up in Ocracoke, I was used to seeing expensive boats line Silver Lake Harbor, but I'd never actually been on one. With what I'd consider a full apartment below deck and enough room to host a crowd up top, it had to have cost as much as a house.

It practically was.

But it sure beat the ferry, and the sunshine on my face was fucking sublime.

The third? Macon had finally revealed our final destination once we reached land, and I was so fucking pumped.

"Are you for real right now?"

"Yep." He grinned like a loon.

We'd passed Bodie Island Lighthouse and were coasting along Roanoke Island, the location of the famed Lost Colony.

The tourists loved that shit.

"I didn't think you were actually serious."

"Hell yeah, I was. I told you, Marin and I are the real deal," he said sincerely. "We've had this planned for months."

I patted him on the back as Eli pulled us all into port. "Good for you," I said. "But I'm warning you now. If you cry, I will totally make fun of you for the rest of your life. And probably make a video."

He looked me over with an amused expression. "You know, the best man is supposed to be supportive."

"I am supportive. I'm manning you up so you don't whine like a little bitch in front of all your friends and the tattoo artist."

"You know"—he rolled his eyes—"now that you mention it, I do feel manlier."

"See?"

"Billy and Eli rented out the whole shop for us, so we have the place to ourselves if we want it." It was like he could see the question on the tip of my tongue. "It's a good shop. They did a ton of research."

I smirked at the realization of how well he knew me. "Damn, that's some good friends."

"You gonna get anything?" he asked.

And just like that, I had an idea.

"Yeah," I told him. "But you're gonna have to help me out."

———

"Did you tell her you were doing this?" I asked my brother as the tattoo artist slapped the Saniderm bandage over his fresh ink.

Although he'd originally said he just wanted her name, Macon had thankfully gone for something a bit more creative. On his forearm, in bold script, two words now etched his skin.

Only her.

Below it, their wedding date was inked out in a simple font.

My brother looked down at it and grinned. "Nope."

"Dude, you're either gonna get really fucking lucky or she's going to drown you in pregnancy tears."

"Hoping for the first one, but probably gonna get a mix of both, honestly." He laughed. "Her mood has been all over the place lately. One minute, she's climbing me like a tree, and the next, she's sobbing over a grocery store commercial. It's fucking weird."

"Is it the one about the neighbors coming together for a cookout?" Eli asked, leaning over to check out Macon's tattoo. "That one gets me every time."

Most of the guys had opted out of ink today, choosing to just enjoy the day with Macon. But Billy and Eli had taken the opportunity to get their ring fingers done with a simple matching design.

There was a whole lot of sentimentality going on today.

And Macon and I were about to add to it.

"So, you ready for number two? Or do you need a break?" I asked, a challenging note in my voice.

"I'm ready whenever you are."

I'd given him hell for it, but he'd handled the pain exactly like I'd thought he would. Effortlessly. Macon had probably been trained to handle all sorts of shit in the military. This was nothing.

I gave a heads-up to the tattoo artist, a quiet, burly guy named Mark. He had tattoos from his neck down to his ankles. He was friendly, but for the most part, he kept to himself, never butting in or asking questions.

"Dave is gonna take you so I can go on my break. That all

right?" Mark asked, motioning to the younger guy, who'd mostly been behind the counter, messing around on his phone since we had gotten here.

"Yeah, man. It's all good." I'd looked up their Instagram accounts, and they were both solid artists with a decent amount of experience. This simple design would be a walk in the park for either of them.

"Why don't you want to get a bro tat with me?" Taylor asked his brother as Macon and I headed toward the front to grab a quick bite.

Dave needed time to set up so we took advantage and joined everyone congregated around the food. As if renting out an entire tattoo shop wasn't enough, Billy and Eli had thrown in catering, too. Because why the fuck not?

"Don't you want to bond?"

"We bond every fucking day." Dean rolled his eyes. "It's called owning a business together."

"I think that might be his way of saying he's sick of you." Jake laughed as he stuffed the rest of his pork slider in his mouth.

When I'd given my brother shit about inviting Jake Jameson of all people to his bachelor party, he'd just shrugged and told me it was just a strategic move.

"It's nice to have a doctor on board," he'd said.

Was it that hard to admit he just liked the guy? Stubborn asshole.

"I don't know how he could be," Taylor offered, grabbing a handful of grapes from a giant platter of fruit. "I'm only there half the time now that we have the hotel. You should have seen the shit Lani made me do for that bachelorette party today. So many fucking flowers."

"I hope she has a good time," Macon said, his expression softening as his thoughts turned to Marin.

"She will. Lani pulled out all the stops."

"Thank you," Macon said to Taylor before turning to everyone else. "Thanks to all of you. We couldn't have pulled this wedding off without all of your help." He spared a glance at Jake. "Even you, asshat."

Jake raised his water bottle in the air with a grin. "Just here for the food, loser."

They should just get those matching BFF bracelets and get over themselves already.

"I'm ready for you guys," Dave announced behind us.

"Don't twitch, Macon!" Dean joked as we walked away. "I hear that spot can be sensitive."

"Nah, that's just your ass," he said over his shoulder.

"Straight guys making ass jokes?" Eli quipped. "It really *is* a bachelor party."

A chorus of laughter followed as Macon and I headed towards Dave's station. I was in the hot seat first, and we'd already gone over design and placement earlier with Mark. Since most of my arms were already heavily inked, I thankfully hadn't had to explain to Macon why I needed this particular tattoo out of plain sight.

Although I didn't think the placement was a concern for him. When I'd told him what I wanted us to get, he'd grown quiet and pulled me into a tight hug. I'd seen him eyeing my Creed tattoo more than once, and I knew this meant a lot to him.

"I didn't catch your name," Dave said, plopping down on the seat in front of me.

"Zander," I offered. "And this is my brother, Macon. He's the groom."

"Congrats," Dave said, although there wasn't much enthusiasm behind the word. "Show me where you want this again."

We spent the next several minutes making sure the stencil was exactly right, and then he had me lie down on my side and got to work.

"So, are you ready for Friday? That's when everyone starts to arrive, right?" I asked my brother, enjoying this bit of time we had by ourselves.

"Marin's parents and siblings get here on Thursday night. And then we do the rehearsal and shit on Friday." He nodded his head, his face splitting into a wide grin. "But, yeah, I'm ready. More than ready."

"And then everything that comes after?"

"You mean the baby?" he asked before letting out a snort. "Fuck no. Not even close. But we'll figure it out."

"Just figure it out as you go and hope for the best?" I repeated his words from the coffee shop back to him, making him grin.

"Yep. Although, for this, I might read a few of those baby books, just to give myself a leg up."

I resisted the urge to laugh, not wanting to move. "Good idea."

The familiar sting of the tattoo gun bit into my side as Dave worked, and I realized I needed to say something. "I'm leaving the morning after the wedding," I told him. "I have to be in New York for something; otherwise, I wouldn't be bailing so soon."

He held out his hand to silence me. "It's okay, Zander. You don't have to feel guilty for having a life and a career. We'll always be here."

I swallowed down the jagged lump in my throat. I hoped he meant that.

I had to hand it to Billy and Eli—they sure knew how to throw a party.

Even a sober one.

The boat, the ink shop, the food—it was all top-notch. We'd even managed to pull Dean to the dark side at the very last minute when he finally caved and got some old-movie quote scrawled across his collarbone.

When I'd thrown a confused look at his brother, Taylor had just shrugged and said, "It's a Cora thing."

We thanked Dave and Mark profusely and tipped heavily, so they made off with a killing. They took tons of pictures for all of us, and by the time we headed back to the boat, we had just enough sunlight to make it back to Ocracoke.

It was exactly what I'd needed with my brother—time.

Every moment we spent together felt restorative, like the wounds of our past were knitting back together, and I no longer saw him as the man who'd left me.

I saw myself.

An eighteen-year-old kid who would have done anything to get away from a terrible situation, even if it meant leaving everything and everyone behind. I realized now that I'd unfairly placed the blame on my brother, but in reality, our father was the root cause of our pain. His neglect and abuse had driven us both to make decisions we were too young and unprepared to make.

But we'd survived. Life had driven us apart, but we'd survived nonetheless.

And now that we were back together, I'd do anything for this family of mine.

When we docked in the harbor, I drove back to an empty house. Elena wasn't back from the bachelorette party yet, so I used the free time to take a quick shower. Afterward, I threw on a pair of dark jeans and a T-shirt and headed out to the living room. I had a few emails to respond to, so I took a seat on the couch and typed out my replies. Just as I was finishing, I got a text from Lance.

LANCE

Ridge went after the blogger, and the article was taken down. Just keep your head down until the concert.

ME

Won't be hard to do in Middle of Nowhere, North Carolina. Thanks.

LANCE

Can I get a zip code for that?

ME

Funny. Have you considered retiring and becoming a comedian?

LANCE

I have, but my Tilly's shoe habit is too expensive.

ME

I think you mean your shoe habit.

LANCE

Oh, right. My bad.

The media will eventually die down, but when this officially breaks, be prepared. It's gonna be a shitstorm. So, just enjoy your brother's wedding and stay out of sight.

ME

Yes, sir.

A shitstorm.

I swallowed audibly. It wasn't anything I hadn't known.

Lance and Ridge had been preparing me for what would follow after the official news broke. Since I was relatively unknown, my life would be ripped apart by the press.

Any little crumb. Any piece of the puzzle. All up for grabs.

We'd made it harder for them, keeping my real name hidden behind legal paperwork. But with this level of scrutiny, it was only a matter of time. It would only take one person to reveal my real name.

And when they did…

My stomach churned when I thought about the information they might print.

Dead mother. Alcoholic father. Runaway.

Would journalists come down here and harass my family? Follow them? The thought of Macon and Marin's perfect little life here getting turned upside down because of me was unfathomable.

This was why I should have stayed away.

The tattoo on my side seemed to burn at that very thought.

You should tell them…

You should tell her…

I wasn't sure how much longer I could keep this secret. The last few days with Elena had been like a fever dream. Both of us were fucking kidding ourselves if we thought this thing between us was normal.

I'd done the casual thing.

I'd fucking thrived in it, and what I felt for Elena was nowhere near casual. It felt…permanent.

I'd been honest with her in that studio. I had no idea where we were headed. I had no idea where she and I would be in two weeks, let alone two months, but knowing that didn't make me want to stop.

From that very first kiss in that bridal shop, I had known I was done for.

But I knew the shitstorm my life was headed into in a few weeks. She didn't.

If she did, would she still be all in? Or would she be slamming on the brakes, ready to walk away?

What a fucking nightmare.

How would I even begin to explain it all?

Hey, so funny story…

I'm about to join one of the biggest bands on the planet, where I'll be obsessed over, under constant scrutiny, and never be able to go out in public again without being recognized.

Wanna be my girlfriend?

I scrubbed a hand down my face as I reached for the fridge. But before I could get there, Elena walked through the front door. It had only been hours since I'd seen her, but my heart raced at the mere sight of her.

My eyes slowly raked down her body as she closed the door behind her.

"God-fucking-damn," I murmured. "Is that what one wears to the spa?"

When I'd left this morning, she'd still been in a robe, blow-drying her hair after we spent far too long getting it wet in the shower.

She was wearing green again, but the fabric stretched tight across all her luscious curves. If someone asked me how to explain her dress, the only thing I'd get right was the way it clung to her body and the fucking hot-as-hell triangular cut-out that exposed her stomach.

"It was a bachelorette party," she corrected me with a grin. "And I only had it on half the time. The rest of the time, I was naked."

Well, hell.

She placed her small Louis Vuitton bag on the table by the door. It was different from the one I'd seen her with yester-day, and I secretly wondered just how many she'd packed for her three-week vacation.

Did she collect purses like I collected guitars?

If so, we might have a storage problem in the future.

Fuck, why am I thinking about the future already?

"How was the bachelor party?" she asked, taking a step toward me.

"Surprising," I answered, making her brow quirk. "Eli and Billy rented out a tattoo shop for the day."

Her eyes widened. "Please tell me Macon got a tattoo?"

I nodded, pulling out my phone to show her the pictures.

Her hand went to her mouth. "Oh my God, Marin's gonna lose her shit."

"In a good way though, right?"

"Oh, yeah. She's probably stripping him naked this very minute."

That's a visual I didn't need.

She swiped through a few more of the pictures before pausing. "What's this?" she asked, seeing a photo of Macon and me, bare-chested and side by side.

She didn't even wait for me to answer and just lifted my shirt to inspect it herself.

I laughed at her lack of patience. Her fingers trailed down the five letters that spelled my last name. They ran down my left rib cage in bold, blocky lettering.

She looked back at the picture and smiled. "You're a good brother, Zander."

"I share a tattoo with my adopted family. Seemed fitting that Macon and I have one, too, considering he practically raised me after my mom died."

"Well, it's really sweet, and I know it means a lot to him."

"It means a lot to me, too," I told her.

"Did anyone else get anything?"

I scrolled through the rest of the pictures, showing her Eli's and Billy's ring tattoos. She gushed over how cute they were, and then when I showed her the movie quote Dean got, her eyes lit up.

"*The Princess Bride!*"

"You know it?" I looked at the three words everyone was so obsessed about. *As you wish.* I didn't get it.

"You don't?"

"I didn't exactly watch a lot of movies, growing up."

Her lips pressed together, and her expression softened. "We're gonna have to add that to the list."

"The list?"

"Of things we're eventually going to do together."

Eventually? It was one word, but it brought so much hope with it.

"Okay."

I slipped my phone into my pocket and reached for her. She curled her arms around my neck and let out a contented sigh.

"I believe we are on our own for the rest of the night."

My eyes darkened as my grip tightened around her. "The whole night? Damn, what will we do with ourselves?"

"Karaoke bar?" she mused.

"No." I shook my head. "Never again. My ears won't survive. But I wouldn't mind going out."

Her brow rose. "Really? After being winked at by the coffee shop owner, you want to go back out into society?"

I shrugged. "We're only going to be here a few more days, and I want to take you out on a date. They'll gossip regardless."

She stilled in my arms, and I realized what I'd said. Our time was running woefully short.

"About that…" I should just tell her. Fuck the contract. Fuck everything. All that mattered was her.

She placed her hand on my chest. "I don't want to talk about it right now," she told me. "I know we need to—and soon." Really soon. "But right now, I just want to enjoy an evening out. And then maybe an even better evening in." Her eyes sparkled with mischief.

I wanted to argue with her.

I wanted to make her listen because if I didn't do this right now, I wasn't sure I'd have the courage later.

But instead, I just nodded and swallowed down my secret in silence.

"What's your favorite color?" I asked her as we waited for our food.

We'd decided to go back to Portofino since neither of us had really gotten the chance to eat much the night of the engagement party. The place was fairly busy tonight, and we were lucky to have gotten a table.

Although was it really luck when you knew the owners?

"You can ask me anything in the world, and you go with

what's your favorite color?" A hint of amusement crossed her face.

The low lighting and the intimate setting made Portofino a perfect date spot. Our table was situated in a corner, giving us the illusion of privacy.

I shrugged. "I want to know everything about you. Besides, it's an important thing to know about a person. What if your favorite color is sad beige? I can't marry a monster, Elena. Think of the children. Kids need color in their lives."

She snorted out a laugh, shaking her head. I couldn't take it anymore. I reached out and took her hand in mine.

So much better.

"Says the man who dresses in all black."

"I wore gray yesterday," I scoffed. "And that Led Zeppelin shirt I had on the other day totally had a rainbow on it."

"Well, to answer your *very important* question"—she grinned—"I guess I'd say it's red. It makes me feel powerful. But I do look pretty damn good in black."

"Yeah, you do," I agreed, remembering her pinned against that mirror in that black satin gown. *Fucking imprinted in my brain.* "I think you look pretty damn amazing in every color, Louie." I made a point to drag my eyes over the bodice of her green dress.

I was really looking forward to taking that off later.

But to be fair, there wasn't a single article of Elena's wardrobe I hadn't enjoyed taking off of her. Or ripping off her. Or dragging off with my teeth…

"Okay, here's a better one," I challenged her, remembering something from a previous conversation. "You've mentioned bad dates. Tell me about the worst one you've ever been on."

"Oh my God," she drawled. "There are so many."

"Really?"

She nodded. "When I broke up with Chad after several years—"

"Several years?" I gulped. I didn't think I'd dated someone longer than a month.

"Yeah." She waved a dismissive hand.

Meanwhile, my brain was still stuck on the words—*several years*. Not just a couple of years, but *several*.

"It sounds like a big deal, but believe me, it wasn't. I was busy. He was busy. I think we just enjoyed having someone on standby." She blanched. "That makes me sound horrible, doesn't it?"

"No, you're just being honest." I let out a breath of relief. "And if you want the truth, I'd rather have you confess to having a long-term fuck buddy who meant very little to you than some tragic romance you weren't over."

"Don't worry." She patted my hand. "I was over it long before we ended it."

"Good. Now, tell me about that date."

"God, okay. So, as I was saying, after Chad, I tried dating apps for the first time. I know a lot of people have claimed they met their soulmates or whatever this way, but I call bluff."

I laughed.

"Either that or I'm doing it wrong because every guy I've ever met through a dating app has been a total dud."

Five minutes and a story about the professor and a serious case of déjà vu, I was laughing into my napkin so I didn't disturb the other tables around us.

"It's not funny!" She feigned a slap on my shoulder. "I didn't even tell you about the guy who asked me for Uber money."

"It's a little funny," I argued. "But I'm glad those guys were assholes, Elena."

"What? Why?"

"Because they all led you straight to me," I told her. "And believe me, I will never forget a single night with you."

She bit her bottom lip, and my whole body reacted.

"You have quite the way with words sometimes, Zander Green. Have you ever considered singing?"

"Only in the shower and for *very* pretty girls," I lied, hating the fact that I couldn't tell her.

I wasn't just joining Manic as their lead guitarist; I was also providing backup vocals. It was the first time I'd ever get to use my voice professionally, and I was fucking thrilled.

And I couldn't tell her.

"Tell me where you've been on tour," she said as if she'd read my train of thought. "Is there anywhere that you just absolutely fell in love with?"

I thought about it as I took a sip of wine. I wasn't usually a wine guy, but Elena had insisted I'd love it if she chose, and, damn, was she right.

"I've only done a few tours outside the US, and they weren't until recently, when I'd made more of a name for myself. But I've been all over the US. When I first started, it was shitty bands with shitty venues and even shitter buses."

She laughed.

"And the money was shit, too, if you were wondering. But eventually, I built up a decent reputation, and the stages got bigger. That's when I really started to enjoy the traveling part of it—when I didn't have to hole up in crap hotels and save every penny. But anywhere on the West Coast is nice. New England is great, too. I love anywhere with a beach."

She scrunched her nose, and I chuckled. I knew exactly how Elena felt about beaches.

"There are some beaches in the world where overwhelming humidity isn't a thing."

"I've heard of these kinds of beaches." She nodded her head. "Sounds intriguing."

"Yeah?" I could think of at least a dozen beaches I could take her to. "We'll make a beach lover of you yet."

So many possibilities hung in the air as we stared at each other.

But before either of us could say anything more, the waiter came by with our main courses, and as we began to eat, an amicable silence fell across the table.

It was oddly comforting how at ease I felt around her. Sometimes, maintaining comfortable silence with someone was infinitely harder than sharing empty words. Finding someone else who understood that was a rarity.

I was coming to find that Elena, as a whole, was a rarity—one I wasn't sure I was ready to let go of.

"What's your favorite part about being a lawyer?" I asked, realizing how little she actually talked about her career.

I'd practically bored her to death with my love of music and the life I'd made of it, but when it came to her day job…crickets.

She took a sip of wine before answering, "I like the financial freedom it gives me."

"Anything else?"

She bit nervously at her bottom lip. "It keeps me busy."

I studied her for a moment as she pushed a tomato around her mostly empty plate. "You don't like your job, do you?"

She froze in place, staring at that freaking tomato like her life depended on it. It wasn't until I reached out and touched her hand that she settled slightly, her shoulders sagging until her eyes finally met mine.

"No," she finally said. "I hate it."

"Have you ever said that out loud?"

"No," she admitted. "I'm terrified to say it too loud in case my mother might be listening all the way from Texas." She said it in jest, but there was an undertone of anxiety in her voice.

"You really think she would care if you did something else?" Before I realized how that came out, I found myself scrambling. "That's not what I meant—"

"No, I know you weren't saying it to be mean." She let out a sigh. "She wanted Daniel to be the lawyer, but he went into IT. So, I foolishly tried to fill that dream for her, thinking it would win her approval." She looked down at the table. "Clearly, that was a wasted effort, and now, I'm stuck doing something I'm quite good at, but really hate."

"So then, do something else," I told her. "Do something for you."

She snorted. "You make it sound easy."

"Oh, I'm sure it's not," I agreed. "I'm sure it'd be really fucking hard. But it beats continuing to do something you hate for someone who doesn't even deserve it."

"I once told Marin..." She stopped herself, her cheeks actually staining red.

"You once told Marin what?" I prodded. "It's got to be good. I don't remember the last time I saw you blush."

"I'm going to regret this." She pressed her lips together and took a breath. "I once told Marin—over a copious amount of alcohol, mind you—that I might want to write a book. Someday."

God, she was cute when she was embarrassed.

But she really had no reason to be.

"Yeah?" I perked up, leaning forward on the table. "What kind? Kinky romance?"

She rolled her eyes. "You would love that."

"I really would. Can you imagine the kind of research required for a book like that? I'd be so down with that."

A grin tugged at the corner of her mouth. "I'm sure you would be, but no...no romance. Sorry, Trouble. I was leaning more toward thrillers."

"That research sounds less intriguing." I laughed. "But that's actually pretty perfect, Elena. I could see you doing that."

"Yeah?" She seemed about five percent more on board with the idea because of my enthusiasm. It was a start.

"Yeah." I nodded. "You could travel, try new things, finally slow down."

She swallowed as I met her gaze, hoping she could read between the lines of what I was trying to say.

You could travel...with me.

You could try new things...with me.

You could finally slow down....with me.

"If only life were that simple," she said, a hint of sadness in her voice.

"Yeah," I agreed. "If only."

Fuuuck.

It was the day of the rehearsal dinner, and this was the last thing I needed to be dealing with. I'd thought I'd managed to stay just under the radar these last three weeks in Ocracoke.

Obviously, I was wrong.

How had Millie found out? What did she want? I was already being dragged down by the weight of one secret. I didn't need any more.

My gut twisted as I quietly got out of bed, not wanting to wake Elena up. There was nothing I wanted more than to stay in that bed, but fear pushed me into action, and I hastily put on a pair of jeans and a T-shirt, grabbed my keys and wallet, and headed for the door.

I wanted to believe Millie had good intentions. But I also knew the prospect of fame and fortune could make even the best of people do terrible things.

Millie had sent me the name of the trendy clothing and accessory shop she owned along the main drag. I'd driven past it with Hendrix and recognized it from my childhood as the old Beachcombers.

It took only minutes to get there. Since it was still early, the parking lot was empty. I quickly parked and headed toward the door. I expected it to be locked, but with a little shove, it gave way with a perky *ding*, announcing my arrival.

It was a lot nicer than the Beachcombers I remembered—that was for sure. The clothing was a mixture of beach attire, ranging from bathing suits and sandals to more everyday stuff—dresses and shorts. There was everything from candles to jewelry and bath salts.

Elena would love this place.

I found Millie and Aiden standing behind the large wood counter. His arms were around her waist, sliding dangerously close to her denim-clad ass, and while they weren't in a compromising position, I definitely felt the need to avert my eyes.

Millie let out a laugh before she turned. "Oh, good. You're here."

"Well, you beckoned," I deadpanned, making Aiden cough under his breath. He moved down the counter and began sorting a box of small, carved ornaments, placing them on a display.

I guess he's staying then…

Millie leaned over the counter, staring at me with an appraising look.

I folded my arms across my chest and just stared back. "So, you know?"

A smug grin spread across her face. "I've known for a while."

I blanched. "How long is a while?"

"Day after the engagement dinner." She shrugged as she began folding a large stack of shirts. "Saw it online. Some of us on this island actually do pay attention to shit like that."

"You mean celebrity gossip?"

She shrugged again. "I was pretty damn stunned when I saw it. I'd just seen you at the engagement dinner, and then the very next day, your face was on my favorite gossip blog."

"A gossip blog, love? Really?" Aiden chimed in.

"Hey, don't judge me." She looked over at her husband. "Not all of us are into nonfiction and art magazines."

"But your descriptions of the art are just so…" His mouth quirked, making her roll her eyes.

She turned back to me, her blonde hair swishing behind her shoulder. "He likes to listen to audiobooks, but magazines are tricky 'cause he can't see the pictures, so he makes me read the articles and then try and describe the photos," she explained. "He still won't let me forget the sculpture I said looked like a turtle."

"No," he argued, an amused expression painting his face. "You said it looked like a giant turtle with a dildo stuck up its arse."

She snorted. "Same thing."

I double-blinked.

Why am I here?

"Anyway, I didn't say anything at the coffee shop that day because I thought maybe you and Macon were both playing dumb for my benefit—which I'd understand," she explained with a wave of her hand. "But yesterday at the bachelorette party, it became abundantly clear that you hadn't told anyone because Elena doesn't seem to have a clue. No one is that good of an actor."

I grimaced.

"I can't tell them." The words rushed out of my mouth. "I signed an NDA."

She pinned me with her gaze as the puzzle pieces started to fall into place. "You can't tell anyone?"

I shook my head. "I might have been able to tell Macon if he also signed an NDA since he's family, but—"

"Then, he'd have to keep it from Marin."

"Yeah."

How could I ask my brother to keep something like that from his fiancée? No, not just ask—legally bind him to keep his mouth closed.

It wasn't even a solution I'd considered. Not one I'd even bothered asking Saul about.

"So, what was your plan, Zander? To just not say anything and let her find out when everyone else does? Or were you not planning for this to go past the wedding?"

"I don't know, okay?" I shoved my hands in my hair. "I don't know what the hell I was going to do. I didn't plan for this to happen."

"Don't pull that shit," she scoffed. "I was with you in that coffee shop. This was completely premeditated. You knew exactly what stakes were involved when you hooked up with her."

"Yes, but I didn't expect to—"

I choked on my own words as she stared at me until, suddenly, her eyes widened.

"Oh shit. You love her."

"I—" *Fuck.*

The realization hit me like a lightning bolt to the skull.

Somehow, over the past few weeks, she'd become part of me.

I loved seeing her in the morning, leaning against the kitchen counter in my T-shirt, drinking coffee.

I loved the sight of her ridiculously expensive handbag by the front door because I knew it meant she was home.

I loved the way she called out my name when I was buried deep inside her.

I simply loved her.

"Millie, love, did you give the poor man a heart attack? Why is he so silent?"

"I think he just had an epiphany."

"Ah." Aiden chuckled. "Feels kind of like a swift kick to the balls, doesn't it?"

"A little, yeah." My voice came out a little shaky.

"So, what are you going to do?" Millie asked, bringing my focus back, even though my mind was still reeling.

"I don't know," I answered honestly. "Part of me just wants to say fuck it and tell her."

"And if anyone found out?"

I frowned. "I don't know. I'd like to say the guys in the band would be understanding, but the last thing I want to do is break their trust before I've barely had a chance to earn it. They've already been through enough with Mitch."

"You can't be loyal to one without betraying the other."

"Pretty much."

She let out a long sigh. "Well, I thought I'd be a lot madder than this, but I can see how hard this has been for you."

"Do you think it was wrong of me to get involved with her?"

"Wrong? Probably not the word I would use. Reckless? Yes." She turned her head toward her husband. "But we're proof that, sometimes, you can't help who you fall in love with."

"No matter how hard you try," Aiden emphasized.

"You might not be able to tell her about the band, but you can tell her something far more important. Something that will make a difference when the news finally does come out."

I swallowed the lump in my throat. "You're right," I answered. "I've got to go."

CHAPTER FIFTEEN

Elena

I was not a cuddler. I never wanted to spoon, and I certainly was not the kind of girl who enjoyed sharing her bed. Even when I'd been dating Chad, we'd had spent most nights apart—using the old *I've got to wake up early* excuse.

I was none of those things—until I met Zander.

Now, in the middle of the night, my body searched for him. My arms would wrap around his warm body, fitting around it like a puzzle piece.

Like two halves of a whole.

So, where the fuck is he?

I sat up in the empty bed, looking around as I noticed his missing shoes and wallet. Where was my bare-chested guitar player? I grabbed my phone off the nightstand, seeing the text from him.

Coffee shop, huh?

My stomach rumbled at the mere thought.

Mmm, bear claw.

I checked the time and cursed. *Shit, shit, shit.*

No bear claw for me.

I jumped out of bed, thanking myself for having the clarity to take a shower last night.

Or maybe I should thank Zander for that…

Either way, it was one less thing to do. I threw on a pair of linen shorts and a tank. A pair of sandals and a hasty low bun finished the look. A bit of concealer and some mascara, and a few minutes later, my empty stomach and I were headed down the road to Marin's.

It was officially the twenty-four-hour countdown to the wedding day, and I'd promised to be hers for every single minute of it.

Even if it meant giving up my last full day with Zander.

Marin came first.

She was why I had come down here in the first place. Zander was just a bonus. One hell of a nice bonus.

I got to their house and pulled up to the curb. Gravel crunched beneath the tires as I cut off the engine, and the humidity immediately began to fill the car.

I freaking hate summer.

I grabbed my bag and headed for the front door when Macon met me halfway.

"Oh, good. You're here."

"Happy wedding eve." I grinned, pulling him into a big hug.

"Thanks," he answered, giving me a tight squeeze. "Marin is inside with a giant box of doughnuts."

"You're my hero, Macon Green."

He laughed. "I'm off to the station for the morning."

"Working the day before your wedding? That's something I would do."

"It's only a few hours, and I don't have to," he clarified. "I want to. The deputies will be working extra shifts to cover while we're on my honeymoon, and I want to make sure they know it's appreciated."

"I'm sure they know."

"Well, the other giant box of doughnuts in my car will definitely drive the point home."

"It sure will," I agreed.

"Call me if you need anything," he said.

"Why would I need anything?" I asked. "I'm awesome."

"And make sure she drinks some freaking water. She keeps complaining that it makes her pee too much." He rolled his eyes.

"Why do I feel like the teen babysitter being left alone for the first time?" I asked, shooing him away. "We'll be fine. It's just a few out-of-town guests. What could go wrong?"

It was like I was asking fate to screw me over.

ZANDER

Where are you? The house is empty, and I have bear claws.

ME

Bear claws? Damn. I forgot to tell you I had an early start. Marin has a crazy-long to-do list, so she has us running all over the place.

ZANDER

Any chance you'll have a break?

ME

Maybe later in the afternoon. Why?

ZANDER

Just wanted to have a chance to see you before the rehearsal.

ME

I'll text you.

ZANDER

Sounds good. Do you happen to know where Macon is?

ME

He's at the station right now. I think he's headed to the inn later though.

A twinge of guilt tugged at my gut at the realization of how little time I had with Zander. I knew we had to have a conversation—*the* conversation—but neither of us seemed overly eager to bring it up.

Where was this headed?

It wasn't that I was necessarily scared to find out.

Okay, that was a lie.

I was fucking terrified.

I just didn't know what scared me the most—finding out he wanted a future with me or that he didn't.

Losing him now was one thing. It would hurt, but my life would eventually go back to its normal routine, and I'd survive. I was used to being alone. Losing him at some point in the future when our lives were so entangled that I didn't have one of my own to return to? That would devastate me.

So, yeah, I'd been putting it off, but I knew it was a conversation we needed to have.

I was just hoping for some sort of epiphany—a cosmic sign that would point me in the right direction.

But so far, I hadn't found one.

"Okay, so my mom and dad are checked off. I dropped off a gift basket for my brother and sister at the other rental this morning."

"Did you get to meet their dates?" I asked 'cause I was nosy.

"No," she answered. "I just snuck in and left it on the counter. Everyone was asleep, which, according to my mother, is all very scandalous because one does not share a bed with a 'date,' " she said as we walked out of the inn, having just given a warm welcome to Mr. and Mrs. Mueller.

They'd all arrived last night, but they had been in need of

some rest after the long drive, so this was the first time we'd seen them.

I snorted out a laugh as we moved down the path toward my car. "Okay, moving on then. What about your aunt..." *Shit, what's her name?*

Marin gave me a knowing grin. "She's at the resort, as are a few others, and where we should head now."

"Okay, but don't you want to stop for lunch first?" I asked, checking my watch. It was just about noon.

"Nah," she said as we both got in the car. I took the driver's seat and started the engine. "I'm good. I'd rather get all these welcome baskets out of the back of the car first. It's too hot."

Speaking of...

I looked in my rearview mirror and let out a sigh. My car had never looked so...cute and domesticated.

The baskets were ridiculously large, packed to the gills with Ocracoke merchandise, local snacks, and coffee.

It was so over the top.

It was so generous.

And it was so Marin.

We pulled into the packed parking lot of Windows Hotel and Resort, and we both got out. Marin was already on her phone, checking her list, while I pulled open the door to the back seat to start hauling out baskets.

"How many of these do we need?" I asked.

No answer.

"Marin?" I looked over the top of the car and found her still staring at her phone.

"Oh, um..." She paused. "Four. No, wait. Five."

"Okay. I'll take three. You take two."

"Yeah," she answered. "And then maybe when we get in there, we can grab some water and rest for a minute?"

"Whatever you want, boss," I told her.

I balanced a basket on my forearm before grabbing two

more, and I was ready. A quick glance over at Marin told me she was, too.

We both closed the doors with our hips and headed inside.

Lani met us at the door with a bright smile. "Here, let me help you!" she said, ushering us in through the lobby. "Your family is lovely, Marin. And all settled in."

"Thank you," she said, a little breathless.

"You okay?" I asked, turning to her as Lani took the last basket from her hands and placed them on a table nearby.

"Yeah," she answered, although she didn't look it. In fact, she looked a little—

"Marin!" I shouted as her thin frame crumpled toward the ground like a house of cards.

Lani and I both rushed toward her, managing to reach her just before her head hit the hard marble floor.

"Marin!" I shouted again, but she didn't respond.

"I'm calling Jake," Lani said, pulling out her phone. A few seconds later, I heard her frantic, clipped voice as I tried to bring Marin back to consciousness. "Jake's on his way. I called Macon as well."

We set Marin flat on the floor, and Lani went to grab some water and a pillow. I checked her pulse and breathing—all of which seemed normal.

At least I think they do.

What the fuck do I do? Shake her? Slap her?

I'd never felt so useless in my life.

"Come on, Marin," I begged, and just when I was reconsidering that slapping idea, her eyes fluttered open.

"Oh, thank fuck." I breathed a sigh of relief as the sound of a police siren came tearing down the street.

Macon was here.

"What happened?" Marin asked, looking around at Lani and me.

"You pass—"

"Where is she?" Macon's voice echoed as he threw the door open. He sounded like a man possessed, his eyes wild until they locked on Marin. He ran across the lobby and sank to his knees in front of her.

"I'm okay," she assured him as he began checking her over.

"Where the fuck is Jake?" he growled.

"I'm here!" Jake said, sprinting into the hotel with a bag slung over his shoulder. He was a little out of breath, but otherwise calm as he knelt down on the other side of Marin, next to me. "I would have gotten here sooner if some asshat in a police car hadn't cut me off."

The fact that he was making a joke was good, right?

He wouldn't be making a joke if this was a real emergency…

"Sorry," Macon muttered.

"It's okay," he told him as he began checking Marin's vitals, having already been briefed by Lani on what had happened. "I once left a patient mid-exam because I got a text from Molly that she was having some pain. I rushed all the way home. It was heartburn," he deadpanned as he pulled out an O2 meter and his stethoscope. "Even doctors panic when their wives get pregnant."

I stepped back then, letting them discuss what had happened and Marin's symptoms. Eventually, Jake got up and asked me a few things about our day leading up to the fainting.

"I think you're just dehydrated and maybe a bit exhausted," he told Marin. "But I'd like to take you to the clinic to do a quick exam and check the baby's heart rate, just to be safe."

Marin nodded, turning to me, but before she could even open her mouth, I stopped her.

"I got it," I said. "Go take care of that baby. Everything will be fine."

She nodded, and Macon patted my shoulder, silently thanking me.

"Can you text Zander? He was on his way to the station to

meet me for lunch, and then maybe let Molly know I won't be able to help with setup?"

"Yes," I answered, seeing the worry in his eyes. "Don't worry, Macon," I assured him. "I'll take care of everything."

Time to pull out some serious maid-of-honor magic.

There were some conversations you just couldn't have via text.

Telling Zander his sister-in-law passed out in the hotel lobby was one of them, so after Macon and Marin left for the clinic with Jake, I sat down in the lobby and dialed his number.

"Hey, you," he said in that tone of voice that made me think of sex.

"Hey," I answered back in an equally seductive voice.

No. Bad girl.

Not. The. Time.

I shook my head, trying to loosen the brain fog that had me thinking about all sorts of dirty things and instead focused on the marble floor Marin had just been lying on. "So, I am supposed to pass on a message for you from Macon."

"Oh." He sounded mildly disappointed at my tone change.

Dude. Me, too.

"We had a bit of a situation. A mild emergency," I said.

A few people shuffled past me with suitcases, laughing. The sound echoed far too loudly.

"Well, now, you're freaking me out."

Now, I was fixated on the floor. *What if she had hit her head? What if she hadn't woken up?*

"Marin passed out at the hotel."

"What? Is she okay?"

"Yeah," I answered a bit too quickly. "I mean, I think so.

They're at the clinic, making sure. Jake said it was probably just dehydration and exhaustion."

"Shit," he breathed out.

I thought back to those moments leading up to her fall. "I should have known she was pushing herself too hard."

"Don't blame yourself, Elena," he said. "You couldn't have possibly known that was going to happen."

"No," I agreed. "But I still could have forced her to slow down."

"Could you?" There was a touch of humor to his voice.

"Maybe," I answered. "She listens to me about fifty percent of the time. Thankfully, it seems to be the important stuff that sticks, like going after Hot Cop even though it was scary."

"You told her that?" He grew serious, making me realize what I'd just said.

"Um, yeah. She just needed a little push in the right direction." I bit the inside of my cheek. "Anyway, there are still a lot of things left to do before the wedding tomorrow, and I was wondering if you could lend a hand this afternoon."

There was a brief pause. "Sure. What do you need?"

"Can you head to the inn and help with setup? Macon was supposed to be there, so I'm worried they might need an extra hand."

"Yeah," he agreed. "I'll head there now."

"Great. Thank you." A silence held in the air. "I guess we'll see each other at the rehearsal?"

"Elena, we still need to talk about—"

"I know. We will," I answered, feeling my gut twist in a knot. "Tonight. After the rehearsal dinner, I promise."

"Okay. Tonight."

If I had a superhero name, it'd be The Delegator.

Superpower: getting shit done.

I truly believe that if Marin had just handed over her freaking list to me in the first place, it would have saved us both a whole lot of trouble.

We could have spent the day getting facials and drinking mai tais—virgin for her, of course.

After my call to Zander, I'd headed to the Windows dining room for a bit of lunch, and that was when the real magic began. Honestly, it wasn't even that hard. Once everyone heard about Marin, they were more than glad to help out.

When Macon texted me a while later to let me know everything was fine, I realized just how scared I'd been—like I'd been holding my breath underwater.

She was okay.

After finishing my late lunch, I headed out to do a few last-minute errands that weren't on Marin's list, including running to the market and coffee shop. Then, I headed back to the rental and packed up everything I needed for the rehearsal dinner and the wedding.

This was the part of the plan Marin didn't know about, and I hoped Macon was still on board after everything that had happened. I pulled into their driveway and turned off the engine, reaching over to the passenger seat to grab my duffel and garment bag. With everything in hand, I got out and headed to the front door.

I look like I'm moving in.

"Couldn't stay away, huh?" Macon grinned, pulling the door open and saving me the trouble.

"You know how much I love you, Hot Cop," I chided.

"She's in our room, getting ready," he said before pulling me into a hug. "Thanks for being there with her today."

"There's nowhere else I'd rather be. Besides, that's my niece in there." I tilted my head. "You still okay with this? You'll be right next door," I reminded him.

"I know." He nodded, though I could still see a bit of hesitation in his expression.

"We can call it off," I offered. "Plenty of brides and grooms spend their—"

He offered his hand, grabbing my duffel off my shoulder. "No, I think she needs this. You both do," he emphasized.

I snatched the duffel back, making his brow arch. "If you're gonna be chivalrous, go grab the food from the car," I told him. He started to head down the driveway. "But don't steal any!"

"No promises!" he hollered over his shoulder.

I headed on to the master and found my best friend, sitting cross-legged on her bed. Her dark brown hair was freshly washed, and her body was covered in a fluffy pink robe.

"Hey," I greeted her, walking in and plopping down on the bed next to her.

She had makeup spread around her, and she let out a sigh of relief.

"Oh, thank God." She shoved the makeup in my direction. "Please take over; otherwise, I'm gonna look like a clown."

I rolled my eyes. She *did* know how to do her own makeup. She just thought I did it better.

Which was true.

"I'm sorry I scared you today," she said softly.

I'd started looking through her lackluster assortment of makeup and grimaced. She was in serious need of an upgrade.

I reached down and rifled through my duffel until I found my own makeup bag.

"Why are you apologizing?"

"I should have known something was up," she said. "I felt a little dizzy, and my throat was dry."

I picked out a brow pencil and got to work. "You need to take it easy."

"I will," she promised. "Macon's basically my shadow now."

"Well, not for tonight he isn't."

Her brow arched, and I scolded her for moving it.

"Sorry!" she said, trying not to laugh. "What do you mean?"

"We're having a sleepover. It's your last night as a single woman. Do you think I'd let you spend it with your fiancé?"

"I'm not really single—"

"Shhh," I said, and this time, she really did laugh. "Not the point. Macon is going next door with the guys, and we're staying here."

I'd originally planned on having Molly and Millie here but decided to scale back after Marin's tumble.

I wanted her to have fun, but, like, not that much fun. We needed her to have enough energy for the main event.

"But what about Zander?" she asked.

"What about Zander?" My heart rate tripled.

"You two have such little time left."

I shrugged as I primed her eyelids. "It's fine," I told her. "We both knew this day would come."

"So, you've talked about it?"

"No." I let out a frustrated sigh.

"Why not? Is he avoiding it?"

I selected an eye shadow palette and swept the brush over a muted pink shade.

"No, he actually brought it up on the phone today. It's just—"

I brought the brush to her lid, but she steadied my hand and looked at me.

"I know you're scared."

I swallowed back a lump in my throat, nodding. "I just keep thinking about all the horrible things that could go wrong, and I just don't know if it's worth the risk."

I can't lose anyone else.

She squeezed my hand. "I get that. Falling in love with someone is always a risk."

Falling in love…

Oh, holy shit.

A grin tugged at her lips as she understood what was going on in my head. "But I want you to actually think about it. What scares you the most? Taking the risk or the regret or wondering *what if* for the rest of your life?"

Before I got to answer, Macon walked in. "Hey, sorry to break up the party, but we've got a bit of a situation."

"What now?" Marin wailed.

Shit, did I fuck something up? I'd been so meticulous with that list...

"I just got a cryptic and really confusing phone call from Zander. Apparently, there are a few reporters outside the inn, and he's worried they might come here."

"Here? Why?"

"He said he'd explain when we got there," Macon said, his brow pinched with concern. "I told him we'd drop by and grab him clothes. Sounds like he didn't want to leave."

"Is he okay?" I asked.

"I'm not sure," Macon answered honestly.

As we began to gather up our things and prepare to leave, I couldn't help but wonder...

What news story would be big enough to bring reporters all the way to Ocracoke?

CHAPTER SIXTEEN

Zander

I f I happened to believe in God, today would be one of those days that had me seriously asking myself what I'd done to anger the big man upstairs.

Ever since I'd left Elena in that bed this morning, it was like the universe was actively trying to keep us apart.

I couldn't really fault Marin for fainting.

That shit was scary.

When Elena had called to tell me, I had known Macon must be beside himself with worry, which was why this wedding needed to go off without a hitch.

Marin didn't need any more added stress.

With Elena now tasked with overseeing pre-wedding tasks, I headed over to the inn to help with setup. If I could race through this, I was hoping I could make it back to the rental and steal an hour or two with Elena. But Molly had the longest fucking checklist I'd ever seen, and after a few hours, I thought we'd never finish.

It was a small-town wedding, not a fucking coronation.

But it was also my brother's small-town wedding, so I put my frustration aside and strung every fairy light, lined up every chair, and set every place setting for the rehearsal dinner.

It was exhausting.

Around late afternoon, I headed to the back lawn, where the ceremony would be, and looked around for Molly—aka the blonde dictator—to see if she needed anything else before I headed out to change.

I found her barreling toward me instead.

"We need to talk," Molly said, her voice clipped as she grabbed my arm and hauled me toward the house.

Okay…

I knew I wasn't an expert at stringing lights, but I thought I had done an all right job. Mostly.

She manhandled me through the sliding glass doors and toward the front.

"What the fuck, Molly?" I swore as she came to an abrupt stop.

"I just had a very interesting conversation with the uninvited guests who are now parked outside our front lawn, Zander."

I looked out the window and found three men huddled together, talking and laughing. Cameras were strung over their shoulders or around their necks.

My eyes widened.

"Shit," I muttered. "I need to call my manager."

"You do that." Her arms were folded across her chest as her fierce gaze fixed on me. "But first you need to explain why you haven't—"

"Call your sister," I told her. "She'll explain. I need to figure out how this happened."

She opened her mouth to protest, but I already had my phone out, turning away from her and the window.

"Zander," Lance answered, sounding on edge. "I was about to call you."

"Thinking you have some news to tell me."

"You didn't keep your head down, kid."

"What the fuck do you mean?"

He sighed. "Someone got ahold of some photos of you

and your brother in a tattoo shop, and they're making the rounds. Your last name is right there on your damn body, Z."

My eyes pinched closed. "It must have been one of the staff members."

Fucking hell.

I stepped into a small parlor and put him on speaker so I could do an internet search and found them with a few clicks. I flipped through each photo, shaking my head in disbelief at how oblivious I'd been that day.

And naive.

We'd chatted openly in that shop, let the artists take photos for their portfolios, fucking tipped them a king's ransom.

I was so in over my head.

"There are reporters outside," I told him. "My brother's rehearsal dinner is tonight."

The rehearsal was nothing compared to the wedding though. Would they harass every single guest?

What a goddamn nightmare.

"They probably found that information online as well. Did they have a wedding announcement?"

"I have no idea," I told him as I scrubbed a hand down my face. "What do I do? I need them gone. They'll ruin his wedding."

"Well, it's probably going to get worse," he said frankly as I started to pace. "Just ignore them for now and let me get in contact with Ridge. In the meantime, tell your family and friends the same thing and, uh, tell your brother congrats for me."

"Sure."

He hung up with the promise to get back in touch soon while I stood frozen in the empty parlor. This was not how I wanted to tell them.

I let out a sigh.

Lifting my phone back up, I called Macon.

"Hey!" he greeted me. He sounded light and happy. His

fiancée and baby were healthy, and he was getting married tomorrow. Life was good.

I was about to ruin that.

Maybe I should have never come back.

"Hey," I echoed, although with far less enthusiasm. "I need you guys to come to the inn a bit early. Can you do that?"

"Uh, yeah, sure. Why?"

"This is going to sound crazy, but there are a few reporters outside the inn."

"What? No way," he exclaimed. "Why?"

"I'll explain when you get here, but can you swing by the rental and grab my clothes for the rehearsal dinner?"

"Yeah? You okay?" His enthusiasm was waning.

"Yeah, I just don't want to go anywhere."

"Okay, sure." His voice was now full of doubt. "Marin and Elena are getting ready, but I'm sure I can persuade them to pack up and finish there if it's that important?" he asked.

"Yeah, that would be great. I don't want the guys wandering over there."

"All right," he agreed. "See you soon."

"Oh, and, Macon?"

"Yeah?"

"Don't say anything to them when you get here. No matter what they tell you."

He didn't respond, and I wondered if I'd just lost my brother's trust for good.

In another life, Macon could have been a decent bodyguard.

That being said, having to stand there inside the inn, watching my brother protect his fiancée and the woman I loved from the onslaught of those reporters was excruciating.

My hand fisted the doorknob so hard that I thought it might crack.

His face was a grim line as he used the girls' garment bags as a makeshift shield. There were only three of them, but, man, they were persistent, huddled around my family like vultures. Marin's and Elena's expressions were a mixture of confusion and annoyance.

"I'm going to go tell those fuckers to get off my damn sidewalk." Jake stormed toward the door. "I've seen enough movies to know that paparazzi can't be on private property, and if they think I'm some country bumpkin—"

I had to leap back from the door so that I wasn't seen by the photographers as Jake ran down to meet them. He distracted the three men enough that Macon was able to pick up the pace and get the girls inside quicker.

I wonder if that was his intention all along…

The door swung open, and the three of them walked in, dropping a heap of garment and duffel bags on the floor.

"What the fuck is going on?" my brother boomed, his steely gaze turning to me, reminding me exactly why he was sheriff of this county. "One of those guys just asked me what I thought about my brother becoming the newest member of Manic at Midnight."

"You didn't answer him, did you?" I blanched.

His expression hardened. "Of course I didn't. But you gotta help me out here, Zander, because those fuckers seem to know a hell of a lot more about you than we do."

I swallowed audibly as my eyes found Elena's. She was silent. So fucking silent.

Please say something.

But she didn't. She just kept staring at me.

"Why don't you all head to the parlor?" Molly suggested, motioning to one of the rooms off to the left.

Where the hell did she come from?

"I'll have your things brought to the suite you reserved for the weekend. It's where the family wing used to—never mind. You know that."

"Thank you, Molly." Marin gave her an appreciative smile.

We all shuffled into the same blue parlor I'd been pacing in earlier. Molly shut the door on her way out, which gave us some privacy. The curtains had been drawn closed, and several table lamps now gave the room a false sense of darkness. Macon and Marin took a seat on the love seat by the window while Elena took the wingback chair next to them, leaving the large sofa for me.

I tried not to look too much into that and opted to stand instead.

"Where do you want me to start?" I nervously ran my hands through my hair.

"The beginning would be good," my brother answered harshly.

"Right." I let out a breath. "Last year, I was asked to tour with Manic at Midnight after they lost their lead guitarist."

"You mean that horrible guy that—"

"Let him continue, Marin," Macon said, taking her hand.

"It was supposed to be temporary—just until they finished the US leg of their tour. All my jobs are like that—or at least they were, and I liked it that way. I never wanted to be in just one band—especially not a famous one. But something just clicked with Manic, and before long, they approached me with the possibility of staying on permanently."

"Holy shit, Zander," Macon breathed out.

"I told them I had to think about it," I explained.

"You had to think about it?" His eyes widened.

"As you can tell from the shitstorm outside, it's not exactly like accepting a regular job. I had to make sure I was willing to deal with all the madness that came along with it."

"So, when did you decide?" Marin asked as my gaze fell back on Elena.

Still so quiet.

"Right before I left for the engagement party."

"And you never told us?" I could hear the pain in my brother's voice.

"I couldn't tell you," I explained as I once again began to pace. "That thing I said at the cookout wasn't bullshit. I'd signed an NDA. I couldn't say shit. And it wasn't like I had planned on sticking around."

My brother looked away. We'd made amends, but the wounds of our separation were still there. Still fresh.

"So, the tour you're doing in the fall?" Marin asked tentatively. "That will be with them?"

I nodded. "Their international tour. Six months, fifteen countries."

"Shit, Zander." My brother's voice was filled with awe.

"I thought about telling you guys a dozen times regardless of the consequences. Especially when—"

I looked over toward Elena.

She immediately looked away.

"Millie knows," I blurted out.

"Millie?" Marin choked out, and I found Elena silently staring daggers at me. Well, at least that was some sort of reaction. "You told Millie?"

"No," I answered quickly. "I didn't tell her. She just figured it out. Apparently, she has a healthy obsession with celebrity gossip and saw an article about me before my manager was able to pull it."

"Your manager?" My brother looked up at me.

"Well, the band's manager, but yeah."

"You mean the same guy who manages Asher Knight? That manager?"

An amused grin fell across my face. "Wouldn't have pegged you for a Knight Rider, Macon."

His brows furrowed, and Marin snorted before she whispered, "That's what they call his fangirls."

He rolled his eyes, and I laughed.

"I was just trying to point out that even I know who the guy is. This is huge."

"I know." I nodded, blowing out a breath.

I looked over at Elena, who still hadn't said a word. Was she just trying to process it all? Did she hate me?

Could I blame her if she did?

"So, how did all that happen?" Macon pointed toward the front-facing window.

"Pictures of us were leaked from the bachelor party," I told him. It hadn't dawned on me until that moment that his photo was also all over the internet—something he definitely hadn't asked for. "One of those tattoo artists must have recognized me while we were there, and since I used my real name—"

"You go by a different name?" Marin asked.

"Yeah, Zander Tate. Hendrix's dad is my manager, and it was something he suggested when I was just starting out, and it turned out to be a good idea—at least for a while."

Marin was studying her best friend intently and gently patted Macon's hand. "I think we're going to give you two some time alone," she suggested.

"Oh, right," Macon agreed. "I'm going to go contact everyone that's coming and give them a heads-up about our unwanted guests."

Macon gave my shoulder a reassuring squeeze, which did little to lighten my mood because as they left, I found that same quiet version of Elena staring up at me.

I decided to give her time, and so I waited, but when I began to wear a path in the carpet, I couldn't handle the silence anymore.

"Say something," I begged, my voice barely a whisper.

Her eyes closed for a moment, betraying her emotions. "I don't know what to say," she said. "I feel like I'm looking at a stranger."

"I'm still me," I tried to assure her.

She scoffed, rising from her chair to turn her back on me. Her posture was rigid and cold.

"And who would that be exactly? Zander Green or Zander Tate?"

I grimaced at the harshness in her tone.

"You know, I actually tried to look you up once. I wanted to see you perform, but I couldn't find anything when I searched for your name. I just chalked it up to the life of a session guitarist. Never getting any credit for your work and all that. But that's not the case, is it?"

"No," I answered.

"Answer me truthfully." She turned abruptly, stepping forward. "If there had been no contract and you'd been free to tell anyone you liked, would you have? Would you have come down here and announced to your brother that you were going to be a rock star, or would you have done the same damn thing and kept it to yourself?"

I opened my mouth to answer, but found I couldn't. A moment passed and then another. "I don't know."

I'd once told Hendrix I felt something close to relief at not having to tell them, but at the time, I hadn't had any choice in the matter. If I had, would I have told them, or would I have held on to this secret a little longer, relishing the normalcy I got here in Ocracoke?

"I can't deny that this whole thing scares the shit out of me," I told her. "Spending these last few weeks in Ocracoke has been a special kind of torture. On one hand, coming here has reminded me why I fell in love with music in the first place. I was a broken kid who needed a way to grieve, and Macon gave that to me when he bought that old guitar. But being here also reminds me of everything I'm giving up, and I'm terrified I've made the wrong choice."

She looked up at me, her expression softening. "You didn't," she assured me. "Think of all those young kids out there, looking for someone to inspire them. Talent like yours is meant for the main stage."

I didn't deserve her kind words, but I'd take them all the

same. "I didn't want you to find out like this," I told her, taking a hesitant step forward.

Her arms were still drawn tight across her chest. "No? How would you have preferred it then?"

"I don't know, but I would have at least tried to butter you up first with a lot of sex and a ridiculously expensive handbag."

"It would have to be at least two ridiculously expensive handbags. You're incredibly rich now," she quipped. Her arms fell to her sides. "Please tell me you had a good lawyer look over that contract. They'd better not be fucking you over."

A grin tugged at the corner of my lips. "Yes. My agent graduated from Harvard Law and is one cutthroat son of a bitch."

She gave a dismissive shrug. "Duke is better."

I took another step closer to her, and when she didn't step away, I reached for her. She came willingly, looking up at me with such deep emotion.

"What are you thinking?" I asked, cupping her cheek.

"I'm thinking that as a woman, I'm really fucking mad at you," she said as she looked up at me. "But as a lawyer, I understand the complexity of the situation and why you couldn't tell me. As a music fan though, I'm geeking the fuck out over the fact that you're going to be a real-life rock star—even if it's for a band like Manic at Midnight." Her hands slid around my waist, and it felt like heaven. "What are you thinking?"

"I'm thinking about all the times I thought about telling you and wishing I had," I said in a low voice. "I'm thinking I'd do just about anything to earn your forgiveness and that it's been entirely too long since I've kissed you—"

"This morning wasn't that long ago," she argued.

"Yeah, but we're on borrowed time. I'm leaving in a day."

She froze in my arms. "You are?"

I nodded slowly. "The morning after the wedding. I have a

charity concert in New York. It's when the band is supposed to make the official announcement."

Her eyes searched mine. "Why didn't you tell me?"

I brushed a piece of her hair behind her ear. "I knew your focus would be on Marin and the wedding today, and I didn't want you to feel guilty for that."

"But that only leaves us with tomorrow night," she said as she pulled me closer.

"We're not saying good-bye, Elena," I assured her. "Nothing has to change."

"Okay." Her voice was full of doubt, and I was desperate to erase it.

"But since we are short on time, we should probably take advantage of this empty room," I suggested, lifting her off the ground. She let out a little yelp, and I scolded her. "You're gonna have to be a lot quieter than that, Louie."

Her legs wrapped around my torso as I walked us back toward the wall, which was conveniently located next to the door. I flipped the lock, ensuring our privacy, and then got right to it. My hand fisted her hair as my mouth closed over hers.

I worked the buttons of her shorts as I kissed her deeply, keeping her pinned to the wall with my knee. I knew the moment she grew impatient when her fingers frantically found the fly of my jeans.

I barely got her shorts to her thighs before she had my cock out and I was sliding home.

"Fuck, Elena," I cursed in her ear.

"I need you."

I felt those words down to my soul because I didn't think I'd ever stop needing this woman. She owned me. If you cracked me open, it would be her name you'd find inked on my heart.

I fucked her hard, gripping her ass for leverage as I slammed into her body over and over. I stifled her moans with my hand before replacing it with my mouth.

It felt wild.

It felt desperate.

When her orgasm finally claimed her and I felt her fall apart in my arms, I had no choice but to follow.

When it came to Elena Mendez, I realized I'd never had a choice.

From the moment I'd walked in that bar, I had been hers.

"Come on tour with me," I said, my breathing still labored from our lovemaking.

We quickly adjusted our clothing, but I kept her pinned to that wall.

"What?" Her hands pressed into my chest as she stared into my eyes.

"Leave with me on Sunday. I want you there with me for my first concert. For every concert, Elena."

She swallowed, and I could see a myriad of emotions in her reaction.

"I can't just leave," she said. "I have a whole life, a job—"

"That you hate," I reminded her. "You could start over. Pick a different career, write a book, or, hell, do nothing at all."

She flinched. "I can't just be your groupie for the rest of my life, Zander."

"That's not…" I was screwing this up, and I could already feel her retreating. "I just meant that you could have the freedom to do and explore whatever you wanted."

"And if we don't work out?"

"What?"

"It's a logical question, Zander. We've only known each other for three weeks, and you're asking me to give up every-thing for you."

I took a step back, feeling the loss of her touch instantly. "No, I'm asking you to make a life with me. There's a differ-ence. It shouldn't feel like a sacrifice if it's right. Elena, I—"

The sound of knuckles rapping against the other side of the door interrupted me.

"Elena?" It was Molly. "Guests are starting to arrive, and Marin isn't ready yet."

She looked at me, and I merely nodded.

"I'll be right out." She stepped out of my grasp and flipped the lock. "We can talk later," she assured me.

There was something so final when she walked out that door, and it took less than an hour to find out why.

When Lance had warned that things would only get worse, he'd proven why he was a damn good manager.

The large red door to the inn swung open as Billy and Eli stepped inside, looking like two opposite ends of a spectrum. Billy had dressed up a nice pair of dark jeans with a black button-down and boots while his husband looked like a sixth member of The Fab Five. His tan suit, black fitted T-shirt, and loafers no doubt cost more than my mortgage.

"Jesus, what a madhouse!" Billy exclaimed.

"I thought I'd left this bullshit in New York," Eli said, running a hand through his neatly trimmed hair.

"Sorry, guys." I grabbed the back of my neck, feeling helpless as the rest of the wedding party and several of Marin's family members tried to get through.

Jake had managed to get the reporters off inn property, but unfortunately for many of the wedding party, the parking lot was now full, thanks to the inn being at capacity, and they were having to park on the street, which was fair game.

Oh, and we had two more—for a total of five. Five fucking assholes with cameras, all because some other asshole had decided to post a picture of me.

I am not worth all this, I promise.

"Man, it's all good." Eli shrugged, giving me a big smile. "But do you mind if we get your picture?"

I rolled my eyes as the two men laughed.

"What? I heard they're going for a pretty penny online,

and that bachelor party wasn't cheap." His expression changed as if he realized what he'd said. "Sorry about that, by the way. I guess those douchebags kind of sold you out."

"Not your fault," I began to tell him, but then I was interrupted by my cell phone.

"Sorry," I said to the guys. "I gotta take this."

They waved me off, and I ducked into a hallway to answer.

"Lance," I greeted him. "Tell me you've got good news for me."

If he was calling me instead of the band's manager, I had a feeling it was the opposite of good.

"Define good," he said, causing me to groan. "Look, I have a solution, but you're not going to like it."

"Just tell me."

"You told me you wanted these guys gone, right?"

"Yeah," I confirmed.

"Look, the only way they're gonna go is if you go, Z."

"But I'm not leaving until—"

"I know that's when you were planning on leaving, but if you stay, they stay. You're big fucking news right now—not like *Taylor has a new boyfriend* big, but close."

"Thanks for that comparison."

"Just keeping you humble." He laughed. "But seriously, I told you this shit was gonna be crazy, and with you being unknown, everyone's dying to get the scoop. Those guys outside won't stop until they get it."

I stared at the pale beige wall in front of me. "What are you saying?"

"I checked the ferry schedule. You have two options. You can leave tomorrow. That will give you a little more time to spend with your family tonight, but you run the risk of more of those guys showing up on your brother's big day."

"Or?"

"Or you can catch the last ferry tonight with the promise that you'll give interviews to anyone who follows you out of town. This will get them out of town the fastest. Also, you will most likely be photographed on your way to New York, thus stopping anyone from heading to Ocracoke."

"You want me to talk to these guys?" My voice rose, and I tried to check myself.

"We've got to control the narrative here, Z, and that's only going to happen if you get ahead of these reporters. If you don't, they're gonna dig up every damn thing they can about you and spin it however they want. At least if you're the one talking, you can decide how the story is told."

"And the band is okay with this? Ridge?"

"We're going to act as though any and all articles posted about you were our idea and continue with the charity concert announcement as planned."

"But that's—"

"The band is good, Z. Asher, Ridge—all of them get it. This shit happens. It won't be the first time."

I looked back down the hall toward the group gathered there. I could hear the laughter. The joy. The anticipation.

If I left now, I'd miss one of the most important days of my brother's life.

But if I didn't, my presence would most likely ruin it.

Fuck.

"Okay," I agreed. "I'll go tonight."

"I'll book your flight and hotel." Silence filled the air. "You're doing the right thing," he assured me.

Then, why does it feel so wrong?

"Are you going to tell them?"

He knew me so well.

"No," I answered, turning my back on the people I loved. "If I do, they'll just try and change my mind. I'll go through with the rehearsal and then slip out after."

"And Elena?"

I opened my mouth, but before I could ask, he said, "Hendrix told me."

Fucking nark.

"I don't know," I answered, thinking of those frantic moments in the parlor when I'd asked her to go away with me. I'd been so hopeful. So sure it was the right thing. But the look in her eyes gave me doubt, and now, I couldn't help but wonder. "Things between us right now are...tense. Maybe leaving is the best thing I can do for her."

"Leaving is never the best choice, kid. Believe me."

We talked for a few more minutes, going over logistics, and he gave me a few pointers on talking to the press. Then, we hung up.

When I headed back into the main room, I found Elena with my brother and Marin.

Macon greeted me with a lazy smile. "There you are."

"Sorry, had to take a call from my manager."

"Were they able to offer any help on our situation outside?"

I went to stand next to her, but kept my hands to my sides.

Not an hour ago, I'd been inside her, and now, I wasn't even sure if she'd welcome my touch.

"Uh, not really," I lied. "He just said to keep ignoring them."

They both nodded, and I could see Marin trying to hide the worry in her eyes.

Before I could say anything more, the blonde dictator announced it was time to start with the rehearsal part of the evening.

Everyone headed out to the lawn, and I couldn't help but smile when I saw Marin and Macon take it all in—from the twinkling lights to the beautiful arch that framed the bay.

It was going to be a beautiful wedding.

I'd make sure of it.

The wedding party headed toward the front while the close relatives took seats to watch.

The next several minutes were spent going over the order of events. There was a lot of pointing, and by the time it was all over, everyone seemed to know what to do.

"Okay, let's do a run-through!" Molly shouted, and we all scattered across the lawn until she was happy with our positions.

Music started, and soon, the wedding party was headed down the aisle. Eli escorted Millie. Billy escorted Molly, and then I stepped up and took Elena's hand.

I told her this wasn't the end, but as I escorted her down that aisle, I couldn't help but feel like I was saying good-bye to her.

And she didn't even know.

She glanced over at me and smiled, and a small piece of my heart shattered.

Would she understand why I left, or would it feel like a betrayal?

It didn't matter because as I watched Marin walk toward Macon, I knew I'd do anything to make them happy.

Even if it meant that I wasn't.

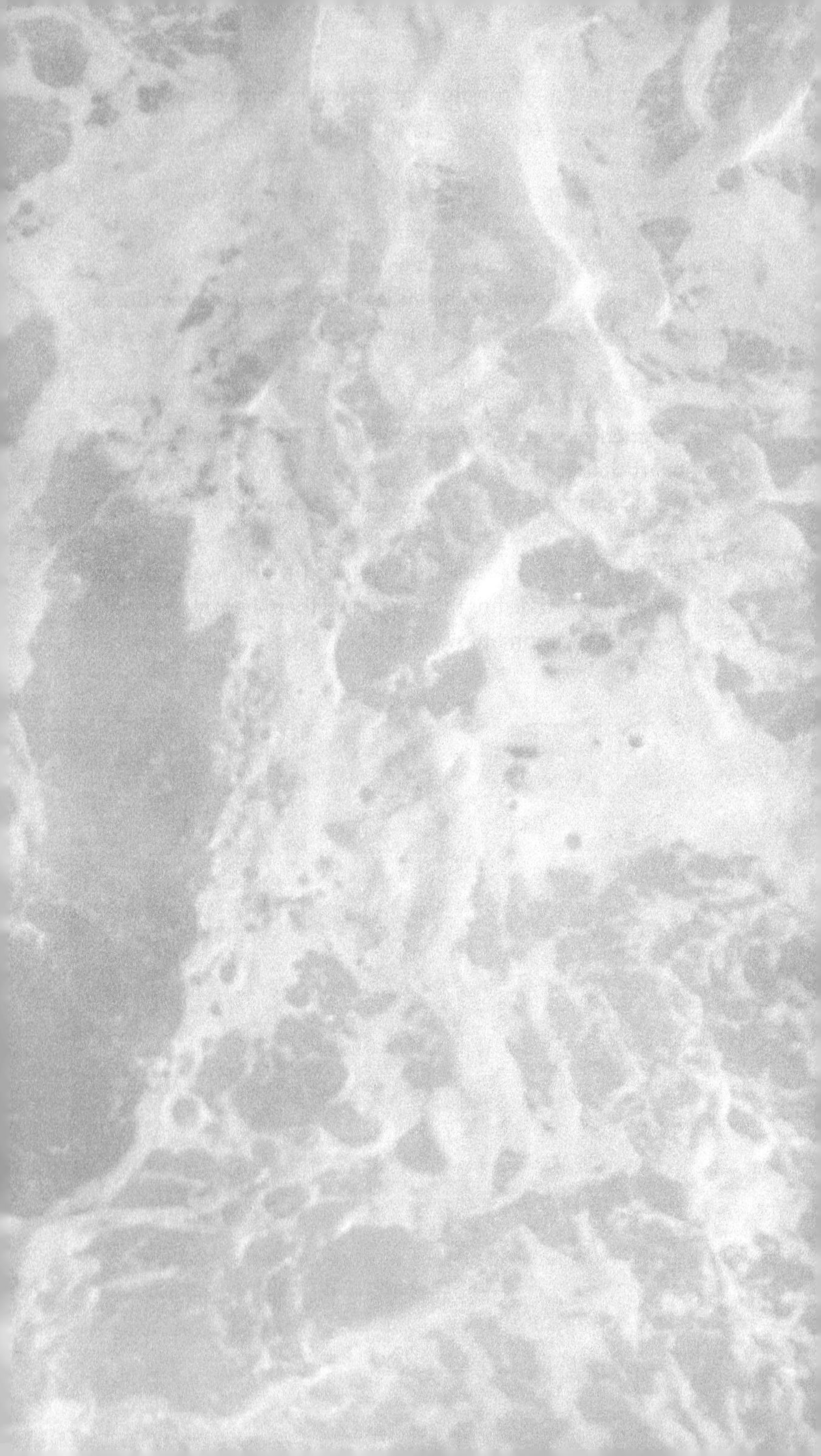

CHAPTER SEVENTEEN

ELENA

"It's your fucking wedding day!" I hollered, jumping on the bed at the ass crack of morning.

Marin groaned.

"Get up, loser!" I plopped down, tucking my feet underneath me as I poked her with my finger.

"Jesus, what time is it?" She rolled over to check her phone, and her groan turned into more of a screech. "You woke me up at six thirty in the goddamn morning? Why?"

" 'Cause it's your wedding day and we have a whole day planned."

"We do?" She eyed me curiously.

"Yep." I grinned. "Come on." I ripped the covers off her. "I'll tell you all about it over a big cup of coffee."

She sat straight up. "Coffee?" Her hair was wild, frizzy curls scattered everywhere. There were pillow marks on her face, and her breath smelled rancid.

Yikes, we have work to do.

"Decaf coffee," I amended.

She grimaced, making me laugh, but she got up all the same. We headed into the kitchen, and I spent the next hour or so plying her with decaf coffee and pastries while we talked about the day.

Her day.

"Your mom and sister want to come over while we get ready," I told her.

"That will be fun."

"And—"

Marin's phone began to ring.

I looked down at it and rolled my eyes. "Seriously. You can't even make it all morning without talking."

She didn't dignify that with a response and instead answered. "Hello, husband-to-be!"

I nearly gagged. She continued to nibble on a doughnut while listening to Macon, and then I heard her respond.

"Really?" She turned to me. "Macon said the reporters in front of the inn are gone."

"Gone?"

She put Macon on speaker so she wouldn't have to play telephone between us.

"No one has seen them since they left last night."

When they had all left before the end of the rehearsal dinner, we'd just assumed they had gotten tired and gone to bed.

I mean, even evil monsters had to sleep, right?

"And they're not anywhere else in town? Maybe they're just late sleepers. Have Zander ask his manager. I'm sure he knows a thing or two about this particular species and their nocturnal habits."

Marin laughed.

"Zander's not here," Macon said matter-of-factly.

"What?" A prickle of unease worked its way up my spine.

"He left the rehearsal dinner early last night 'cause he wasn't feeling well. Didn't he tell you?"

The prickle was turning into full-blown panic. "No, because he told me he was leaving early to go pack a bag to stay at Eli and Billy's house with you."

"Shit," Macon and I said at the same time.

I tried to think back to that exact moment at the rehearsal dinner. I'd been caught up in a rather passionate discussion with Millie about our love for fashion. He'd pulled me aside and said he was headed out, and because of our earlier conversation, I'd sort of hurried him along and—

The look in his eyes right before he kissed me good-bye…

"He wouldn't." I shook my head back and forth, racing to the bedroom to grab my phone where I'd left it on the nightstand, charging.

I walked back out into the kitchen as Macon said, "I'll go check the rental."

"Don't bother," I told him, looking down at the text he'd sent me.

> **ZANDER**
> Enjoy the wedding.

"He's gone."

ZANDER

> **Lance**
> First article went live overnight. You did good, kid.

> **ME**
> No more reporters showed up in Ocracoke?

> **LANCE**
> Several photos of you at the airport popped up on gossip rags, so I think we're good.

> **ME**
> Good.

I looked out toward the water as I sat on the patio of the luxury suite Lance had booked for my overnight stay in Virginia Beach.

By the time I'd caught the last ferry and driven up the coast, it was too late to catch a flight to New York.

So, he'd sent me here.

It was the most expensive hotel in the city—because, according to Lance, rock stars didn't stay at just any hotel.

No, they stayed at the best.

I'd nearly shit myself when I saw the cost per night.

Eggs Benedict?

Wait, what the fuck?

My brain suddenly skidded to a halt as I remembered the last part of his text. *How the hell did he know—*

Someone knocked on my door, and I found myself grinning instantly.

Getting up from the chaise, I padded toward the front of the suite and pulled open the door, not even bothering to check who it was.

I already knew.

"I was kind of hoping to antagonize you a little longer, but then you stopped answering my texts, and we're kind of on a schedule."

Lance Creed stood in the hallway in his typical reformed rock-star style. Jeans, a fitted tee, and a blazer. His gray beard and tats meant he always stood out in a roomful of suits, and he wouldn't have it any other way.

"What are you doing here?" I asked, pulling him in for a tight hug.

"You think we were going to let you go to your first big-boy concert alone?"

"We?"

"Hendrix is downstairs, getting coffee," he explained, pointing toward the elevator before he swung his head back to me. "Jesus, are you going to cry?"

"What?" I scoffed, blinking several times. "No, I have allergies."

You guys came all the way here for me?

A smirk tugged at his lips. "Well, come on, crybaby. Let's go make you famous."

ELENA

Enjoy the wedding.

Enjoy the wedding?

Like that was fucking possible.

To say the day was a bit of a blur was an understatement.

I did my best to be wholly present for Marin, but I knew she could see the devastation written all over my face.

"We're not saying good-bye, Elena."

Then, why did you leave?

Why does everyone always leave?

Marin was the perfect bride. When she walked down that aisle and looked into Macon's eyes, they defined love. Her lace gown fit her petite frame perfectly, accentuating her subtle curves and her tiny baby bump.

Billy effortlessly stepped back up to the role of best man, and Eli had no qualms, walking two McIntyre sisters down the aisle instead of one. If anyone wondered where Zander had gone, no one asked.

Maybe they all just chalked it up to the unpredictable life of a rock star.

By the reception, Macon had begun forcing Marin to take regular breaks, worried the excitement of the day would cause a repeat of the day before. As she was sitting with her feet up, sipping on a glass of sparking apple cider, she pointed to the dance floor.

"Go take my husband for a spin," she demanded.

"I don't want to," I began to argue, not wanting her pity dance.

She nudged Macon out of his seat. "Go on," she said. "If I can't dance with him, someone else should. It's hilarious."

He rolled his eyes but shot Marin one last grin before we headed to the dance floor.

"Don't step on my feet."

"No promises," he warned as he stiffly took my waist like it was on fire.

I snickered, wrapping my arms around his shoulders.

"You doing okay?" he asked.

I nodded a bit too quickly, making him smirk.

I let out a sigh. "Are you?"

"I'm sad that he wasn't here," he said. "But I understand why he left."

"You do?"

"He knew the only way those reporters would leave was if he did," he said without a shadow of a doubt. "He did it for us."

I'd already thought of that, but in my own self-loathing, I'd brushed it aside and cast him as the villain. It was easier that way.

"Why not tell us that then?" I asked. "Why leave in the middle of the rehearsal dinner without even bothering to say good-bye?"

"Would you have let him go?"

The question nearly halted me completely, and I almost stepped on his feet.

No.

I would have barricaded the door and tried to find any other solution that didn't involve him missing his brother's wedding.

Mostly, I would have done anything to keep him from leaving me.

"So, what now?" I asked.

He gave me an incredulous stare. "Fuck, I don't know, Elena. Do I look like a relationship guru? You two need to figure your own shit out. Leave me the hell out of it."

And then he tried to spin me, and my laughs drowned out my sorrow—for at least a short while.

Since I didn't need to be back at work for another few days, I hadn't planned on leaving Ocracoke until Monday. But when I woke up the day after the wedding, with Marin and Macon already on their way to the airport for their honeymoon and Zander…

Nothing about being in that town felt right anymore.

Even so, I still offered to stay and help with the cleanup. Molly, however, just waved me off, sending me home with a bunch of cake and a sad smile.

Yet another reason I was leaving.

Billy, Eli…even fucking Millie. They had all spent the whole wedding giving me *the look*. The one that said, *Gosh, Elena, I'm sorry your crazy-hot rock-star boyfriend dropped you like a hot potato the second he became famous.*

Did I even get to call him that? My boyfriend?

Ugh.

Macon had told me not to worry about cleaning the rental before I left since they had a management company for that. So, I took him for his word and packed up my stuff, all of which was mostly in Zander's room—a place I had avoided since he'd left. That was where I found it.

His leather jacket.

It was spread across the neatly made bed, obviously left behind on purpose.

The fucking asshole.

I pulled the leather to my nose, breathing in his scent until I finally gave in and wrapped it around me. And then I got the hell out of there.

See you the fuck later, Ocracoke.

ZANDER

As soon as we landed in New York, I was whisked off to do sound checks, wardrobe fittings, makeup, photographs, and interviews.

Being a session guitarist, I had only been ever given a glimpse of what bands did during the tour. It was the gritty and intense part, but it barely encompassed a fraction of what was expected of them.

Now, I felt like I was getting a peek behind the curtain and seeing what really went on, and it was mind-boggling.

And exhausting.

"You'll get used to it," Evans—Manic's bass guitarist—assured me as we stood backstage, waiting to go on.

Lance was off with Ridge, doing whatever managers did, while Hendrix got to know the guys better. He'd met them before, when he visited me on tour, and as expected, he fit right in.

"And it's not always like this. We don't do a lot of TV appearances."

"Or group performances," Asher added. "We probably could have eased you in a bit more."

"Yeah, thanks for that." I grinned.

"You seem to be doing all right. You handled those reporters at your brother's wedding like a pro."

I shrugged. "That was all Lance and Ridge. I just did what they told me to."

"And that's the point," Darius, interjected right before his head turned and zeroed in on some girl's ass, his drumsticks twirling between his fingers. That guy had the attention span of a mosquito.

Evans just shook his head and finished Darius's thought. "You handled it like a professional. You listened to your manager, aced your first interviews, and managed to get those tossers away from your brother's wedding."

"Manic, you're up in two minutes," someone announced.

We all nodded as hair and makeup people swarmed us one last time. Asher handed over his drink to his assistant. It looked gross as fuck, but I'd seen him with it before every single performance. He swore it helped his voice.

My phone buzzed in my back pocket, and my heart spiked.

I pulled it out immediately, hoping it was—

It wasn't.

"Oh, good, they got it," Asher said over my shoulder as he looked at the photo my brother had sent.

I looked at him in confusion. Macon and Marin had sent a photo of them in a giant infinity pool overlooking the ocean.

MACON

Thank you so much for the gift. We
missed you.

"What gift?" I asked him.

"I upgraded them to the presidential suite at their resort." He shrugged like it was no big deal.

"Why? How did you even know—"

"People can be very forthcoming when my name is mentioned," he said. "And we're family now, Tate. It's not an easy life, but we take care of each other. Mitch forgot about that. We won't."

And then Darius grinned and said, "Let's go make some girls scream."

I turned back to Hendrix, who was watching from the wings.

"Go make me proud, brother."

"I'm sorry, who are you again?" I laughed.

"That's the spirit."

I walked out on that stage without a backward glance and knew, without a shadow of a doubt, that my life would never be the same.

ELENA

Since the majority of vacation rentals were booked from Saturday to Saturday in the Outer Banks, the drive back was relatively tame. I still hit the annoying back-to-back traffic in Virginia Beach but managed to sail right past Williamsburg.

Small miracles.

By the time I was hauling my suitcase into my apartment, I was bone-tired and in need of food.

I checked my phone for the hundredth time.

It had been over twenty-four hours since the wedding, and he still hadn't texted me.

If Macon was right and Zander had, in fact, left to save the day, why hadn't he reached out?

He'd asked me to go on tour with him. Had he changed his mind? Had my reaction—my reluctance—made him reconsider?

What if Macon was wrong and he'd used the reporters as an excuse to just get away from me?

I checked the time, wondering if I'd made it home in time for his concert. You know, the one he'd asked me to come to, but I'd been to chickenshit to say yes to?

Yeah, that one.

I had to do a quick Google search to figure out what channel it was on. Thankfully, it hadn't started yet, so I flipped on my TV, and while I waited for it to start, I ordered some dinner.

I let out a deep breath.

Being in Ocracoke hadn't felt right, but being here didn't either. The empty apartment felt claustrophobic, and I suddenly remembered the weight of responsibilities I had to face at work.

Deciding I had nothing better to do, I opened my work email for the first time in over two weeks.

"Jesus," I breathed out as I scrolled and scrolled *and scrolled*.

Usually, something like this would push me into overdrive, and I'd pull an overnighter just to see that inbox cleared. But looking at it now, all I felt was an overwhelming sense of dread.

Because I knew once I got back into that routine, there would be nothing else. Work would become my whole life again.

And for once, I wanted more.

I thought about what Zander had told me in that restaurant.

"Do something for you."

It didn't sound any less scary now than it had then. It sounded even scarier when I added a six-month tour with a man I'd only known for three weeks into the mix.

That's if he even wants you …

Luckily, I didn't need to think about that train of thought anymore.

The concert was starting.

Some annoying, overly enthusiastic MC started off by introducing himself—a young actor I'd never heard of. The crowd went crazy, and he preened like a goddamn peacock from their praise. He talked about the charity the bands were supporting, and then each band was listed off while a giant screen ran B-roll footage behind them. The moment Manic at Midnight was announced, the crowd erupted.

The screams were so loud that I had to turn the volume down.

The camera zoomed in on a huge group of girls, all wearing custom Knight Rider shirts with two strategically placed hearts with a picture of Asher's face.

I'll give you two guesses where those hearts were placed.

My attention drifted in and out after that. Some of the bands I liked, so I'd turn it up and listen. Others I was less enthusiastic about, and I'd find myself scrolling social media. At some point, my food arrived, and soon, they announced the second-to-last band. I poked my mandarin chicken, all while an entire kaleidoscope of butterflies looped-the-loops in my belly.

Finally, after what felt like the longest commercial break of all time, Manic at Midnight took the stage.

And I forgot how to breathe.

I leaned forward, my legs tucked underneath me as I watched the front man, Asher, take the mic. He was gorgeous. Tight, lean muscle all on display with only a black vest and low-slung jeans to cover him. There was a reason he had legions of fans.

But all of my attention was on the man to his right.

If I had any doubts he might be nervous, they were washed away in that instant.

He looked like he owned that stage.

This is really happening.

His hair had been given the *just fucked* treatment, and the black jeans and ripped tank he wore made his body look ridiculous.

Mine.

The thought was so intense that I wanted to reach through the screen just so I could lick him in front of all those skanky women to prove my point.

But then Asher stepped up to the mic, his blue eyes blazing. "Hello."

One word, and chaos ensued. Girls were screaming and calling out his name.

Finally, after what felt like five fucking minutes later, he said, "If you haven't heard, we added a new member to our motley crew. You might have seen him lurking around onstage if you happened to join us on tour this year. He's an American, but we won't hold that against him. " Asher grinned, that Scottish brogue working its magic over the crowd. He turned, his mouth still pressed to the mic. "Meet our new lead guitarist and backup vocalist, Zander Tate. Isn't he lovely, ladies?"

Zander did a little medley on his guitar before the camera panned the audience. There were women everywhere, waving signs in the air, screaming his name.

Marry me, Zander!

Asher and Zander, you be the bread. I'll be the jam.

Zander! Remember me from Tucson? Call me!

The last one actually had a phone number the camera had to blur out, but it was enough to make me nauseous. It wasn't like I hadn't known he had a past. But I also didn't want to be reminded about it on live television.

I pulled the jacket I still wore tightly around my body.

The camera was back on the band. Specifically Zander. He was looking at Asher, shaking his head, laughing.

He looked happy, and I found myself swimming in doubt.

He'd spent his entire life chasing this dream, and he'd found it.

He didn't need me riding his coattails.

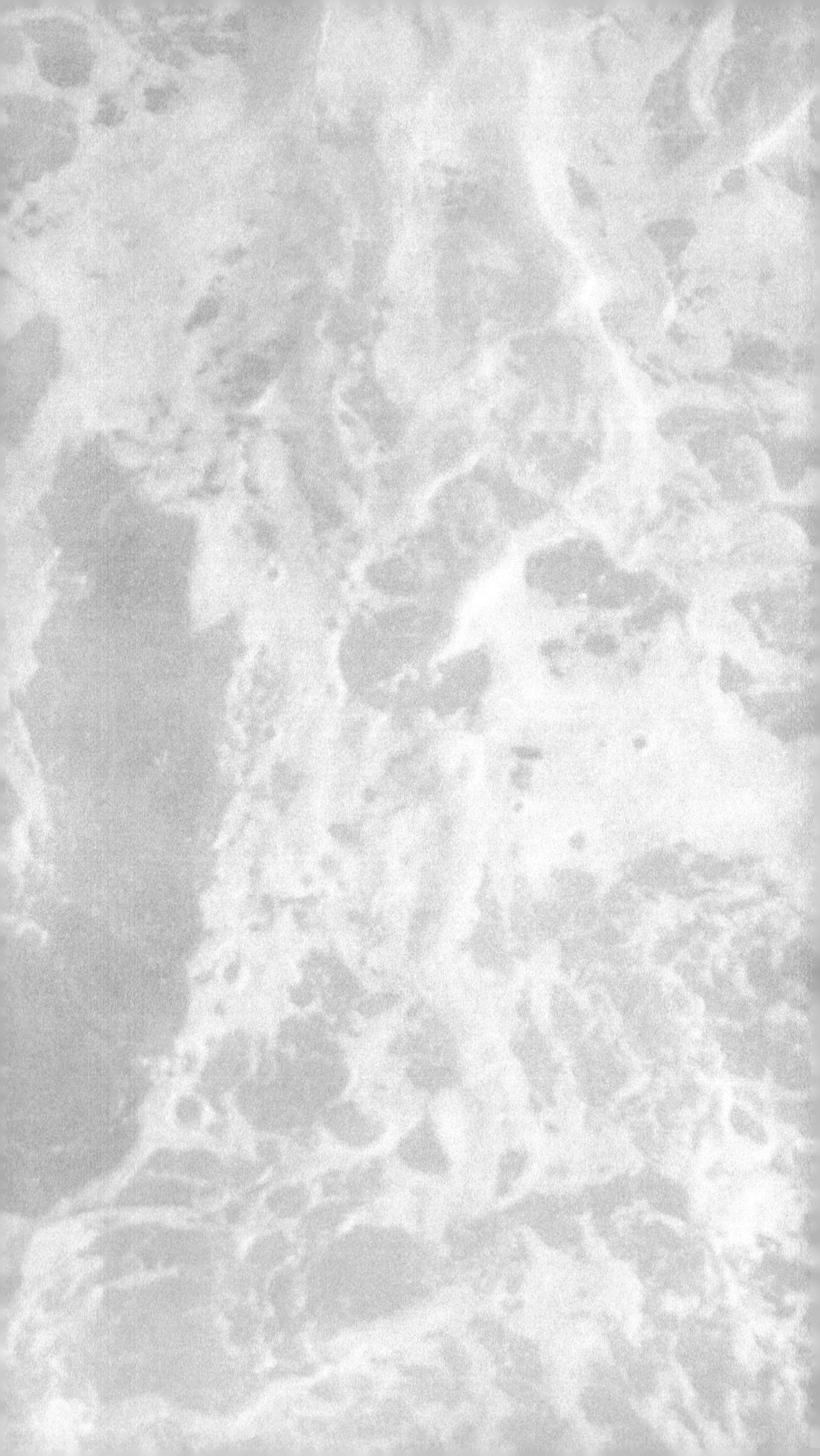

CHAPTER EIGHTEEN

ZANDER

"Okay, guys, let's take five," Asher announced.

"What about we say more like ten?" Darius suggested, spinning a drumstick between his fingers.

"I need at least fifteen. Daddy needs a protein bar," Evans said, setting down his bass.

"If you refer to yourself as Daddy one more time, E—" Asher pinched the bridge of his nose. "Seriously, no one needs to hear that."

Evans cackled as I muffled a laugh. He headed toward the snack counter to grab a water bottle from the mini-fridge.

If there was one thing Asher excelled at, it was providing ample snacks.

We never went without food when he was around.

Since the charity concert, we'd been practicing nonstop in preparation for the tour. It wasn't that there was much difference between the US and the international tour, but it had been a while since we'd played together. It was important that we came together as one on that stage.

Asher had a penthouse in New York, where we'd been staying, and it came complete with a private recording studio and practice rooms.

It's the rock-star starter package, honestly.

It had been a crazy few weeks. I couldn't go out on the street without being mauled by fans. *People* magazine had dubbed me Rock's Newest Hottie—whatever that meant. Macon had said Ocracoke had been flooded with tourists, wanting to see where *the* Zander Tate had been born.

Hard eye roll.

It was easy to see how someone could become addicted to this—the heady feeling of fame. But I wasn't worried. I had enough people in my life to keep me humble.

Almost enough.

I pulled out my phone, and after a moment, it was ringing. But once again, it wasn't her.

It never was.

I answered on the second ring.

"How's my famous brother today?" Macon greeted me.

"I'm good, man. How are you?"

"Well, I had to see your ugly face on the front of a magazine while I was trying to buy eggs yesterday, so I've been better."

I laughed. "Anyone ask you to sign it?"

"No, thank God. I think enough time has passed since those photos of the two of us leaked that most people have forgotten about me. It's a good thing, too. Because if one more woman came up to me and asked to see that tattoo on my rib cage, Marin was going to kill someone."

"That would be awkward for you," I quipped.

"Would definitely make my job a lot harder." He paused, and then I heard him say my name under his breath. "Marin says hi."

"Hi, Marin."

Another pause. More whispering.

"I'm not telling him that. Marin, fuck. I told you, I'm not getting in the middle of this. No, you aren't either. OUCH!"

I pressed my lips together. "Everything okay?"

Macon growled. "My wife feels very strongly that I should tell you that Elena is in town."

I had tried to ask Macon about Elena before, and he'd refused to tell me anything, saying, "If you want to know, fucking ask her yourself."

And then he'd muttered under his breath about how we were just a bunch of idiots.

I perked up. "Why?"

"Would you fucking stop kicking me? I'll tell him."

"It's the anniversary of Daniel's death, and she decided to spend it with Marin. She, uh…she cut ties with her parents last month. Officially."

That was a surprise. I'd always hoped she might have the courage to do it one day, but never expected it to be so soon.

Macon and I both knew how complex emotions could be when dealing with a toxic parent. It had taken me weeks to finally work up the courage to ask Macon what had happened to our own father. I was so terrified his answer wouldn't be definitive enough for me and that I'd be too scared to ever go back to Ocracoke. But he wasn't coming back. He'd landed himself in prison somewhere in South Carolina. He couldn't touch us anymore.

"Is she okay?"

"Yeah, she's good," he answered. "I think it was harder to sever the connection with her father, obviously. He never hurt her directly, but he also never defended her either."

"Maybe someday, he'll figure out what he's missing out on," I said. "But if not, she's better off."

"Tell him about the—"

"I will. Give me a second."

"Tell me about the what?"

"He can hear everything you're saying, babe. You might

as well just tell him yourself," Macon said to Marin, a touch of amusement in his tone.

She must have grabbed the phone because she was suddenly louder in my ear. "She didn't just come here for Daniel. She came here to celebrate. She quit her job."

I froze. My eyes were fixated on the New York skyline, but my mind was back on that island.

"Do something for you."

"Zander?"

"Yeah, I'm here," I managed to say.

"Look, I don't know why you didn't call," she went on. I opened my mouth to say something, but none of the reasons I had to offer up were good enough. "But I wanted to tell you something she told me before it's too late."

"Too late?"

"She saw your dreams come true on that stage, Zander, and she couldn't compete. So, she focused on the one thing she could control—her own. She quit her job, cut ties with her parents, and finally started doing things for herself, but—"

"But what?"

"She misses you."

I swallowed hard, finally realizing what a complete idiot I'd been. "I gotta go."

"Zander—" She called out my name in confusion.

"My dreams didn't come true on that stage, Marin," I told her. "They came true the night I met her."

"Well then, where the hell are you going?"

"To book a flight," I said.

ELENA

"What did you not understand about the word *no*?" I asked my best friend for the fourth time.

She shrugged, pulling into the parking lot like she'd lost her damn mind. "You said we could do whatever I wanted today. This is what I want."

"I really should have put parameters on that," I groaned as we both stepped out of the car. "How the hell did Macon get out of this?"

"He's spending the night with Billy and Eli. They haven't had a guys' night since we got back from the honeymoon."

"So, he gets out of this because he has a penis? That's what you're saying?"

She rolled her eyes as we both headed for the door.

It had been an emotional weekend.

Friday marked the sixth anniversary of Daniel's passing.

We'd spent some time at the memorial, where Daniel's name was etched, along with the twelve others who were lost that day. We placed flowers, and Marin left a small painting. After, we headed back to Macon and Marin's and made a big meal full of Daniel's favorite—nachos—and then spent the night sharing our favorite stories of my brother.

If my mom or dad had tried to contact me, I wouldn't have known.

I'd blocked their number two weeks ago, and I'd never felt freer.

We were barely to the door, and I could already hear someone butchering Carrie Underwood's "Before He Cheats."

"I think a few guys had better watch their cars tonight." Marin snorted out a laugh. "That girl sounds pissed."

"Sorry to be the bearer of bad news, Marin, but most men suck." I pulled the door open, and the sound of the pissed-off girl's voice doubled.

"That's not true," she argued as I let her move past me, and we headed toward the bar.

"You're still in the honeymoon phase of marriage. You're not allowed to have an opinion."

She pursed her lips as we found two empty seats. "And you're still in the *I'm so stubborn I refuse to text Zander* stage.

The next act went up, a guy intent on belting out "Bohemian Rhapsody."

Haven't we all had enough trauma?

"He hasn't—"

She rolled her eyes. "Yeah, yeah. I know. He hasn't texted you either. But has it ever occurred to you that maybe he's just as scared as you are?"

I scoffed as the bartender came our way. "Scared of what? He's not the one who has to watch grown-ass women throw panties at his feet."

Okay, I hadn't actually seen that, but it didn't mean it hadn't happened.

The bartender took our drink orders—or mine. Marin stuck with a Coke, avoiding the virgin drinks tonight. She'd gotten a few judgy looks on her honeymoon and decided that was enough of that.

People needed to mind their own damn business.

"I'm just saying," she went on, very much not minding her own business, "perhaps you're both being a little stubborn."

She gave a pointed look at the leather jacket I wore, and smiled.

I let out a huff as the man onstage finally finished.

"You already said that. And I'm not stubborn," I argued. "He's the one who left. He's the one who asked me to go with him and then bailed without a single word."

"And you're the one who is too scared to demand an explanation."

I opened my mouth to rebuke her, but instead, I just whined like a child. "Why are we even here? You're not even paying attention and—"

My mouth fell open as *he* took the stage.

"What the fuck?"

"That's why we're here," Marin said smugly.

The crowd roared, recognizing their local boy immediately. He took a minute, positioning a single stool in the middle of the stage, and then took a seat. He had a guitar strapped across his broad shoulders.

So fucking sexy.

Shut up. We're mad at him.

"Hey, everyone," he said, making the crowd go even crazier.

It was like an encore of the charity concert, except we were in karaoke hell and he was playing the role of Asher Knight.

He was so much hotter than Asher Knight.

"I hope you don't mind me coming and crashing your evening." Every single phone was out and recording. "But you see, I met this girl at one of these karaoke nights. Not just any girl. *The* girl."

My heart fluttered rapidly in my chest as his eyes met mine.

"And I've been trying to find a way to tell her exactly how I feel, and since she has a thing for my mouth—shit, sorry, I mean, my voice."

The crowd erupted in laughter, and I just shook my head as a cocky grin crept across his lips.

"I figured this might be the best way to do it."

People were starting to figure out who he was looking at, and several phones were now pointed at me as I watched him. I tried not to be nervous, but as he strummed the first note, everything and everyone else seemed to just melt away.

Tears stung the back of my eyes as he sang a slow, haunting version of "Take on Me" by A-Ha. By the last note, I probably looked like a damn raccoon from the layer of mascara that had run down my face, but I didn't care.

I ran to him, launching myself into his arms the second he set his guitar on the ground. He caught me, thank God, as thunderous applause filled the bar.

When his lips met mine, it felt like coming home, and I

knew in that moment, we'd be able to handle anything as long as we held on to this feeling.

"Nice jacket." His voice was possessive. Raspy. So fucking hot.

"Did you miss it?" I looked up at him like it was the first time. Like I was memorizing every detail.

"No, I missed you." He brushed hair behind my ear. "You quit your job."

"I sold my apartment, too," I added with a smirk.

He cupped my chin as people still clapped and cheered.

"Are you saying you're homeless, Louie?" He grinned.

"Yep." I feigned a pout. "My handbags and I are all alone."

"Sounds like you need a place to stay."

"What do you have in mind?"

"Well, several places actually. How do you feel about Spain? And London? Maybe Paris?"

I bit my lip as a slow smile spread across my face. "You might regret that when you see how much luggage I bring."

"You haven't seen my guitar collection yet."

"We're gonna need a really big house," I said.

"I'm a rock star now. Let's get three."

He kissed me again. This time, it was deeper. Slower. When he pulled back, his eyes were so intense that they stole my breath. "I love you, Elena. I should have told you that weeks ago. I knew it then. My life has been hell without you."

My lips wobbled at the sound of his words. "I love you, too, and you were right; it wasn't a sacrifice, giving up my shitty job and my lonely apartment. I'm ready to start this life —this adventure—with you."

"Then, let's get out of here," he suggested. "I'm sick of all these cameras, and there are about a hundred different things I want to do to you right now that are definitely not appropriate for the internet."

"I mean, they might be." I laughed. "Depending on where you look."

"No one gets to see any of this," he said as his hand slid down my ass, "but me."

I bit my lower lip as heat bloomed in my belly. "Let me go say good-bye to Marin, and I'll be right back."

"Okay," he said, but then his grin turned mischievous. "Just don't run off this time."

"Never," I answered. "I'm yours. Forever."

EPILOGUE

ELENA

"I think they're onto us," I said, motioning to the car on my right.

Zander glanced in my direction, looking ridiculously hot in his black baseball hat and aviator sunglasses. His forearm rested on the steering wheel, even though the engine had been off for a while now.

"I think they're onto the fact that you really love that ice cream." He raised that pierced brow.

"It's really fucking good."

"I can tell. That's the same noise you make when I have my head buried between your thighs."

"It is not!" I argued, causing him to laugh.

"No?" His eyes heated as he leaned forward. "Should I give you a demonstration?"

"Now, you're just asking to be caught. If we end up with a mob following us to the inn, I'm blaming it on you." I playfully tried to shove my ice cream cone in his face, but he managed to dodge it effortlessly.

"God, Molly would have my balls."

"She would," I agreed. "And since I'm quite fond of them, you need to behave."

Zander and I had spent the most amazing six months in Europe and beyond. Touring with a bunch of single rock stars had turned out to be an easier adjustment than I'd anticipated. Traveling in luxury accommodations everywhere we went definitely helped. Seriously, those boys lived the high life in every way.

But it was more than that. After getting over my initial shell-shock of meeting them, I found a certain kind of kinship with the members of Manic at Midnight, and seeing the bond they'd formed with Zander only made me love them more.

None of them had ever seriously dated anyone, so I officially became the adopted sister of the group, and I was all for it. They even asked me to join their legal team, and as tempting as it was, I had to pass. While the leap from criminal to contractual law could technically be considered a career move, it would have hardly been a challenge.

I was done playing it safe.

It had taken months of hyping myself up, but eventually, I had gotten myself in front of a laptop and started plotting a story which lead to an actual outline. Many months of self-doubt, tears, and late nights later, I had my first rough draft. My suspense-thriller was a bit sexier than I'd planned on, but when you had a muse like Zander Green, who could really blame you?

Now, I just had to figure out how to sell the damn thing.

After six months of touring, you'd think I'd get tired of it all, but I never did. Every time Zander took that stage, it felt like the first time. I'd never get over the sight of him, all hot and sweaty, with his mouth against that mic as he played his guitar. He'd turn his head, catch my gaze, and give me the most panty-melting smile, knowing the effect he had on me.

I was fairly certain I'd shoved him in every bathroom, closet, and dark corner I could find just so I could get those post-concert quickies in.

"So, let's place bets now," he said as I finished my last bite. "Initial reaction to our big news—happy or pissed? Or maybe a combo situation?"

I grinned as butterflies erupted in my stomach. "I guess we're about to find out."

ZANDER

Thanksgiving hadn't really been a thing when I was growing up.

Let me rephrase that. *Holidays* hadn't really been a thing when I was growing up.

My mom had tried—or at least, that was what Macon told me—when we were younger. He said she'd sometimes try to make a fancy dinner for Thanksgiving or buy us a few nice things for Christmas, but quickly learned it wasn't worth my father's wrath when he realized how much it had cost.

We couldn't be wasting money on food and clothes when he had booze to buy after all.

The first time I sat down to a proper Thanksgiving dinner was after I met the Creeds. I had barely started working there, and I was convinced they'd only invited me out of pity, but I didn't want to upset my boss.

He was mother-fucking Lance Creed.

That was the day that I realized a family could be something more than blood. Their table was filled with other "strays," as I liked to call them—people who had come into their life and become ingrained in it.

Just like I eventually did.

For a long time, I thought the Creeds would be my only family, and then I went back home to finally burn the bridges of my past.

Instead, I'd found my future.

"We're here." Elena looked at me with anticipation in her

eyes. It wasn't the first time we'd been back to Ocracoke since we'd left for the tour a year ago, but it was the first time since—

"Let's go, Trouble!" she demanded, throwing the door open. "I want baby snuggles."

I chuckled, quickly following her. "Okay, but you're gonna have to beat me there." I took off in a run, hearing her curse behind me.

Marin and Macon's daughter, Naomi Danielle Green, had been born this past December and was the perfect mixture of the two of them. Since Elena and I were now home-based in Los Angeles, we didn't get to see her as much as we would like, but Marin and Elena spoke on the phone at least once a day.

Which was why our little secret was killing her.

We didn't bother knocking.

The house was filled with people anyway. Molly had been trying to make this particular dream a reality for years—a By the Bay Thanksgiving.

She and Jake had invited their entire family, their friends, and their friends' families.

It was chaos, and I was pretty sure the blonde dictator was loving every minute.

There were screaming kids everywhere, and I narrowly missed one colliding with me the second we walked through the threshold.

Elena snorted out a laugh. "You're no superstar here, Trouble."

"Thank God for that." I grinned.

"We're here," Elena hollered. "Where's my niece?"

"Outside," I answered her, seeing everyone gathered on the lawn, enjoying the mild fall weather.

I knew the moment Marin spotted us when we stepped outside.

A high-pitched feminine squeal filled the air, and the two best friends met in a giant hug.

A smirk tugged at my lips because I knew what was about to go down.

Macon came up to us with Naomi on his hip.

Elena immediately reached out with her hands. "Gimme."

Naomi gave her a slobbery smile, her fist halfway shoved in her mouth as Macon handed her over. I'd thought it would be weird to see my brother as a father, but he was sort of a natural at it. Considering neither of us had been shown, growing up, what a good father was supposed to be like, it gave me hope that I might be up to the job.

When the time came, obviously…

"How was your flight?" Macon asked as I took a look around the lawn.

Molly wasn't kidding. Everyone was here. Dean and a very pregnant Cora were playing a game of cornhole with their daughter while Lani and Taylor watched on. Their son was in his arms, half asleep.

"It was good. Quiet."

"I can't believe you flew here on a private jet." He rolled his eyes.

"Asher insisted," I told him, shrugging. "He wasn't using it, and I doubt I would have made it here unscathed otherwise."

"He has a point."

"Oh my God! It's—"

"Are you going to do that every time I see you?" I turned to see Millie coming up with Aiden.

She held his arm as his service dog flanked the other side.

"Hell yes, I am," she teased. "Got to keep you humble."

"That's what I have my w—"

Her eyes widened as her head snapped down to look at my left hand. Marin must have heard as well because, suddenly, she was staring at Elena, her mouth gaped wide open.

"What the fuck is that?" Marin pointed to the glittering

diamond ring on Elena's hand—and the platinum band beside it. "Did you—"

I looked over at Elena and broke out into a giant, shit-eating grin.

"We got married."

"You got married?" Marin practically shouted.

"When?" Macon asked.

The lawn went silent.

Well, I guessed that was one way to tell everyone.

"Last month," Elena answered.

"You've been married for a month, and you didn't tell me?"

I had to hold back a laugh, noticing the way Marin hadn't included Macon in that sentence.

"We wanted to tell you in person," I explained.

And we were kind of enjoying our month-long honeymoon…

But that was clearly irrelevant right now.

"Why didn't you tell us, you know, when it happened? We could have been there."

"You know I never really wanted a wedding, Marin," Elena said, her voice softening as she placed a tender kiss on our niece. "I know it's not how you would have wanted it, but believe me, it was exactly how I did. It was perfect."

It *was* perfect.

I'd been wanting to propose for a while. I just didn't know how. That fucking ring had been burning a hole in my pocket for weeks. One particularly tame day in LA, we were walking down the street and happened to pass a bridal shop, and it hit me.

I sent her off to go grab us coffee—something I hated doing because I always got recognized—and I darted into the bridal shop.

I pulled out my phone and showed them the photo of Elena in that black dress, and sure enough, they had it.

When she came back, I had the dress and the ring and a proposal.

We had flown to Spain, and I'd married her in the same dress she had worn when we shared our first kiss.

Luckiest man in the damn world.

Marin eyed her friend for a moment, and then, suddenly, tears were falling down her cheeks. "You're really married?"

Elena nodded, her own eyes glassy. With all the emotions flowing, Macon decided it was time to snatch back the precious cargo and pulled Naomi into his arms.

"So, we're sisters again?"

"We never stopped being sisters," Elena pressed. "But, yeah, we even have matching last names again."

Marin let out another squeal and then launched herself at me, throwing her arms around me. I grunted from the impact, making everyone laugh.

"You're the best brother-in-law ever!"

"Thanks?"

She let me go and turned back to Elena. "You must tell me everything. Do you have pictures? You didn't do a court-house thing, did you?" The questions kept coming as the two of them headed for the house.

Elena flashed a mischievous smile over her shoulder, and I laughed.

Wait until they find out she's pregnant.

ACKNOWLEDGMENTS

I'm going to make this somewhat short and sweet because I'm currently recovering from wrist surgery and one-handed typing takes forever!

My husband deserves extra praise this time around as he is currently doing pretty much everything around the house while I'm in a cast. Nearly twenty-three years of marriage and he's still my favorite person on the planet, guys.

As always, there are a few people who helped make this book possible and I am always grateful for their talent and love.

Jovana Shirley—my lifelong editor. Thank you for being so crazy anal. Like the copious notes you keep on my books… it's wild.

Katy Nielsen—my proofer. Thank you for your dedication and friendship.

Barbara Martoncik—Thank you for your last-minute help and long-term friendship.

Juliana Cabrera—my cover designer. Thank you for working so hard to get those tats just right!

Devin McCain—My discreet cover designer. Thank you for stepping in and creating these gorgeous covers and making my discreet cover dreams come true.

Nazarea Andrews/Inkslingers PR—my publicist, who took this release on at the last minute and hit the ground running.

Lastly, thank you to all of my readers—both old and new. You make my words come alive.

ABOUT THE AUTHOR

J.L. Berg is the USA Today bestselling author of the Ready Series, the Lost & Found series, and many more. Originally from California, she now resides in central Virginia with her high school sweetheart, two children, and three dogs. When she's not writing, she enjoys spending time with her family or indulging in her love for Doctor Who. J.L. Berg is represented by Jill Marsal of Marsal Lyon Literary Agency, LLC. For the latest book updates, audio news, and more, be sure to visit her website.